THE CHEMICAL REACTION

66
Dy
Dysprosium
162.50

Fiona Erskine

POINT BLANK

A Point Blank Book

First published in Great Britain, the Republic of Ireland and Australia
by Point Blank, an imprint of Oneworld Publications, 2020
This mass market paperback edition published 2021

Copyright © Fiona Erskine 2020

The moral right of Fiona Erskine to be identified as the Author of this work has been
asserted by her in accordance with the Copyright, Designs, and Patents Act 1988

ISBN 978-1-78607-930-5
ISBN 978-1-78607-734-9 (ebook)

Printed and bound in Great Britain by Clays Ltd, Elcograf S.p.A.

Oneworld Publications
10 Bloomsbury Street
London WC1B 3SR
England

Stay up to date with the latest books,
special offers, and exclusive content from
Oneworld with our newsletter

Sign up on our website
oneworld-publications.com

MIX
Paper from
responsible sources
FSC® C018072

To Jonathan – Happy Thirtieth Wedding Anniversary

Science tells you love
is just a chemical reaction in the brain
Let me be your Bunsen burner baby
let me be your naked flame!

John Otway, 'Bunsen Burner'
from the album *The Year of the Hit*, 2002

元素週期表

1	2	3	4	5	6	7	8	9	10	11	12	13	14	15	16	17	18
1 H 氫 1.008																	2 He 氦 4.003
3 Li 鋰 6.941	4 Be 鈹 9.012											5 B 硼 10.811	6 C 碳 12.011	7 N 氮 14.007	8 O 氧 15.999	9 F 氟 18.998	10 Ne 氖 20.180
11 Na 鈉 22.990	12 Mg 鎂 24.305											13 Al 鋁 26.982	14 Si 硅 28.086	15 P 磷 30.974	16 S 硫 32.066	17 Cl 氯 35.453	18 Ar 氬 39.948
19 K 鉀 39.098	20 Ca 鈣 40.078	21 Sc 鈧 44.956	22 Ti 鈦 47.867	23 V 釩 50.942	24 Cr 鉻 51.996	25 Mn 錳 54.938	26 Fe 鐵 55.845	27 Co 鈷 58.933	28 Ni 鎳 58.693	29 Cu 銅 63.546	30 Zn 鋅 65.38	31 Ga 鎵 69.723	32 Ge 鍺 72.631	33 As 砷 74.922	34 Se 硒 78.971	35 Br 溴 79.904	36 Kr 氪 83.798
37 Rb 銣 85.468	38 Sr 鍶 87.62	39 Y 釔 88.906	40 Zr 鋯 91.224	41 Nb 鈮 92.906	42 Mo 鉬 95.95	43 Tc 鎝 98.907	44 Ru 釕 101.07	45 Rh 銠 102.906	46 Pd 鈀 106.42	47 Ag 銀 107.868	48 Cd 鎘 112.414	49 In 銦 114.818	50 Sn 錫 118.711	51 Sb 銻 121.760	52 Te 碲 127.6	53 I 碘 126.904	54 Xe 氙 131.294
55 Cs 銫 132.905	56 Ba 鋇 137.328	57-71 鑭系元素	72 Hf 鉿 178.49	73 Ta 鉭 180.948	74 W 鎢 183.84	75 Re 錸 186.207	76 Os 鋨 190.23	77 Ir 銥 192.217	78 Pt 鉑 195.085	79 Au 金 196.967	80 Hg 汞 200.592	81 Tl 鉈 204.383	82 Pb 鉛 207.2	83 Bi 鉍 208.980	84 Po 釙 [208.982]	85 At 砈 209.987	86 Rn 氡 222.018
87 Fr 鈁 223.020	88 Ra 鐳 226.025	89-103 錒系元素	104 Rf 鑪 [261]	105 Db [262]	106 Sg [266]	107 Bh [264]	108 Hs [269]	109 Mt [278]	110 Ds 鐽 [281]	111 Rg 錀 [280]	112 Cn 鎶 [285]	113 Nh 鉨 [286]	114 Fl 鈇 [289]	115 Mc 鏌 [289]	116 Lv 鉝 [293]	117 Ts 石田 [294]	118 Og 气奥 [294]

57 La 鑭 138.905	58 Ce 鈰 140.116	59 Pr 鐠 140.908	60 Nd 釹 144.243	61 Pm 鉕 144.913	62 Sm 釤 150.36	63 Eu 銪 151.964	64 Gd 釓 157.25	65 Tb 鋱 158.925	66 Dy 鏑 162.500	67 Ho 鈥 164.930	68 Er 鉺 167.259	69 Tm 銩 168.934	70 Yb 鐿 173.055	71 Lu 鑥 174.967
89 Ac 錒 227.028	90 Th 釷 232.038	91 Pa 鏷 231.036	92 U 鈾 238.029	93 Np 錼 237.048	94 Pu 鈽 244.064	95 Am 鋂 243.061	96 Cm 鋦 247.070	97 Bk 錇 247.070	98 Cf 鉲 251.080	99 Es 鑀 [254]	100 Fm 鐨 257.095	101 Md 鍆 258.1	102 No 鍩 259.101	103 Lr 鐒 [262]

PROLOGUE
AUGUST

Fine art auction, London, England

A hush fell over the auction room as the final lot was brought to the table. A dark-suited man carried the case with exaggerated care. He placed it on a plinth, donned cotton gloves and carefully unpacked Lot 66. With a flourish, he swept aside the green velvet cloth to reveal a jade statue on a honey-coloured base.

A murmur of excitement rippled round the room.

'Ladies and gentlemen, Lot 66.' The auctioneer mounted the rostrum and adjusted his microphone. Despite his youth, eccentric taste in bow ties and foppish blond hair, there was no doubt who controlled the room. Cool blue eyes appraised the audience, a mix of art lovers, private investors, journalists and the odd incongruous pensioner perhaps seeking warmth or the company of strangers. He waited for complete silence before continuing. 'A Qing dynasty wedding cup. Approximately three hundred years old, this is the very finest Chinese jade mounted on a base of xenotime, and the only one of its kind.'

The jade statue glowed under the spotlights: milk-white nephrite, almost translucent, with the faintest tinge of sea green. The wedding cup consisted of two slender cylinders, each one the diameter of three fingers. A dragon encircled the male chalice, its jagged spine winding around the outer edge in a graceful helix, head raised, mouth open to reveal sharp teeth. The female vessel was laced with flowers and strings of tiny, perfectly carved pearls. A phoenix, wings spread to embrace the male and female sides, drew them together. So much intricate detail, and yet the wedding cup stood only two hands high and two fists wide on its polished crystal base.

The auctioneer flicked a lock of hair from his forehead. 'The

Qianlong Emperor ruled China from 1735 to 1796. A man of great taste – poet, musician, sculptor, collector – a warrior and a consummate politician, he was exquisitely sensitive when it came to objects of art, inventively barbaric regarding the murder of his enemies. A man of his time? Or a demonstration that for great men,' he paused and smiled at a woman in the middle row, 'and great women, the appreciation of beauty goes hand in hand with success.'

Video cameras relayed an image of the object onto giant screens as the white-gloved assistant rotated the plinth. He turned it slowly to allow everyone in the room, and the more serious bidders connecting remotely from homes and offices far away, a chance to admire the magnificent workmanship.

'Do I have an opening offer? Ladies and gentlemen, who will start the bidding for this splendid object?'

The auctioneer tossed back his blond locks and stared directly into the camera.

In Vladivostok, Russia, a ship's horn boomed out of the darkness. The long mournful chord echoed between the cliffs of the Ussuriysky Gulf.

Dmytry Zolotoy gripped the arms of his chair, light-headed with excitement as he watched the London auction on the screen. One arthritic hand strayed to his shirt, open at the neck, following the links of a chain to a jade pendant. He had waited half a century for this: the chance to square the circle, the moment to put things right, to make himself whole again.

He twisted his silver propelling pencil and wrote a number on the pad in front of him before pushing it across the desk towards his secretary.

She raised a perfectly shaped eyebrow, so thin and smooth it might have been painted on. '*Sterlingov?*'

He gave a sharp nod. '*Da.*'

She spoke into the phone, glossy crimson lips pursing and

stretching in elaborate enunciation. 'One million pounds sterling,' she said.

Dmytry surveyed his private office, chest tightening with each tick of the mantelpiece clock, an invisible vice squeezing his ribs against his spine. What if the line of communication broke? Why hadn't he sent someone to London in person? Someone like Timur, the only one he really trusted. Why? Because Timur was with his swim team, winning medals for Russia. Timur wasn't ready for this, for all the baggage that went with it: not yet.

His secretary was talking into the phone, replying to some question.

'*Prinyato?*' His jaw began to ache.

She covered the mouthpiece with her hand and nodded. '*Horosho.*'

The auctioneer held up a hand. 'I have a bid of one million pounds.' If he was surprised by the opening bid on his screen, almost double the reserve price, he betrayed not a flicker of emotion. 'Any advance on one million pounds?'

A nod from the audience, a heavyset man with one hand clamped to an earpiece.

'Two million.'

A young Chinese woman raised her auction brochure.

'Three million.'

The male bidder nodded again.

'Four million pounds. Am I bid five million?'

Sun Chang paused to admire the lights of Hong Kong twinkling over the dark water of Kowloon Bay. A faint rhythmic splashing from the deck told him that his daughter had already arrived. He drew up a lounger and waited for Mico at the shallow end of his rooftop swimming pool.

'Dad!' She raised herself from the water.

He held out a towel. 'How was the shoot?'

'Cancelled,' she said.

'Again?'

Mico climbed the tiled steps and swapped the towel for a bathrobe, so large and fluffy that her slim body disappeared into its folds.

'Five.' Sun Chang said into his phone.

'Work?' she mouthed.

'Pleasure.' He gave her the auction brochure open at Lot 66. 'What do you think?'

She studied the picture of the Qianlong wedding cup. 'Incomplete.'

'What?'

'The lids are missing.'

He peered more closely. 'How come you know so much about Qianlong jade?'

She blushed and looked away.

Sun Chang frowned and opened his laptop, clicking onto the Art Police website. There it was, an old photo from the Kaifeng Museum. The same exquisite cup, but with a tiny flower covering the female vessel and a circle of dragon fire atop the male one. He zoomed in on the image, inspecting the object rotating slowly under LED lights in London. Sure enough, he could make out two tiny holes, eyelets where hinges of silver thread would once have secured a little cover for each cup.

'Damn, you're right.' He sighed.

Mico inspected the photo. 'It *is* beautiful, though.'

'The buyer will be held to ransom by whoever has the missing lids.'

Mico peered over his shoulder. 'Last photographed in the 1930s. Before the Japanese invasion, the Great Leap Forward, the Cultural Revolution. Two lost discs of white jade, each the size of a coin. They'll never be found.'

'So, should I keep bidding?'

In China, Ru turned up the volume on her new smartphone and listened.

'Six million.'

The tiny screen was only a few centimetres wide. There was no need for better resolution. The jade statue on the xenotime base was as familiar to her as her own hands.

'Seven million.'

She stroked the jade brooch pinned to her collar; the carved flower was all she had left.

'Eight million.'

Several of the bidders had dropped out, but two remained, each one determined to win. And two was all it needed.

'Nine million.'

In Vladivostok, Dmytry's hand began to shake as he wrote a new number. He tried to lift his left arm to steady his right, but it remained obstinately at his side, as if made of lead.

The silver pencil clattered to the floor. He grasped the pendant that hung from a chain around his neck, clutching the carved circle of dragon fire as if it might save him.

He shuddered and exhaled a rasping breath, his skin ashen and damp.

'*Gospodin!*' His assistant dropped the phone and ran to his side. '*Chto ne tak, nezdorovy?*'

'*Doktor . . .*' Dmytry gasped.

'Do I have eleven million pounds?'

'Ten million, five hundred thousand?'

'Ten million, two hundred and fifty thousand?'

'Ten million, one hundred thousand pounds?'

'Any advance on ten million pounds? Ten million pounds it is, ladies and gentlemen.' The auctioneer raised his gavel and looked around the room. 'Lot 66 sold for ten million pounds. Going, going . . .' He struck the lectern with the gavel. 'Gone!'

In the London auction house, the journalists crowded the lectern, trying to see the screen.

'Can you give us the buyer's name?'

'Do you have a name, sir?'

'Who's the buyer?'

The auctioneer threw his head back, the untidy mane of blond hair bouncing up and down. He tapped his nose. 'The buyer wishes to remain anonymous.'

'The seller, then?'

'The seller's name, sir!'

'Provenance, please?'

A retired metallurgist was the last to leave the London auction house by the front entrance, lingering to get a closer look once the crowds had cleared. Although far from immune to the beauty of the jade carving, his principal interest was the xenotime base. Quite extraordinary close up, the photographs didn't do it justice. He'd never seen such large and flawless crystals of the rare metal phosphate. He wished he'd brought his Geiger counter, to gauge the radioactive content. Rare earth ores from China, monazite and xenotime, had always arrived in his lab as greyish-brown powders or dull lumps of partially crushed rock. Pure translucent crystals were unbelievably rare.

He chuckled to himself as he collected his hat and umbrella. If the prices of rare earths continued to rise at the same crazy rate as they had these past few months, the xenotime base might soon be worth as much as the jade statue.

He pulled up his collar and stepped out into the rain.

The woman from the middle row slipped out sometime later, by the back door, unseen.

PART I
SEPTEMBER

Twenty nautical miles from the Crimean coast, Black Sea

Dark clouds raced in from the east, the yacht creaking and sighing as it sped towards land in a desperate attempt to outrun the approaching storm.

Jaq grasped the wheel, the varnished wood smooth and warm under her hands, staying the course, filling the sails, running for shelter. The yacht was a living thing beneath her bare feet, bucking and twisting, stretching and straining, rolling and slewing.

A crimson glow lingered above the hills as the sun dipped below the wine-dark sea. Calm water lay ahead. Chaos and darkness, behind.

The rendezvous had gone smoothly, the 'cargo' picked up in the Crimea, delivered at the appointed time and place, twelve nautical miles from shore.

Mission accomplished.

A flash of silver lightning split the sky, illuminating the deck. *One . . . and . . . two . . . and . . .*

Giovanni worked around her, trimming the spinnaker sheet, keeping the huge sail filled as the boat rolled, wrenching every ounce of speed from the *Frankium*.

Five . . . and . . . six . . . and . . .

She looked up at the sails, perfectly set like the wings of a massive bird, propelling them over the ocean.

Ten . . . and . . . eleven . . . and . . .

They worked well together, just the two of them. Jaq setting the course, both hands on the wheel, keeping the wind behind them, optimising their speed. Maximising tension, minimising resistance. Constant small adjustments. Watching and listening, sensing, anticipating.

In contrast to Jaq's pool of stillness at the helm, Giovanni darted from side to side, a lithe dynamo in constant motion. Synchronised motion. Perfectly attuned to each other's needs. In and out of bed.

His dark curls blew about his face in the wind, eyes glinting in the gleam of the running lights, brown irises merging with dilated black pupils as he adjusted his vision to the gathering darkness. His skin was tanned by sunshine, weather-darkened by a life lived in the open air. He wore a striped T-shirt, the fabric plastered to his broad chest, damp with sweat and sea spray, the long sleeves rolled back to reveal muscled forearms. His blue chinos ended above bare ankles. Rubber soles squeaked as his white plimsolls scooted across the teak planking of the foredeck, his compact, wiry frame twisting and turning, bending and stretching.

They couldn't carry this much sail if the gusts increased. At her signal, Giovanni clipped his harness to the jackstay and started forward to drop the spinnaker. The symbol on the billowing white nylon – a black box containing the letters Fr, the chemical symbol for the eighty-seventh element in the periodic table – wrinkled and folded as the nylon sail spooled onto the deck. Giovanni bagged the sail and dropped it down the forehatch.

Fifteen . . . and . . . sixteen . . . and . . .

A massive wave lifted the stern and the boat rolled. The wind snuck behind the mainsail and forced it hard against the preventer. It rattled, straining to break free.

Jaq spun the wheel, trying to stop the boat from broaching, but it wasn't responding.

'Gybe!' Jaq bellowed.

Giovanni ducked as the preventer snapped and the boom scythed across the deck, the mainsail rattling like machine gun fire before billowing out on the other side. The boat righted and steadied itself as she brought it back on course. Giovanni waved a fist in mock anger.

That was close. Too close. The boat was answering the helm

again but it felt sluggish, no longer smoothly responsive and finely tuned. What had changed?

Giovanni must have sensed something too. '*Troppo scuro!*' he hollered. '*Troppo agitato!*' Too dark. Too risky. She mimed her reluctant agreement to reduce sail. He put a reef in the main and rolled in some of the staysail.

Twenty-five . . . and . . . twenty-six . . . and . . .

The yacht pitched and yawed, the waves rolling past the hull as it barrelled downwind. A shudder ran through the craft from prow to stern.

Twenty-eight . . . and . . . twenty-nine . . . and . . .

Thunder cracked and boomed, the roar of an angry sky dragon, threatening from on high.

Twenty-nine and a half seconds. Jaq did the mental calculation. Thunder and lightning happen at the same time, both caused by an electrical discharge from heaven to earth. Or cloud to sea, in this case. The delay in perception is only due to the different speeds at which light and sound travel. Speed of light 299,792,458 metres per second: instantaneous to all intents and purposes. Speed of sound 343 metres per second. Twenty-nine and a half seconds between the light and sound reaching them meant the storm was ten kilometres away and closing. It would hit the boat long before they made land. And hit them hard. With winds approaching 100 km/hr, 50 knots, they had less than six minutes. All around was darkness; only the rasp of sea spray on her skin, the shrieking wind howling across the Black Sea.

Had she been wrong to release the crew? Essential to the rendition, but after capturing The Spider – the criminal mastermind behind a chemical weapons factory – and rescuing his prisoner, double agent Camilla Hatton, Interpol had taken over. Sending the crew away with Interpol had seemed the obvious thing to do. More than obvious – necessary. The crew were mercenaries, soldiers not sailors, the right men for a dirty job. Task complete,

Jaq wanted nothing more than to forget the mission, forget the bloodshed and forget her own part in it all.

After the lightning, then the thunder, came the scent, borne on gusts of wind, the familiar metallic smell of ozone, the telltale chemistry of the sky.

And another scent. Testosterone and sandalwood. Giovanni appeared beside her. 'It's getting wild.'

Jaq cocked her head and appraised him. 'Shall I tie you to the mast?'

A shadow passed over his face as he handed her a life jacket. 'Put this on.'

She pulled it over her head and tightened the buckle. 'When this storm is over, let's find a quiet bay somewhere and—'

She stopped as his expression darkened. What did she see there? Something new. Was it fear? No; Gio was in his element out here in the storm. Something had changed between them. Gone was the easy intimacy, replaced by a new reserve.

'What's wrong?'

He put a finger to her lips.

'I need to check something.' He turned away and dropped through the hatch.

Jaq stood alone on the deck, fighting the untrammelled forces of nature. No time to think about Gio right now. The yacht was increasingly hard to handle. Even with reduced sail she was struggling to maintain course, to keep the wind in the sails, to stop the boat broaching again.

Giovanni popped his head up from the hatch, his eyebrows meeting in a frown.

'Water in the cabin,' he shouted. 'I'm going down to investigate.'

Lightning split the dark sky, fingers and tongues of silver all around. The shriek of wind in the rigging vied with the crash of the sea against the hull of the yacht. The waves were getting bigger and stronger, foaming salt water sluicing down the deck.

The boat vibrated from the aftershock of another thunderclap. And kept on quivering. Jaq stood still. The juddering beneath her feet felt different. Not the familiar tremors of the craft yielding and rebounding. Something less elastic, something tearing and wrenching. Something below the waterline, dampened by the sea and yet violent enough to be sensed on deck.

A sudden screech, louder than the wind, than the waves, louder than thunder. The boat itself was crying out. Rebelling. Out of control.

The boom heaved across and then back, the yacht pitched and yawed. She was falling, sliding across the sea-drenched deck, halting her slide by grabbing the jackstay. Jaq lay panting, opening her eyes wide to make sense of the dark shape that rose up in front of her.

No time for panic, or for despair – the boat was going over.

'Gio!'

Hand over hand, she hauled herself up the tilting deck away from the water.

The boat continued to heel as another massive wave caught her broadside.

Merda! One choice, two options.

Option one was to use the motion of the boat, dive under the starboard rail as the boat turned upside down, use the swell from the capsize to throw herself clear, facing the full fury of the sea.

Option two was to stay where she was. Easier for a rescue vessel to find. Remain in the boat. Allow it to roll over her. Swim to an air pocket, pull herself out of the water into a cave protected from the waves. Hope that it would not sink, rely on the inherent buoyancy, trust in a well-maintained compartmentalised design to ensure that the *Frankium* remained afloat.

Trust. Could she trust anything connected to Frank Good, the owner of this wretched craft? Given the evidence so far? Was there even a choice?

Jaq took a deep breath. As the deck thundered overhead, she

plunged into the water. The shock of immersion gave her new strength. She swam down, kicking wildly, scooping the water in mad, desperate strokes as the wounded boat completed its death roll. As she emerged a huge wave crashed over her. Tumbling and turning, she surfaced, only to be buffeted by a new wave, at the mercy of the angry sea.

Something rose beneath her, erupted from the water and arced through the air. The life raft had launched itself and inflated. By the time she reached it, she no longer possessed the strength to haul herself on board, but she caught a tether and clung to the side.

A flash of lightning lit the upturned hull of the *Frankium*, bobbing on the waves, a pale sea creature.

No sign of Giovanni. She had to get the raft to the upturned boat and send him a signal.

She started to swim back towards the yacht, towing the raft behind her, but the currents were against her, arms aching as the distance only increased.

How to get out of the water and into the raft? It was no use fighting the waves. Could she use them? She positioned herself between the next wave and the raft, hoping to surf above it. Bad idea. The force of the wave slammed her into the side, knocking her breath away so that she almost lost hold of the rope. *Burra!* If at first you don't succeed, try something different.

Many years ago, she had learned how to right a kayak. Johan, then her instructor, now her best friend, had superb upper body strength, but she always beat him in the timed drills. Brains over brawn. Use the buoyancy as your friend; let physics do the work. Time to apply that here. Once her breathing was almost back to normal, she repositioned the raft between her and the next wave, tipping the side towards her until it was almost perpendicular, grabbing the ropes inside. As the wave passed underneath, the raft scooped her up and she collapsed, like a flapping fish, into the bottom of the vessel.

She lay on the rubber floor for a few minutes, gathering what was left of her wits, then scrabbled around for the paddles and a waterproof pouch of survival gear: flares, water, energy bars, first aid kit, compass, rope, a handy-billy block and tackle, knife.

Where were they? She checked the compass. North led back to Crimea, east to Russia, west to Bulgaria, south to Turkey, the direction they had been heading. There was no sign of land – black ocean pitched and heaved in all directions – and no sign of her captain.

'Giovanni!'

The worst of the storm had passed, the intervals between lightning and thunder extending, the intensity decreasing, the wind dropping, the waves subsiding.

She let off a flare. If Giovanni was already in the water, then he'd soon find her. She unwrapped an energy bar and washed it down with a swig of fresh water. Then she wrapped herself in a blanket, took up the oar and paddled towards the upturned boat.

As she drew closer, she could see the rudder and skeg, but where was the keel? The huge underwater fin stuffed with five tonnes of lead had only one job – to keep the boat upright. Nothing remained but a tear in the hull and jagged holes where the keel bolts should be.

'Giovanni Fantucci!' she yelled as loud as she could. She brought the life raft alongside the stricken, upturned yacht to where the cabin should be, and struck the side with an oar. Was it her imagination, or was there a faint noise in return? She knocked again, twice this time.

Then listened. Nothing.

She tried again, smashing harder, scanning the water, expecting him to emerge: his flashing white teeth and dark brown eyes. And then came the reply. Three faint taps, three scratches, then the taps again. Dot dot dot, dash dash dash, dot dot dot. SOS. Giovanni was under the wrecked boat and needed help.

Heart racing, cold hands fumbling, she threaded the life raft's painter around the rudder shaft and tied a bowline. She set off another distress flare before diving into the dark water. Her life jacket fought against her, pulling her back. She surfaced and removed it, tossing it back into the life raft before diving again, using her hands to pull herself under the boat, jackknifing under the rail and swimming up through the companionway into the cabin. If she didn't find air soon, she was not sure she could make it out again. Her lungs were bursting, close to the point of no return. She took a gamble, let go of the rope and kicked upwards.

A hand came down and caught hers, guiding her into an air pocket. She took a breath. *Deus.* He was alive. She took another breath. And another. *Bolas*, it was worse than she thought. There was barely enough room for Giovanni, and the water was up to his shoulders. The air, what little of it there was, was stale. No: worse than stale. Oxygen-depleted.

'Lucia?' he whispered.

Who was Lucia? No time for that now.

'It's Jaq. I've got the life raft. Can you swim out with me?'

'Trapped,' he gasped. 'Can't move.' He was panting hard.

Merda. Alive, but only just. And her presence was using up his oxygen supply. She felt around his body. One arm was wedged at a strange angle between a loose floorboard and the base of the mast. She tried to yank the fallen board free, but even before he screamed, she knew his arm was trapped and broken.

'I'm going to get you some air. Then I'm going to get you out of here.'

No reply.

'Gio. Don't leave me. Don't give up. I need you.'

Silence.

'Lucia needs you.' Whoever she was.

'Lucia.' He sighed.

How could she get air to him? There was nothing in the life raft: no oxygen tank, no scuba mask, no tubing. Even the life rings were foam-filled.

Could she open an air hole from the top? The knife would never pierce the hull. She had no drill, no saw, no blowtorch.

A plastic bowl floated past, followed by an empty Tupperware box. Tupperware. Suddenly she knew what to do.

'Gio!' she whispered. 'I'm going to get you out of here.' Jaq kissed his cold cheek. The stubble rasped against her lips. She took a shallow breath and dived down.

She used the position of the mast to guide her to the locker. She yanked it open and scrabbled around until she found it: the little Tupperware box confiscated from a man who'd tried to kill her. She stuffed the box into the waistband of her shorts. You never knew when a kilo of Semtex might come in handy.

There was only one way to free him. It might kill Giovanni. *Deus perdoa-me.* But if she did nothing, he would die anyway. Alone in a cold, dark cave, suffocating in his own exhalations. She was out of other options. Better a bang than a whimper.

Jaq was going to blast what remained of the *Frankium* to smithereens.

And pray that she didn't kill her lover.

Melrose, Scotland

The river crested a weir and cascaded into a dark pool beside the old mill. Sleek trout swam in wide circles, the toffee-coloured water stained by peat and topped by a creamy foam from decaying vegetation: green figwort and sand leek, water mint and forget-me-not, yellow cress and flowering rush.

An osprey circled the pool before turning west, soaring over the old Cistercian monastery in a parallel wooded valley. Beech trees and sycamore, ash and oak, chestnut and hawthorn, Scots pine and larch formed a dense wood that sheltered and concealed the exclusive clinic operating in the heart of the Scottish Borders.

Inside the medical wing, a man with a white coat and stethoscope sat at a desk taking notes while his patient, the owner of the yacht *Good Ship Frankium*, lay on a brocade couch and stared at a plaster rose in the ceiling.

'In conclusion, Mr Good, you think you're ready to go back to work?'

'Yes.'

Not that he'd needed sick leave at all. The halfwits in Zagrovyl Human Resources had forced him to take time off. Claimed he'd been behaving erratically. *Ppffit!* One person's erratic was another's proportionate response to events. After all he'd been through, everything he'd done to protect the company, his actions had been wholly reasonable.

Yes, there was the unfortunate incident during the team-building event. He could see how it might look from the outside. But the fault was with the team. Left alone, he could handle anything, even the flashbacks. It was other people he couldn't stand. Especially the idiots from the Teesside factory. All fake concern to his face while they stuck knives in his back.

He wasn't sick; Zagrovyl wanted to keep him out of the way during the investigation. And it suited him to lie low for a while. Until it was safe again.

Frank had made a show of resisting, driving a hard bargain, relenting only after his employers agreed to fund this place – a golf retreat. The executive health insurance wouldn't cover it, but Zagrovyl owed him. Big time. And although he hadn't needed the time off, he had to admit he felt better for it. Calmer, leaner, fitter, stronger.

'How about the nightmares?'

A mistake to discuss his subconscious with this overpaid shrink. He'd have to be more careful.

'Manageable.'

Still waking him up. Always a version of the same dream. Trapped in a silken web, unable to move, he screamed himself awake, drenched in sweat. Nothing a shower couldn't fix.

'And the tremors?'

Frank held out one hand and then the other. Steady as a rock. The solo golf practice had improved his muscle control as well as his stroke.

'Fine.'

Fine, so long as he didn't think about . . . He stuffed both hands under his buttocks as he tried not to picture her, the woman who had caused all the trouble.

'Excellent.'

The doctor bent down to check his blood pressure.

'Hmmm. Still high. Let's give it another few days, shall we? Stay off the stimulants – coffee, tea, alcohol. I'll adjust the medication, and then we can review next week.'

'I'm ready to leave.'

'I can't force you to stay, but you're not ready to go back to work.'

Arrogant bastard. What did he know about work? Or whether Frank was ready? The pulse in his temple began to throb as he felt the anger rising.

'The weather is fine. Play some more golf. Take time for yourself. Take a trip. Catch up with old friends.'

Old friends? Ha! The only social event in his calendar was a funeral.

'You can continue as an outpatient at my Newcastle clinic. We can work on relaxation techniques. Discuss what might provoke a stress response. Find strategies to recognise and master the triggers.'

Triggers. The Spider was in custody; Frank's lawyer had written with the news from Interpol. The man who had tried to trick Zagrovyl into supplying a chemical weapons factory was going to prison for a very long time. It was safe to come out of hiding. Safe to go back to work. There was only one potential trigger at large. Dr Jaqueline Silver.

Recognise and master.

Frank closed his eyes and sent up a silent prayer that she wouldn't make it back.

Somewhere in the Black Sea

Jaq didn't pray. In her experience, praying was a waste of time. Even as a child, before she had completely discounted the notion of an omniscient, omnipresent deity, praying still struck her as futile. It usually made things worse. Praying was passive, waiting for someone else to help you out. Better to face up to the problem, explore options, plan a solution and take action.

She surfaced to find that the clouds had cleared to reveal a full moon and a rash of stars. The storm had passed, leaving a beautiful night sky and calm water. Gulping great breaths of air, she hauled herself back into the life raft.

Face up to the problem, explore options, plan a solution and take action.

Giovanni was suffocating, and she had no way to get fresh air to him. If he couldn't leave the boat, then the boat was going to have to leave him. And the only way she could think of to make that happen was to blow it up.

She peeled the lid from the Tupperware box, inhaling the faint scent of almonds.

But could she detonate the Semtex? The success of plastic explosive is in part its stability. The main components, cyclotrimethylenetrinitramine – RDX and Pentaerythritol tetranitrate – PETN, don't explode if you drop or heat them; they are waterproof and resistant to minor shocks. PETN is difficult to ignite and burns slowly. RDX burns more easily, producing large volumes of gas. The trick is confinement – leave nowhere for the hot gases to go, build up the pressure and temperature of a deflagration and force a transition to detonation.

She assembled the things she needed. From the first aid box, Vaseline, crêpe bandages and cotton wool. From the survival box, the flares and an aluminium cylinder with screwed caps on either end, containing nautical charts.

Her best hope for detonation was the rocket flare, packed with propellants. Would the shock wave have enough energy? If the impact wasn't enough, then she'd have to rely on a secondary ignition. And even if she succeeded, would it do enough damage to open the hull?

Setting aside the rockets, she inspected the handheld flares, two each giving orange smoke or white light. Excellent. There was no list of ingredients, but they would be packed full of magnesium, strontium nitrate, charcoal and potassium perchlorate. Just what she needed. She worked quickly, stuffing the aluminium cylinder in layers, giving herself the best possible chance.

Once the improvised bomb was fixed to the weakest point of the hull, as far away from where Giovanni was trapped as she dared, she fashioned a conical funnel with the laminated nautical charts. Satisfied that the target was wide enough to hit, she retreated to the life raft.

The rocket flare had a plastic base, easily unscrewed to release the ripcord. She crouched down low, resting the flare tube against the side of the raft in line with the opening of her explosive device. *Here goes. Now or never.* She took a deep breath and pulled.

Sacana! The recoil knocked her off balance and the flare went wide, missing the opening to the aluminium tube before screaming across the surface of the now-mockingly calm water, flaring briefly before sinking beneath the dark sea.

No choice; she'd have to get closer. Yes, it was risky. If she was successful, and the Semtex detonated, the blast might kill her. If the energy from the rocket propellant was insufficient, but it started a fire, then she was in with a chance of moving back in time.

Giovanni's best hope was if she activated the flare at point-blank range. The highest-risk option.

And if she lived and he died? What sort of a solution was that?

In her professional life, Jaq was a meticulous planner. In her personal life, she lived for the moment. Giovanni was exactly the sort of man you needed to skipper a yacht packed with explosives. They'd had a bit of fun to celebrate the successful completion of the mission – so what? Would their relationship last once they got back to shore? And did it even matter? She couldn't stand back and let him die.

She climbed back onto the upturned yacht and knelt on the hull, resting the flare tube inside the opening of her pipe bomb. As she pulled the ripcord, she threw herself back into the sea.

Under the water, she opened her eyes. Nothing but darkness. No bright lights, no vibration, no boom. She'd failed.

She surfaced with a heavy heart.

It took her a moment to register the light twinkling from the end of the aluminium tube. A fire. Something had ignited. But would it be enough? The light was burning brighter now. Magnesium to magnesium oxide. Time to get away.

She swam in long straight strokes, surfacing every few yards to breathe, resisting the temptation to look back.

BOOM!

Fragments of the *Frankium* pelted the surface of the water all around. A splinter of fibreglass grazed her cheek. *Plip, plop, splash.* The most welcome heavenly shower imaginable. As it abated, she swam back, through a cloud of smoke and ash. There wasn't much left of the boat, but where was Giovanni?

She dived again, hands outstretched, searching frantically. He'd been wearing a life jacket. She was sure of it. She surfaced at the same time as the yellow jacket bobbed up on the other side of the life raft. *Oh, Gio, please be alive, please, Gio, don't leave me now.*

She swam to him and brought an ear to his cold mouth. He was breathing. *Graças a Deus.* She checked him for injury. An obviously broken right arm – just as well he was unconscious – but no other sign of surface injury. How to get him out of the water and into the life raft? She was shaking too much to even try right now. Instead she tied his life jacket to the life raft, gathered provisions and placed them where she could reach them. She returned to the water and wrapped her arms and legs around his cold body to share warmth and closed her eyes.

'Jaq?'

'Gio? *Ragazzo*, am I glad to hear your voice!' She grabbed the water bottle and pressed it to his lips. 'Here, drink this.'

He gulped and coughed. Securing it with his left hand, he gulped again.

She unwrapped an energy bar. 'Now, eat.'

He tore through one, and then another.

'What happened?' he asked between mouthfuls.

'What do you remember?'

'The storm. Reefing the sails on the boat . . .' He looked around. '*Dove cazzo è la barca?*

'You don't remember it breaking up?'

'No.'

'Or how I got you out?'

'The last thing I remember is pulling in the sails. Then waking up in the sea, tied to this poxy life raft.'

'Do you think you can get in?' she asked.

'With your help.'

It wasn't easy. The water had numbed the pain of his broken limb, but as he tried to manoeuvre himself over the side with one good arm, he passed out, half in, half out. Now all she had to do was pull him in.

Did she have the strength? Strength is overrated. Power has never been about muscles. The powerful of the ancient world used slaves to do physical work. Modern humans use tools. And gears. The average adult man can lift 30 kilograms easily. The average adult woman about two-thirds of that. So, all you need for complete equality is a two-thirds geared pulley. Giovanni would weigh about 75 kilograms. And Jaq had the handy-billy, a block and tackle with a double pulley and ratchet. Easy-peasy.

She clipped one end to the webbing straps on the far side of the life raft, clipped the other end to his life jacket and hauled him in.

Giovanni regained consciousness, yelping with pain as he hit the rubber deck. She tried to make him comfortable, fed him analgesics from the first aid kit, paracetamol and ibuprofen, cursing at the lack of morphine.

Dawn was coming, and with it the welcome sound of a boat. Jaq stood up and waved at the Bulgarian coastguard. When she looked back, Giovanni's face had lost all colour.

'Not long now, Gio. Rescue's here. Hang on in there.'

He was drifting off again. She needed to keep him awake.

'Who is Lucia?'

A little colour returned to his face. 'Lucia?'

'When you were trapped. You said her name.'

He looked away. 'A girl.' He corrected himself. 'A woman back home. I should have told you.'

'I understand.'

'No, you don't.' He screwed up his face. 'I've been a bastard.'

'To Lucia perhaps, but not to me. I've got someone back home as well.' Not quite a lie. There was someone she loved completely and unreservedly, though it was wholly unrequited.

'You forgive me?'

'Of course.' Although Lucia might not. Would he tell her? Up to him. None of her business.

'Thank you, Jaq.'

'Hey, we just had a bit of fun, right?'

No reply.

He was unconscious when the rescue boat pulled alongside.

PART II
SEPTEMBER

Beijing, China

A hush fell over the room as the door opened. Yun kept her eyes down, following the points of her jet-black shoes, modulating the click-clack of stiletto heels on polished floor tiles to maintain an even rhythm. Careful not to falter as she stepped onto silk carpet, moving from a geometric grid of burnt umber to swirling almond and aquamarine curves, her footfall softened to a swish, swish until she reached her seat and stopped.

A man cleared his throat. *Hhggaarrkh*. The phlegmy rasp echoed around the cavernous room, punctuated by the ping of spit hitting a copper bowl.

She mastered her disgust, placing her cerise handbag on the tan surface in front of her, adjusting the long edge to line up with the short side of the wooden table, sat down and bowed her head.

'Madam Yun, thank you for coming.' The tone was terse, anything but welcoming. 'I think you know everyone.'

She raised her eyes slowly, neck muscles straining to lift a head leaden with anxiety, facing her accusers at last. The performance committee, twelve men and one woman, sat at tables set out in a horseshoe around her. The chairman, a civil servant, wore a charcoal-grey business suit. The politician to his left was dressed in a blue tunic and loose trousers, and the woman to his right wore a summer dress patterned with bright flowers of magenta and cinnabar and leaves of viridian green. The other ten wore, like her, police uniform. Only one surprise among the depressingly familiar faces of her superiors: Yan Bing. What was her former deputy doing at her disciplinary hearing? Telling lies again? This could be even worse than she feared.

Her hands began to tremble; she clasped them together.

'Madam Yun, please state your job role for the record.'

'I am Chief of the Ancient Art Section of the Anti-Smuggling Division of the Ministry of State Security.'

'And your remit?'

'My team are entrusted with preserving the ancient heritage of China for the benefit of the Chinese people.'

The chair turned to his secretary. 'Head of the Art Squad.' Painted fingernails clacked on a keyboard.

'And have you been effective in that role?'

'We have had many successes.' She began to reel them off. The backpackers caught at the border, their rucksacks stuffed with Neolithic clay pots; the sea containers prevented from leaving with bags of plastic granules insulating Ming dynasty porcelain; the Hong Kong gang caught red-handed in a fishing boat.

The chair interrupted. 'Indeed, the committee would like to applaud you for your work.'

Say one thing, mean the opposite. The eyes of the committee looked away, one after another. Only Yan Bing met her gaze, dark eyes glittering, wrinkling at the corners as his mouth twisted in a smirk.

'Which is why we would like your . . . ahem . . . advice on this matter.'

The chairman tapped a pistachio-hued file that lay open in front of him and removed a newspaper cutting. Sepia-tinted paper. English characters.

The Qianlong wedding cup. She hung her head.

Had it been a mistake to go public? Her vigorous attempts, on behalf of the Chinese government, to have the sale stopped had created headline news and significantly raised the profile of the auction. It had certainly brought it to the attention of her superiors.

'What do you know about the auction of ancient Chinese jade in London last month?'

All her efforts. Too little, too late. 'My department used all legal means . . .'

Yan Bing muttered to his neighbour, loud enough for all to hear, 'When our treasures have been stolen, what use are legal means?'

The chair glared at him and held up a hand before continuing, his voice low and steely. 'Tell me the history.'

'The Henan Museum jade collection was originally assembled by the Emperor Qianlong around 1775, although some pieces are much older. It was last seen in Kaifeng in 1937 before Museum Director Wang Jun packed the collection away for safekeeping.'

She didn't have to spell out the threat. The Japanese invasion.

'And Wang?'

'He perished soon after, along with the last of his family.' A tragic tale. His wife and sons died in the war, his daughter during the Great Leap Forward. Wang Jun and his only surviving relative, a granddaughter, drowned in the floods at the end of the Cultural Revolution.

'And yet . . .' He flicked through the file. 'It seems that the pieces appeared in the West only very recently.'

'Yes.' Careful now. 'At the Drottningholm Palace museum in Sweden, the University Museum in Durham and Museu de Arte Antiga in Lisbon. All acquired pieces from the Qianlong jade collection in the last decade.'

'So where was the collection? Between 1937 and 2000?'

'It's not clear. But we are working with the museum authorities to return the pieces to China.'

'What about the prize piece, the wedding cup?'

She dropped her eyes. 'Unfortunately, that was a private sale. We have not yet identified either the seller or the buyer in order to begin negotiations for recovery. But we are confident—'

'At the start of your tenure,' the politician sitting to the right of the chair interrupted, 'we estimated that 1.64 million Chinese antiquities resided in 200 museums in 47 foreign countries. And now?'

'The new figures are disputed . . .'

'How many treasures have you brought back?'

'We are making great progress in Norway, and . . .' She began to list the countries with treaties under negotiation.

The politician raised his palms to the ceiling as she tailed off into silence. He turned to the chair. 'None,' he barked, and pointed at the secretary. 'Record that.' The secretary tapped a single character into the computer.

A uniformed officer piped up. 'In fact, the situation has worsened, has it not?' His thin, reedy voice grated and rasped like a corncrake. 'For every single treasure you try to recover, thousands more are smuggled out under your nose. Foreigners continue to rape and pillage our heritage. And what do you do? Go to international conferences.'

A few members of the committee muttered their disapproval.

She sat forward, hands on the desk in front of her. 'The bilateral exchange of art treasures requires delicate diplomacy.'

The ripple running around the room told her she'd made a tactical error. What had Mico told her? Watch your language. Dress it up.

'Delicate diplomacy, bilateral exchange. Hmmm. That is your style, is it not? Perhaps, Madam Yun, it's time for a different approach. Less careful, gentle and consensual. More vigorous, aggressive and muscular.'

Her lips tightened and her eyes flashed with anger as she processed the subtext. *You have failed because you are a woman. Too soft. Not hard enough.* It didn't matter that she'd made more progress than any of her male predecessors, didn't matter that they were on the verge of a breakthrough in Europe. No; one bloody public auction in London and everything was her fault.

She jumped at the snap of paper. 'Madam Yun.' The chair closed the file. 'I believe my comrade is right. It is time to try new ideas and new methods. Perhaps we need new blood.' His eyes rested on Yan Bing, who gave the briefest of nods.

Please, no. Anyone but him. 'Yes, sir.'

'You are an artist, are you not?'

'My degree was in fine art, yes.'

'Very impressive.' His tone said everything but. 'The Women's Federation are rolling out a new programme. They have contacted us, asked if you could be released to develop the schools' ancient art curriculum . . .'

Her mouth opened in an involuntary *Oh!*

'In Chongqing.'

Exile. She swallowed, her mouth suddenly dry.

'What shall I tell them?'

'Sir, I would be honoured to be considered for such a post.' Say the opposite of what you mean. 'However, there are serious internal issues to investigate.' She looked directly at Yan Bing. 'And I believe I am the best person to resolve them.'

The chair waved a hand dismissively. 'Madam Yun, it's time for a change. A new approach.'

That meant Yan Bing. Two could play at his game. What had Mico said? Be bold. It was now or never.

'I know how to get the complete collection back.'

'The Qianlong jade? All of it? Guaranteed?'

She straightened her back. 'I guarantee it, sir.'

'How much time?'

She made a quick calculation. 'One year.'

'Too long.' He sighed and waved a hand at the secretary. 'Write to the All-China Women's Federation. Inform them that we will give our answer after the Spring Festival.'

The Spring Festival, only four months away. Impossible. Unless . . .

'Madam Yun, you will focus on this task and this alone. Yan Bing will take over operational duties on a temporary basis.' *Temporary if you succeed. On a permanent basis if you fail.*

She raised her chin and made eye contact. 'The collection will be back in China before the Lantern Festival.' The fifteenth day of the Spring Festival.

And this time she meant exactly what she said.

For, if she failed, it wasn't just her life that was over.

As dusk approached, visibility worsened. Under the Beijing street lights, the smog sent out sulphurous tendrils, ancient orpiment, the King's yellow, making her eyes water. Darkness fell early in Beijing.

Yun coughed, dislodging the sharp needles in her nose and throat, and dabbed at her watering eyes.

'You're late tonight,' the driver said.

A tinge of complaint? His job was to drive her wherever she wished. Whenever she wished. A perk of office, one of the few. Her hours were long and unpredictable.

'Busy day?'

Fishing for information? Perhaps the driver was one of Yan Bing's cronies. Yan Bing could always count on a loyal following in the force. Notorious for rescuing waifs and strays from juvenile detention, he bypassed normal admission processes to give them police jobs, or placed them undercover as informers and enforcers. One of the many reasons she had removed him from her department. She gripped the armrest as the car swung out of a side road into the Beijing traffic and considered the return of her former deputy. Her nails dug into the soft leather, knuckles whitening as she berated herself. She should have prosecuted him, not offered him a transfer. And now he was back for revenge. Were they right, the performance committee? Had she been too soft in the past? Well, all that was over now.

As the car nosed into a snarling jam, twenty million people on the move, she ignored the driver and composed herself, softening her work face, slipping into her role as Mimi's mother.

Mimi had her whole life ahead of her.

Or did she? What if her daughter fell into the clutches of the All-China Women's Federation and their flagship New Era Sunny Women Program, designed to teach women how to dress to please, how to use make-up to entice, how to sit, walk, bow, pour tea, limiting aspiration to homemaking and caring for parents, children and, crucially, husbands?

The cunning bastards. As personalised torture went, the punishment assignment had a particularly sharp edge. Yun had never made a secret of her feminism; Mao had brought China kicking and screaming into twentieth-century equality and she had made it her personal mission to protect and defend the progress. But now, in the twenty-first century, it was slipping away. Women were being encouraged to take a back seat, to reconnect with older Confucian traditions of beauty and passivity.

The faint strains of a Shostakovich study filled the stairwell as Yun opened the street door. She listened to Mimi's cello as she waited for the lift. Inside the flat, two paper cartons of noodles sat on the kitchen table, one empty, the other still in its takeaway bag, the throwaway chopsticks facing her in pointed rebuke. The hunger pangs had morphed into something different. She tipped everything into the bin, moving quietly so as not to disturb her daughter's practice, before tiptoeing to the bedroom. She removed her police uniform, hanging it up in the closet before turning on the shower.

When she emerged from the steam, wrapped in towels, Mimi was already sitting on her bed.

'What happened?' she demanded.

'Hi, darling, how was school?'

'Why didn't you tell me?' Mimi stood to face her; they were almost the same height now. 'Have you really been sacked?'

Yun turned away to towel her hair. 'No, of course not.'

'You mustn't let that happen.' Mimi stamped her foot. 'I won't get into the conservatoire.'

If Yun lost her government job, and her Beijing residency, Mimi would lose her place at the special music school. What sort of a life was there for them in Chongqing? A landlocked industrial megalopolis. Mimi would have to start from scratch.

'Who's been talking?'

'Jaja and Feng.' Mimi scowled. 'I don't like them any more.'

'It's just idle gossip. Ignore it. Everything's fine.' She smoothed back her damp hair and held out her arms. Mimi stepped into the embrace, reluctant at first, the slight adolescent body crumpling against her mother, dissolving into sobs. Great theatrical sobs.

'All the practice. All for nothing. I can't bear it.'

Oh, child, if only you knew. If only you understood. So many worse things in the world to bear.

'There's nothing to worry about.' The half-truths came easily, a silken river from a newly forked tongue.

Yun pulled away and held Mimi at arm's length. Fifteen years old. A child of new China. A girl who had only ever known food on the table, a roof over her head, a soft bed to sleep in, hot water for washing, four grandparents and an extended family to adore her, clothes and shoes whenever she needed them, toys whenever she wanted them, a TV, tablet and smartphone, music lessons, a car to take her to school. Were they spoilt, this new generation? Or was this normality returning, after so many turbulent years?

We must make sacrifices, yes. But do we have to sacrifice our children?

After Mimi went to bed, Yun made the call. Mico was the only one who could help her now.

PART III
OCTOBER

A village five miles south of Middlesbrough, England

Frank kept half an eye on the weather as he drove to the church. Autumn in Teesside meant grey skies and rain. Just like winter, spring and summer. October rain might be slightly warmer than January rain, but the seasons in the north-east of England were barely distinguishable.

Today, just to confound him, the afternoon was turning out crisp and bright, the silver weathervane at the top of the spire shimmering in the sun.

A perfect day for a funeral.

Catch up with old friends, the doctor said. A funeral was the ideal place to start socialising again, to take one small step towards complete recovery.

Frank reversed into a tight space next to the village green. A little stream ran beside the high street, corralled into a steep-sided canal fringed with willow trees. Pretty village. You had to say that for the North. Outside the ghastly industrial towns there were plenty of attractive places. Although, strictly speaking, this one was in North Yorkshire. A different class of place. If he'd known he'd be in the Zagrovyl job this long, he might have considered buying a house out here, in a hamlet like this. You could get a lot of living space for your money compared to Sussex. A thought for the future. For now, the serviced apartment in Eaglescliffe was more convenient for a single man. An eligible bachelor on his way to an interesting date.

He'd agreed to play the organ as a favour to the family – well, as a favour to Sophie, who had some confused idea that Frank and her father had been friends. Business acquaintances, yes, but apart from money they had little in common. Charles Clark was obsessed with batteries. All he could talk about. Boring as hell. Fortunately, he'd buggered off to China to set up a factory there. Frank had barely noticed his absence. And then the old man got ill and came home to die. It had all happened fast. At least he hadn't lingered.

Frank was here to keep an eye on his investment. Apparently, Charles had left everything to his daughter, Sophie. Rich, easy on the eye and grieving. A winning combination.

He twisted to grab his folder of sheet music from the back seat and swore at the brief pain in his lower back. He'd chosen the programme to impress. Sophie had reeled off a list of music her father loved. Simon and Garfunkel, Lloyd Webber, the Carpenters. Charles had execrable taste. Frank had substituted a more appropriate programme. One that showed off the full range of the glorious instrument. And his skill. You couldn't go wrong with J. S. Bach.

He ambled up the path to the vicarage, taking a shortcut across the lawn and onto the terrace so he could peer through the french windows of the grand Victorian rectory, but the shutters were closed. He walked away from the house, past a tidy vegetable patch, avoiding the beehives buzzing with activity, and skirted an orchard heavy with fruit.

The church door opened on to rows of empty pews. At least an hour before anyone else arrived. He climbed up to the organ loft and adjusted the seat with mounting irritation. Whoever had been performing here before was a fucking midget.

His phone pinged, amplified and echoed by the ancient stone walls. He blinked at the screen, too bright for the soft light of the chapel. Aha! So, she was on her way back, was she? Jaqueline Silver. The murdering engineer who almost cost him his job, his health and his sanity. He read her brief message and a surge of anger swept over him. The scar on his left leg began to throb, and the ringing in his bad ear turned to white noise.

Frank switched off his phone and took two tablets. The doctor told him to count to one hundred, but he preferred to use music to manage the madness.

A chorale prelude from *Orgelbüchlein*, J. S. Bach's *Little Organ Book*, helped his breathing return to normal. '*Christum wir sollen loben schon*', the tempo in inverse proportion to his heart rate as the muscle memory in his fingers took over and moved the melody through visceral harmonisation to a glorious final chord.

He set up the sheet music for the funeral and cracked his knuckles. A fine instrument.

With an even finer organist.

Ljubljana, Slovenia

The plane began its descent, crossing the invisible border between Austria and Slovenia. It banked on approach to Ljubljana, the broad fertile valley of the river Sava a riot of autumn colour: russet, crimson, amber, copper and gold.

Jaq gazed out of the window at Mount Triglav, the rocky peak sparkling in the sunshine, white with the first snow of the season. Her thighs and calves tightened involuntarily. Muscle memory: only a few months ago she had been skiing down the high slopes.

This visit was time-constrained – meet with her lawyer, sign some court documents at the police station, ensure her record with Interpol was wiped clean, collect her passport and possessions and say goodbye to Slovenia.

And to everything that might have been. And could never be.

In a cramped office, behind tinted windows, the immigration official frowned at the document before scrutinising the face of the woman in front of him.

'You are Dr Jaqueline Silver?'

'Yes.'

'Any other identification documents?'

'No.' Her Portuguese passport lay at the bottom of the Black Sea. This piece of paper was the best the consular official in Sofia, Bulgaria had been able to manage: a one-way warrant to Slovenia to collect her British passport, currently in a police safe in Ljubljana.

'You're married?'

Separated, awaiting divorce, but that was more information than she was willing to share. What business was it of this bureaucrat?

Legally speaking, she was still married to Gregor Coutant. Morally speaking she had a step-granddaughter she was anxious to meet. OK, make it simple.

'Yes.'

'Is your husband meeting you?'

'No.'

He looked up, narrowing his eyes.

'And your luggage?'

She handed him the letter from the UN office. 'I was shipwrecked.'

He read the letter carefully, his eyes slowly widening. 'You OK?'

'I'll survive.'

He stamped the document and waved for her to go. 'Good luck.'

Brooding, lost in memories, she almost walked straight past the slim, fair-haired policeman.

'Dr Silver.'

She stopped and held out a hand.

'Detective Y'Ispe.'

It was good to see him again. Will-O'-the-Wisp, the Slovenian police detective who had believed in her innocence long after everyone else had decided she was guilty. The man who had carried on investigating while others tried to silence her.

'Safe flight?'

Strange question. The safest thing she had done in the last six months was to take an airplane from one European airport to another. Only twenty-three fatalities among 2.4 billion passenger flights last year. Safer than a trip by train or a journey in a car, orders of magnitude safer than a spin on a motorbike on forbidden roads, a jump from a crashing helicopter or a dive from a capsizing yacht in the Black Sea.

'Fine.'

Why was he here, at the airport? She hadn't told him the exact arrival time, offering only a window of dates for a return to Ljubljana.

'Your lawyer told me which flight you were on.'

Could everyone read her thoughts as well as Will-O'-the-Wisp? Or was it his profession that gave him special insight? He was good at his job. And looking much more relaxed than last time they met.

'He'll meet us at the station.'

Outside the small airport, a police car idled: stripes of white, red and blue and a coat of arms with three mountain peaks and three stars – the Slovenian flag. Will-O'-the-Wisp opened the back door for her before getting into the front next to the uniformed driver. They drove into the old town through narrow streets, bouncing over cobbles, past brightly painted houses: salmon pink, lime green and sunflower yellow under terracotta tiles. Most of her time in Ljubljana had been spent behind prison bars. People had conspired to keep her there.

Her court-appointed Slovenian lawyer was waiting for her in an interview room. A man who stank of ketosis – the giveaway smell of the committed alcoholic. He looked as if he had slept under his usual hedge. Perhaps his shaking hands could not be trusted with a razor or hairbrush. Rumple Stubble the Useless.

Not quite so useless, as it transpired. He'd done a thorough job. The documents he had prepared exonerated her completely; the consolidated statement was accurate and concise. All charges in Slovenia – professional misconduct, breaking bail, evading capture, contempt of court, manslaughter and murder – had been dropped.

Once the paperwork was complete, a police constable brought out the things she had left behind. Before her arrest, she'd been employed as an explosives expert, setting off controlled avalanches to keep the slopes safe for skiing and snowboarding. There wasn't much to show for her season at Snow Science: a suitcase of clothes, a carton of books and CDs, a crate with her stereo, assorted kitchen items and a sealed padded envelope marked private.

She unzipped the suitcase and recoiled at the smell of mildew. Her clothes were neatly folded: ski jacket, salopettes, thermal vests and long johns, coat, hat, gloves, colourful pashmina scarf, a party dress, assorted underwear, a business trouser suit, several blouses, T-shirts, sweaters, a pair of faded jeans, gym kit, swimming costume, knee-length leather boots, running shoes and climbing boots. The whole case stank. *Cladosporium*, the microscopic fungus with its invisible branching mitospores had permeated everything, feeding on moist fibres and producing volatile organics like trichloroanisole, detectable to the human nose at parts per trillion.

She removed the Shetland hat and sniffed it; the familiar scent of peat fires and wet sheep persisted, the natural antimicrobials in the lanolin having protected it. Perhaps she should go back to Sullom Voe. Even in winter, the outer isles had a magic that was hard to resist. Despite the short days and long nights, the gale-force winds and angry seas, it was a place she would happily return to.

Hat retrieved, everything else was replaceable. Best to start afresh. She zipped the suitcase back up and placed it on the floor.

The books and CDs were in better shape. She flicked through, picking out a few to keep – those with memories attached, such as *Perry's Chemical Engineers' Handbook* (sixth edition) and Parliament's *Mothership Connection* (remastered). The rest could go to charity, along with the old stereo and all the kitchen equipment except the Bialetti Dama, the stove-top espresso maker that Johan had given her.

She left the padded envelope to last. Her peripatetic childhood meant that she had been able to keep only a few things that she really valued, and this package held most of them.

She opened it and explored the contents with her fingers. The Portuguese ceramic tile was intact, and everything else safely wrapped.

A green marble rolled out; she caught it and held it up to the light.

The first thing Jaq remembered, really remembered, was the crocodile in the garden. His unblinking green eye, a vertical slit of black in a circle of jade shot through with golden threads, pulled her in. Close up, she could see the knobbly reptilian skin, the rows of yellow teeth, the nostrils that flared, and was repulsed and fascinated in equal measure.

She'd been playing outside the family home in Luanda, Angola. Her brother had climbed a tree, but she was too small to reach the first branch and was bored with trying. Glimpsing movement and a flash of green at the bottom of the slope, she'd run off to investigate. It wasn't as if she was unaware of the danger – they'd been warned many times – but crocodiles didn't usually venture so far from the river.

Curiosity drove her tottering down the bank; she couldn't have been more than three or four years old. The strange animal in the long grass was smiling at her, so she smiled back. She remembered wanting to touch its skin, to see if it was warm or cold, rough or smooth, wet or dry. The crocodile moved fast, but Sam moved faster.

He saved her life.

Which was more than she'd done for him.

Lock it down. Lock it in. She wrapped the marble in its square of bubble wrap, put it back in the envelope, sealed it and pushed it into her bag.

Will-O'-the-Wisp was waiting for her.

'Everything in order?' he asked.

'Yes. I've taken what I need.' She patted her bag, bulkier than before. 'Can you dispose of the rest?'

He peered into the room behind her. 'Sure.'

'My passport?'

He opened a drawer and took out a brown folder. Extracting her passport, a slightly battered booklet in burgundy and gold, he handed it over. She checked it and then put it in her bag.

'Will I be OK to travel?'

'Interpol case closed,' he said.

'Thanks for everything.' She stood and held out her hand.

'Perhaps you need a ride to Kranjskabel?'

He'd assumed she would return to Karel, her former lover. The pang of regret twisted her stomach. He was mistaken there, but she would play along.

'It's OK. I can take the bus.'

And she could. But she wouldn't. She had moved on. She had everything she came for: her passport, the personal stuff that mattered. What she didn't need now were complications. An early night, and then she was on the next plane to England.

Will-O'-the-Wisp didn't insist.

'I guess it's goodbye, Jaq.' He held out a hand. 'Until you stumble across some more criminal masterminds in my backyard.'

'Always happy to help.' She shook his hand.

'Try and stay clear of explosions.'

She smiled. 'I'll make it my New Year's resolution.'

A sea of travellers washed through Manchester airport, ebbing and flowing like the tide. Johan was waiting in Arrivals. She tried, and failed, to hide her delight.

'Sorry, it's only me.' His arms were strong, and his chest felt reassuringly solid as he pulled her into a warm embrace. She pulled away first.

'Emma wanted to come,' he said. 'But someone had to stay with the kids.'

'I'm so glad to see you.' And she was. Indecently glad.

They walked towards the exit.

'How's Giovanni?'

It was Johan who had suggested his Italian climbing buddy as skipper for her last mission.

'He'll live.' She frowned. The Bulgarian hospital had not been the most comfortable, but the orthopaedic surgeon knew what he was doing. 'Broken arm reset.' She'd stayed with her increasingly irascible skipper – a sure sign he was on the mend – until the doctors confirmed the success of the operation, and then skedaddled a few hours before Lucia arrived to fetch him home. Giovanni's fiancée sounded lovely on the phone; kinder to leave them alone.

Talking of kindness, maybe she should head straight back to her flat.

'You didn't have to come and meet me. I can get the train to Yarm.'

'I'm driving you to the farmhouse.'

'Are you sure?' Lake Coniston was one of her favourite places in the whole world, but it was Johan and Emma's family home.

'Emma's strict instructions.'

Jaq smiled. Emma was a true friend. One she didn't deserve.

'Just for tonight then.'

'Our home is your home.' He draped an arm around her shoulders and drew her closer as they walked. 'You stay as long as you want.'

If only it were that simple.

Charles de Gaulle airport, Paris, France

Frank slammed his case onto the conveyor. Taking a flight was another step back to normal life. It was proving more taxing than he'd bargained for: insufferable Paris.

It was fuckwit day at airport security. An entertaining day out for delinquents with nothing better to do than stare at the walls of whatever asylum they normally inhabited, but intolerable for anyone wishing to travel. The group of construction workers in front of him were arguing over the bottles of brandy and eau de toilette in their hand luggage. The combination of surly Frenchwomen choreographing the ridiculous security dance and bovine Poles who didn't understand the steps, had caused the queue to snake right back to the doors.

There was something peculiarly passive-aggressive about the worst airport in the world. He could overlook its ugliness – a concrete monstrosity – if the interior functioned. But no, the signs that confidently directed you to the Charles de Gaulle airport train disappeared as you approached. The driverless rapid train wasn't remotely rapid. And even if you did manage to get to Terminal 2, you then had to walk mile after and mile, only to arrive at 2F and be directed to a bus stop outside.

'Terminal 2G.' Frank thrust his boarding pass at the uniformed security guard.

The man sniffed and pointed at the exit with a sign that said NAVETTE.

'Shuttle, monsieur.'

'I don't travel by bus.'

The man shrugged and turned away.

Frank hailed a taxi. It followed the free shuttle bus, driving halfway to Paris before depositing him at the pauper's terminal: 2G.

'Twenty euros,' the driver announced. Daylight robbery. Normally he would charge this to Zagrovyl. So long as he had a receipt, what did it matter? Could he justify the meeting with his personal insurance broker as company business? He was only following doctor's orders, after all.

Take a trip.

Past security, the departure lounge was so crowded there was nowhere to sit. Talk about no frills; there wasn't even a business lounge. He found a spot away from the rabble and checked his phone.

An update from the insurance company. A concise summary of yesterday's meeting to discuss his claim. All things considered, the Paris meeting had gone quite well. The French were remarkably sanguine about the loss of an expensive yacht. Gallic shrugs all round. The fact that someone else had been at the helm when it sank didn't seem to perturb them at all. After all, top businessmen like him were far too busy for the long crossings; they had crew to move the yacht from port to port. Open-sea sailing was boring and dangerous. Ports were where the real action happened, yacht marinas full of beautiful women in search of wealthy men.

Unfortunately, rather than just paying out, the insurers seemed to think they might recover the wretched thing. The claims handler wanted to speak to the crew – a bad idea. The underwriter wanted to initiate a salvage operation – even worse. They wanted a full maintenance history and any recent surveys. Disastrous.

Through the window he could see the airplane taxi towards the gate, *Jump!* in large letters along the side. Frank wasn't sure what offended him most: the stupid name, the jokey font or the exclamation mark calling attention to the fatuous name. Johnny Foreigner really didn't have a clue about branding. And no concern for accuracy. Given the delays, they might as well call it *Limp!* or *Crawl!*

There was risk in this insurance claim. Instead of signing over his interest in the late *Good Ship Frankium* to Assurance Actif, there was another option.

Jaqueline Silver had signed an agreement when she borrowed his yacht.

All things considered, it would be much easier to hold her to the contract.

And bleed her dry.

Teesside, England

Yarm High Street was abnormally quiet, businesses taking a holiday to avoid the mayhem that was about to descend in the form of the annual fair. Jaq crossed the river, swishing through a carpet of dry leaves as she climbed the hill to the north. She bent to pick up a chestnut, peeling back the spiky green casing with its soft white insulation to reveal a glossy nut inside. She slipped it into her pocket for Ben.

Her destination, Natalie's hairdressing salon on West Road, sat back from the main road between Yarm and Stockton, the front room of a Victorian terraced house hidden away above the railway viaduct. Since leaving Cumbria, where she had spent a week recuperating, Jaq had been busy sorting out her life: doctor, dentist, utility meter readings, mortgage, tax, insurance and MOT (failed), overdraft application (denied), fitting a new lock on the garage door, a deep-clean of her flat, a telephone catch-up with her stepdaughter and offers to help with the new baby (declined). Putting off the meeting with Frank Good for as long as she could.

Natalie was waiting at the window, her hair completely different – short and purple – but her welcoming hug as warm and rib-crushing as ever.

'So, what's it to be then?' she asked, twisting her mouth in disapproval as she inspected her client.

'Have I left it too late? Will you have to shave it all off?'

'Don't be daft.' Natalie scowled. 'You're so lucky. You have gorgeous hair. It just needs a trim and some conditioning.'

'Will you fix it?'

'That's my job.'

Natalie washed Jaq's hair and then smothered it in conditioner.

'Been anywhere nice?'

'Let me see.' Jaq counted off on her fingers. 'A Slovenian prison, a brothel in Belarus, the Chornobyl nuclear power complex and a yacht in the Black Sea.'

'Hmm, the yacht sounds all right.'

'It sank.'

Natalie threw her head back and laughed. 'Now I see why your hair needs attention.' She rinsed away the conditioner and wrapped Jaq's head in a towel. 'Did you get the job done?'

Jaq grinned. 'Done and dusted.' The Spider would be standing trial at the International Court of Justice in The Hague.

'That bloke who was following you last time, the one with the black beard?'

Jaq shivered at the memory of The Spider's henchman. 'In prison.'

'You going to tell me about it?'

'Over a glass of wine?'

'Training tonight.' Natalie harrumphed. 'Anyway, I'm on the wagon. Not drinking. My body is my temple, and all that.' She got to work with a comb and scissors.

'How's the kung fu?'

Natalie and Jaq had met at a self-defence class. Of similar height and build, they had been paired in a fight, but Natalie had won easily. And then shown Jaq how.

'Passed my exams. I'm an instructor now.'

'Brilliant!' Jaq clapped her hands. 'When did that happen?'

'Last year. I'm saving up for more training. In the meantime, I still need this.' She gestured around her tiny salon. 'The day job.'

Jaq focused on her rapidly improving reflection in the mirror.

'You work miracles in here, Nat.'

'You should see my kung fu action.'

'Can I come along?'

'Tuesdays and Thursdays.' Natalie named a local school hall. 'Still got your togs?'

Jaq shook her head.

'No problem, I can lend you some. But first.' The whir of a fan and a blast of hot air as Natalie raised the hairdryer. 'Let's get this lovely hair of yours back into shape. Hot date after this?'

Jaq checked her phone. 'A meeting in Gateshead.'

'Business or pleasure?'

'Definitely not pleasure.'

'Oh, that sort of meeting. Someone I know?'

'I hope not.' Jaq sighed. 'A prize bastard.'

'Better look your best then,' Natalie said. 'Straighteners, too?'

Why not? Keep him waiting. Because this would be her very last meeting with Frank Good.

London, England

The blond auctioneer was still in his dressing gown when the doorbell rang. He slid his fingers under soft fur and gently moved the sleeping cat from his lap. Knotting a silk cord around his waist, he peered through the spyhole. A quiet street, but you could never be too careful.

A young Chinese woman stood on the doorstep.

He left the security chain in place as he opened the door a few inches. Xiǎo Māo followed him, rubbing herself against his leg.

'Bernard Ashley-Copper?' The voice was soft, the accent heavy.

'Cooper,' he corrected her. 'How can I help you?'

'A message for you. May I come in?'

Bernard hesitated. He was expected at Jude's party later and he still had work to do.

'A message from whom?'

She swivelled to show him the large sports bag, the strap diagonal across her slight body, open to reveal an ice-blue velvet cylinder. 'From the Emperor Qianlong.'

More treasures from China. Goody. Bernard glanced up and down the street to check that she was alone. A curtain shifted opposite. Nosy parkers.

Xiǎo Māo meowed and skittered away from the blast of cold air as Bernard released the chain and opened the front door.

'Please.' He stepped back and gestured with a silk-robed arm. 'Come in.'

Gateshead, England

The three bridges over the Tyne, visible from the esplanade of the Sage Gateshead concert hall, perfectly exhibited Frank Good's approach to problem-solving.

The first bridge, a green arch anchored by two granite towers, stood high over the river. It didn't matter what sailed up the grey water underneath – and let's face it, it was little enough these days – the stone structure remained aloof, above it all, uninvolved in the day-to-day seedy details of Geordie commerce.

Detachment was Frank's default setting.

A pair of fat birds, white-bellied with ghost-grey wings dipped in ink, soared above the southern tower and swooped towards the river below, crying *kittee-wa-aaake, kittee-wa-aaake.* He turned his good ear away to check the voicemail.

The second bridge, a pontoon built on the remains of an ancient Roman crossing, lay almost at water level. When a ship needed to pass, the painted red and white superstructure pivoted on a central platform, swivelling until it was parallel to both shores. This was Frank's second strategy. Get out of the way. Maintain a low profile when a problem snowballed and drew attention from lords and masters above. It was rarely worth the effort to stand and fight the approaching shitstorm. Smarter to step aside and let someone else collapse. Take the credit when all went well; let someone else take the fall. Play both sides. A little forward planning was required, but there was never any shortage of 'brave' individuals ready to tackle something head-on.

People like Dr Jaqueline Silver.

An involuntary shudder ran down his spine at the message on his phone. She was on her way. Not long now.

The third bridge, the most recent, was a white metal structure, which the locals called the Blinking Eye. The modern bridge was built to twist; huge pistons tilted the curved deck to form an arch over the water. This was his third approach: set a trap. Hover above, watch and wait until the unsuspecting target blundered into the shadow.

Then pounce.

Sometimes, he combined all three problem-solving methods.

He'd first come to Newcastle, some months ago, to get the contract drawn up. The Teesside lawyers had been too obstinate to draft it the way he wanted. But this city had a proud maritime history, long since destroyed, and his money talked. Smoggies, Mackems and Geordies: the towns were only a few miles apart and yet the natives of Middlesbrough, Sunderland and Newcastle regarded each other with suspicion and ridicule. Useful knowledge when it came to manipulation. He pocketed his phone and strode back in through revolving doors to resume his meeting with the corporate sponsorship director of the Sage Gateshead.

'Bottled water, wasn't it?' A willowy man in a pale fawn suit sat at a circular table, a tray with two bottles in front of him. 'Wasn't sure if you wanted still or sparkling, so I brought one of each.'

Frank took both. He didn't really want either, but it was important to start the relationship on the correct footing. If they wanted his money, they would have to work for it.

'So, Mr Good, you wanted to talk about sponsorship?'

Frank looked him up and down. With his hair so black it was almost blue and his long, pale body, he could have tumbled out of a Scottish Bluebell matchbox. 'I'd be interested in understanding the options.'

'Can you tell me a bit more about what Zagrovyl do?' Match Man inspected Frank's business card. 'You'll understand that the board of trustees is supersensitive when it comes to industry. We are committed to reducing our carbon footprint and making a positive environmental impact in everything we do.'

Frank suppressed a sneer. This absurd dome of curved glass and steel had been paid for by the corporation taxes of Zagrovyl and other successful businesses. And yet these pygmies thought they could pick and choose, sniff the money and refuse the notes that stank of industry.

Zagrovyl International supported Carnegie Hall and the Sydney Opera House. No way were they going to approve charitable funding in this backwater, however good the acoustics. A global company needed global visibility.

'I'm considering a personal donation,' Frank said.

'Ah, I see. Well, that should be no problem.'

Match Man ran through the various packages, ranging from millions of pounds to name one of the concert halls, through thousands for a music education suite in the basement, down to hundreds to name a seat in the auditorium.

'Level 2, Row AA, Seat 17. Is it available?'

'Excellent choice.' The man blinked a couple of times. 'I can check, sir. What about—'

'Only that one.' Frank checked his watch. 'I have another meeting now.'

Match Man sprang to his feet in confusion and disappointment.

'It was great to meet you, sir,' he said, extending his hand. 'I'll check on the seat availability and get back to you. I do hope we can count on you for further support.'

'I'm sure you do,' Frank said, dismissing him with a wave of his hand.

Frank remained seated as Match Man scuttled off. He perused the new season classical programme. A little heavy on the Romantics and light on Baroque, but there were some interesting options.

A pulse started beating in his bad ear as he spied Jaqueline approaching from a distance, striding across the concourse full of unshakeable, misplaced confidence. No broken limbs, no obvious cuts or bruises; in fact, she looked better than she did before the shipwreck.

He'd tried to describe Jaqueline Silver to a private investigator once but stumbled over the contradictions. Too tall for a woman, but well proportioned. Athletic in movement but curvy in form. Southern European in appearance – long dark hair and olive complexion – but English in manner. Beyond the first flush of youth yet with sexual energy undimmed. Magnificent or monstrous? Delectable or dangerous? Radiant or radioactive? People in the café, men and women, looked up to follow her progress across the concourse. However you described her, she was hard to ignore. So what? Definitely not his type. His throat tightened.

Of course, it would have been much cleaner if she had gone down with the yacht. Even neater if she'd taken her prisoner with her. But that would have raised questions; a fatal accident inquiry might delve deeper into the condition of the vessel before it sank. He took out his handkerchief and dabbed at the beads of sweat forming on his brow.

Her footsteps slowed as she approached. He could feel the effort she was making, as if the air had turned to treacle. He smiled internally at the flicker of distaste that flitted over her face as she spotted him.

'Hello, Jaqueline,' he said.

'May I?' She took the seat opposite him without waiting for his assent. 'I guess you already know what happened?'

Straight down to business.

In some ways it was refreshing. No small talk, no false enquiry – how are you; fine, thank you, and you? – no comments on the weather. His pulse slowed a little.

He let her talk, assessed her version of events. She was mercifully brief.

'So,' he said, 'in summary, you borrowed my yacht and then wrecked it in the Black Sea?'

She answered him between gritted teeth. 'That yacht was unsea-worthy. You nearly killed me, Frank.'

'Now, now. Calm down,' he said. 'Don't get hysterical.'

She failed to rise to the jibe, fixing her eyes on his with a long cool stare of distaste.

'Your boat had a serious structural problem.'

'When you ran it aground.'

She shook her head. 'We were twenty miles off the coast.'

'Tsk, tsk.' He shook his head. 'I doubt that. Perhaps your map-reading skills need improving.'

She was hard to goad, but he relished the challenge. Over the years, he had collected a rich resource of trigger phrases. He'd never met a woman yet who didn't react eventually. Sometimes with anger, more often with tears.

'It was a bad storm, but nothing out of the ordinary.'

'You were at the helm when it went down?'

'I'm not here to fight with you, Frank.'

'So, you have the money you owe me?'

That silenced her. This was the moment he'd been waiting for, the moment to spring the trap. The Blinking Eye descending before the quarry was clear, ensnaring it. He opened his briefcase and pulled out the contract.

'Remember this, Jaqueline?'

The contract she'd signed before taking the yacht consisted of ten pages of dense legalese, old-fashioned maritime language.

He flicked over five pages to the annexes, small print in a font so tiny he strained to read without his glasses. He didn't need to read them, having dictated these clauses in the first place.

'"The signee agrees to protect, defend, indemnify and hold harmless from and against any and all loss, liability, damages, claims, demands, and expenses (including without limitation, court costs and legal fees) which may arise out of any claim relating to or resulting from the use of—"'

'That's ridiculous!'

'"In the event of damage or loss to the *Good Ship Frankium*, irrespective of cause, fault or circumstance, the consignee agrees to pay compensation equivalent to the full replacement value of an equivalent yacht—"'

'You must be joking.'

'"With fixtures and fittings and additional equipment as listed below: navigation system, VHS radio, outboard motor . . ."'

'I want you to tear up that contract.'

Frank laughed, a short, scornful burst of mirth. 'You pay me the money you owe me, and you'll be released from the contract.'

'I gave you the benefit of the doubt,' Jaq said, her voice low and quiet now. 'Assumed you were an incompetent owner who knew nothing of the faults that nearly killed me. But if you pursue this, I'll counterclaim for attempted murder.'

'Be my guest.' He sat back and spread his legs wide. 'Lawyers are expensive, and you already have one lawsuit on your hands.' He'd checked with his adviser. The private prosecution, brought by the families of men who'd died at Seal Sands, her former workplace, was likely to drag on for years. 'I think you'll find that I have deeper pockets than you.'

She shook her head slowly. 'You wanted me to go and fetch The Spider.'

'I expected you to bring my yacht back in one piece.'

'It wasn't my fault—'

'The excuse of scoundrels. And women. When will you learn that equality means not just equal opportunity but equal responsibility?'

'You tricked me.'

'Perhaps you should have read the contract before you signed it.'

'I'll fight you, Frank.'

He jutted his chin forward, eyes blazing. 'I look forward to it.'

She rose abruptly, the chair clattering to the floor.

'Of course, there is an alternative.' He flicked over the page. 'In the event that you are unable to raise the funds, you can offset the debt by working for me.'

She retrieved the chair and righted it. 'You are a despicable, manipulative monster,' she hissed.

'Get used to it, Jaqueline.' Frank Good smiled. 'I own you now.'

He sat back in a glow of satisfaction, watching her storm out. He had to hand it to her; she was tough. Which made it all the sweeter. Nothing more satisfying than impending victory over a worthy adversary. Whatever the medical advice, he was ready to get back to work.

Match Man accosted him as he was leaving for his appointment with the doctor who stood between him and Zagrovyl.

'Mr Good, so glad I caught you.' He beamed. 'Good news. Level 2, Row AA, Seat 17 has not yet been sponsored.'

Frank carried on walking. 'I've changed my mind.'

Teesside, England

The fair was back in town. A big wheel, ghost train, carousel, dodgems, roller coaster and a cantilevered catapult that swung out across Yarm High Street, narrowly missing the tops of the Georgian terraced houses as it looped the loop over the river Tees at white-knuckle speeds.

A little boy sat at the window of Jaq's flat, a glossy brown conker in his hand, wrinkling his snub nose and licking his lips at the hint of hot sugar in the air outside: candyfloss and toffee apples.

'Can we go to the fair now, please?'

Emma shook her head. 'Sorry, darling.' She stroked the fair hair of her baby daughter, fast asleep on her lap. 'We can't go yet.'

Jaq watched Ben's shoulders slump, but he said nothing.

Emma turned to Jaq. 'Where's that contract you wanted me to look at?'

Jaq pulled out the file. She couldn't meet Emma's eyes. This was the moment she'd been dreading. She stuck a yellow note onto the front and wrote on it. *I can take Ben to the fair if you like.*

'You sure?' Emma mouthed.

'If you're OK with it?'

'Let's ask him.' Emma whistled. 'Ben, d'you want to go to the fair with Aunty Jaq?'

A bundle of energy leapt up from the window and grabbed Jaq's hand.

'Off you go, then.' Emma kissed him as he passed. 'Take care.'

Outside the flat, they pushed their way through the crowds, past the Roma caravans with fortune tellers, straight to the merry-go-round. Jaq let the little boy choose a horse and hoisted him on before taking the saddle on the one behind.

'Again!'

After the third session, Jaq enticed him away to the candyfloss centrifuge and the big wheel. It wasn't very big, but it towered over the houses. Each time their little pod made its slow progress into the sky, Ben waved and shouted at the windows of Jaq's flat, hoping for a glimpse of his mother. Jaq texted her friend and by the last circle, Emma was leaning out of the window, blowing kisses at her son.

Ben spotted the giant soft toys from the air, pointing excitedly at lions and tigers and a giraffe. As soon as they were back on land, he made a beeline for the shooting gallery.

'I'm gonna win a present for Mummy,' he announced. 'And Jade.' A definite afterthought. His relationship with his little sister wasn't entirely straightforward. Understandable, really. Promised a playmate, all his baby sibling had done so far was sleep, cry, eat and poo, demanding almost constant attention from her parents. And yet Ben was clearly fond of Jade, bringing her well-meaning if unsuitable presents – interesting stones, unusual insects, telling her stories, singing her songs with the words all muddled up.

Jaq wondered how Sam had felt about her, his little sister. She remembered her big brother as a friend and ally, her protector until she became his. And then she hadn't done a very good job. The mock Kalashnikovs, model AK47s of the shooting gallery brought back a flood of unwelcome memories.

'How old are you, sunshine?' The gruff voice brought her back to the present as Ben clambered onto a stool, reaching out for a rifle.

'Four and three-quarters,' Ben announced proudly.

'Sorry, mate.' The stall owner took the gun from him and pointed at the sign. 'Eight years or over.'

Ben bit his lip. 'The fair is not fair at all.'

She could have offered to shoot for him, but the thought of handling a gun, even a poor replica, made her stomach turn. Jaq took his hand. 'Come on, I know something better.'

His eyes opened wide at the wriggling goldfish slowly suffocating in plastic bags beside the coconut shy. Jaq paid for a heap of missiles – little bags of sand sewn into rough sacking – and kept paying until between them they finally managed to topple a coconut.

He chose a little fish with red fins and a gold back, the underbelly spotted with white. A sick little *Carassius auratus*. Jaq felt a momentary pang of conscience, but Emma would know what to do with it.

Ben carried his prize aloft and they headed back to Jaq's flat.

Rosalie the fortune teller sat on the steps of her caravan, a little wooden house on wheels, elaborate carvings of flowers and dragons around the circular opening, the sides freshly painted in bright red and green.

'Cross my palm with silver, and I'll tell you the future.' Her voice was low and musical, and Ben stopped to stare.

Gold rings dangled from her ears and a jewelled comb sparkled in her long black hair, the coils twisted into a bun on top of her head. Her eyes slanted upwards, dark with kohl, and red lipstick contrasted against gleaming white teeth and smooth, tanned skin. She wore a dress with a tight bodice and flared skirt, clean white petticoats tumbling out beneath the embroidered hem.

'Shall I tell you your fortune, young master?' She beckoned to Ben with a long finger, the nail a curved talon painted purple with a gold star in the centre.

Ben regarded her with curious fascination. 'What about my fish?' he asked. 'Can you tell his fortune?'

'Indeed,' she cackled. 'Come inside.'

Ben looked up at Jaq in excitement and she didn't have the heart to pull him away. Anyway, she was curious to know what a Roma fortune teller made of the poor fish's chances of survival. She pulled out a pound coin, but the woman held up ten fingers. *Outrageous.* Jaq haggled until they reached a compromise.

An oil lamp made their shadows flicker and dance as the woman ushered them inside the caravan and let the heavy curtain fall. She pointed to brocade cushions on the floor and took up position behind a low stool. Ben held his fish aloft, the gold scales bright in the soft light.

'What's his name?' Rosalie raised a velvet cloth to reveal a glass globe.

'Rosco Bulldozer.'

Jaq suppressed a smile.

'A fine name,' the fortune teller said, straight-faced. 'A noble name. For this fish is a prince among fishes. He has come a long way. Do you know where this fish came from?'

'The sea?'

'From China. Rosco is descended from the royal fish of the Qing dynasty. His imperial forebears swam in the jewelled pools between the palaces of the Forbidden City.'

'Where's his crown?' Ben peered through the plastic, the lens of water making his eyes even larger.

'Rosco's grandfather gave up his royal privileges to be with the love of his life, and they swam away together.'

'To come to Yarm Fair?'

'To find you. But Rosco will not be with you for long,' she said. 'So, you must heed the five lessons he teaches.'

She held up a hand, her long fingers heavy with rings, little sequins and stars sparkling in the varnish of her painted nails.

'Number one – we all need space. Give him a big tank of water to swim in, the biggest one you can find. Give him the illusion of freedom and he will settle into his captivity.'

Jaq looked at Ben to see if he had understood. He was staring at the woman, nodding sagely.

'Number two – keep him clean. Change half his water and brush his tank every week. And that goes for you too, young man, for the master must set an example.'

'I brush my teeth three times every day,' Ben said proudly, opening his mouth to display a fine set of baby teeth.

'Number three – don't feed him too much. Greedy fish get slow and sick, and that goes for the master, too.'

'I'm not greedy,' Ben said, surreptitiously wiping a pink thread of candy floss from the edge of his mouth.

'Glad to hear it.' Her eyes sparkled as she held up her ring finger. 'Number four. You must do a good deed every day.'

'Every day? Even school days?'

'Every day.'

Ben wrinkled his nose and dropped his eyes, thinking hard. Eventually he looked up and nodded.

'Number five.' She held up her pinkie. 'Can you read?'

'Yes,' Ben said, then cast a sideways look at Jaq. 'A bit.'

'Then you must read to your fish out loud. Every single day. He only speaks Chinese right now. You must teach him English. And the best way to do that is to read him stories.'

Ben opened his eyes wide. 'Will he speak back to me?'

'Not out loud. But you'll hear him in your head. Watch the patterns he forms as he swims. Right now, he is speaking to you in Chinese characters. Once you teach him your language, he'll spell words for you. But only if you treat him right. Lots of space, keep him clean, not too much food, be good, read to him every day. Got it?'

'Got it!' Ben turned, ready to go.

Good advice. Money well spent. Maybe the so-called Roma fortune teller was an ichthyologist, or a primary school literacy champion making a bit of extra money at half-term. 'Thank you.' Jaq stood up with a smile.

Ben pulled back the curtain and the light from the lamp flickered.

'Wait!' The woman grasped Jaq's hand and ran a finger over her palm. 'Your son.'

Jaq tried to pull her hand away. 'Ben isn't my son.'

Dark eyes bored into her soul, a beam of dizzying intensity. There was sadness in those dark eyes, but also a hard edge, a glint of anger, a tinge of madness.

'Your son is looking for you. He's out there. Searching. A son in danger.'

'I don't have children.' Jaq wrenched her hand free and turned to follow Ben, who had already descended the wooden steps and was running towards the crowd.

'Ben, wait!' Jaq shouted, jumping down after him. The last step tilted, and she tumbled onto the cobbles. As she picked herself up, a wave of people surged past and Ben disappeared.

Heart beating nineteen to the dozen, Jaq raced after him. But he was nowhere to be seen. *Amor de Deus.* Where was he? He couldn't have gone far.

'Ben!'

What would Johan say if she lost his son at Yarm Fair? It was amazing that he trusted her near his children after the near drowning in Lake Coniston. Ben seemed to have recovered from his misadventure, but now she'd put him in danger again. One moment's inattention and he was gone.

The fortune teller called after her. 'Find him!'

Fat lot of help that was. Oh, Christ. What if the fortune teller was part of some gang? Gaining Ben's trust so that an accomplice could whisk him away from under her nose? Bile rising in her mouth, her stomach clenched as she pushed deeper into the crowd.

'Oi! Steady on. Watch where you're going!'

Jaq ignored the protests, elbowing her way through the crowd, pushing and shoving, every muscle straining. Where was he?

'Ben!'

And there he was. High above the crowd. Sailing towards her. A big grin on his little face, Rosco Bulldozer held aloft, still swimming in his tiny polyethylene prison. Safe on the shoulders of his father.

'Johan!'

Jaq fell into the arms of her best friend and, for a moment, all was right with the world again.

The meal was simple, hastily assembled. Pizzas from the deep freeze (with extra olives, anchovies, capers, jalapeño peppers for the adults), accompanied by a packet of pre-washed salad tossed with a dressing of Dijon mustard, olive oil and cider vinegar. The goldfish was installed in a clean washing-up bowl and Johan took the children to bed, leaving Emma and Jaq alone.

'I can't believe you signed this!' Emma put down the bundle of papers and stared at Jaq, her blue eyes wide with astonishment. 'Why didn't you check with me first?'

'There wasn't much time.'

In truth, there had been time enough. But Jaq had caused her friend enough trouble, enough danger.

'Is it bad?'

'I won't lie, Jaq.' Emma leafed through and pointed at a paragraph on the final page. 'In the event of damage or loss you agreed to pay the cost of repairs or the full cost of a replacement yacht.' She sighed. 'There's no provision for dispute resolution. It's not good.'

Good. Frank Good. A misnomer if ever there was one. Neither frank nor good.

'There was something structurally wrong with the *Frankium*. There's no way a storm, even of that intensity, could have caused it to sink.'

'Can you prove it?'

Jaq shook her head. The *Frankium* lay in pieces at the bottom of the Black Sea.

'At least no one was badly hurt,' Emma said.

'Giovanni might disagree.'

Emma laughed. 'If he's anything like Johan, he'll bounce back quickly enough from a broken arm.'

'He could have been killed.' It was a close call. And if they'd been down below when the yacht disintegrated, they would both have drowned. Was that Frank's plan all along? Had he booby-trapped the yacht? 'I'm going to fight this.' And nail Frank.

Emma flicked through. 'As your friend, I would say why not? As a lawyer, I would have to advise caution. It's not my area of expertise. You'd have to hire specialists. It could be very expensive. My recommendation would be arbitration, make a direct appeal, try for a settlement.'

'Negotiate with that bastard? Never! I'd rather pay him his filthy money.'

'How?'

'I'll sell this flat.'

'Do you have any idea how much yachts cost? It's a lovely flat, but I doubt the money you'd get would come close to what you would need.'

Johan joined them, walking on tiptoe, closing the door softly behind him.

'Do they need me?' Emma made to stand up.

He shook his head. 'It's OK. I read one of the new books Jaq bought for Ben. They both went straight off to sleep.'

'Does that mean I chose well, or badly?' Jaq asked.

'Perfectly judged.' Johan smiled and joined his wife on the sofa.

Jaq sprang to her feet. 'Wine, anyone?'

Johan and Emma exchanged glances. 'Go on then,' Emma said. 'A very small glass of white.'

'And a large red for me.'

Jaq removed a bottle of Pinot Grigio from the fridge and then uncorked a bottle of Rioja. Johan fetched two large crystal goblets and one tiny sherry glass from the sideboard.

Jaq poured the wine, refraining from comment on the marital portion control.

'Cheers!' They chinked glasses. 'OK, bring me up to speed.'

Emma outlined the mess Jaq was in – a sunken yacht and a contract that held her liable for the cost.

'So where are they with the salvage operation?' asked Johan.

Jaq sighed. 'If Frank has anything to do with it, the yacht will never be recovered.'

Emma shook her head. 'If the boat is insured, then it won't be his decision. The moment he makes a claim, it becomes the job of his insurers.'

'After negotiating with the Russian, Ukrainian, Georgian, Romanian, Turkish and Bulgarian maritime agencies. So it's not going to happen any time soon, and the longer it stays underwater, the poorer the evidence.'

'I know guys who do underwater survey work, contracts from insurance companies – North Sea, mainly,' Johan said. 'They might appreciate a job in warmer water. Even if they can't bring the yacht to the surface, they might be able to get some under-water pictures to prove your case.'

That was the great thing about Johan and Emma. They believed in her. At times, more than she believed in herself.

'The trouble is . . .' Jaq hadn't told anyone yet. 'I did sort of blow it up.'

They both turned to look at her.

'Giovanni was trapped, and I had to get him out.'

Johan chuckled. 'That's the spirit!'

Emma looked aghast. 'You blew it up?'

'Only after it capsized.' Jaq took a gulp of wine. 'Without evidence, it's my word against Frank's. With evidence of an explosion, it's going to look even worse.'

'You need a good lawyer.'

Jaq touched Emma's shoulder. 'I've got a good lawyer.'

Emma reached up and squeezed her hand. 'No, you need a specialist lawyer.'

'Can you recommend one?'

'I can ask around, but it's not going to come cheap.'

Johan fetched the bottle of red and filled Jaq's glass and his. 'What about the UN? The Organisation for the Prohibition of Chemical Weapons. You went on their behalf, after all.'

'Strictly unofficially. They'd have to deny all knowledge of a rendition from Ukraine. Anyway, Frank Good is a bloody hero in their eyes. They need his testimony, and they're unlikely to want to alienate him before the trial.'

'What about the woman you rescued?' Emma asked.

Jaq noted that Emma hadn't touched her drink. 'Camilla Hatton.'

'You saved her life. Maybe she could help with legal fees.'

'Or maybe I need to find a job.'

And, as she confided to Rosco Bulldozer, contentedly swimming round her washing-up bowl after everyone else had gone to bed, a very well-paid job at that.

Newcastle, England

Frank sat in the dark of the gentlemen's club and nursed his tonic water, scowling at the barmaids.

The elation he'd felt after the showdown with Jaqueline Silver had all but evaporated in the doctor's surgery. He might be medically fit, but Zagrovyl were putting new obstacles in the path of his return. It was almost as if they didn't want him back. Ludicrous. Clearly, there was some conspiracy against him at the Teesside factory.

The TV screen above the bar flicked over to the news. He watched the ticker tape headline.

Scotland Yard launch murder investigation after victim of frenzied stabbing bleeds to death in his luxury Chelsea home.

Frank drained his glass. He'd come to this city centre haven in the hope that a dose of recreational titillation would chase away the blues, but he'd felt no stirring of interest in any of the hostesses so far.

His phone buzzed and he glanced at the number – Sophie Clark, the heiress. He grabbed his phone and slipped into the corridor, away from the thumping music.

'Frank, am I disturbing you?'

'Not at all.' He'd never been more delighted to leave a topless bar. 'In fact, I was about to give you a call. To see if you'd like to go out for dinner sometime.'

The silence at the other end went on too long, broken by a small voice. 'It's too soon, Frank.'

Too soon for what? Was there some sort of unwritten protocol?

The number of days or weeks after a funeral before you could resume normal activity? And if it was unwritten, how was he expected to know?

'Of course, Sophie.' He tried again. 'I've been thinking about you, worrying about you.' Thinking and worrying about your money. 'I'd love to help you through this difficult time.'

'I know. It's why I called.' Sophie sighed. 'I need some advice on the joint venture.'

The Chinese operation. 'But of course!' Frank still had a sizeable investment in Charles Clark's business. Time to get it back. With interest. Frank grinned. Happiness is when your interests and those of your target align. 'How can I help?'

Frank listened to the outline of Sophie's problem.

'What about getting an expert to visit the factory and find out precisely what the Chinese partner is up to?' he asked. 'Then you can negotiate from a position of strength.'

'Oh, Frank. That's such a good idea. Do you know any factory experts?'

Frank clenched his free hand into a fist.

'Well, as it happens,' he said, 'I think I know exactly the right person for this job.'

Durham, England

The mist from the river Wear enveloped the city of Durham in a cold, grey blanket.

Jaq left the bookshop and walked across the Elvet Bridge. She continued through the centre of Durham and up the hill to CCS – Chemical Contract Services. Not the snappiest of names, it made her think of latrines, but then Vikram was not the most imaginative of entrepreneurs. Solid and dependable, exactly what she needed right now.

A young man sat at reception.

'Dr Silver to see Vikram Dhawan.'

'He's expecting you.' He stood up and pointed. 'Straight through to the boardroom.'

The CCS office was a no-frills affair. The top floor of a flat-roofed concrete office block that had seen better days. She passed the drawing office and a server room, before the door at the end of a dimly lit corridor flew open to reveal Vikram in the doorway. Silver hair, copper skin, a striking man in his sixties, Vikram had made his fortune in the oil industry before returning to the town of his birth.

'Jaq!' He pumped her hand in enthusiasm. 'Good that you could come at such short notice.'

A morning of updating her CV and LinkedIn profile and telephoning all her local contacts had yielded a disappointing response. No one in Teesside had any work to offer her, although she suspected the problem was her reputation rather than the lack of vacancies. The call from CCS had taken her by surprise. Durham was only thirty miles from Middlesbrough, but clearly isolated from the jungle drums of Teesside gossip.

She'd first met the owner of CCS at a charity fundraising ball. In a sea of hypocrites, his passion for philanthropy, coupled with a refreshing transparency on how the networking benefited his business, had turned a dull evening into an enjoyable one.

'You're between jobs?'

They sat at either side of a table made up of three desks that didn't match: not in colour, not in width and not in height.

'Yup.' She handed him the CV she'd cobbled together.

He flicked through, muttering as he read. 'Chemical engineer… ICI… process safety… Teesside University lecturer… explosives licence.' He looked up. 'What are you looking for?'

'A good rate.' It paid to be straight with Vikram.

'Can you travel?'

'I'd prefer to stay in the UK for a while.'

'Explosives-related?'

'No.' She suppressed a shudder at the memories of the last explosions. One had killed a murderer. Another had saved Giovanni. If anyone knew what she'd done on either of those occasions, her licence would be swiftly withdrawn. And never reissued. 'I'd prefer something else.'

He tapped the CV with a manicured fingernail. 'You've run manufacturing sites, led capital projects, worked in research groups, taught process safety – seems to me you're a bit of a Jaq of all trades.'

She laughed as if no one had ever made that joke before.

'How do you feel about project management?'

A damp patch on the ceiling caught her attention as she murmured something non-committal. Johan claimed that for an engineer to become a project manager, they first had to undergo a lobotomy. Otherwise they couldn't live the lie of compressed schedules, reduced budgets and shrunken teams. Mind you, since leaving the army, Johan felt that way about most forms of management, indifferent to the reality that it paid much better than engineering.

'No problem.' Who cared, so long as the rate was enough to pay all the lawyers Emma was lining up? 'D'you have something in mind?'

'Leave it with me.'

Back in Yarm, she sat at her computer and searched for flights to Lisbon. A visit to her only surviving relative was long overdue. No direct flights from Teesside airport, so she'd have to go via Amsterdam or drive to Manchester. A spreadsheet of options was called for, the ideal displacement activity, perfect procrastination. LinkedIn was buzzing with notifications. She scrolled through, discarding most. A few gems from ex-students. One, Tarun Nayaran, was getting married. Another, Ning Dan, was changing jobs. She sent them both messages of congratulation then checked the BBC news, flicking past a story about a brutal knife attack.

CHELSEA MURDER INVESTIGATION

The victim of last night's fatal stabbing has been identified as Bernard Ashley-Cooper, aged 33, a fine art auctioneer.

Emergency services were called to Mr Cooper's opulent Chelsea home, worth over £1 million, after neighbours reported a disturbance involving animal cruelty.

A spokesman for Scotland yard said . . .

Her phone rang. Vikram. That was quick.

'I have a project management role that might interest you.'

'I'm listening.'

'Shetland.'

Remote and peaceful; exactly what she needed. And a long way from London, where people were stabbed in their own homes. She knew Shetland well: the northernmost islands of Scotland harboured the main terminal for North Sea oil.

'Oil or gas?'

'Neither. A new wind farm.'

The march of new technology, clean technology.

'What's the salary?'

Vikram named a generous hourly rate. Jobs on Shetland attracted a premium. More than enough to keep the wolf from the door.

'Sounds ideal.'

'Before you decide, I have a potential new client. One I'm rather keen to secure. Would you join us for lunch on Friday?'

'Why me?'

'Jaq of all trades.'

She laughed.

'Look, you'd be doing me a massive favour. All my senior technical people are out on jobs. I need someone credible to stand in. Just for lunch, OK?'

'Who's the potential client?'

'Krixo.'

'Never heard of them.'

'An ICI sell-off. It changed hands a few times and then there was a management buyout.'

No surprise there. Most ex-ICI companies in the area had been through several changes of name. She had colleagues from Seal Sands who had changed employer half a dozen times without ever changing workplace.

'Where do they operate?'

'UK and China. The UK head office is at the Wilton Technology Centre in Teesside. Manufacturing is in Shingbo, Shandong Province.'

A LinkedIn notification popped up on her screen, a reply from Dan. Serendipity.

She sent him a new message, adding, *Do you know anything about a company called Krixo in Shingbo?*, attached her private electronic business card and signed off.

'Are you still there?'

'Yes, sorry. What do Krixo do?'

'Green energy stuff. Superstrong magnets for wind turbines. Batteries for electric vehicles. That sort of thing.'

'I'm not interested in going to China.' Too crowded, too noisy, too unpredictable. Peace and solitude were what she craved more than anything else. 'Shetland sounds just right for me.'

'I know, but I think you might enjoy the lunch . . .' Vikram named a Michelin-starred restaurant.

'Wow, you must really want to impress them.'

'They're paying.' He laughed. 'I could really use your help on this one, Jaq.'

She clicked back to the airline page. There was a cheaper flight on Saturday.

'Just lunch?'

'Just lunch.'

'And after that?'

'After that, I put you forward for the Shetland job. Sole candidate. It's a shoo-in.' So, lunch was a precondition? OK then. She adopted her smoothest tone.

'I'd be delighted to have lunch with you and your client.'

Because that was the sort of reply a good project manager would give.

She hung up the phone and booked a return flight to Lisbon.

Thirsk, North Yorkshire, England

A fire roared in the grate, glittering coals shifting to release tongues of azure and tangerine flame. The retired metallurgist sat back on the sofa and opened his book, adjusting the reading light to inspect a coloured map.

His wife stuck her head round the sitting room door, white hair curling under a woollen hat. 'John, you do know I'm going out tonight?'

He frowned, a flicker of irritation passing across his brow. 'Book group?'

'Every Wednesday.'

'What nonsense are the girls discussing tonight?'

'It's not just for women, you know.' She came into the room, their dog trotting along behind her. 'You could come along too.'

'I could.' He gazed up at her. 'But I don't like the novels you read.'

The dog padded across the room towards her basket.

'Then suggest something else.'

He held up his book. 'Such as the latest monograph on Australian ore deposits?'

She sighed. 'It would do you good to read some fiction for a change.'

He shook his head. 'A waste of time.'

She bent to kiss his forehead. 'Will you be OK?'

The little dog turned round and round in her basket, flattening some invisible bumps, before settling in front of the fire.

'Jenny and I will be just fine, thank you, darling.' The dog sighed in agreement. 'Drive carefully.'

*

He must have nodded off, which was unlike him, whatever Kay claimed, because suddenly the fire was low, and Jenny was no longer in her basket but scratching and barking at the front door.

The bell rang again. It took two goes to hoist himself to his feet, a groan of pain escaping as ankles and knees and hips took the weight. Kay must have forgotten her house keys.

He opened the door wide, stepping back in surprise at the sight of a young woman on the doorstep. She held an ice-blue velvet roll in her small hands.

'Professor John Tich?' she asked.

'Tench,' he corrected. 'Good evening, miss. And you are?'

'May I come in?' She spoke so softly, and with such a strong Chinese accent, that he understood her question more by lip-reading. Perhaps she had been one of his students, though he didn't immediately recognise her, but then he had never been very good at names or faces.

Jenny barked a warning, but he ignored her. It was cold in the doorway and he needed to put his hearing aids in and his spectacles on if he was to find out what she wanted. Such a slight young thing, she hardly posed a threat.

'This way. There's a fire on in the library. Can I get you a cup of tea or a glass of sherry?'

Teesside, England

The restaurant was nothing much to look at. A former drovers' inn on the main road between Darlington and Barnard Castle, the cramped eating area looked more like an austere living room than a palace of fancy nosh.

Sophie Clark and Vikram Dhawan were already seated by the time Jaq arrived. The boss of CCS had failed to mention how young the managing director of Krixo was. Or how beautiful. Early twenties, blonde, five foot two – one metre fifty-seven in new money – immaculately turned out in a tailored pink dress, kitten heels and a jaunty fascinator. She reminded Jaq of the cardboard cut-out dolls that you could adorn with paper clothes using little folded tabs to hook the garments onto the shoulders and hips. Clothes that you coloured in first.

Sophie was certainly coloured in. Her fair lashes were dark with mascara, the matching bruises of purple eye shadow above her amethyst eyes mirrored by kohl below. The natural blush of young healthy skin glowed through a light foundation and dusting of powder. Her perfect rosebud lips shone with crimson gloss.

Vikram dragged his gaze away from Sophie long enough to make the introductions.

'Dr Silver.' Her voice was surprising, deeper and more nuanced than Jaq expected.

'Call me Jaq, please.'

A waiter appeared with three flute glasses. He filled them from a bottle of English sparkling wine, accompanied by a long and involved explanation of the provenance.

They clinked glasses.

'To business!' Sophie announced.

The first of twelve courses arrived. A single scallop, topped with grapefruit, ponzu and micro-herbs, served on a tiny white porcelain stand. One slurp and it was gone, the taste of the sea so intense and fresh that Jaq could almost hear the crashing waves and smell the salt air.

Sophie wrinkled her nose at the raw seafood. She seemed keener on the paired wine, calling for another glass of the English champagne.

'Where are you living now, Sophie?' Vikram asked.

Sophie beamed. 'Wynyard.'

Home of Premier League footballers and business successes.

'At least until probate is sorted out. Then I'm thinking of the Bahamas.'

Jaq disconnected from the conversation and scanned the room. A middle-aged couple with heads close together, lost in intense conversation. A quiet family group, three generations from wrinkly to pimply, who seemed comfortably familiar with staff and surroundings. A trio of businessmen more interested in their mobile phones than the food or one another.

She reconnected with the pros and cons of buying off-plan in Barbados as new wine arrived with the quenelles of offal wrapped in artichoke. Jaq followed the server's instructions and popped it into her mouth, a savoury Baked Alaska bursting with meat juices. Gone in a few seconds, leaving a taste of land. Earthy and surprising, and utterly, utterly delicious.

Sophie drank her wine, nibbling at the edges of the little parcel of food on the smooth wooden platter. Their host's continuing discomfort at the unusual fare perplexed Jaq. What had Sophie imagined a Michelin-starred tasting menu would serve? Or had she chosen the most expensive restaurant in the area in order to impress? Impress who – Vikram? A waste of money. Vikram would be equally happy eating in a pub. How on earth had Sophie managed Eastern food?

'Have you spent much time in China?' Jaq asked.

Sophie nodded. 'I helped my father set up the joint venture. He was a brilliant scientist, but I brought the business acumen.' Again, that defiant tilt of the chin, as if to say *that's my story and I'm sticking to it; you want to fight about it?*

Jaq sipped her wine and allowed a tiny glimmer of sympathy to slip through her instinctive distrust. Poor unhappy Sophie. It must be boring being quite so beautiful. Perhaps she really was a business whizz. How tiring it must be when people only saw the superficial charms and ignored the brains underneath; how infuriating when they assumed it was her father who had built the business rather than this tiny, fierce young woman. OK, she would cut Sophie a little slack. Innocent until proven guilty. Capable until proven otherwise.

'Did you like Shingbo?' Jaq asked.

Sophie wrinkled her nose. 'I based myself in Shanghai.'

Aha, that explained it. The most Westernised city in China. Quite possible to live on McDonald's burgers and Kentucky Fried Chicken. You could probably even get a parmo and chips.

Not here, though. Three rustic earthenware dishes appeared, each containing a single Lindisfarne Oyster, cooked, as the server informed them, in a sous vide at 62° centigrade and garnished with English wasabi. Back to the sea, with the meltingly smooth texture of barely denatured protein, delicate and fresh, followed by a whack to the back of the head as the myrosinase metabolised. *Tsuun!*

Intent on her own food, Jaq pretended not to notice when Sophie slipped the oyster into a napkin she raised to dab at her lips. What a waste. She waited until their host made her excuses and minced to the bathroom. Presumably to dispose of the scallop and oyster concealed in her expensive handbag.

Jaq turned to Vikram. 'Who suggested this restaurant?'

'Sophie, of course. Good, isn't it? Glad I'm not paying though.'

'She's not eating anything.'

'Watching her figure?'

Jaq gave a snort of irritation. 'No, but you're doing plenty of that.'

Vikram grinned. 'I love my job.'

'What does she want?'

'Why don't we ask her?'

Clicking heels on parquet floor – short steps, restricted by her tight skirt and pointy shoes – announced Sophie's return in time for the signature dish: razor clams with almond and celeriac, dotted with tiny brown shrimps. The wine was Japanese, lemony and sharp – who knew that the Japanese produced such fine wine?

'Can you tell me more about what Krixo do?' Jaq asked.

Sophie must be used to the question, responding with an elevator speech on the crucial role of rare earth metals in green energy, leaving Jaq none the wiser.

Vikram leaned back and folded his hands over his stomach. 'And what are your plans for Krixo?'

Sophie leaned forward. 'We plan to double in size every year for the next ten years.'

Vikram's eyes lit up.

As did Jaq's when the next course was served, raw beef with caviar: folds of thinly sliced, finely marbled meat piled high, ruby-red pillows for the tiny black beads of caviar hiding under nasturtium leaves.

The waiter replaced their glasses and described the wine for the next course.

'All the expansion to happen in China?' asked Vikram.

'That's the exciting bit,' Sophie said. 'It made sense to start in China. It's where most of the rare earths are mined. But Krixo...' she corrected herself, 'but my father also developed advanced recycling technology. Do you have any idea how much precious metal Britain throws away every year? Materials that could be recycled and reused. He wanted to open a demonstration plant in Teesside. And that's where I need your help.'

Vikram beamed as the spring salad was served. It was a work of art: swirling pea shoots dotted with orange nasturtiums and violet periwinkles lay on a bed of crinkly black kale, pale lambs' lettuce, emerald wild rocket and watercress sweetened with circles of pink radish and red cherry tomato.

Sophie talked on as the main courses came, sea bream with smoked cod roe followed by pigeon breast. Jaq listened intently, the project suddenly as interesting as the food.

Rare earths – the technology metals, seventeen elements with extraordinary properties – are not actually rare at all, just difficult to get at. Most are present in the earth's crust, but so tightly bound to other minerals, and so widely dispersed, that it is very expensive to extract them.

Green energy relies on rare earths – energy-efficient light bulbs, solar panels, wind turbines, rechargeable batteries – and so does modern communications technology.

And yet, we throw away our old phones, our spent batteries, consigning them to landfill for want of a simple, cost-effective process to extract and recover the key materials.

'Fascinating,' said Vikram, although most of his fascination appeared to be with Sophie herself.

'There's one teeny, tiny problem,' said Sophie, her eyes lighting up as the trio of desserts arrived.

'And what might that be?' asked Jaq.

Sophie plunged a spoon into the black olive and chocolate mousse and sighed.

'It's so terribly difficult to get the joint venture partner to agree to anything. We don't see eye to eye, and . . .' Sophie turned and pouted at Vikram. 'I need help.'

'Joint ventures are notoriously difficult in China,' he said, author-itative and supportive. He tapped the thin wafer of caramelised liquorice and it shattered into the lime cream below. 'But we have a lot of experience in this area, don't we, Jaq?'

Long and bitter experience, yes. Jaq nodded and bit into a chocolate shaped like a skull. You win some, you lose some. Sophie's project had just revealed its true face.

Sophie glanced around before dropping her voice to a whisper.

'That's why the next phase will be Krixo alone, without the joint venture.'

'Does the joint venture partner know that?' asked Jaq.

'No.'

Her lovely shoulders drooped, and she took a sip of dessert wine.

'The only way to negotiate is from a position of strength,' Sophie said.

Strength? What did she mean? Jaq glanced at Vikram.

'So, Sophie,' Vikram said, 'you asked for help. Give us an idea of the scope of the work.'

Sophie's chauffeur-driven limo arrived before Vikram's taxi. Her driver paid the bill while Sophie said her rather tipsy and effusive goodbyes. Jaq waited until she was gone before wiping the crimson lipstick from her cheek and ordering a double espresso.

'You said it was just lunch.'

Vikram made a rueful twist of his lips. 'I don't know anyone else as capable as you.'

'I don't do industrial espionage.'

'Come on, Jaq,' Vikram said. 'You've worked with Chinese joint ventures before. You know how tricky things can be. Keep an open mind.'

'I don't trust her.'

'She liked you.'

'What she was asking me to do was to approach a Chinese development agency under false pretences and visit a factory she claims to own. I can't do it.'

'It'll be tricky, I know, but money is no object, you saw how generous—' began Vikram.

'That's not tricky, it's downright dishonest! I've had enough of investigating dodgy companies. I've put my friends in danger, and I'm not doing it again. Give me a technical problem and I'll solve it, give me a project and I'll manage it, give me a team and I'll lead it, but no more mysteries.'

'Jaq, you are overreacting, imagining things.'

'It doesn't smell right . . .'

'Stick to facts, Jaq.'

'The fact is, I'm not doing the Krixo job. I'm going to Shetland.'

'Triple rate.'

'Whatever the salary, the answer is still no.'

Vikram turned away from her.

'Bugger it. How am I going to find someone else?'

'I'm sorry, Vikram.' *Sorry you have such poor judgement. Sorry you can't see through the superficial charms of a client to the murky layer of risk below. Sorry you can't see that no job is better than the wrong job.*

'Make one trip to China for me, OK? Business-class flights, five-star hotel, all expenses paid.'

She shook her head. 'I—'

'Quadruple rate.' He put a finger to his lips. 'One trip. Fact-finding, that's all.'

Good money, better than she'd ever earned before. Two months' salary for a fortnight's work. Could she do it? Could she override her gut feeling, ignore all instinctive doubts and misgivings? For what? Money? No, however tempting it sounded, she wasn't going to let filthy lucre cloud her judgement.

'I'm an engineer, not a spy.'

Vikram sighed. 'I don't want to lose this client.'

She stood up to leave.

'Think about it over the weekend,' he pleaded. 'I'll call you on Monday.'

Outside the light was fading. Jaq unlocked her bicycle and checked the lights.

No way was she going to China.

Enough of adventure. She was just an engineer. Engineering was all she wanted to do.

PART IV
OCTOBER

70

Yb

Ytterbium

173.04

Shingbo, China

The early-morning fog cleared to reveal a fleet of ships sailing down the Qiantang river towards Hangzhou Bay. The boats were moving faster than the lorries. A line of vehicles stretched back down the road in a queue several miles long.

Yan Bing, acting head of the Art Squad, directed operations from the back of a police car. If his source was correct, and given the effort that had gone into extracting the information, he had no reason to doubt it: the delivery would arrive today. A small parcel, the size of a shoebox, containing the Qianlong wedding cup. Early interception, and secret storage until after the Spring Festival, would ensure Madam Yun's banishment and his own job security.

Sweet revenge.

The area was too flat for covert surveillance; a police car was visible from miles away, and even an unmarked car would arouse suspicion. Better to hide in plain sight. Yan Bing's men had closed the east and west gates, and the river provided a natural boundary to the north. By setting up diversions to direct traffic through the south entry, he ensured all traffic entering the industrial park had to funnel through his inspection point.

It was set up to look like a normal search. His men were reviewing documents, checking axle weights, the security of the tarpaulins, and shaking a little cash loose as compensation for the trouble.

He inspected the queue of traffic: buses packed with workers, three-wheeled trucks brimming with vegetables for the factory canteens, lorries and tankers for the raw materials that didn't come by ship or rail, the odd bicycle. Yan Bing ignored them all, leaving his men to go through the motions. He knew exactly what he was looking for.

The buzz of excitement as the first international courier van approached soon fizzled out: nothing but documents, express-release bills of lading, letters of credit – no parcel of the right size.

It was almost lunchtime before the next suspect appeared: a young man in the back seat of a taxi.

Yan Bing signalled to his deputy that he would deal with this one personally. Smoothing his uniform and setting his cap at a severe angle, he took his time before springing from the car.

The taxi driver, an old man with a paunch, stood by his vehicle, trembling hands holding out a sheaf of papers. Yan Bing ignored him and walked around the taxi. Front seat empty. Nothing on the back seat except the passenger. He banged his truncheon on the window.

'Get out.'

The taxi driver opened the door for the startled passenger.

A young man emerged. Clean-shaven, short hair, good teeth, dressed in a crisp white shirt, pressed grey trousers and polished black shoes.

'Papers!' Yan Bing inspected the ID card: Ning Dan, a Shanghai resident.

'What's all this about?' The man was well spoken, just the trace of a city accent. An air of confidence that spoke of easy money, a rich family or a lucrative job. Probably both; one begot the other.

'I ask the questions.' Yan Bing brought his face closer, sniffing cologne. 'Where are you going?'

'Krixo factory,' the driver answered on behalf of his passenger, anxious to curry favour. 'From the railway station.'

Yan Bing returned the ID card and addressed the driver. 'Open the trunk.'

He watched the suspect as the driver fumbled with the catch. He betrayed no sign of anxiety. A cool customer. Or innocent.

The trunk was empty.

Yan Bing smashed his truncheon against the taxi in frustration. His deputy approached. 'Shall I issue a violation?'

'Triple.' Yan Bing named a spot fine that would wipe out the taxi driver's income for three months. Something to encourage care in his future choice of passenger. Unsurprisingly, the driver chose to make a donation to the police orphans and widows fund instead.

It began to rain. Yan Bing sheltered in his car as he ate lunch, a dish of noodles from a mobile vendor taking advantage of the traffic jam like flies to shit.

As he slurped the last of the broth, something about the taxi passenger nagged at him. Something in the boy's manner. His confidence, bordering on arrogance. The way he kept his hands in his pockets. What was he hiding? Yan Bing made a call. Ning Dan. Check him out.

The rest of the day dragged on. A few more couriers were stopped at the checkpoint, none with anything of interest. He was almost asleep when the call came.

Ning Dan. Engineer. Educated abroad. Recent contact with England. Internet traffic and calls being monitored.

Of course; the smugglers were smarter than he'd realised. The messenger wouldn't bring the Qianlong wedding cup here. He would be carrying a key to a safe-deposit box, or a verbal message with the location for the drop.

Yan Bing ordered his men to suspend operations and sped towards the Krixo factory.

Time for another conversation with Ning Dan.

Lisbon, Portugal

A storm was blowing in from the tropics, hitting the Azores hard overnight and now approaching mainland Europe at its most westerly point, just north of Lisbon. The air was heavy, humid, pressing on Jaq as she emerged from the metro at Rato and walked towards her mother's nursing home. The smell of roasting chestnuts wafted over from a mobile brazier. A woman shuffled half a dozen blackened fruits into a corner of old newspaper – *Diário de Notícias*. An ancient man with bow legs hobbled towards her waving a sheet of lottery tickets. Nothing much had changed.

The cemetery gates were closed, so she took the long way round, climbing Rua de Estrela, the cobbles slippery after a shower of rain, and turned right at the top of the hill to reach the convent.

The mother superior came out to greet her.

'*Bem vindo.*' Welcome back.

Jaq shuddered. The very sight of those grey robes, the white wimple, the heavy wooden rosary and cross, was enough to transport her back decades, back to the childhood stolen from her in this place.

'*Anda cá, menina.*' Come here.

The appellation *menina*, literally translated as 'girl', was more a term of endearment than an attempt to infantilise a grown woman. Or was that exactly the problem? Had she become so used to being patronised by the nuns that she failed to register the ideological undercurrent? Mafalda had been at another convent when Jaq had been incarcerated here. She was not responsible for the things that happened. Except in so far as she was part of the same church, the same organisation that denied women control over their own bodies. The same organisation now caring for her mother.

Jaq bit her lower lip and approached the old woman. She allowed the mother superior to embrace her, returning the kiss on one cheek, then the other, marvelling at the smoothness and softness of the old woman's skin. The nun's grey robes rose in a gust of wind, the tails of her wimple flapping against the stone arch.

'Come and see me before you leave.' The tone of voice made it clear the mother superior had issued a command, not a request.

Jaq bent her head and pressed forward against the wind. The scented garden was thirsty for rain, releasing the aromas of lavender and sweet basil as she hurried past.

Dona Rosa, the nursing sister, a wide-hipped woman with skin the colour and patina of a coffee bean, waited for Jaq at the entrance to the new dementia wing.

'I'm concerned about Dona da Silva.' Her dark eyes crinkled, and perfect white teeth gleamed through full red lips as she outlined the issues. 'She's more communicative . . .'

That was a change. The last time, Angie had not said a word, spending the whole visit staring at a wall.

'But increasingly erratic. Her delusions and paranoia are getting worse.'

'She knows I'm coming?'

'She's looking forward to seeing you.'

Jaq doubted that very much. It would take more than a change of ward for Angie to welcome the daughter she blamed for everything.

They walked together to the day room. Several men and women sat slumped around a wide-screen television. Most in easy chairs, a few still in wheelchairs, waiting for the hoist that was busy lifting a man who resembled a bundle of sticks. Those who were awake stared at the flickering screen of the TV. One woman was sleeping, a trickle of drool running down her cheek. Another was rocking to and fro, keening softly. Angie sat bolt upright in her wheelchair, her eyes glittering.

'Maria de Jaqueline,' she said. 'About time!'

Jaq swallowed hard. It was a relief to have her mother back, even if it only meant reprimands. It was almost reassuring to be chastised. Better than being abandoned again.

'Mãe.'

'Don't call me that!'

'Angie.' Jaq stepped forward awkwardly, unsure if her mother would accept a kiss.

'Keep away from me!'

Everyone in the room turned their attention from the soap opera on the screen to the unfolding real-life drama.

'Let's give you some privacy.' Dona Rosa grabbed hold of Angie's wheelchair and set off down the corridor at a furious pace.

Angie's new room was smaller than the old cell. There was barely room for the single bed, nightstand and an easy chair. But instead of a barred window that looked out on to a stone wall, french doors opened on to the garden. Or would when the weather permitted. Right now, the glass panes in aluminium frames rattled against the door jamb.

Jaq sat on the bed as Dona Rosa helped Angie into the chair. 'You look well, Angie.' It was true. When Jaq had last visited, her mother had looked much frailer. Now a spark of life had returned.

Her mother sniffed. 'What do you care?'

Rosa intervened. 'Dona da Silva, your daughter has come a long way to see you.'

'Leave us.' Angie waved her hand, dismissing the nurse.

Dona Rosa stood up and indicated a buzzer on the end of a long white cable that snaked across the bed. 'Just press this if you need me.'

Jaq waited until the door closed softly. 'How are you feeling, Angie?'

'Terrible.' Angie pointed an accusing finger at the door. 'That woman is torturing me.'

'Dona Rosa?'

Angie leaned forward, hard eyed glittering, little flecks of spittle mottling her lips. 'She is the devil.'

Deluded. No point in reasoning with her. Try distraction.

'I brought you something.' Jaq unpacked the iPod and portable speaker. She set it up on the nightstand beside Angie's bed.

'What is it? Give it to me!'

'Wait.'

'Ha! That's a fine imprecation coming from you. She who couldn't wait.' Angie's voice was harsh. 'You never had an ounce of self-control.'

Jaq pressed play and suddenly there was music in the room. The piano notes soft at first, then rising in confidence and tempo as Schubert's glorious impromptu swirled around them.

Angie stopped talking and listened in silence, her hands moving with the music. When the first étude finished, Jaq pressed pause.

'Maria João Pires?'

'Yes.' Her mother knew not only the piece but the artist. Some parts of her brain were functioning properly.

Angie tutted. 'Overrated.'

'I disagree.' Jaq sighed. 'Who would you like to hear?'

'Sam.'

Tears prickled her eyes. In truth, her brother had been an indifferent pianist, but she would do anything in the world to hear him play again.

'But you killed him, didn't you?'

This again. They'd been through it all so many times. There was no point in protesting, no point in arguing. No room for reason. Jaq pressed play again and Angie closed her eyes.

They sat together, listening to the other études, finishing *Le Voyage Magnifique* with a sublime allegretto. 'Darling.' Angie was smiling now, the sudden change from spite to charm unnerving. 'Get me my pills.'

Jaq looked around. 'What pills?'

'My painkillers.'

'You are in pain?' Jaq asked.

Angie groaned. 'I'm always in pain.' She began to cry. 'Terrible, terrible pain. It's eating my bones from the inside. Excruciating, unbearable . . .'

'Let me get the nurse.' Jaq pressed the buzzer.

'No! They don't understand pain.'

Dona Rosa appeared at the door.

Angie pointed at her daughter. 'She stole my pills!'

Dona Rosa laughed, a long throaty chuckle. 'You know that is not true, Dona da Silva.'

'Give me my painkillers, I want them now!'

Dona Rosa entered the room and checked the sheet at the end of the bed. 'You've already had them. You can have more at 6 p.m.'

'I'll be dead by then.' Angie pointed a finger at Jaq. 'Why is she here?'

'Your daughter is here to see you, Angie.'

'In trouble again, ha!' The old woman made a crude gesture, ramming the index finger of one hand into a circle made from the middle finger and thumb of the other. '*Puta!*

The anger rose, impossible to quell. *In trouble, yes, but not that sort of trouble. You made sure of that.* Why should the force of the anger take her by surprise? She should know by now, recognise the signs. There was no point in trying to fight it. Jaq stood up. 'I'm leaving now, Angie.'

'Go,' Angie screamed. 'And don't come back.'

Jaq walked briskly through the garden, striding into a cloud of swirling leaves. The rain had started, fat drops driven sideways by the wind. As she approached the exit, a pale face appeared at the office window and a disembodied hand tapped on the glass. She suppressed a sigh and entered the office.

'I'm afraid we need to talk about funding for your mother's care.'

Jaq swallowed, but her mouth was dry. 'Funding?'

Aunt Lettie had taken care of everything when she rescued Jaq from this place. The Lisbon properties belonging to her mother's family had been sold to pay for her mother's care.

'I thought the annuity covered everything.'

'Times have changed, and costs here have risen faster than inflation. Your mother's dementia is much worse. She's more aggressive, and needs special care.'

'But the money she brought with her?' The nuns had access to Angie's bottomless box, the one Jaq was allowed to borrow from, but prohibited from seeing inside.

'I'm afraid we gave you the last of the cash when you visited earlier this year.' Escaping from Slovenia, en route to Belarus and Ukraine, pursued by Interpol, she'd been grateful for the lifeline, never imagining it was finite.

'There's nothing left?'

'Personal stuff, a few papers and letters, some trinkets and mementos.'

'How big is the shortfall?'

The nun patted Jaq's arm. 'Let's discuss the options.'

The storm had passed by the time Jaq left the convent office, the sky washed clean. The turmoil had passed to Jaq. She needed thinking time.

Few people knew about the tunnel which connected a storeroom in the basement of the British Hospital to St George's church. The key was in its usual hiding place, exactly where she had left it. Emerging into the British Cemetery, she walked slowly between cypress trees and took her seat on a bench opposite the elaborate grave of the fifteen-minute baby. A stone cherub held a chain that linked the family tombs, each stone ziggurat marked with a simple cross.

Her eyes fell to the inscription.

In loving memory of the son of Manuel and Alice Nunes Correia, who died on 4 February 1905 aged 15 minutes. Thy will be done.

It wasn't her baby buried here, although his life had been equally brief. They took him away from her, telling her that it was for the best, a blessing in disguise, for how could an unmarried teenage mother be expected to cope with a child? They blamed her for his death, the wages of sin, demanding to know the name of the father. She never told them. She never even told her mother. Especially not her mother.

Thy will be done. What a cop-out.

She rarely thought about Mr Peres. On discovering that she was not the only girl in the class who was 'special', she'd made sure he would never teach chemistry again. After that, she held no bitterness, no rancour towards him. Their brief affair was legal and consensual, if unethical on his part, but he'd gifted her with an appreciation for the power of chemistry. A superpower which had allowed her to earn an independent living, never to be dependent on anyone else, ever again.

Now she needed money. A lot of money. The costs of her mother's care were shocking. Was there an alternative? Not in Portugal; the state provision was minimal. Bring Angie back to England? Was it any better in England? Could she find a dementia home willing to take a violent, deluded, aggressive patient? And if the only option was private, the costs would be even higher. The Shetland job would just about cover her own living costs plus her mother's care. But not the legal costs to fight Frank Good.

Who could she turn to?

The banks had already rejected her approach.

Johan, her best friend, had no money to spare, not with a family to support and everything invested in his outdoor adventure business.

Nat would help if she could, but the sums of money were daunting.

Gregor, her soon-to-be-ex-husband, was out of the question. He was making the divorce complicated enough without letting money taint it further. And he had a granddaughter now – Lily – a child whose special needs came first.

As she waited to board the flight at Lisbon airport, Vikram called.

'About the Krixo job,' he began.

'I'll do one trip.'

He sighed with relief. 'Thank you, Jaq. This job seems tailor-made for you.'

A little frisson, a premonition of danger, made her shiver. *Tailor-made, or a trap?* Too late; she had financial commitments that couldn't be avoided now.

'One trip. Then I go to Shetland. OK?'

'Already arranged. Angus has approved your CV. You start as soon as the Krixo job is done. I won't forget this . . .'

She cut him off and switched the phone to flight mode.

One trip to China. Just one.

Anything to free herself of Frank Good.

Vladivostok, Russia

The palace towered over the bluff, high above the town of Vladivostok. Stone walls sheltered the ornamental shrubs from the Pacific monsoon to the east and the Siberian High to the west. Sunlight glinted on tall windows, the transoms lining up with the gaps between mature trees to give unimpeded views of Golden Horn bay. The wide stone stairs – partially covered with a curving steel ramp – led through fluted Doric columns and under a smooth architrave with carved triangular frieze to a double doorway. The customers arrived through this portal, some still walking, many in wheelchairs, a few on stretchers with fluid drips and oxygen masks, to this place of respite. To days, weeks, even months of peace and kindness. Before moving on . . .

The old man rocked by the window of his room on the second floor. *Groan, clack, swish, squeak.* Back and forward, the runners of the old oak chair catching on the rug in front, then slapping against the wooden floorboards behind. Back and forward, syncopated to the rhythm of his laboured breathing. He turned his face towards the sea and a shaft of sunlight illuminated his cloudy eyes. His lips moved silently and his fingers twitched, his brow furrowing as if searching for some memory.

His hand reached into his dressing gown, brushing aside the button that would summon medical assistance. Since the heart surgery, it wasn't the doctors who were keeping him alive, it was the unfinished business. Slow fingers traced the golden chain down to the pendant and stroked the jade, tracing the circles of dragon fire with his pinkie as his heartbeat slowed and his breathing returned to normal.

So little time left, and so much still to do.

He resumed rocking in his chair. *Groan, clack, swish, squeak.* The sun hid behind a cloud and he shivered, pulling up the soft felt of his dressing gown collar to cover his scrawny neck. Waiting. But what was he waiting for? What hope, after so long?

The doctors had no explanation for the unexpected side effect of the surgery. Cortical blindness, they called it. Unusual but not unknown. All in his head, apparently. Now he relied on visitors for news of the outside world, both auditory and olfactory.

He smelt the chlorine before he heard the knock. The boy spent so much time in the swimming pool that he must be half dolphin by now. The old man stopped rocking and smoothed his remaining strands of hair.

'Come in, Timur!'

Dmytry was ready for the waft of cool air as the door opened and closed, the confident bounce of rubber soles on wood, the warmth and strength of the young man's embrace. He pushed Timur away and moved his nose down and to the left. Beside the hypochlorite there was soap, glycerine scented with rosin. And something else. Mint? Menthol. Deep heat cream.

'Trouble with the shoulder again?' he asked.

'How did you know?' Timur laughed. A screech of wood on wood as he pulled up a chair, a sneeze of dust as he sat on the cushion and then the warmth returned with an outstretched hand. 'The physio wants me to stop competing for a while, give it a chance to recover.'

Dmytry squeezed the young man's hand with his withered claw. 'Is it snowing?'

'Not yet.'

'This will be my last winter.' He hated the sound of his own voice, so thin and querulous compared to the younger man's rich bass rumble.

'Nonsense!'

'I won't make it to the spring.'

'Of course you will.'

'I failed,' he said.

'No, *Dedushka*, you—'

'I broke my promise.'

'Hush, rest now.'

Dmytry sighed. 'I left it too late.'

Timur brushed his brow with soft lips. 'Why don't you let me help you?' The voice was low and gentle. 'Your secretary told me that you were bidding for something when . . .'

'When my heart stopped me.' Ironic, really.

'What was it you wanted to buy?'

Wanted? That made it sound frivolous, a toy for a rich man. He didn't want it. He needed it.

'A piece of Chinese jade.'

'I don't understand.' The voice was gentle. 'Why was it so important?'

What to tell him? After all this time, after all the lies. Here was the one person left in the world who thought well of him. Loved him, even. Could he throw that away? Now, when he needed it most?

'Is it connected to my father?' Timur asked.

Interesting. Useful. Perhaps he didn't need to tell the truth. Perhaps the young man's curiosity was enough. 'In a way, yes.'

'Then why don't you let me track down the buyer for you?'

'What about your training?' Elite athletes couldn't afford to take time off.

Timur hesitated a fraction too long. 'My shoulder, remember?'

What choice did he have? He could no longer complete this alone.

'You would make a journey for me?'

'Anything, *Dedushka*.'

The old man released his hand and his words flowed like water.

PART V
NOVEMBER

71

Lu

Lutetium
174.97

Teesside to China

The afternoon sun glinted on the little Fokker 70 as it banked over the river Tees and turned east on the short flight to Amsterdam. From seat 1A, Jaq looked down at Teesside airport. Or Durham Tees Valley as it was now called, courtesy of a ruinously expensive rebranding exercise. *Absurdo.* Nestling in farmland between Darlington and Yarm, the airport was miles from the city of Durham. What was wrong with Teesside, anyway?

The fields gave way to industry: Billingham and Seal Sands, then south over Teesport to Redcar and Wilton. Depressingly little activity to be seen. The dark spaces, whorls of scar tissue left by long-demolished factories, outnumbered the bright lights and healthy plumes of steam rising from the working ones. Manufacturing had once thrived here. Now it was moving east. To the Far East.

Just like Jaq.

The cabin crew unfurled a curtain between Rows 3 and 4. Only three passengers travelling business class, and each had a row to themselves.

Flicking through the newspaper she had picked up in the airport, she stopped at the article.

BRUTAL ATTACK LEAVES RETIRED UNIVERSITY LECTURER FIGHTING FOR HIS LIFE

An elderly man was attacked in his own home on Thursday night.

John Tench (76) is in a critical condition in hospital with multiple knife wounds.

Kay Tench (73) returned from her book group to discover her

*injured husband and dog in their North Yorkshire home and called
999.*

The dog did not survive.

*A local resident, who did not wish to be named, said: 'I can't believe
this has happened, it's quite a shock. I have lived in this village for
thirty years. Who would hurt a dog like that? It's inhumane. You don't
expect things like this to happen here.'*

*Witnesses or anyone with information about the attack have been
urged to contact police.*

Was England becoming more violent? Knife crime was endemic in
big cities like London. Was it spreading to rural areas as well? Jaq
shuddered and closed the newspaper.

'Good evening, Dr Silver.' The KLM cabin attendant had done
her homework. 'Can I offer you a meal this evening?'

Jaq rejected the proffered tray of food – too early for dinner.
She sipped black tea and looked out at the grey North Sea. A wind
farm lay a few hundred metres offshore. Serried ranks of slender
white stalks, with trefoil petals moving slowly. Each wind turbine
containing a permanent magnet made with up to two tonnes of
rare earth metals. Rare earth metals from China.

Jaq released her seat belt and retrieved her bag from the
overhead locker. She flicked through the information Vikram
had compiled. The glossy brochures with the Krixo logo – three
green recycling arrows inside a triangular flask – were aimed at
investors rather than engineers; the technical information was
sparse.

As the plane began its descent into Schiphol, she checked the
connecting flight details. Over two hours before the flight to
Shanghai. Not quite enough time to pop into Amsterdam city
centre, but plenty to enjoy the most civilised airport in Europe.

From the business lounge, gazing out through huge windows at the
planes landing and taking off, Jaq considered her official mission.

With the death of Charles Clark, his daughter Sophie had become the 49% owner of a Chinese joint venture. The mysterious majority partner, Wang, never seen in person, was resisting any changes. Sophie wanted to negotiate 'from a position of strength'. Jaq's job was to visit the industrial park incognito. By working through the consultancy CCS, there was no need for anyone to know that the real client was Sophie.

She checked her emails and sent a message to Dan, her former student.

Arriving Shanghai tomorrow, then Shingbo for a few days. Any chance of meeting up? Jaq

She left the business lounge in plenty of time for her flight. She stood apart from the queue and observed the milling crowd. With her class of ticket, or even the frequent flyer miles collected, she could have jumped to the front. But the plane wasn't going without her, and she preferred to stretch her legs in the airy departure hall than be jostled in a line or confined to a seat. She had little luggage – her bag and a carry-on trolley case – and preferred to board at the end to minimise time spent inside a cramped, pressurised aluminium tube.

The young priest joining the business-class queue caught her attention. His face managed to be both sharp and delicate at the same time: dark hair shaved at the sides with a buzz cut over the top, dramatic eyebrows – tapering black slashes over slanting green eyes, high cheekbones, a straight nose, square chin and full lips. His flowing cassock couldn't entirely hide the grace with which his body moved beneath the black silk, and the neck emerging from his white preaching bands revealed well-developed trapezius muscles more usually associated with a swimmer than a cleric.

Since when did priests travel business class? Is that what they used the congregational pennies for these days? The money left over from paying lawyers to cover up the latest scandal? Or had the faithful donated their air miles to a man on a mission? She failed to suppress a smirk when a check-in assistant scanned his boarding pass and gestured him towards the back of the economy queue.

As the final stragglers boarded, she approached the counter and was directed left down a special gangway. Seat 72B was on the upper deck of the Boeing 747, a wide seat with plenty of legroom.

A Chinese cabin attendant with boyish features offered to hang up her jacket and returned with a bag of complimentary toiletries: toothbrush, toothpaste, lip balm, hand cream, comb, ear plugs, eye mask, flight socks. The cabin crew distributed flutes of chilled champagne. Jaq made her preparations. Phone, computer and e-reader set to flight mode. Luggage stowed. Headphones plugged in. Quilt unwrapped. Pillow plumped. Boots off, flight socks on. Seat belt fastened. The aisle seat beside her was still unoccupied when the safety video started and the plane began to taxi towards the runway. Jaq stretched her legs.

Once the plane was airborne, Jaq flicked through the in-flight entertainment options. Audiobooks, recorded music collections and 'live' concerts, HBO box sets, Hollywood and art house films, nature documentaries. From the galley she could hear the tinkling of glasses. Work, eh? There were worse places to be stuck for eleven hours. On quadruple time.

'Excuse me, madam.' The boyish attendant offered a hot hand towel and the dinner menu. 'We have a passenger who is eligible for an upgrade. Do you mind if he takes this spare seat?'

A frisson of irritation washed over her. *Do I mind? Yes, I do bloody well mind. Can I say so? No, of course I can't.* Ten minutes into her first long-haul business-class flight and she'd already become the sort of person she despised. Corrupted by privilege.

'Fine.'

She regretted her generosity when he returned with the priest, who took his seat beside her.

'Good evening,' he said.

'Hi.' She put on her headphones.

The purser returned with the drinks trolley. Jaq was going to need something stronger than champagne to get through this flight without picking a fight. Subjects to avoid: transubstantiation, denying women rights over their own bodies, child abuse and the callous neglect of the world's disenfranchised by their omnipotent, omniscient, omnipresent, non-existent deity.

She took off her headphones. 'Gin and tonic, please.'

'Same for me,' the priest said.

So, alcohol wasn't a problem for these men of the cloth. What happened to self-restraint and denial of earthly pleasures?

He clinked his crystal tumbler against hers. 'Cheers!'

'Cheers.' A little devil rose inside her. 'We may as well introduce ourselves, since we'll be sleeping together.' She extended a hand. 'Jaq Silver.'

'Timur Zolotoy.' He took her hand in a firm grip. The sleeve of his cassock rolled back to reveal an intricate lattice of tattoos.

A priest with a past?

'What takes you to Shanghai, Jaq Silver?'

None of your bloody business. The silence stretched into discomfort.

He spoke again. 'I'm going to look for work.'

'Oh, you count it as work, do you?' She could remain silent no longer. 'I assumed yours was more of a vocation.'

'Well . . .' He sipped his drink and wrinkled his brow, the dark eyebrows joining. 'I enjoy the girls and the dancing, but I only strip for the money.'

She spluttered a mouthful of gin back into the tumbler.

'Never judge a book by its cover, Jaq Silver.' He fluttered his thick, dark lashes.

'You're a stripper?' She did a double take. 'Disguised as a priest?'

'Master of disguise.' He smiled, his parted lips revealing a gold molar. 'This is one of many stage outfits, and by far the most comfortable for travelling. Since we'll be sleeping together, I thought full disclosure was only fair.'

The smell of hot bread announced the arrival of food. Her

neighbour turned his attention to the selection of wines, choosing a Gewürztraminer to go with the seafood appetiser. Dry and spicy, good choice. Jaq took the same.

The smoked salmon and prawns came with a side salad. Jaq shook the little glass bottle, mixing the copper-coloured vinegar with the green-gold olive oil, then added salt and pepper from a pair of miniature Dutch clogs. By the time she'd buttered the sesame-topped roll her companion had already cleared his plate.

'So, you're a chemical engineer?'

'How did you . . .?' Immediately defensive.

'You really want to know?' He raised one eyebrow. 'You won't be offended by my observations?'

She debated her options. It was a long flight, and now she was intrigued.

'Go on.'

He flashed his green eyes at her. 'You're the only woman in business class. You are travelling alone, so it is probably for work.'

'What deep insight,' she mocked.

'You aren't wearing any make-up.' He raised his perfect straight nose and sniffed the air. 'Or perfume. You don't colour your hair and you dry it naturally. You don't care what other women think, so I'm guessing you are a big shot in a predominantly male environment. So far so good?'

So far so bad, and painfully true. How many female bosses had she come across in her working life? None, if you excluded Camilla. Plenty of bright young scientists and engineers, but how many senior colleagues? Few of her age. Where did those younger women go?

'No sign of a manicure.' He nodded at the hand holding her glass. 'You shouldn't bite – there's stuff under your nails that isn't good for you.'

She put down the gin and curled her fingers into the palm of her hand to hide her ragged cuticles.

'Metal fragments under the nail of the pinkie, paint under the middle finger and sawdust under the thumb.'

Really? She'd changed the lock on Aunt Lettie's garage door, filed the burrs, sanded the new jamb and painted, which would explain the swarf and other fragments, but she wasn't going to give him the satisfaction of checking whether he had really seen it.

'I'm guessing you live alone.'

And so what? She was beginning to regret giving this cheeky bastard permission.

He pointed at the shoes under her seat. 'You travel wearing work boots to keep your carry-on luggage light. Those anti-static soles and steel-reinforced toecaps must weigh a bit.'

Jaq's feet were not abnormally small for a woman, but she had never encountered a construction site that stocked adequate safety boots in her size.

He tapped the boarding pass on her armrest. 'You're travelling from Teesside. The North-East of England must have the highest concentration of chemical manufacturing in England.'

What's left of it.

'So, I guess you are an executive in the chemical industry, off to kick ass in China. Right?'

'Wrong,' she said. But an alarmingly creditable attempt.

The attendant cleared their plates, changed their glasses and served the main course.

'Am I losing my touch?' He turned to her and wrinkled his nose. 'Completely wrong?'

She sipped the new wine. A rich Malbec. Robust and velvety at the same time. It was possible for strength and softness to coexist. 'Partly right,' she relented. 'I trained as a chemical engineer.'

He clicked his fingers and rolled his shoulders. 'Score!'

'You really figured all that out from those small clues?'

'My job is to please.' He dug into his food. 'To please, you must understand. To understand you must observe.'

'Seriously?'

'No.' He grinned. 'I might have caught a glimpse of your frequent flyer profile. The rest was guesswork.'

Despite all attempts to hold it in, her laughter escaped in a throaty chortle. At last, something she believed. Then a moment of doubt.

'You asked to sit next to me.' She'd been here before. Beautiful young men with ulterior motives taking an unusual interest in her. What did he know? Her last mission had been hushed up, governments reluctant to reveal the extent to which they had lost control of the trade in chemical weapons. One or two newspapers had run speculative articles. Could he have targeted her because of past misadventures?

He shook his head. 'Relax, this was the only free seat in business class. Some dude missed his connection.'

She turned and looked behind her. The upper cabin appeared full. She scrutinised his face. 'So, how did you get into your current line of work?'

His green eyes sparkled. 'You mean, why is a nice boy like me working as a stripper?'

'Exactly.'

'I used to swim. For my country.'

The accent was Eastern, though his English was perfect. 'And your country is?'

'Russia.'

She nodded, impressed despite herself. Russia trained formidable athletes.

'We were paid in prize money. Then I injured my shoulder.' He rubbed his left shoulder with a large right hand. 'When things got tough, the prize money ran out. The swim team were far from home. Someone offered me a way to make a quick buck. I enjoyed it. Maybe more than the swimming.' He grinned. 'So, in a nutshell, Jaq Silver, I do this for the money.'

You and me both.

'And I'm not alone. There's not a country in the world where I can't find a superb athlete looking for a bit of work on the side.'

A stripper in every port.

'Although not all of them can dance.' He yawned. 'But all the international travel gets a bit much. Which is why I persuaded this lovely gentleman here,' he beamed at the cabin attendant, who blushed as he cleared away their plates and glasses, 'to find me a seat in business class.'

The cabin attendant said something, and Timur replied in fluent Mandarin.

'Lovely talking to you both,' he returned to English, 'but I badly need my beauty sleep.' Timur pressed the button to turn his chair into a flat bed. 'Goodnight, Jaq Silver. Sweet dreams.'

'Anything else, madam?' the steward asked. 'Coffee, a liqueur?'

Jaq suppressed a burp. 'No, thanks.'

'Sir?'

But the Master of Disguise was already asleep.

The huge Boeing 747-400 had started its descent when she woke after a full, unbroken eight hours of sleep. And what dreams. Delicious.

She glanced at the empty aisle seat. Her extraordinary travelling companion had vanished. Returned to his assigned seat for landing? Perhaps she had dreamed the whole mad encounter. Touchdown so smooth, only the deceleration signalled that the huge plane was on the ground.

As she was collecting her things, she found a business card in her right safety boot. A thick purple border and violet letters: *Timur Zolotoy. Masters of Disguise.* A contact number and a handwritten message.

> *Lovely to meet you, Jaq Silver. Come to the show one day.*
> *I'll save you a hot seat.*
> *And a private dance.*

Hong Kong, China

A plane banked as it flew over Hong Kong and turned west to the airport at Chek Lap Kok. On the rooftop of a penthouse above Kowloon Bay, a slight woman in flowing robes flung a curved sword high into the air. The steel blade caught the setting sun, sending out flashes of rose and amber as it spun. Mico arched her back and executed a backward somersault, landing on her feet just in time to catch the plummeting weapon in the leather sheath slung across her back.

She removed the blindfold and shook her ponytail free. The remnants of the silken hairband, sliced open by the blade, fluttered to the floor.

'Bravo!' Stretched out on his lounger beside the pool, Sun Chang applauded, his eyes crinkling with affection for his daughter. 'How was your trip? I haven't seen you since you got back.'

She wrinkled her nose. 'Terrible flight. I hate long haul, so many hours sitting still. It messes up my training.'

He laughed.

'Don't you get bored? Training all day?'

She skipped over to him, bare feet squeaking on the polished wood floor. 'Don't you get bored, drinking beer all day?'

He raised his cheek for her kiss, belching as she bent towards him. Wrinkling her nose in disgust, she brushed his forehead with her lips before turning away and settling herself on another lounger.

'This is work. A new brand.' He pushed the frosted glass towards her. 'Here, try it.'

She patted her lean stomach. 'Too many calories.'

'Aha, thought you might say that. This is a special light beer, our new brand for women.'

She picked up the bottle from the table between them and inspected the label.

'Why the rabbit?'

'Hop!' He chuckled to himself. 'Don't you see? Beer is made with hops – rabbits hop, girls love cuddly rabbits.'

'Little girls don't drink beer. Your target is adult women.' *Careful.* Her sexual politics, and preferences, were a taboo subject. 'Your idea? The rabbits?'

'Yes. D'you like it?'

She didn't say what she really thought.

'Let me taste.'

He handed her the glass.

It was surprisingly good. Bright, bubbly, clean. 'I like it.'

He clapped his hands with delight.

'I have business in Shanghai next week. Some foreign guy who insists on a face-to-face meeting.' He handed her a card with a purple border: Timur Zolotoy. 'I might need a translator. Fancy coming along? You could take a look at the launch plans for Hop! Give me your professional opinion. As an adult woman.' He sighed. 'An adult, unmarried woman.'

'Dad . . .' she warned.

'You're almost thirty, Mico. You can't put it off for ever.'

'Maybe I haven't found the right person yet.'

'Then consider the ones I find for you. Meet them. Give them a chance. Yang's cousin is a millionaire already, and my accountant has a son just back from Harvard . . .'

'If you bring this up again, I'm moving out.'

'It's hard for me to understand your generation.' He sighed. 'Meet me halfway. Come with me next week? Get to know more about the beer business.'

Why not? She owed her father that much. They didn't need her on the film set; her new fight scenes would be shot on location at the Shaolin Temple. And she could make a side trip to see Yun in Beijing. Her heart raced with happiness at the prospect.

'I'll think about it.'

Shanghai, China

Shanghai Pudong airport stretched as far as the eye could see. A bridge connected the two terminals across multi-lane roads to a central train station. Pedestrian conveyor belts, crammed with people, ferried a river of travellers in both directions.

Disembarking ahead of the masses, Jaq marched straight up to an immigration desk. She presented her passport and landing card with trepidation. How much police information was shared? Given her history, would they turn her back at the border? If she was refused entry, then there was nothing she could do except get on a plane back to Europe. She would have fulfilled her obligation to Vikram and Sophie, enjoyed an excellent meal and a good sleep and earned enough to keep her mother in care.

The immigration official, a young Chinese woman ramrod straight in an impeccable uniform, stamped her passport and waved her through. Jaq emerged into a cathedral of light: huge glass panels held in a vast lattice of white-coated metal tubes rising to a high vaulted roof, the afternoon sun diffracted and tempered to an even glow.

She eschewed the travelator, choosing to walk, glad to stretch her legs. Her little trolley made a clicking noise as it rolled towards the Transrapid. Vikram had booked a hotel limousine transfer, but Jaq cancelled it, preferring to make her own way. After hearing so much about the fastest train in the world, she wasn't going to miss an opportunity to experience it for herself. Magnetic levitation – another successful application of rare earth magnets.

A sleek white train hugged the platform: pointed nose, tinted windows, orange and blue go-faster stripes. The doors slid open with a sigh, and Jaq stepped inside.

She checked her emails. A short reply from Dan with an address, a date and a time. Tonight, in the centre of Shanghai. She put the address into her phone.

The doors locked with a soft click and the train began to float forwards. Jaq ran through each stage. First, lift – the repulsion between two similar magnets that allows the train to rise above the rails. Next, stability – the compensating forces that stop it veering sideways or flipping over as it lifts. And finally, propulsion – the repulsion between magnets that drives the train forwards, free of friction from rails or wheels, thanks to the lift.

The magnetic river was a British invention. Eric Laithwaite, a professor at Imperial College London, built the first full-size working model in the 1940s – a single linear motor giving lift, stability and propulsion. How tragic, how predictable, that such a groundbreaking piece of British engineering could only be commercialised by others. Her adopted country was famous for the brilliance of its engineers, infamous for its inability to value them or their inventions. Because of men like Frank Good. Men who had no interest in progress or innovation, men who only cared for short-term self-interest, who only saw this year's bonus.

The train sped past marsh and open fields. The speedometer on the ceiling clicked up to 100 km/hr in less than a minute. Jaq was pushed back into her chair. Newton's second law: force equals mass multiplied by acceleration.

The ride was smooth, even as the speedometer hit 200 then 300 km/hr; there was no noise or vibration. Only the wind outside, rushing over the smooth aerodynamic shape. A strange sensation; keep your eyes on the horizon, or middle distance, and it felt much like any other train ride. But if you tried to focus on the side of the track, everything became a dizzy blur. The train tilted as it rounded a bend, then straightened up and uncoiled, moving faster and faster. Four hundred km/hr and rising. No vibration, nothing inside the carriage to suggest the true speed. The speedometer settled at 431 km/hr, and the sleek white train zoomed towards the skyscrapers of Shanghai.

Without the acceleration, everything felt normal. Newton's first law: it's as natural to be in motion as it is to be at rest. Without friction, without resistance, moving forward takes no more energy than remaining static. There is no reason not to continue.

Indefinitely.

So much easier to travel, to stay on the move, embrace the new, never look back.

The hotel sat a few blocks back from the Huangpu river. A white-gloved, top-hatted flunkey opened the door on to an elegant lobby. Beyond the leather armchairs, a sweeping stone staircase led up to the master suite: a bedroom with a curtained four-poster bed, a bathroom with double sink, rain shower and enormous free-standing claw-footed bath, a small study with office chair, desk and laptop docking station already connected to a keyboard, screen and printer, and finally a sitting room with brocade sofas, glass tables, a huge TV and quadraphonic sound system.

Jaq locked the door, stripped off and headed straight for the shower. Lost in the pleasure of hot water pummelling her skin, she did not emerge for a while.

So, this was the suite that Sophie reserved year-round, guaranteeing its availability at forty-eight hours' notice. Krixo must be doing well to run to such extravagance.

Wrapped in a bathrobe, Jaq drew back the curtains and gazed out at the busy street below. Daylight was fading fast. Time to move.

She checked her phone for the address where Dan had suggested they meet. Very close. There was something vaguely unsettling about the brevity of the message. The fact that he didn't ask if it was convenient. Dan was an engineer, not given to flowery language, but he was always polite and had a superb command of

English. It wasn't like him to be so curt. He must have been in a hurry.

Better not be late. She dressed, pulling the Shetland hat over her wet hair, and left the hotel, heading towards the Bund, Shanghai's famous waterfront, admiring the Gothic, art deco and beaux arts buildings, the nineteenth-century banks, custom houses, shipping lines, insurance brokers, consulates and boutique hotels on the Puxi side of the river: Old Shanghai.

Initially a British settlement, it was one of the five treaty ports conceded after the First Opium War in 1842, giving the British the right to continue creating Chinese addicts with poppy from India and Afghanistan. Other nations followed, and Shanghai soon became an international trading settlement.

New Shanghai now towered over the old. Giant skyscrapers reared up from the Pudong side of the river. The old stone buildings lurked, conventional, squat and dim in comparison to the new neo-futuristic architecture, a glorious extravaganza of cutting-edge engineering. Europe in decline; Asia ascendant. Exactly as her students, like Dan, had predicted.

Checking her watch, she walked briskly to the rendezvous, a café on the riverside with open windows. The clientele were mainly elderly tourists with a few younger Chinese people, most of them female. No sign of Dan. She waited outside for a few more minutes, then dialled his number.

A Chinese woman inside the café sprang to her feet and hurried out towards her.

'Dr Zliver?'

'Silver, Jaq Silver.'

'I'm Dan's sister, Lulu.' The young woman marched back into the café, turning her head and beckoning. 'Come.'

Jaq followed. No sign of Dan. Perhaps he was parking a car and had sent his sister on ahead.

'Sit down.' She spoke with a strong accent but the command in her voice was unmistakeable.

'Is Dan coming?'

'No.' Lulu's face crumpled. 'He's vanished.'

Jaq sat down opposite her. Lulu wore her hair in a short bob, a glossy black frame for a striking face – high cheekbones, small nose, thin lips, pointed chin. Difficult to judge age, but she looked to be in her late twenties. Small and slim, she wore a frilly white blouse, a short tartan skirt, opaque turquoise tights and wedge-heeled shoes. No obvious family resemblance, either in features or fashion sense. But then Dan was a boy who wore the same clothes – jeans, T-shirt and padded anorak with fur-lined hood – for the four years he had spent at Teesside University.

'Vanished?' Jaq put her hands flat on the table. In the last few hours? Since he replied to her message? 'Today?'

A waiter approached, and Lulu ordered green tea for them both. 'Two weeks ago.'

Two weeks ago? 'So, it wasn't Dan who asked to meet here?'

Lulu shook her head. 'It was me.'

'Why?'

'I thought you might know something.'

'But I've just arrived.'

'You see, he went on a day trip to Shingbo and didn't come back.'

'For work?'

The expression in Lulu's eyes was hard to read. Hostile. Almost accusatory. Why?

The tea arrived in glass beakers, the dark leaves unfurling slowly, rising and swelling before falling.

'He was very happy.' Lulu stirred sugar into her tea. 'He'd received a message from his professor . . .'

It took a moment to realise who Lulu was talking about. When had she sent a LinkedIn message to Dan? Almost three weeks ago.

'Asking him to visit a factory.'

'Not exactly.' Stay calm. An innocent request for local information. Krixo might have been in the news. Dan might have ex-colleagues working there, or his company might use the same specialist contractors. 'I asked a general question. Did he tell you why he was going to Shingbo?'

'No.' Lulu shrugged. 'That's what I was hoping you would tell me. Why did you send him?'

Jaq shook her head. 'I didn't send him anywhere.'

'Then why did he go?'

Jaq took a sip of her tea. A leaf stuck to her upper lip and she removed it with a small, thin paper napkin.

'I have no idea, I'm sorry.'

'I called his work. In case they'd sent him on to Ningbo or somewhere else.'

That would explain things. A sudden change of plan.

'They hadn't heard from him either. He didn't go to work on Monday. That's when I started to get worried.'

More alarming. Dan had a strong work ethic. 'And then?'

'I checked his computer. No activity. He hasn't used his email or WeChat or anything. I saw your message on LinkedIn saying you'd arrived.'

And pretended to be Dan to meet me. The actions of a desperate sister? Or something more sinister? An invisible band tightened around Jaq's throat.

'And then I looked back through his LinkedIn messages and saw that it was you who'd sent him to Shingbo.'

Jaq sighed. No point in repeating that she'd done nothing of the sort. Lulu appeared fixated on the idea.

'Does he know you have access to his computer? His passwords?'

'We share a flat.'

'But he could have other profiles, for private stuff.'

Lulu scowled. 'I called all his friends. No one has heard from him.'

'Does he have a girlfriend?'

'No.'

'Boyfriend?'

Lulu shot her a look laced with venom. 'No.' Emphatic. 'I called the police.'

'What did they say?'

'They told me I had to wait a month before they'd log a missing persons report.'

'And his phone?'

'Turned off. Goes straight to voicemail. I've left messages, but he doesn't call back.' Lulu looked away.

'What about your parents?'

'You don't know?' Lulu dropped her gaze. 'They died last year. Within a few days of each other.'

'I'm so sorry.' Jaq extended a hand in comfort. Should she have known? How could she? She didn't even know that Dan had a sister. When did the one-child policy start in China? Around 1980? Although rural parents were allowed a second child if the first one was a daughter. Perhaps Lulu was a little older than she appeared. No wonder she was so brittle. She'd lost both parents and now her brother had disappeared.

'Why did he go to Shingbo?' Lulu persisted.

'Look, Lulu, I can't believe that Dan's disappearance is related to an innocent question about a chemical company, but I'm going to Shingbo tomorrow morning. I'll try to find out whatever I can.'

Lulu nodded. 'I will come with you.'

Jaq shook her head. 'Thanks, but it's not necessary.'

'How will you communicate? Do you speak Mandarin?'

'It's all arranged.' Jaq fished out the card Vikram had given her. SEITA: Sino-Euro Interpretation and Translation Agency. 'I'm meeting my translator tomorrow morning.'

Lulu's phone beeped. 'I have to go.' She shouted something to the waiter, who brought the bill.

Jaq paid. 'How do I contact you?'

Lulu gave her a card and a long stare: direct, hard, almost angry. 'Call me if you need anything. Anything at all.'

Shanghai to Shingbo, China

Jaq slept deeply, and was woken by her alarm at 7 a.m. She ordered breakfast in her room and checked her messages. One was from Lulu, reiterating her offer of help.

When breakfast arrived – boiled eggs with no egg cup, fruit and black tea – it came with a message in a solid silver clip.

SEITA regret to inform Dr Silver that the translator has been taken ill and no replacement is available.

Merda. How was she going to manage? The translator had been meant to arrange the train tickets and travel with her.

Midnight in the UK. Too late to call Vikram? But what choice did she have? He had chosen SEITA. He was ultimately responsible for the cock-up. He'd have to fix it.

She rummaged in her bag for her business card holder, a slim silver envelope, dimensions slightly larger than a standard business card with a picture of the Transporter Bridge and her initials embossed on one side, a magnetic flap on the other. At the front were her new cards. *Dr Jaq Silver, CCS, Project Director.* A meaningless title if ever there was one.

At the back were the cards she had collected recently. Lulu's plain white card with nothing more than her name and number. Lulu was desperate to help, but far too emotionally invested in her brother's disappearance to be objective. It wouldn't be fair to ask her. The SEITA card was not there – had Lulu given it back? Not that it was any use. The translation and interpretation service promised everything but delivered nothing. She paused at the thick, glossy card with a purple border, smiling at the idea of

Timur as interpreter, imagining a trip to Shingbo with the Master of Disguise. He was looking for work, after all. *No, not that kind of work. Don't be absurd. Get a grip.*

Her fingers closed around Vikram's card and she punched the number into her phone. No answer. She dialled again. This time, a sleepy voice answered.

'Jaq, do you know what time it is?'

'Sorry to wake you, but I need help.'

'What's up?'

'Translator has bailed. I'm sure I can get to Shingbo on my own, but not sure how useful it will be without someone who speaks English.'

'Leave it with me.'

Vikram rang back ten minutes later.

'The Shingbo Development Corporation are sending a car. They have their own translator – he'll meet you when you arrive.'

Jaq switched her phone to silent and went back to bed.

A grey limousine pulled up a couple of hours later, the young male driver impeccably turned out in a well-cut black uniform with gold braid, sunglasses and peaked cap. He introduced himself as Pang Mo, and although he spoke limited English, his hand gestures were perfectly eloquent.

It took forever to get out of Shanghai, the traffic nose to tail on the corkscrew expressway that led to a river crossing. Jaq checked her phone. A missed call from Lulu. And a text.

Everything OK?

Jaq texted back. *Everything fine. On my way to Shingbo.*

Once they were free of the megacity, the ride was smooth and the air began to clear. As they rose up out of the mist that fringed Hangzhou Bay, she had a clear view of the offshore windmills: slim metal columns topped by three blades, rotating slowly. With the old technology, it would have taken thousands of these monsters to generate the same amount of power as the smallest conventional power plant – coal, gas, even nuclear. But with rare earth magnets, the technology was changing fast, and with it the promise of clean energy, green energy, wind energy.

A colleague at Teesside University had explained the economics of wind power to her. The trouble with the first wind turbines was the speed. The huge blades describe a full circle every three to six seconds. A conventional generator, the bit that turns the wind energy into electrical energy by spinning magnets inside copper coils, had to run ten times faster than the blades. So, a gearbox high in the nacelle converted the low speed of the windmill into the high speed demanded by the generator. But it's not easy to maintain high-speed bearings on top of a hundred-metre structure several miles offshore. In a place specially chosen because it is very, very windy. Despite design improvements, the wind–electricity conversion rates remained low, the maintenance costs high. Huge subsidies had been required to produce green energy.

Then came the superstrong magnets. So powerful that the generator could rotate at the same speed as the blades and still produce a satisfactory electrical current. Direct drive meant no gearbox, lower weight meant a lighter structure, simpler design meant less maintenance. Net result – cheaper wind farms, improved conversion efficiency, and suddenly green energy need not be impossibly expensive energy.

Just one catch.

The new magnets needed new metals, rare earth metals. The rare earth metals are never found in a concentrated form. You need to shift an awful lot of rock to get a few grams of neodymium and praseodymium, dysprosium and terbium.

Which was where companies like Krixo and their advanced recycling technology came in.

Ping.

The electronic box on the car windscreen beeped, and Jaq blinked at the white light of a flashing camera as the car passed smoothly through an electronic tollbooth. As they crossed the Qiantang river and descended from the expressway towards Shingbo, she could see the vast sprawl of an industrial estate reserved for high-technology investment. Some of the plots were already occupied. She pulled out the Krixo brochure and checked the location graphic. It was a conceptual rather than an accurate map, but the Krixo factory would sit beside the river, on the seaward side of this bridge. The car slid to a halt, joining a queue to exit the toll road. She thrust the brochure towards the driver, pointing at the location dot and the Chinese address for Krixo. He smiled and nodded and once they were through the toll road, he made a sharp left and drove along a wide, empty road between the industrial estate and the shoreline.

Down by the estuary, the mist rolled in. After a few kilometres she saw the first signs for Krixo through the fog: three green recycling arrows inside a triangular flask. A line of lorries queued up by the side of the road, wooden shipping crates on their flatbed trailers. The car slowed to a halt outside an elaborate wooden gate, replete with sinuous carved dragons, brightly painted in red and gold. She peered through the extravagant arch to the factory inside.

Visibility was poor, but she could just make out four buildings around a small lake with a vigorous fountain – the cooling sink and fire water reserve. Each building was about thirty metres long and six storeys high, the exterior walls painted a light pink with a terracotta roof. Perhaps Sophie had some say in the colour scheme? A gust of wind blowing in from the sea made the grey fog swirl and clear. She looked up to see wisps of steam emerging from a tall chimney, the tip painted red and white, towering over a double extraction column and a row of stainless-steel tanks, each with KRIXO stencilled in large red letters in English and Chinese. The fog thickened again, and the letters disappeared. So far, so conventional; it looked like any other high-tech chemical plant. Most of the sophisticated recycling activities must be kept out of sight, inside the large pink buildings fanning out north, south, east and west from the central turquoise fountain.

Another gust of wind, the fog thinned and she saw that dark blue utility sheds and warehouses formed a secure perimeter. Yellow cranes were busy at one corner of the site. What were they building? Perhaps Sophie was right to be concerned about the secretive behaviour of the joint venture partner.

Not a soul in sight. She checked her watch: midday. It must be lunchtime. All the workers would be in the canteen, eating the main meal of the day and then preparing for a short siesta. China might be the hardest-working country in the world, but lunch was lunch.

The driver got out of the car and opened her door.

The site was fenced, but the security didn't look unusually heavy. Could she go and take a closer look? Better not draw attention to herself. She was here for a week. Plenty of time to visit Krixo under the official auspices of the development agency. With a translator.

Jaq shook her head at the driver. She waved her itinerary and pointed to the address of the hotel. The driver nodded and got back into the car.

As they drove away, a pair of uniformed security guards emerged from the factory and stared at the retreating car before the mist closed in again.

Teesside, England

Take time for yourself, the doctor said. What did that even mean? Frank was used to working eighty-hour weeks, racing across Europe, making things happen, meting out reward . . . and punishment. It wasn't that he didn't enjoy his own company – he was by far the most cultivated and interesting person he knew – but he preferred seeing himself through the eyes of others. Adoring or fearful, it was all the same to him. Without a social mirror, he was already bored. It was time to get back to work.

He picked up the phone and dialled.

'Nicola.' He imagined the scowling face, the shithouse-rat eyes of the dumpy HR director. 'Frank here.'

'Frank? I'm sorry, Frank who?'

If it was designed to irritate, it certainly had the desired effect. 'Frank Good.' Your old boss, as if you didn't remember.

'Ah, Frank. I was just about to write to you.'

Write? Why the bureaucracy?

'We'd like you to attend a disciplinary interview, that is, if you're well enough.'

Disciplinaries were always the most fun. They must have missed him. Perhaps they had saved up some juicy sackings for him to administer. A good way to get back in the saddle.

'Fighting fit,' he said.

'You have the right to bring a trusted colleague.'

Why would he want to bring a trusted colleague? The epitome of an oxymoron.

'In any case, we would advise you to seek legal advice.'

'Legal advice?' He sniffed. 'Why?'

'It's all in the letter,' Nicola said.

He could get nothing more from her and hung up, confused.

Frank didn't want to think about what was in her letter, so he opened the local newspaper.

VICTIM OF KNIFE ATTACK DIES

North Yorkshire police have launched a murder investigation following the death in hospital of an elderly academic assaulted in his own home. Professor John Tench (76) succumbed to the injuries inflicted in a frenzied knife attack.

Police spokesmen refused to confirm that the victim had been tortured, but an RSPCA spokesman confirmed that a dog belonging to Professor Tench was killed during the attack.

Frank shuddered and turned to the business news. Aha, here was something more interesting: Graham Dekkers, President of Global Operations for Zagrovyl, was visiting the Teesside factory. A straight-talking South African, Graham owed Frank a few favours.

Here was an opportunity too good to miss.

Time to go over Nicola's head.

Shingbo, China

The modern tower block was unremarkable from the outside, but the interior decoration of the Shingbo hotel was anything but subtle. Jaq counted twelve chandeliers between the entrance lobby and lift. The two in her room cast a diffuse light onto the striped carpet, gilt dado rails, heavy dark furniture and fake fur throw covering the emperor-sized bed.

The translator, Lai Lang, had been waiting in the lobby when she arrived, and assisted her with the check-in. A slight young man with a broad smile, he spoke excellent English. Dinner, he informed her, was booked for 6 p.m. in the same hotel, the head of the Shingbo Development Corporation evidently unable to wait for their scheduled meeting tomorrow.

She spent the afternoon trying not to fret. How was she going to survive an intimate dinner with the very agency she'd been sent to hoodwink? What if they asked questions she was unable to answer? How soon would it be before they spotted that she was a fraud? Twigged that her motives went beyond the stated brief? Why had she agreed to do this? How had she got herself into this mess?

She needn't have worried. Mr Smiles, her translator, had failed to mention that dinner would involve a large number of people. As she entered the banquet hall at the appointed time, sixty men, and a handful of women, turned and bowed to her. The translator guided her to a circular table that seated twelve. Business cards were exchanged, and she was seated between the head of the development corporation and the deputy mayor of Shingbo.

A waiter approached.

'Do you drink alcohol?' Mr Smiles asked.

Jaq hesitated. There were times when it was easier to pretend she didn't touch the stuff, especially when she needed her wits about her. Women in Asia could generally get away with refusing to drink; it was more difficult for men in a business setting, unless they invoked religious beliefs. But she sensed it might be a long and tedious night, and right now, she could really use a drink.

'What do you recommend?'

'I'd avoid the liquor, Moutai, it's pretty strong. Wine?'

'Perfect.'

The waiter poured a splash of dark liquid into a large wine glass. Was she meant to taste it first? She looked around, but he had retreated with the bottle.

The deputy mayor clinked his glass with hers and proposed a toast.

'*Zūnjìng de kèrén, huānyíng,*' he bellowed.

The translator spoke more softly. 'Honoured guest, welcome.'

The plump man in the Chinese tunic continued to declaim, barely pausing to allow Mr Smiles to translate.

'Welcome to our new industrial park, welcome to the seven hundred and sixty square kilometres of reclaimed land, to the seven new bridges, to the fifty-eight kilometres of new road, to the housing for one hundred thousand people. We welcome you from the bottom of our hearts and we hope that you prosper!'

'I am delighted to be here,' Jaq replied. 'Thank you for the invitation.'

Mr Smiles spoke for a few minutes. So much for Mandarin being a concise language.

Ganbei!

Bottoms up. Jaq copied the others and drained her glass, trying not to grimace at the sour taste of the liquid billed as wine, suddenly grateful that the serving was so small.

'What did you say?' she whispered.

He coloured slightly. 'Do you really want to know?'

'Yes.'

'Something along the lines of, "it is an honour to visit your magnificent industrial park. I admire the effort that has gone into reclaiming the land from the treacherous estuary. I am impressed by the supreme skill of the engineers in designing and building the new bridges and roads and houses. Truly this is an enterprise of great merit".'

Jaq grinned. 'Spot on.'

An army of waiters brought silver platters heaped with delicacies, placing them on a rotating glass disc in the centre of the table. The deputy mayor leaned over and placed an iridescent wobbling lump of translucent putty onto her dish.

'What is it?' she whispered to Mr Smiles.

'Jellyfish.'

She suppressed a shudder as she tried to get her chopsticks to work, pushing the slithering raw mess into a cave under the raw vegetables that the Inward Investment Director was merrily piling onto her plate.

Her glass was refilled, and it continued to replenish itself after each toast, the welcomes becoming more elaborate as each member of the deputy mayor's team stepped forward to salute her.

Ganbei!

Although Jaq had a strong constitution, by the time the deputy mayor came to make the most important toast, she was feeling a little light-headed.

'We welcome the beautiful big engineer to our industrial park. She has skin like a peach and hair like silk. We hope that she has good sense as well as height, and will not ask the questions that have no answers. That way, she will leave us as big and healthy as when she arrived,' he said.

Ganbei!

Jaq stared at her smiling translator. Was that a threat? Or a challenge?

She stood up.

'Gentlemen, all questions have answers, whether we like them or not. I look forward to finding out more.'

Mr Smiles translated.

The assembled company smiled and clapped.

Ganbei!

'What did you say?' she hissed.

'Does it matter? They won't remember a thing in the morning.'

'Tell me.'

'"Gentlemen, you are as handsome as warriors, as strong as lions, as clever as scholars. I will take your advice in all matters, including which questions I should ask".'

'But it's not what I said.'

'Don't worry. Enjoy the evening.'

Enjoy was not the right word. Endure would be better. The banquet was about competitive humiliation. The food was not about pleasure, it was about who would be shamed first, who would be unable to overcome their natural revulsion as the dishes came around on the lazy Susan, who would gag and refuse. Dishes made from increasingly exotic animals, chosen for rarity rather than taste or tenderness. Dishes made with increasingly unusual body parts: feet, beaks, genitals, entrails, tentacles. Usually raw.

At least some skill had gone into the presentation of the food. Sculpted vegetables adorned the tray of greasy testicles; sprays of wild flowers framed the plate of chicken feet. The drinking games were a cruder licence to bully.

The man on her left was trying to toast one of the younger functionaries. Both men were already drunk, but the younger man was attempting to refuse more alcohol. A cry of scorn rose around the room, and men began thumping the table.

Ganbei! Ganbei! Ganbei!

The young man blushed and drained his drink in a single gulp.

Ganbei!

The moment he sat down, the next member of the mayor's entourage approached him, demanding a toast. One after another descended on him. Now that they had identified the weakling, he became the victim. The pack scented a kill. A blood sport, appropriate entertainment for the collective state of inebriety. When he was carried out unconscious, the uproarious laughter guaranteed that he would be selected for similar treatment at future banquets, until he could get himself moved to some new post or had expired from cirrhosis of the liver.

Jaq was longing to escape. 'When can I leave?'

'I'll say you are tired. But first you need to return the toasts.'

'I can't face any more of that wine. Can I try the rice spirit?'

'Are you sure?' He summoned a waiter, who brought a thimble and filled it from a glass jug. The clear liquid was oily and thick; it smelt of vomit, but tasted sweet. And packed a punch.

'How strong is this? Like whisky?'

'Stronger. Ready?'

'As ready as I'll ever be.'

With her smiling translator's help, Jaq toasted each of the dignitaries at her table in turn. As she moved from one to the next, the waiter filled her small glass.

Ganbei!

She suspected she would regret it in the morning.

The smartly dressed driver was already waiting in the lobby when Jaq dragged herself down for breakfast. Was she late? Had she slept in? She couldn't remember the instructions from the night before. And now something was hammering in her head so loud she couldn't hear herself think. She skipped breakfast and followed the driver. The car took them out of town, stopping at the Inward Investment Development Office. Mr Smiles was waiting.

'Good Morning, Dr Silver. Did you sleep well?'

'Very well,' she replied, although she wasn't sure it was, strictly speaking, sleep. More like an alcohol-induced coma. She certainly didn't feel rested. Everything ached. Nothing that a litre of water and a couple of paracetamol wouldn't fix.

The translator led her up a curving flight of stairs to a palatial meeting room. Under a dozen chandeliers, a vast mahogany table stretched in all directions, decorated with alternating flower displays and pyramids of fruit. Trumpeting lilies and towering gladioli were interspersed between crescents of melon, discs of pineapple, giant strawberries and miniature plums. Or were they tomatoes? On the table in front of each carved mahogany chair stood a microphone, a glossy brochure, an anglepoise lamp and a teacup. She blinked at the bright light and attempted to suppress her nausea at the esters and terpenoids emanating from the ripe fruit.

People filed in to take their seats. Some she remembered from last night. Additional participants, younger and with a more even gender distribution, sat on two rows of chairs between the table and the back wall. There must have been a hundred people in the room.

After everyone was seated, the deputy mayor entered the room, flanked by the Director of Inward Investment. Tea was served to those at the top of the table. Jaq sipped it gratefully.

After much fussing with cables, the video started, a lavish one-hour production with dramatic music and English subtitles. It was replete with details of the industrial park. Far too many details. Jaq might be an engineer, but she was not terribly interested in learning how many tonnes of concrete or metres of copper cable had gone into the park. She was more interested in visiting Krixo.

Once the video had finished, the speeches began. Jaq barely listened to the translation. Every speech seemed to be repeating the numbers in the video. She tried not to wince each time the other participants in the room broke into ear-splitting applause.

Swish, swish. At the softer noise behind her, Jaq turned to see a cleaner, face turned away, hunched over a rustic birch broom. She seemed to be sweeping the room mid-meeting. Jaq looked at the deputy mayor, in full flow now, half expecting him to wave the old woman away, but no one else seemed bothered by the interruption. Such menial staff must be invisible to the important men and women around the table, in the same way they ignored the two pretty attendants topping up the teacups every time anyone took a sip. Her thoughts were interrupted as the translator paused, staring at her expectantly. Clearly, she was supposed to say something in reply to his effusive welcome.

She clicked the button underneath her microphone. 'Thank you,' she said.

Mr Smiles made a long speech.

The young man was good at his job, a cultural as much as a linguistic go-between. Whatever it was that he said was met with approval and a round of deafening applause.

The chairman spoke again.

'The committee would like to hear about your company and your potential project.'

Damn you, Sophie Clark, for forcing this charade. Jaq cleared her throat.

'I work for a company that is exploring an investment in China.' She read from the spiel that Vikram had prepared, pausing to allow Mr Smiles to do his stuff. 'We are particularly interested in the Special Economic Development Zone No. 2.'

A quick exchange of glances, then a heated conversation began.

Jaq tried to focus on the body language, but the noise of the old woman directly behind her, the swish-swish of her unnecessary broom, was strangely disconcerting. Perhaps because she seemed to be focusing on such a small area. Had Jaq spilled something? Stepped on something smelly that needed clearing up? Jaq glanced at the floor and lifted her feet to inspect the thick crêpe soles of her safety boots. All clean. Could it be because she was a foreigner? Preventative infection control?

The chairman stood up and directed a burst of noise at her, more like machine-gun fire than his previous mellifluous oratory.

'Zone No. 2 is full,' Mr Smiles translated.

Funny. It didn't look exactly full yesterday. But perhaps the empty land was already reserved. That settled that, then. No future for Sophie's expansion plans.

Jaq shrugged. 'But there is space in one of the other new zones?' she asked.

The chair beamed. 'Of course.' The incomprehensible language became softer again. 'The committee would like to ask you some detailed questions about your project.'

Here goes.

'What is the turnover of your company?'

Vikram had warned her about this. His little consultancy would appear puny in comparison to some of the giants in this zone.

'I'm afraid that is confidential. It's a private company.'

'And the projected capital investment?'

At least she had an answer for this one. 'About ten million dollars.'

A young woman tapped at a calculator and announced a number in renminbi to the assembled company. There was a general murmur. Excitement? Disappointment?

She decided to ad-lib. 'But with the long-term potential for ten times that figure.'

They brightened visibly as this was translated.

'How much land?'

She looked at the brief and applied a factor of ten.

Again, the crestfallen looks.

'Initial or final?'

'Initial,' she lied, and they brightened up again.

Jaq tried to concentrate as they explained the mechanisms for foreign investment, the cost of land and services and the legal framework. By the time they broke for lunch – a more intimate gathering of only fifty people – she was ravenous. Hungry enough to eat the bony fish in a cloying, sweet sauce, slices of chicken with skin and bone and entrails still attached, strawberries with salt and vinegar and a dessert of sugared tomatoes. She passed on the offer of rice – served last and only to those still hungry – feeling much better disposed.

A Chinese man in a Western-style dark suit entered the room. Unusually tall, with a striking triangular face, he strode across the room as if he owned the place, a Bluetooth earpiece winking in his ear. As he stopped to whisper in the ear of the deputy mayor, the scent of star anise reached her nostrils.

The deputy mayor bellowed something at Mr Smiles.

Jaq watched closely as he translated. Conflicting emotions passed across his face.

'Pang Mo made a detour on the way here, yesterday?'

'Who?'

'Your driver.'

'Yes, I asked the driver to go past the Krixo site.' She pulled the brochure from her bag. 'I have heard a lot about it.'

Mr Smiles stuttered as he translated. A young man, barely out of university, he had not faltered until now. The deputy mayor appeared to bat his words away with abrupt hand gestures before barking back.

'We have no Krixo site in the industrial park,' Mr Smiles translated.

Jaq held up Sophie's brochure. Krixo was written in English on one cover and in Chinese characters on the other. She held it out towards him.

He didn't take it, didn't even look at it.

'You are mistaken,' he said, smiling at her determinedly.

The deputy mayor turned away.

Jaq turned to her other neighbour, a portly young man. He reminded Jaq of a pink grapefruit, his skin rosy and pockmarked with large greasy pores. She handed him the Krixo brochure.

His small eyes narrowed and he pursed his thick lips.

The man in the dark suit grabbed the brochure from him and tucked it inside his suit jacket.

'Be more careful,' he said in perfect English before turning and walking away.

'Hey, give me back . . .'

Mr Smiles put a hand on her arm and whispered in her ear, 'Leave it for now.'

'Who the hell was that?'

'Police. Best not to cross.' He rose to his feet. 'I'll try and find out what is going on.'

Mr Smiles had not returned by the time the tour started. A new translator took his place, a sour-faced woman with English as precise as it was unimaginative. Not that there was much call for erudition, the litany of dates and numbers remorseless as they toured Zones 3 to 5. Jaq dutifully admired bridge pontoons and drainage ditches, river port foundations and tunnel excavations, asking a stream of trivial questions to keep herself awake as they toured half-built worker accommodation.

'Tomorrow we will visit the technical school and new hospital.'

'And some working factories? I'd be interested to speak to other tenants. Maybe one or two of the foreign joint ventures?'

The woman conferred and then assented. 'Yes.'

'Tomorrow?'

'Yes, yes.'

At the end of the day, she was returned to the hotel. Another dinner was planned, but she excused herself, claiming pressure of work. Not entirely a lie; the UK would be waking up now and she had some calls to make.

Mr Smiles was waiting for her in the hotel lobby.

'Can we talk?'

'Sure.' She led him to the bar. They ordered soft drinks.

'What is your connection with Krixo?' he asked.

She studied his face. Had he looked so pale and drawn this morning? She hadn't been in a fit state to take any notice.

'The company is headquartered in the UK, close to where I live.' Not a word of a lie. 'It's very successful, could be a good model for our project here.'

'But you are mistaken. There is no such company in Shingbo.'

'*You* are mistaken. There is. I saw it.'

He shook his head. 'Not any longer.'

There was little point in arguing. Perhaps they had twigged that she was working for Sophie, the joint venture partner. If nothing else, she was now certain that Sophie was not being paranoid. Wang, the Chinese joint venture partner, was clearly up to something. Why else would they try to hide? In that sense, her trip had already been useful and her work for Sophie was done. She had no real interest in Krixo. Except for the strange story from Dan's sister. Perhaps Mr Smiles could help her. Change of tack.

Their drinks arrived. Jaq stirred her luminous yellow pineapple juice – more tartrazine than fruit – and the ice cubes clinked against the glass.

'You know I worked as a university lecturer for a time?'

'You are a teacher.' He made a little bow of respect.

'I had many students from China over the years. One of them has gone missing.' Jaq handed him Dan's LinkedIn profile photo that she had printed before leaving Shanghai. 'Ning Dan. Last seen on his way to catch a train from Shanghai to Shingbo.' She gave the date and times. 'I'm sure there is a simple explanation, but his sister is worried about him.'

'I see.' He bit his lower lip. 'What is his connection to the factory you keep talking about, this Krixo?'

'His sister believes that he was going to visit it.' *The factory you say doesn't exist.*

'Why?'

The million-dollar question. Had he felt the need to travel to Shingbo on her behalf? All she'd asked for was information. Had he found something that made him curious? Compelled him to make the journey? To visit Krixo in person?

'I don't know. Will you show the photo to that policeman who took my brochure?'

Mr Smiles shuddered. 'That would be a very bad idea.'

She looked at him, surprised.

'Why?'

He waved a hand, vaguely. 'Better if I ask around. On one condition.'

'Which is?'

'You stop asking questions about Krixo.'

Damn you, Vikram. Damn you, Sophie. She'd done what they'd asked her. Given the communication difficulties, it wasn't too hard to agree to stop there.

'It's a deal.'

She had no interest in Sophie Clark's joint venture, other than reassuring herself that Krixo had no connection with her student's alleged disappearance.

Her only concern was for Dan.

The temperature had fallen overnight, but the day dawned bright and mild, a clear sky over the fast-expanding town of Shingbo.

Jaq had slept badly, finally giving up before dawn. She retrieved a one-piece swimsuit, hat and goggles from her suitcase. The hotel had a decent-sized lido, not the sort of overheated footbath that often masqueraded as a pool in international hotels. She swam for an hour.

After a breakfast of noodle soup, she searched the chandelier-infested lobby for her driver, but it was a new chauffeur who arrived with the sour-faced female translator. They drove first to a technical college, touring every classroom before lunching with the principal and some local business leaders, none of whom spoke any English, or at least admitted to it. Next was a half-built hospital where Jaq was invited to admire the cutting-edge medical technology not yet installed, before a driving tour of power stations and effluent treatment plants. The final visit took her to a white goods assembly line. Her request to see some chemical plants had been accepted with smiles and nods and then completely ignored.

The final dinner was to be another lavish banquet, attended by hundreds of people, with a formal signing ceremony. Vikram had instructed her to sign a Memorandum of Understanding – an empty set of promises to work together in partnership. There was nothing more she could do. The next phase was up to others.

All she had discovered was that Krixo was super-secret. So sensitive that the development corporation preferred to deny its existence rather than explain why she was not allowed to visit. But she had seen the factory with her own eyes.

She was no further forward in finding out what had happened to Dan.

In the car, she tried Mr Smiles' number. When he didn't respond to a text, she tried calling him, but there was no reply.

As they entered the banqueting hall, she scanned the room. No sign of Mr Smiles, and when Vinegar Face took up position behind her seat, her heart sank. It looked as if he wasn't coming.

Jaq turned and smiled. 'Will I have a chance to say goodbye to . . .' She paused and searched for Mr Smiles' name. 'Lai Lang?'

'Who?'

'The other translator.'

'I'm afraid that won't be possible.'

'Please.' She touched the woman on the arm.

Vinegar Face got up and moved to an adjacent table, interrogating a white-haired man. A hand flew up to her mouth and then her shoulders sagged, her body language still eloquent with shock as she slumped back into the seat behind Jaq.

A lively conversation ensued. The table seemed divided on something. Debating what to tell this nosy foreigner. Her heart sank. How bad could it be? Had he been sacked? Was it her fault?

'What is it? What's wrong?'

The deputy mayor spoke, and Vinegar Face translated.

'I regret to inform you that our colleagues, Lai Lang and Pang Mo, were in a traffic accident.'

Jaq's mouth became dry. 'Are they OK?'

'It's bad.' Vinegar Face's eyes widened, like a rabbit in headlights. 'They are both in hospital.'

Darlington, England

A flutter of yellow leaves drifted down to join triangular nut husks prickling the mossy bank. The row of mature trees, smooth grey trunks supporting a continuous yellow canopy, lined either side of a private road leading to the stables of a vanished stately home. Refurbished as a boutique hotel and spa, glass corridors connected the modern wings to the original stone structure, now crowned by a helipad. A small white ball soared above the Georgian stone before disappearing back to the lush green golf course nestling between the hotel and a wide bend of the river Tees.

Frank Good put his foot down and accelerated along the avenue of beech trees, speeding over smooth new tarmac before braking sharply in front of the grand entrance. He tossed his car keys to the uniformed doorman, nodded at the smiling receptionist and strode towards the library.

The door stood slightly ajar and Frank took a moment to appraise the man sitting beside the fire. Polished: from his shoes, through his buttons, to the light tan on his broad forehead.

'Frank!' Graham sprang to his feet, right arm extended, shaking hands with an iron grip. 'Good of you to drop by.' He spoke with a languid Afrikaans drawl, but there was nothing lazy about the Zagrovyl president of Global Chemical Operations.

One last chance. Important to take the lead here.

'I heard you were visiting,' Frank said. 'I wanted to give you my news in person.'

Graham gestured to the leather sofa facing the fireplace, at right angles to his wing-backed chair. On a low walnut table stood a glass cafetière with two green and gold cups on matching saucers.

'Coffee?' Graham pressed the plunger and the scent of roasted beans mingled with beeswax and woodsmoke.

Frank removed his raincoat, handing it to the waiter who had followed him in, and barked an order over his shoulder. 'Peppermint tea.'

As he took his seat, Frank glanced dismissively at the bookshelves above the fireplace. Colour-coordinated book spines sold by the metre: Dickens, Thackeray, Walter Scott. All Fake. A log toppled to one side of the grate in a shower of sparks. The open fire was genuine, at least.

'So, Frank.' Graham filled one coffee cup. 'How are you?'

Careful. The one thing to avoid was any taint of the loony bin, the slightest suggestion that his prolonged absence was anything but the physical recovery of a wounded hero. Frank stretched his legs and sat back, letting his suit jacket fall open to emphasise his excellent physical shape. He'd worked out on the retreat, spent hours in the gym, lost weight and gained muscle. He was looking better than ever.

'Fighting fit, and ready to get back to work.'

'Good, good.' Graham's expression belied the words, or perhaps the coffee he was sipping had an unusually bitter taste. 'I was thinking . . .'

Never a good sign.

The waiter interrupted, bringing a silver pot of hot water. From a wooden box of individually wrapped tisanes, Frank made his selection, tore open the plastic packet and extracted a gauze bag containing dried leaves before opening the lid of the silver pot. He slipped the packet of overpriced herbs into the water and let the lid fall with a metallic ring. Red hot. He waved his burning fingers in the air. Bloody awful design.

'Maybe it's time for something new . . .'

Something new? So, they didn't want him back in Teesside, running Zagrovyl's European Chemical Operations? Good. A change of scene, a new challenge, that was exactly what he needed.

'In Special Projects, perhaps?'

Frank bit his lip. Special Projects. The lame duck brigade, the department stuffed with the broken, the useless, the has-beens, the delusional – blind to the writing on the wall, deaf to the warnings of colleagues, shunted towards meaningless tasks, then gardening leave until finally they got the message that some faces just didn't fit.

Not the case here.

'You understand that I was sent to Teesside to turn things around,' Frank said. 'Lasting change takes time, and results can get worse before they get better.'

'The Teesside results are fine. In fact, the operation seems to have turned a corner in the last few months.'

The last few months? Since he'd been forced to take sick leave? He crumpled the wrapping and hurled it at the fire. It bounced off the grate and plopped onto the granite hearth.

'What are you implying?'

'Chuck can explain.'

Chuck, Frank's American boss, was a lily-livered lickspittle of a man, slave to company policy, cautious to the point of paralysis, incapable of grasping an opportunity, unable to take a calculated risk: one useless tosser.

'Chuck's a nice guy.' Frank spread his hands and waggled them a little to illustrate the lie. 'But we all know who makes the real decisions.'

'You're out of line, Frank.' Graham put down his cup with a firm clatter. 'Look, I'll level with you. The team seem more productive in your absence.'

Frank snorted. 'Who've you been talking to?' Not that he needed to ask. Graham would have toured the Billingham site with Eric, the wannabe engineer, a man unable to construct anything except towers of paper excuses, and would have looked at financials with the pessimistic bean counter, Robin, a man who could only see the downside to every row of numbers. 'I'm a tough guy, exacting when it comes to performance, ruthless on delivery. That won't have won me any friends in the factory.'

'An understatement.' Graham frowned. 'There have been serious complaints from the female staff.'

Not hard to imagine who. There would be an HR report from value-pack-knickers Nicola, based on whimpers from Shelly, his one-time PA, and vitriol from Raquel, the frigid dyke who replaced her. Maybe even wild accusations from Dr Jaqueline Silver. And what would those complaints all have in common? Hell hath no fury like a woman scorned.

'Best to make this clean.' Graham leaned forward and flicked the little ball of packaging into the fire. It flared, green and violet. 'Perhaps a new opportunity outside of Zagrovyl?'

Frank's jaw dropped. They thought they could fire him? Seriously? After all he'd done to protect this bloody company. After risking his life for Zagrovyl. He stared at Graham and saw that the top man didn't know the truth.

'What about the ongoing threat?'

'Threat?' Graham's cool grey eyes appraised him. 'HR have plenty of experience in dealing with harassment claims of this kind. Thank you for your concern, but we can handle things internally.'

'Not that.' Frank took out a handkerchief, wrapped it round the metal handle of the teapot and poured pale green liquid into his cup. 'The plot to defame the company. The misuse of Zagrovyl chemicals. We need to be prepared for an investigation.'

'A police investigation?'

'With OPCW.'

Graham raised a quizzical eyebrow.

'The Organisation for the Prohibition of Chemical Weapons,' Frank explained. 'You might prefer to have me on your side than on theirs.'

Graham stared at him and blinked once, twice before springing to his feet. 'Excuse me.' He had his phone out before the door closed behind him.

Frank sat back and sipped his mint tea. Disgusting. The doctor had advised him to avoid all stimulants including coffee, tea and alcohol until he'd finished the treatment, but this was testing the limits of his control.

He opened the newspaper that Graham had been reading before his arrival.

AUCTIONEER NAMED AS MURDER VICTIM

The man murdered in his exclusive £3 million Chelsea home on Wednesday has been named as Bernard Ashley-Cooper. Ashley-Cooper (34) was not married and lived alone in the two-reception-room, three-bedroom house.

In a statement, the Met said: 'Police and animal welfare officers were called at approximately 22.21 hours to reports of a violent disturbance. Officers attended along with the RSPCA. The victim, who has been formally identified as Bernard Ashley-Cooper, was found in his own home with multiple stab wounds. An ambulance arrived at 22.51 hours, but despite the best efforts of medical teams, he was pronounced dead at the scene shortly after 23.00 hours.

'A post-mortem will take place in due course.

'Detectives from the Homicide and Major Crime Command are investigating. A crime scene remains in place. No arrests have been made at this early stage, and enquiries continue.'

A high-profile art historian, Ashley-Cooper gained recent notoriety as the auctioneer presiding over a controversial auction of ancient Chinese artefacts with the September sale grossing over £100 million.

The Chinese government launched a challenge to the sale, alleging that the ancient artefacts were stolen during 'periods of confusion' in China, and should be returned.

Wealthy expatriate Chinese are increasingly investing in ancient Chinese paintings, porcelain and sculpture, and the value of these items has soared.

A police spokesman refused to speculate as to whether the victim had been tortured before he died, but the RSPCA confirmed that a dismembered cat, which was believed to belong to the victim, was also found at the scene of the crime.

A three-million-pound mansion in Chelsea. That's what his old flat in London would be worth by now if he hadn't had to sell it. The unfairness still rankled.

A movement in the corner of his vision made him turn towards the fire. A spider crawled out of the basket of logs and made its way towards the oak skirting. About the size of his hand, with spindly black legs and a glistening brown bulbous body, it ascended in quick, jerky movements. The scar on his left leg began to throb. Beads of sweat formed on Frank's brow, dripping over his eyebrows and running down his temples. He closed his eyes, fingers trembling as he fumbled for the tablets in his inner jacket pocket. He swallowed three and counted out a fugue. When he opened his eyes, the spider was gone. The doctors might not be able to stop the nightmares, but their magic tablets vanquished the daytime panic attacks. Mustn't let anyone see him like this. The handkerchief felt hot against his face as he wiped away the telltale rivers of sweat.

By the time Graham returned to the library, Frank's heart rate had returned to normal.

'Sorry for the interruption.' Graham stopped and peered at him more closely. 'Everything OK, Frank?'

Frank suppressed a shiver. 'Everything's fine.'

'It seems that there was some important information kept from me.' Graham's sunny bonhomie had been replaced by tightly controlled anger.

'That's exactly what I feared.'

'I think you'd better start from the beginning.' Graham poured himself a fresh cup of coffee. 'Tell me exactly what happened.'

Frank steepled his hands, his long fingers forming a Gothic arch.

'I discovered Zagrovyl materials going missing from the Smolensk factory in Russia, diverted by a previous employee named Pauk Polzin.'

'The Spider? But you hired him.'

Should he come clean and admit that The Spider had tricked him? Best not. Frank tapped the side of his nose. 'Keep your friends close, and your enemies closer.'

'I see.'

'Once The Spider thought he was on my team, he became careless and I was able to track the missing materials to an operation in Ukraine.'

'Chernobyl.' Graham shivered. 'Isn't that still radioactive?'

Frank nodded. 'That's exactly why The Spider chose it as a base for a chemical weapons factory. The tracer signals, designed to prevent misuse of stolen chemicals, got lost in the zone. I went in after him.'

Graham nodded slowly. 'Wasn't that dangerous, Frank?'

'I did what was necessary to protect Zagrovyl's reputation.'

'What happened to the illegal factory?'

'Closed down.'

'And The Spider?'

Frank smiled. His master stroke. His silver bullet. Dr Jaqueline Silver.

'That's what I've been so busy with these last few months. Helping to find him.' A slight exaggeration; he hadn't been involved directly, but he had provided the means for Jaqueline to go and sort things out by lending her his yacht, the *Good Ship Frankium*.

'The army cocked up the first mission and The Spider escaped. But thanks to my help, he's now been apprehended. Last news I received, he's in Turkey under NATO custody, awaiting extradition to The Hague for trial.'

'I heard something of this, but no one made me aware of your role in resolving it.' Graham leaned forward and put down his coffee cup. 'So, even after all this, you prefer to stay with Zagrovyl?'

'I dread to think how OPCW would view it if you let me go.' Tantamount to an admission of guilt.

'You think there will be an OPCW investigation of Zagrovyl?'

'I'm sure of it.'

'And what can you offer in our defence?'

'If I'm given a promotion?'

Their eyes met. He saw in Graham's slow nod that he understood the compact.

'I have evidence to show that Zagrovyl played no part in any criminal activities.'

Graham stood and walked to the bay window, crossing through rays of autumn sunshine. 'Is that a river down there?'

'The Tees.' Frank joined him at the window. 'It rises in the Pennines, gives Teesside its name and provides that golf course with its water.'

Graham turned to Frank. 'Do you play?'

The Zagrovyl president's reputation as a golfer preceded him. 'Not as well as you.'

Graham checked his watch. 'I need some time to think. I leave tonight, but I'm heading back soon. Can we meet again?'

Frank turned away to hide the smirk of triumph. 'To continue this discussion on the golf course?'

Graham clapped him on the back. 'Damn right!'

A gust of wind whistled through the trees, brittle leaves rustling and rattling as they fell, swirling at the doorman's feet as he limped across the car park. The man had the cheek to offer up the keys and point to where the car was parked. Frank had told him in no uncertain terms that he expected better service from a five-star hotel that enjoyed the patronage of Zagrovyl executives.

He raised his coat collar and averted his face from the breeze as he descended the steps to his approaching car. Wind. The one thing about sailing that he'd never liked. The loss of the *Good Ship Frankium* might be a blessing in disguise.

The doorman handed him his keys. Frank tipped him with a coin, a deliberate insult and a clear warning. He slid into his car and accelerated towards the avenue of trees.

Shingbo, China

Jaq tossed and turned all night, unable to sleep. Traffic accidents might be common in China. All that sudden wealth, so many powerful new cars. Could this be a coincidence? Who was she kidding? This was her fault. She'd poked a hornet's nest and let others take the sting. And what did this mean for Dan? If he'd really visited Krixo, a company so dangerous that everyone pretended it didn't exist, then had he met the same fate as the smiling driver and spectacled translator? *Mãe de Deus*. Was he in the hospital as well?

Morning dawned with a sickly yellow light. Jaq skipped the breakfast buffet, the smell of fish sauce from the noodle station too astringent for her early-morning constitution, grabbed a banana and went to reception to see about finding her own transport.

'I want to hire a car.'

'Check out?'

'No.' Jaq mimed the action of driving. The young woman behind the desk wrinkled her eyebrows in puzzlement and beckoned to a colleague.

'Check out?' he asked.

'Avis? Hertz?'

He looked blank.

She produced a green Enterprise loyalty card in case he recognised the logo. 'Car hire?'

He shook his head. 'Miss need,' he paused to think, 'China driving licence.'

She produced her driving licence. 'This one is international.'

He shook his head vigorously. Not valid in China, apparently.

'Then I need a taxi.'

He brightened considerably.

'Airport?'

'No.'

'Train station?'

'No.'

'Where go?'

Jaq took the city brochure and marked a cross where the economic development zone met the estuary, a few blocks east of the bridge. As close as she could get to the Krixo site from memory. 'Here.'

The concierge bit his lower lip, his skin suddenly paler. He reached out to take the map from her and retreated behind the counter as he dialled. Evidently there was no response from the first taxi firm, because he dialled a second number, speaking rapidly, then listening intently. '*Howda, howda.*'

'Wait,' he said, his smile suddenly forced, his hand shaking as he handed back the map.

Jaq took a seat where she could watch the road outside the hotel. Most of the traffic was powered by motorbike, Vespa-style scooters with elaborate fairings, their riders wearing a sort of quilted straitjacket worn in reverse, the arms fixed over the handlebars, the inside protecting the front of the driver from wind and rain. The same noisy two-stroke engines were used to power three-wheelers, little trucks carrying sheets of glass and metal window frames or sacks of rice and bundles of leafy vegetables.

Every time a taxi approached, she jumped to her feet, but one after another sailed past. *Santos.* She felt so bloody unprepared, deeply ashamed at her lack of progress learning Chinese, frustrated by the impenetrability of the most widely spoken language in the world. Was it the jet lag? Travelling too fast? Had the slice of her brain, or corner of her soul, that endowed her facility with languages been left behind somewhere over Outer Mongolia? She was reeling it in, but far too slowly.

After twenty minutes' waiting, she resolved to go outside and hail a cab herself. Could you flag one down, or did you have to find a taxi rank? Normally she did some research before travelling, but this trip had happened so fast. Now she felt ashamed at herself for spending the journey drinking and chatting to a male stripper, when she could have been reading and preparing.

As she stepped into the street, someone called her name. Vinegar Face came rushing towards her.

'You need to go somewhere?'

'Yes.' Jaq pointed to the map. 'I want to go here.'

She'd been willing to leave Krixo alone when this was a paid job for Sophie Clark. But she couldn't ignore the chance, however small, that she'd led Dan into danger.

Vinegar Face scrunched up her nose. 'That is not possible.'

'Why not?'

The translator looked back at the hotel, casting around for some sort of explanation.

'Roadworks. Closed off. Nothing to see.'

Jaq gave up. She didn't want to go to the Krixo site with Vinegar Face anyway. Invent an excuse.

'I wanted to swim.'

Vinegar Face's jaw dropped and then she burst into peals of mirth.

'You can't swim in the river!' She laughed. 'It's too dangerous. This hotel has a pool. Much cleaner, much safer.'

Jaq slapped her forehead and made a joke of her idiotic plan. Stupid foreigner. Had she got away with it?

The hotel swimming pool suddenly seemed like an excellent idea. Thinking time.

The water was nicely cool, and she swam front crawl to warm up. Within a few lengths, the monotony of the stroke gave her freedom to think. Was it true that she couldn't hire a car in China? What about one of those little motorbikes? Did you need a driving licence for one of them? Or a tuk-tuk three-wheeler? How to get hold of one?

It was clear she needed help. Who did she know in China? There were other students who'd returned from Teesside, but no one near Shingbo. And after what happened to Mr Smiles and his driver, could she really put someone else in danger?

Timur looked as if he could handle most situations. Was he still in Shanghai? Still looking for work? And what made her think he would drop everything to come and help her? Drop everything, he might. No; Timur would be too much of a distraction.

There was only one other person who wanted to find out what had happened to Dan badly enough to take the risk.

Lulu, his sister.

Jaq dialled her number.

Shanghai, China

The roar of Shanghai traffic flooded into the room as Mico opened the triple-glazed window and stepped out onto a narrow balcony. The studio overlooked a canal, patches of green weed waving at her from the still grey water. She shivered; it was colder here than in Hong Kong.

They were waiting for her back in the soundproofed video suite, five anxious creatives, all men, all eager for approval of the advert that would launch Hop!, the new light beer for women.

'So, Miss Mico, what do you think?'

She smiled. 'Did Sun Chang approve the concept?'

'It was his brief. D'you like it?'

She pursed her lips. Her father couldn't be allowed to lose face. On the other hand, he was a businessman first and foremost. The fact that he'd asked her to look at his pet project meant that he was in some doubt.

'I think pink flowers, yellow butterflies and blue rabbits might be great for selling pencil cases, but we are talking about beer here.'

'The target demographic is women aged eighteen to thirty-five, and the consensus—'

'Hopping cartoon rabbits with big round eyes aren't going to sell beer. We need to attract the rebel girls, or at least the ones who would like to think of themselves as rebels.' If they didn't have to study and work and clean and cook and take care of Grandpa.

The publicist sniffed. 'So, what do we need to change?'

Everything. 'How do we inspire a bit of daring, a bit of fun?' She handed him a pamphlet. 'We had a visit from a rather enterprising young man yesterday.' Timur Zolotoy. 'With an interesting value proposition.'

The publicist stroked the purple border of the booklet with a manicured fingernail, his eyes widening as he took in the photos. He muttered something and pointed to the door. The other four men filed out of the room.

'We can't advertise with naked men. The new rules on decency forbid—'

'The new rules on decency forbid naked women. They say nothing about naked men. Or about private clubs.'

'I don't understand.' He flipped the pamphlet closed and sat back in his seat.

'Look.' She struggled to remember his name and coughed to hide the memory lapse. 'Women are sick of being told what to do. We aren't stupid. All that execrable blue bunny rabbit advert tells them is that they are being targeted by cynics to make money. They have grown up believing that beer is bad for you, unladylike, something only men drink. Why don't we use that, turn it in on itself? Make this campaign about independence, taking control. Do you see?'

He scowled. 'No.'

'Hop! can be naughty but nice. Low-calorie, with a frisson of danger. Bubbles for the free spirit.'

'You don't like the advert.' He coughed and looked around. 'I don't like it either. I was only following the brief. But we're running out of time to make something completely new.'

'Then let's do it differently. Let's use word of mouth and WeChat. Why not launch Hop! with an exclusive show that will tour China? Western men will take their clothes off for Chinese women. Hop! beer will be served in champagne glasses to female-only audiences. If we find the female social media influencers and excite them, we can associate beer with having a good time.'

The publicist smiled. 'You think it would work?'

'I'm absolutely sure of it.' She picked up the brochure and smiled at the picture of Timur. 'News will spread like wildfire.'

And provide the perfect cover.

Shingbo, China

The traffic flowed smoothly through the centre of Shingbo, the wide boulevards oversized for the population. For the moment, at least. Build and they will come.

Lulu's high-heeled shoes clattered into the hotel lobby. A cloud of perfume enveloped Jaq along with a spiky greeting full of recrimination.

It was hard to believe this was the same woman from the café in Shanghai. The angular face was even more striking with make-up and her hair pinned back. Gone was the student attire, the bohemian clash of colours and styles: the woman who entered the hotel lobby was impeccably turned out in a fitted navy-blue dress, with a turquoise silk scarf that matched her soft bag.

They found a corner in the bar. The same corner where Jaq had last talked with Mr Smiles.

Lulu leaned forward, eyes shining. 'Tell me everything.'

Where to start? 'The translation service cancelled.'

'You should have called me.'

'The Shingbo Development Corporation sent a car and provided a translator. Both men are in hospital now.'

'What happened?'

'The officials claim it was a car accident, but I find that hard to believe.'

'Why?'

'I asked the driver to make a detour. I made him drive past the Krixo factory on the first day.'

'What sort of place is it?'

'I only saw it through the gate.' Jaq described the layout as seen from the road, through the fog. A relatively new, well-designed

163

and, judging by the large cranes, carefully maintained manufacturing site. 'A typical high-tech chemical plant.'

'Had they seen my brother?'

'I didn't get a chance to find out. When I asked to visit, the officials claimed the factory didn't exist.'

'But you saw it!'

'Exactly. Which is why I think the driver got into trouble.'

'And the translator?'

'I showed him Dan's LinkedIn photo. He was going to ask around, see if anyone recognised him.'

'And did they?'

'I don't know. Both of them met with . . . an accident.'

'Have you been to the police?'

'I think the police are involved in some way in whatever is going on.' Jaq told Lulu about the tall policeman and his strange behaviour; how he had taken away her Krixo brochure and warned her, in perfect English, to be careful. 'I'm really worried.' Jaq ran a hand through her hair. 'When you first contacted me, I couldn't believe that your brother's disappearance had anything to do with Krixo. But now I'm not so sure.' In fact, she was positive it did.

'You think he's in danger?'

The danger might be long past. His disappearance might be permanent, terminal. But Jaq couldn't say that to his sister.

'I don't know.'

'Jaq, I still don't understand. Why did he go to that factory? What did you ask him to do?'

'Nothing!' The frustration crept into Jaq's voice and the word came out louder than she'd intended. 'I didn't ask him to go.'

'So, why did you mention it to him?'

Perhaps Lulu deserved a better explanation. 'I'm doing consultancy work. I was curious to find out what sort of company Krixo is.'

'And what sort of company is it?'

A dangerous one. 'I'm none the wiser. No one will take me there, and I don't speak the language. I can't even hire a car.'

'You want to go to the Krixo factory now?'

'I want to go to the hospital first. Check that those guys are OK.' Jaq paused, scrutinising Lulu's reaction. 'And see if Dan was ever admitted there.'

Lulu put her head in her hands.

They took a taxi to the old hospital. Judging by demand in the crowded waiting room, the new hospital was badly needed. Lulu pushed to the front of a queue that snaked into the corridor. She returned shaking her head.

'No chance of visiting your driver or translator. They're in intensive care. Restricted visiting. Close relatives only.'

'What about your brother?'

'No record in his name,' she said.

What if he was brought in unconscious? Without ID? They wouldn't know his name then. 'We need to show them a photograph.'

'I already did.' Lulu pointed to her phone. 'They've never seen him.'

It must have been a rather cursory check. What if a different shift was on duty when Dan was brought in? What if he'd been injured? Hard to recognise? Jaq's stomach twisted as she opened her mouth to suggest they canvass other members of staff.

'We need to get out of here.' Lulu grabbed her arm and marched her to the door. 'Let's go and pay the Krixo factory a visit.'

'You sure that's a good idea?' Jaq said. 'Think carefully before you get involved. This might be dangerous.'

'We're talking about my little brother,' she said. 'I'm involved whether I like it or not.'

Every taxi refused point-blank to take them to the factory address. Eventually they gave the address of the hotel, and then Lulu tried offering extra money mid-journey. The car screeched to a halt and the driver demanded they get out. They had to walk the last few blocks back to the hotel, Lulu hobbling slowly in her high heels.

'Can you drive?' Jaq asked.

Lulu shook her head. 'Only a scooter.'

'Can you get us one?'

'I'll try.'

It was dark by the time Lulu had sorted out their transport.

'Here,' she said, opening her suitcase in Jaq's room. 'Put these on. We'll be less conspicuous.'

She handed Jaq a pair of cloth slippers and a dark trouser suit: the ubiquitous collarless jacket and loose trousers, too wide at the waist and too short in the leg. Jaq made a belt from a silk scarf.

'Stuff your hair in this and hide your eyes.' Lulu handed her a cap and dark glasses.

'How do I look?'

'Like a giant foreigner trying to pass as a local. Keep your head down. Drop your shoulders, hunch your back. Take smaller steps.'

'Like this?'

'Just as well it's dark outside.'

Lulu's suit fitted her perfectly. Without her high-heeled shoes, she only came up to Jaq's chest.

They took the service elevator to the basement and slipped out through a storeroom. A three-wheeled truck was waiting for them, a couple of sacks of rice and a catering drum of oil in the back. Lulu handed the driver some notes in exchange for the keys.

Jaq climbed in and shuffled along a bench to the passenger side. Lulu started it up, stalled twice and then narrowly missed a car as she accelerated onto the main road.

'Maybe I should drive,' Jaq ventured.

'If you like. You don't need a licence for one of these.'

They swapped places.

'Know where you are going?'

'More or less.'

Jaq possessed an inbuilt compass. She could sense direction –
north, south, east and west – even without sun or stars to guide her.
Having looked at the map, she had a good idea of the direction, but
wanted to avoid the motorways in this comically underpowered
truck. She headed for the river, doubling back when they found
themselves on the wrong side of a tributary and had to retrace
their route to find a crossing, but when she saw the lights of the
Changtai expressway overhead she knew they were near.

'Under the bridge, and then it should only be a couple of
kilometres further on.'

Lulu shivered, although whether it was from the cold or nerves,
Jaq wasn't sure.

The road was closed – at least Vinegar Face and the taxi drivers
had been telling the truth about that – but Jaq manoeuvred
the little truck around the barricades and cones. The darkness
thickened. No street lights on this section of road, or no working
ones. Where was the factory? They should be able to see it by
now. She drove carefully on the uneven road surface, jolting over
potholes and ruts. She didn't remember it being this bad in the
car. When she reached the bend in the river, she knew she'd gone
too far.

'Sorry, Lulu. I overshot.' She turned round and headed back,
halting at each intersection. No sign of a gate. No turquoise
fountain or pink buildings; no blue warehouses or yellow cranes.
Strange.

Jaq got out of the three-wheeler. She walked away from the
road towards the river. Sure enough, the road ran right beside the
estuary. On the seaward side it dipped away sharply, and she could
hear the black water lapping noisily, a brackish smell rising from it.
The factory should be on the other side. She crossed the road and
walked towards where the gate should be. But there was nothing,
only darkness. An empty plot of land. No fountain or chimney,
no rows of storage tanks, no extraction columns or cranes. She
scratched her head. How was it possible?

'The Krixo factory was here. I'm sure of it.'

'That's not possible.' Lulu sounded irritated. 'We must be on the wrong road.'

'I was so sure, but . . .' Jaq was beginning to doubt herself.

'It might be easier to navigate if we could see a few landmarks.'

A tall chimney with red and white bands, for one.

Lulu's teeth were chattering now. 'We can come back when it's light.'

Jaq took a step forward and winced. Something sharp under her left slipper. She bent down and extracted a nail that had pierced the thin sole and slipped between her toes. An ordinary, rusty, iron nail. Nothing special. The kind you find everywhere in the world. The kind that causes serious injuries in the wrong footwear. It was bad enough being out here in the dark, but in these flimsy shoes, it was madness.

'You're right. I'm sorry.'

As Jaq drove back, she became more certain, and more confused. More certain that she'd taken the right road. More confused that she couldn't find the factory.

How was it possible for the factory to exist one minute and disappear the next?

How was it possible for a factory to vanish?

Beijing, China

They met in Jiangshan Park, in a pavilion on the top of a hill, an artificial hill built from earth excavated from the moat below.

Yun opened her arms and Mico rushed towards her. To a casual onlooker the embrace might be the fond reunion of sisters or cousins. There was no one close enough to see the kiss, hear the sighs or feel the heat as their bodies connected.

After a while they separated.

'Come away with me,' Mico whispered.

'You know I can't.'

'Why not? Because of Mimi? She can come too.'

'And where will we live?'

'With me!'

Yun stroked the younger woman's cheek. 'Mico, you live with your father. If he knew the truth about . . . us, what would he do?'

'I can find us a place.'

'In Hong Kong? On the salary the studio pays you? Really?'

'We could go to London, Vancouver, Melbourne – where do you want to live?'

'I want to live in China. This is my country. For better or for worse. I can't leave it, can't tear the soul from my body.'

'Even if that means exile to Chongqing?'

Yun went silent.

'You won't be allowed to travel.'

'So, let's finish what we started.'

Mico grinned. 'You saw the newspaper reports?'

Yun nodded. 'I'm so proud of you.'

'Let's get to work.'

Yun extracted the dossier from a cerise handbag. 'This won't be easy.'

'Easy is boring.' Mico took the folder and flicked through the photos of the jade collection: a white jade water pitcher with matching cups, a bowl embossed with carved fish, a horse, an elephant, a dragon. She paused to admire the simple, clean curves of a spinach-green water buffalo. 'Beautiful.'

'How will you do it?'

'I have people. They know other people. It can be done. We've made a good start.'

'But at what cost?'

'Leave that to me.'

Yun stood and paced. 'I'm doing this for Mimi.'

'I understand.'

'Do you? You don't have a child of your own.'

'You're beginning to sound like my father.'

Yun stopped and frowned. 'Is he still matchmaking?'

'He's unstoppable.'

Yun took her hand. 'Will he ever understand?'

Mico gazed down at the Forbidden City and sighed. 'It's beyond his comprehension.'

Shingbo, China

Lulu appeared to think that it would be natural to share Jaq's room. After all, the bed was stupidly wide.

Not an option.

Jaq paid for an additional room. They ate a hasty dinner in the hotel restaurant, which was about to close as they arrived, Lulu loud and irritable, Jaq quiet with fatigue and worry.

Despite her anxiety, Jaq slept soundly, waking before dawn full of energy, convinced that she'd taken a wrong turn in the dark, and that today everything would become clear. She dressed quickly in the ill-fitting trouser suit from yesterday, but with socks and safety boots instead of cloth slippers.

Too early for breakfast, Jaq slipped a note under Lulu's door and made her way to the basement. The three-wheeler was in the same bay where they'd parked it last night, the keys still under the bench. The owner would have to wait a bit longer to retrieve his truck. It took her twenty minutes in daylight to do a journey that had taken twice as long last night. This time she took a different route, hoping to approach the factory from a back road, driving towards a distinctive chimney with red and white bands. But there were several such chimneys, and none of them the right one. Once again, she found herself on the rutted road beside the river. Once again, she drove to the spot where the Krixo factory should have been, only to find an empty plot of land.

Jaq walked through the gap where the gate had been. The ground was broken and uneven. Where the production buildings should have been, she saw a glint under the soil. Scraping away the earth with her steel-capped toe, she uncovered a metallic object and bent down to pick up the stub end of a welding rod.

Welding rods look a bit like sparklers: thin cylinders of metal coated in a protective layer of sintered metal sponge. The thin end is inserted into the jaws of a metal clamp. A voltage is applied from a portable generator. When the other end of the rod approaches the workpiece, an electric arc connects them, the heat melting both the tip of the rod and the metal to be joined, allowing molten metal to fuse exactly where it is needed.

She examined the stub carefully. The code was written in English characters, truncated where it had been used, but there was enough to identify the material. She put it in the pocket of her jacket. She used her toe to move the earth and found several more stubs and some wire.

Taking her time, she got out her notebook and divided the site into squares. She started in one corner and began to assemble little piles, scraps and other debris. Shards of glass, fragments of brick, strands of reinforcing bar, lumps of concrete, tile chippings, shiny washers. It was surprising how much there was when you really looked closely. What appeared to be barren earth was a treasure trove of clues.

Once she had assembled a significant pile, she wrote the grid location, tore the page from her notebook and photographed the objects with the grid reference using her phone. Broken terracotta tiles where the production buildings had been, a torn piece of blue sheeting near the perimeter warehouses.

She stuffed the pockets of her jacket with the more intriguing finds. An FEP-encapsulated Viton O-ring, the translucent alabaster fitting for a PVDF pipe, a curl of celluloid cut from a radiography film, multicore instrument cable – purple, green, yellow, red and grey strands. A bolt that, judging by its weight, was neither carbon nor stainless steel. A chip from a turquoise tile. A torn business card with a purple border, some scraps of paper with Chinese writing. These were the crumbs that might lead her to the truth.

And then she found it. To anyone else it would have been rubbish. A torn plastic bag about fifteen centimetres square with a sixteen-digit number and barcode on the label. Along with the supplier's logo. A design she recognised. The swirling Celtic pattern representing a selkie, the mythical creature that changes from a seal in water to human on dry land. A logo belonging to an engineering company with a factory not far from Teesside.

Her heart raced. Was this the proof she needed?

Intent on scavenging, she didn't hear the police car until it pulled up opposite her. She put on her dark glasses and turned away.

Merda. Too late. A man was approaching in a dark suit. The tall policeman who had pinched her brochure. The one who spoke English.

'Good morning, Dr Silver.'

'*Ni hao.*' The only Chinese phrase she'd learned. 'I'm afraid we haven't been introduced.' She extended a hand.

He did not take her hand or give his name. 'You know that this is private property and you are trespassing?'

'I'm leaving.'

'Indeed you are. I'm taking you to the station.'

Bolas. 'You're arresting me?'

'The train station. You are no longer welcome in Shingbo. I'm not sure why you came, or what cock and bull story you concocted for my gullible friends at the development agency, but now it is time for you to leave. I trust I won't see you again.'

'I need to return this vehicle. Collect my things.'

'That will be arranged.' He pointed to the car. 'Unless you want to become intimately acquainted with a police cell, I suggest you come with me.'

'What happened to the Krixo factory?'

'There is no factory here.'

He was right. There was no doubt about it. All that was left was rubble and rubbish.

'What happened to my translator? And his driver?'

'A tragic accident.'

'Will they be OK?'

'You don't know?' He stared at her, face impassive. 'They are both dead.'

Jaq froze. A chill rose through her body, starting in the soles of her safety boots, working its way up through legs that were suddenly jelly, a stomach full of concrete, arms trembling, the hairs standing on end under her cloth cap.

Lang Lai, the smiling young translator and Pang Mo, the sharp-suited driver. Dead. Because of her? What hope was there for Dan?

She stumbled and the tall policeman put out an arm to steady her. She jumped away as if he'd tasered her, the momentary weakness replaced by cold, hard anger.

Lulu was waiting for her outside the train station, hunched in the back of a police car, ashen-faced. A uniform handed Jaq her luggage. She opened her case to find that someone had folded everything with considerable care. Her laptop was in the padded compartment of her bag along with cables and adaptors. Toothpaste and unscented roll-on deodorant in a sealed plastic bag. Passport and wallet in a secure pocket. Nothing missing.

The tall policeman opened the door for Lulu, barking at her in sharp, clipped phrases. Was he as furious as he sounded? Lulu said almost nothing in reply to the verbal machine-gun fire.

They were escorted to a platform and directed to board the train that pulled in a few minutes later.

As the train slid out of the station, Jaq leaned over to Lulu. 'Are you OK?'

Lulu raised downcast eyes to look at her through long lashes. 'I'll be glad to get out of here.' She shuddered. 'There is something . . . unwelcoming about this town.'

An understatement if ever there was one. This was not the first time Jaq had been run out of a town. Not a great feeling. But at least in the past she'd had a pretty good idea why. Right now, she was mystified. The train gathered speed, the speedometer hitting 300 km/hr as they rushed north. Back to Shanghai. Back to civilisation. A metro system. Independence. Jaq pulled the scratchy collar of the borrowed clothing away from her neck with filthy fingers, the idea of a thorough wash in the luxury suite of a boutique hotel suddenly appealing.

'Did you find it? The Krixo factory?' Lulu asked.

'It's gone.'

'How is that possible? Are you sure you went to the right place?'

'I'm sure.' GPS coordinates do not lie, even if everyone else does.

Lulu sighed. 'Dr Silver, all this would be so much easier if you would tell me the truth.'

Should she be more open? Did she owe it to this worried woman to confess that, although she was officially contracted to innocent Vikram and the anodyne CCS, the real client was Sophie Clark, foreign partner in the Krixo joint venture? And that Sophie was suspicious of the activities of her Chinese partner? Rightly so, as it transpired. And how would revealing this to Lulu help them in any way? In truth, the only thing that mattered now was Dan.

'I told you.' Jaq sighed. 'CCS are looking at projects in Shingbo for Teesside companies wanting to build in China.' Deserting the North-East economy in droves, rats leaving a sinking British ship for the bright lights of a billion Chinese consumers. 'Krixo was held up as an example of a successful joint venture. My boss wanted me to see if it was all as good as the brochure made out.'

Lulu wrinkled her nose. 'But it turned out that Krixo was just a fake?'

Could that be the explanation? Had Jaq been fooled by a phoney factory? A stage set? Cardboard cut-outs? It was daylight when she had first stopped at the gates of Krixo. Yes, there had been fog, visibility wasn't perfect. OK, there had been no people around, but then it was lunchtime. Had she heard anything? Smelt anything from the factory? No – and that was odd, but the wind had been blowing in from the sea. Had the chimney really been producing steam, or were they simply tendrils of mist from the river? Had Jaq seen what she believed should be there, rather than what was actually there? Had her brain turned a two-dimensional fake into a three-dimensional image? It was the only possible explanation. No one could demolish a working factory of that size in a few days. And even if they could, it would be impossible to remove all traces. Almost all the traces. She put her hands in her pockets and her fingers closed on the empty, torn plastic bag. The tall policeman had been in too much of a hurry to search her pockets or delete the pictures from her phone. She had solid evidence. The factory had been there, and now it was gone.

'It wasn't a fake,' Jaq said.

'How do you know?' Lulu's voice was peevish, irritated. 'What did you find?'

What indeed? An empty plot of land. A few scraps of rubbish. Why not show Lulu? Jaq's confidence in the significance of her discoveries was reinforced by the determination of the police to kick her out of town. Why not share this with Lulu? Because it didn't bode well for her brother. Pang Mo, the driver who had made a detour past the Krixo factory on her request, and Lai Lang, the smiling young translator who had taken Dan's picture to make enquiries – the very people who had tried to help her – both of them were dead. If that was the fate of those who innocently brushed up against the peculiar activities of shape-shifting Krixo, then what hope was there for an engineer who turned up at the factory gate asking more pointed questions? It didn't look good for Dan.

Jaq gestured around the busy train carriage and then shook her head. *Not here, not on the train, not in public.*

'Nothing?' Lulu asked.

'Nothing,' Jaq replied, for the benefit of any eavesdroppers.

Lulu leaned back and closed her eyes.

Gridlocked traffic outside Shanghai Hongqiao train station made underground public transport a more appealing option. Modern, clean, fast and efficient, with signs in English as well as Chinese, there was a metro station right next to Jaq's hotel. But Lulu had booked a car and insisted they shared it. Perhaps just as well. They needed to talk in private. Did Lulu already know the fate of the driver and translator? Had she already figured out the sinister implications for her brother? For herself?

A black car pulled up. The uniformed driver jumped out and opened the passenger door. A short, muscled man with a stern, square face under his chauffeur's cap, he looked as if he spent more time lifting weights than sitting in Shanghai traffic. Lulu rattled off directions. The driver stared into his rear-view mirror and grunted something in reply. An argument ensued. Jaq had no idea what was being said, but Lulu appeared to prevail. The driver cleared his throat and spat out of the window before manoeuvring into the traffic.

Jaq waited until they could no longer see the station. 'Who was the man who made us leave Shingbo?'

'Police.' Lulu's shoulders slumped. 'Of sorts.'

'Explain?'

'He works for the Chinese Ministry of Public Security,' she said. 'His name is Yan Bing, acting chief of the Art Police.'

'What do the Art Police do?'

'They look after China's national treasures. Make sure that our ancient cultural heritage isn't being smuggled out of the country and sold abroad.'

Pity the Art Police weren't involved in the crimes against taste in hotels and restaurants. All those chandeliers, all that gilt and fur and velvet, all those acid colours. High time restrained elegance and understatement made a comeback. 'Where are the Art Police based?'

'Beijing.'

'So, what was he doing in Shingbo? And what's the connection to Krixo?'

Lulu shrugged.

'Lulu, I'm sorry to tell you this.' Jaq swallowed. 'Yan Bing gave me some bad news. He told me that the driver and translator, the ones who helped me, are dead.'

'I know.'

Did that explain Lulu's utter dejection?

'How did you know?'

'Yan Bing told me.'

So that was what the angry exchange was about.

'Did you ask him about your brother?'

Lulu looked at her, a strange, almost calculating expression. 'Why did you go without me?' A ball of pent-up frustration seemed to explode from her slender frame. 'Why didn't you tell me you were going to the factory site? Wake me up so I could go with you?'

What difference did it make? Why was Lulu so annoyed? Was she projecting the fear about her brother onto something else? Or had Yan Bing given her a hard time for allowing Jaq to roam unaccompanied around the industrial estates of Shingbo? Hardly a treasure trove of ancient Chinese art. Why would he care?

Jaq shrugged. 'I was up ridiculously early. I thought—'

'Next time,' Lulu hissed, 'ask me first.'

What was this about? 'Are you worried about the truck? Whether the owner gets it back?'

'I couldn't give a rat's arse about the truck. Or the snivelling driver.'

Jaq recoiled at the vehemence. Dan and his sister had clearly been raised in different stables. The gentle student she had known and respected would always put others before himself. And look where that had led. A lump formed in her throat.

The driver turned south-west. Away from the centre. The wrong direction.

A prickle of alarm turned to a shiver. 'Where are we going?'

'I need to go home,' Lulu said. 'The driver will drop me off and then take you to your hotel.'

They travelled in silence for a while. The driver pulled off a motorway and drove along a canal into a leafy estate. Lulu got out at a metro station, Qixin Road.

'I'll call you later.' She turned down a side street.

Jaq felt about as enthusiastic at that prospect as Lulu sounded. They were no further forward, and further apart than ever.

The road ahead was blocked by an altercation between a man pulling a handcart laden with plastic waste and an open-topped sports car. After an eternity of hooting and jostling for position the traffic became gridlocked. The driver swore, swung the car across the central reservation and turned back the way they had come, crossing the road again at the metro station to find a route that wasn't gridlocked.

By chance they caught up with Lulu, walking beside a uniformed policeman, too engrossed in conversation to notice them. At a noodle shop, she opened a street door and disappeared inside. As the car passed the café, Jaq looked back to see the policeman salute towards the building. She craned her neck in time to see Lulu pull back from a first-floor window, directly above the noodle bar. A second policeman emerged from the street door, clapped the first on the back and the two officers walked off.

Something about Lulu had troubled her from their very first meeting. And now the strange little cameo she had witnessed proved that her gut reaction had been correct. Why had Lulu got out at the metro station and not been dropped off outside the flat she shared with Dan? Who were the two policemen? Why had one saluted Lulu? Was Lulu really who she said she was?

There was only one way to find out.

Shanghai, China

The black car dropped Jaq back at the boutique hotel. Jaq locked the apartment door behind her and started to run a bath. She pulled off the borrowed clothes, desperate to rid herself of the ill-fitting, coarse fabric, to wash away the dirt from the abandoned industrial site.

She laid out her findings in the basin and then sank into the hot water.

Dan. Where are you? Why did you go to Shingbo? What happened to you? She closed her eyes and lowered herself under the water. Had he been murdered? Had they dumped him in the river? Would his body ever be found? An image of a bloated corpse floating in the estuary, nibbled by eels and torn by diving gannets, made her cry out.

The sharp peal of a phone snapped Jaq from her ghastly daydreams. The strident bell of her room phone, not the soft music of her mobile. She stepped into a bathrobe and padded into the sitting room.

'Hello.'

'Madam, we have a call for you.'

'Who is it?'

'A Mr Gao Ding from SEITA.'

The translation agency. Calling to apologise? Well, she had better things to do.

'No, thanks.' She put the phone down.

She returned to the bath and washed, rinsing her hair in the shower. Then she cleaned the treasure trove from the Krixo site. The chip of turquoise tile that had once been part of a fountain, the bolt, welding subs, O-rings and fitting, the torn plastic bag with the Selkie label. She took pictures of them on her phone and then wrapped them in tissue before packing them away in a corner of her suitcase.

She started up the desk computer. Some search websites were blocked, but there were plenty of alternatives, although not many in English. She clicked through a sea of pictograms – elegant, fluid, beautiful and totally incomprehensible – until she found a tourist site with a metro map and plotted her route.

Jaq dressed quickly in jeans, T-shirt, jumper and boots and strode out in the direction of the metro station. At the metro, a group of giggling students offered to help. She got out at Qixin Road and took a moment to orientate herself. It didn't take her long to find the noodle shop. A huddle of people waited on the pavement outside, the smell of ginger and soy borne on clouds of steam billowing from huge woks inside.

The lights were on in the flat above.

Jaq dialled Dan's number. Lulu answered.

'It's Jaq. I'm outside.'

Lulu appeared at the window. A hand flew to her open mouth. Was it surprise or fear? Perhaps both.

'Wait.'

Jaq rattled the street door, but it was locked. The noodle bar customers eyed her with frank curiosity.

After several minutes, Lulu emerged from the main door and closed it behind her. Her expression had changed in the time it took her to descend a flight of stairs. The shock was replaced by a broad smile of welcome.

'Jaq,' she trilled. 'I was about to call you.'

'You have some explaining to do.'

'I have news . . .' Lulu said.

'How did you get Dan's phone?'

'Listen . . .'

'You're not Dan's sister, are you?'

'It doesn't matter,' Lulu protested.

'So, who are you? What are you doing in his flat?'

'I found him. He's OK.'

Jaq reeled back. 'You found Dan?'

'You were right. It was all a misunderstanding. He never went to Shingbo, never visited the Krixo factory.'

Struck dumb with relief, Jaq let out a long sigh.

'He met a monk on the train. He didn't get off at Shingbo. They got talking and he stayed on the train, went with the monk to a Buddhist retreat, a mountain island.'

Wait a minute, wasn't this all a bit too neat, too convenient? 'I have to see him, talk to him.'

'Of course! He's just getting dressed.'

Jaq stared at Lulu and then up at the open window. 'He's here?'

Lulu nodded and opened the door. Jaq pushed ahead of her, taking the stairs two at a time, bursting into the flat at a sprint. If you could call it a flat. It was just a one-room bedsit: a worktop barely wide enough for the rice cooker and single gas burner on top, the fridge below. A futon rolled under a table with two chairs, and sitting in one of them, a young man in a bright orange robe.

'Darling, look who is here!' Lulu was behind her.

'Dr Silver.' He looked up and made a little bow. 'I am very sorry to have caused you so much trouble.'

She took in his shaved head, sunken eyes, gaunt cheeks and bare feet. A shadow of the student she had once known, but there was no disguising his lilting, musical voice. Ning Dan. No doubt about it; she had found her old student. Alive. *Graças a Deus*.

Jaq came forward, pulling out the other chair, removing an ice-blue velvet roll which she placed on the table before sitting down. 'Where have you been? Everyone has been so worried.'

'I haven't been well.' Indeed, he looked terrible, pale and drawn. Always a thin boy, he was now almost skeletal. There was a grey tinge to his skin.

'I had to get away from the pollution in Shanghai. All the disulphur oxide was making me ill.'

Disulphur oxide? Did he mean SO_2 – sulphur dioxide? *Don't be a pedant.*

'How are you feeling now?' Jaq asked.

'Much better.' Dan ran the palm of his hand over his shaved head. Jaq could almost feel the soft bristles. 'Remember how you used to tell us about the dangers of bottling things up? How if you weren't careful, the stress level rises until breaking point? Like in 1975.'

What on earth was he talking about? She lectured students on process safety. She'd never been a pastoral tutor. What was up with the guy? Poor Dan, he sounded positively deranged.

'That's why I had to get away from the city.' He turned to his sister. 'Lulu, you need to be careful. They put out a 71-71 alert last week. They found iodine, promethium, osmium, tellurium, even rhenium in the air!'

'That's enough chemistry!' Lulu softened the sharp rebuke with a nervous laugh. 'Tell Dr Silver where you were all this time,' Lulu demanded.

'A monastery!' He wrinkled his mouth, but the intended smile failed to materialise. 'The ideal place. Solitude. Meditation.' He wrote something on a pad in front of him. 'And puzzles. Lots of puzzles.'

He bent his head and concentrated. Scribbling numbers, row upon row of numbers. Manic. Frantic. Lulu walked round behind him and removed the pen and pad. She whispered something to him and pointed to the ice-blue velvet roll on the table.

'I'm sorry,' he said. 'I get confused sometimes.'

'Why didn't you tell anyone?' Jaq asked.

He bowed his head. 'I'm sorry. Oddo–Harkins rule – no outside contact allowed.'

Oddo–Harkins rule? Surely that was related to chemistry, not visiting hours. Poor lad, he was in a bad way.

'You're still not well, are you?' Lulu put into words what Jaq was thinking.

'Dan, is there anything I can do?'

'You've done what you can.' He tried to smile, but his mouth trembled. 'Lulu will care for me now.'

A flicker of triumph passed across Lulu's face before her sharp features softened to an expression of infinite tenderness. She bent forward and wrapped both her arms around Dan. He closed his eyes and leaned back into her embrace, appearing to fall asleep. Jaq looked round at the tiny room with space for only one bed. And the penny dropped.

Of course, Lulu and Dan were lovers, not siblings. Cohabitation before marriage was still frowned upon in China. That explained so much. The rest didn't matter.

'I'll care for him now,' Lulu whispered.

'He needs a doctor.'

'I'll take him myself.'

Dan's eyes opened.

'You should go now, Dr Silver,' he said. 'Stay safe.'

Occam's razor. The simplest explanation is the most likely. Dan had only recently lost his parents. He had needed time and space to grieve. The more conventional your outward behaviour, the more rigid your response to trauma, the more likely you are to snap. Was it surprising that the poor boy had suffered a breakdown? He'd met a sympathetic monk on a train and asked for help. There was nothing wrong with that. Lulu had overreacted, and so had Jaq.

Just a false alarm.

All that mattered was that Dan was safe, her mission for Sophie Clark was complete and now she could go home.

Vladivostok, Russia

Snow was falling on Vladivostok. A flurry of fine white crystals that melted as they hit the poorly insulated old buildings. The transition from autumn to winter swift and irreversible. A tram turned the corner at the top of the hill, a shower of sparks glittering against the grey sky as the diamond-shaped pantograph bounced against the overhead cable.

Dmytry Zolotoy sat at the window of the hospice, wrapped in a blanket, ears alert to the slightest noise that penetrated the acoustic insulation of the snow: the screech of metal on metal as the tram braked, the pneumatic hiss of the opening doors, the crunch of size twelve boots on fresh snow with that familiar gait – limber, athletic, purposeful – emerging from the narrow street, crossing the road and striding across the frozen lawn, greeting the security guard with a musical, deep-voiced '*Dobriy den*'.

A surge of impatience flooded his atrophied veins at the prospect of Timur's return. At least there was one thing in his life that he had done right. Champion swimmer, an athlete who made money from doing what he was good at, a boy any father would be proud of.

And he brought news.

He pictured Timur removing his overcoat and pulling off his snow boots, waiting for the arpeggio of soft-shoed feet on the marble stairs, the pause at the door, the rap of swim-soft knuckles on wood.

'*Voyti! Zakhodi*,' Dmytry shouted.

The door opened. Visitor slippers padded across on the polished wooden floor. The scent of menthol followed Timur into the room, mixed in with coffee and apricots.

'Breakfast at Pelmetov?'

'You know all my secrets, *Dedushka*.' A warm hand tucked the blanket round Dmytry's lap where it had fallen away. Dmytry tilted his face for the embrace. Velvet lips on dry skin.

'I saw you at the window. How are your eyes?'

Dmytry turned his head away. 'No change.'

'You were waiting for me?'

'Ever since I got your news.' Dmytry grasped his hand. 'You found the buyer?'

'I found the buyer.'

'Will they sell?'

'It's complicated. More like a trade.'

'Trade? For what?'

'A jade horse, elephant, dragon, water buffalo . . .'

As Timur listed the objects, Dmytry's heart beat faster. How was this possible? Was someone playing games with him? It must be a coincidence. This couldn't be Nina's collection.

'I know where to find them.'

'But how will you . . .?'

'We have events coming up.'

'Championships?'

'More like demonstration events.' Timur coughed. 'Followed by an all-China tour.'

Dmytry felt a tingle of excitement. Could the magnificent boy really do in a few months what this old man had failed to do in fifty years?

'You would do this for me?'

'I'll do my best.'

No, best was not good enough. This was the last chance. This time they must succeed.

'The lovers' cup is a link to your father.' The trouble with lies is that they take on a life of their own. The time for truth had long gone. Why hadn't he told the boy everything while he was still young? Because he was afraid. If Timur knew the truth, might it change him? How could it not? With all that baggage, could he have grown into the fine, confident young man he had turned out to be? A surge of irritation festered into cruelty. 'And unless we find it, we can never be sure who he really was.'

'Then I'm going to get it back.' Timur clenched his fists. 'Whatever it takes.'

PART VI
DECEMBER

63
Eu
Europium
151.966

Durham, England

The squat grey cathedral loomed over a river wreathed in mist. The train slid to a halt at Durham station and Jaq got out, shouldering her bag and setting a brisk pace for the exit.

She arrived early at CCS, hoping to catch Vikram before the meeting, but he'd already left for a client lunch. Jaq accepted the offer of coffee from the young man at reception.

'Hello, Dr Silver.' He smiled. 'How was your trip to China?'

She hesitated, but there was no malice in the open, friendly face.

'Interesting,' she said. 'Do you have an empty office I could use while I wait?'

'Of course.'

He carried her coffee to a small room, bare except for a desk and chair, closing the door as he left.

She took a seat and opened her bag, extracting the report for Krixo with the evidence in sealed bags, followed by a bundle of letters, mainly bills that had arrived in her absence, plus this morning's delivery: an overdraft warning from the bank and a handwritten missive from Dan. She opened the rice paper envelope and read the letter again.

Dear Dr Silver,

My sincere apologies for causing you such trouble and inconvenience during your recent visit to China. I am greatly ashamed that I was unable to act as a host and show you around my city.

As you know, I have not been well. Please ignore any messages you received from me during my illness. I have seen a doctor and I'm much

*better now. I have decided to return to the monastery to complete my
recovery.*

No outside contact is permitted.

I am sure you will understand.

Respectfully yours,

Ning Dan

She bit her lip. The disquiet she felt on first reading the letter
wouldn't go away. A conspiracy of silence. Was she imagining
things? Dan had asked her to leave him alone. Why did that make
her uneasy?

She sighed and laid out the evidence bags in a row beside the
report. The only tangible object that was even remotely convincing
was the torn plastic bag with the Selkie logo on a label containing
a barcode and sixteen-digit number.

A high-tech engineering company, Selkie – the name was a play
on the word seal – made specialist mechanical seals in a factory
not far from Teesside. She flicked through her contacts until she
found Martin's number. Before he joined Selkie, they had studied
together, classmates in King's Buildings when she was doing her
MSc in Edinburgh.

Martin sounded delighted to hear from her, bombarding her
with questions about what she was up to. If only she knew.

'How's the family?' she asked. Darned if she could remember
his wife's name.

'Mary's well, and the kids are doing fine.'

Mary. Of course. A metallurgist, they'd all hung out together at
Clark's Bar. How many kids? She was such a bad friend, incapable
of keeping track of things that simply didn't interest her. She interrupted him before he could launch into details.

'I have a part number on a bag with a Selkie logo. Would that be
enough to trace the customer?'

'Depends if it's from a standard seal or a special. What are the first four digits?'

'6066.'

'A special, then. Yes – it's a bespoke seal, relatively easy to trace that back to the customer, to the specific order even.'

Result.

'The full number is 6066-2157-3958-7071.'

'Ah . . .' The sound of air being sucked in through teeth. 'Sorry, Jaq, I can't give you the information you are looking for.'

'Why not?'

'Customer confidentiality.'

'If I told you I'm working for Krixo, would that make a difference?'

'Krixo? You're working with Sophie Clark?'

'Small world, isn't it. How do you know her?'

'She visited a few times in the summer, a 3D printing job.'

Odd; Sophie hadn't struck her as the kind of person who would be interested in mechanical seal parts.

'So, the number I gave you, was it part of a seal supplied to Krixo?'

'I'll need permission from Krixo before I can confirm that.'

'I'm meeting with Sophie this afternoon. Just tell me I'm not wasting my time.'

He laughed. 'You aren't wasting your time.'

Good enough.

Sophie and Vikram arrived an hour late for the meeting, reeking of alcohol. The English owner of a missing Chinese factory looked remarkably unruffled. High-gloss heels, tailored skirt suit, manicured nails, pink chiffon blouse, perfect make-up, smooth, shiny hair. There was no antagonism in those amethyst eyes, just a tinge of curiosity. Amusement, even?

Vikram ushered them to the boardroom and pulled out a chair for Sophie before taking his seat at the head of the table. Jaq sat opposite Sophie. The room had changed since the last visit: gone was the mismatched furniture, replaced by a stylish beech table and chairs. There were new pictures on the walls. Had Sophie's fee purchased all this? About time Vikram passed over the share of Sophie's money that was due to Jaq.

'So.' Vikram put his hands behind his head. 'Jaq, I think you have some explaining to do.'

Jaq took a deep breath and turned to Sophie. 'You've read my report?'

'I'd rather hear it from you,' Sophie said. 'From the beginning.'

Jaq outlined the first sighting of the Krixo factory, the tedious meetings with the development corporation, their refusal to acknowledge the existence of the rare earth recycling factory, her visit to the empty site and being run out of town. No point in mentioning the false alarm with Dan; he had no connection to Krixo.

Sophie looked down and fiddled with the gold clasp of her patent leather handbag. 'Go back to when you drove past the factory. What did you see?'

Jaq described the scene as best she could. The elaborate gate, the turquoise fountain, the pink production buildings and blue warehouses, the columns, tanks and chimneys.

'Was the factory working?'

'I couldn't see any people, but there was steam coming from the chimney, so I guess so.'

'Did anyone see you?'

'A couple of security guards as we were driving away, but we didn't stop to speak to them.'

'And you didn't go back the next day?'

'I repeatedly asked the Shingbo Investment Bureau to take me on a formal visit, but they were more interested in showing me half-constructed bridges, model workers' flats, fridge factories, further education colleges . . .'

Sophie grimaced. 'And the endless banquets?'

'Alas, yes.' Jaq sighed at the memory of raw jellyfish. 'They denied all knowledge of a Krixo operation. I couldn't get anyone to take me back there. When I tried to go alone, by taxi, the hotel contacted the development agency and they sent a translator to stop me.'

'What reason did they give?'

'They claimed it didn't exist.'

'Why didn't you use the translator Vikram set up for you?' Sophie asked.

'SEITA cancelled. Let me down at the last minute.'

Vikram interrupted. 'Bloody annoying. They even had the cheek to send an invoice. I'm not paying a penny.'

Sophie resumed the interrogation. 'But you managed to go back?'

'Yes. But the factory had gone, nothing left but bare earth.'

'I can't believe it. You are seriously telling me that you saw the factory operating and a few days later it had vanished?'

'I didn't believe it either.'

'Millions of dollars' worth of equipment?' Sophie shook her head. 'It's not possible. Maybe you went back to the wrong place.'

Jaq shook her head. 'I collected some interesting bits and pieces.' She fished in her bag and brought out the treasures, each one in a clear polythene bag.

'Looks like rubbish to me,' said Sophie.

'These aren't the sort of materials you'd find on a normal building site.'

'What do you mean?'

'Look at this one.'

In the bag was a black band coated in transparent plastic.

'What is it?'

'An O-ring.'

'What is it for?'

'Sealing.'

'Ceiling?'

'When you join two hard things together, you need something soft in the middle. To avoid leaks. The black material is Viton. But Viton swells up in contact with some solvents. So, it's encapsulated in FEP.'

'FEP?'

'Fluorinated ethylene propylene. It's expensive. You don't use it unless you have to.'

'What would you use it for?'

'Joining pipes carrying solvents like acetone.' A key solvent in the Krixo recycling process.

'And this.'

Jaq showed her a ring of translucent white plastic.

'I'm pretty sure this is a PVDF fitting – polyvinylidene difluoride. It's expensive, not just the material itself but the installation. Difficult to weld and floppy, so you need more pipe supports. You'd use it if you were handling chlorine gas or strong acids.'

'There was a chlorination plant.'

Jaq brought out the final proof. The plastic bag with the Selkie label and code. The full logo was a Celtic knot, a circle with the long flowing hair of a human swirling into the tail of a seal.

'I spoke to Selkie. They can trace the order from this part number. I just need your permission—'

'What?' Sophie paled. 'You contacted Selkie?' She banged her small fist on the table. 'How dare you?'

Jaq sat up straight and spread her hands, turning her palms upwards. 'They wouldn't tell me anything, but—'

'Do not, on *any* account, speak to Selkie again.'

Vikram shot Jaq a warning look.

'I'm so sorry, Sophie. Jaq will do nothing more without your express permission. Right, Jaq?'

'Of course,' Jaq said.

What had just happened there?

'What else?' There was a hard edge to Sophie's voice.

'I found this in the centre of the site.'

Jaq brought out another bag, fragments of turquoise ceramic tiles and a white chip that might be marble.

'The fountain!' said Sophie. 'Oh, no.'

For Jaq the last bag held the least conclusive evidence. The plot of land had been reclaimed from the estuary, and tiny fragments of ceramic and marble could easily be found in general rubble. Unlike FEP and PVDF. But she had guessed that Sophie would be more convinced by this, and she was right.

'Show me the photos again,' said Sophie, reaching to get something from her bag.

Jaq unlocked her phone and flicked through the pictures she had taken and downloaded into the report. All of them showed a barren plot of land from different angles. Some included shots of a pathetic little pile of debris, all that was left of a multimillion-dollar investment. Intent on talking through them in detail, it wasn't until Vikram put a box of tissues on the table that Jaq noticed Sophie was crying.

Sophie wept elegantly. Tears rolled down her cheeks, but there was no snuffling or sobbing. Even the mascara seemed to stay in place, although the white paper handkerchief came away from her eyes daubed with purple.

'All I have left of my father is a pot of ashes. It is too much to bear that his life's work has been reduced to rubble as well.'

'I'm so sorry,' said Jaq. 'I would not have believed it possible if I hadn't seen it with my own eyes.' They worked fast in China. A fully functional factory on Monday had completely disappeared by Friday.

'I don't have the strength to fight any more.' Amethyst eyes flashed. 'I am going to dissolve the joint venture. Will you act as a witness for me?'

'I can certainly confirm what I saw, yes.'

'That's all I need.' Sophie straightened up as if a great weight had been removed from her fragile shoulders.

'Vikram, can I have a word?' Jaq asked.

'Not now.' He waved her away and attended to his client.

As Jaq waited at the station for the Eaglescliffe train, she checked her phone. Three missed calls and two voicemails. A message from Emma inviting her to spend Christmas in Coniston. Jaq smiled and shook her head. Simultaneously a very lovely and a very bad idea. A briefer message from her mother's care home, asking her when she planned to make the next payment.

On the opposite platform, the London train pulled out of the station, heading north to Inverness. From Aberdeen it was an overnight ferry to Shetland. And as soon as Sophie released her from this bizarre contract, that was where she was headed.

She pulled the Shetland hat over her ears and wished she was already there.

On the platform opposite her, a young man stood still. The wind whipped his long hair into writhing red snakes, and he stopped to gather it into a band. As he lifted his head, the red curls now secured in a topknot, he looked directly across the tracks. He hefted his large sports bag and moved towards her like a gymnast, his movements controlled, precise, almost languid.

Beauty is a powerful tonic. You know it when you see it, and sometimes it is uplifting to soak it in. A displacement activity, watching this young Adonis with his perfect physique on his way to a date with some lucky partner, she followed his progress towards the subway and reappearing on her platform, striding towards the exit and the footbridge that led into town.

She couldn't control her response, it was a chemical reaction: phenylalanine to tyrosine to levodopa to dopamine to norepinephrine. The neurotransmitters increasing her heart rate and blood pressure, triggering the release of glucose from energy stores.

As he drew level, striking hazel eyes found hers. He smiled and she looked away, embarrassed to have been caught staring.

What was she playing at? He was far too young for her. And students were always off limits, even now she was no longer a university lecturer.

Once he was out of sight, Jaq called Vikram to ask when she would be paid.

Teesside, England

Driving over the brow of Thorpe Hill, Frank paused to survey the container ships sailing into Teesport. A plume of smoke belched from the chimney of the moribund Redcar steelworks. He scanned the dark satanic mills, the flares and steam plumes from Wilton and Billingham until he found the prilling tower and storage spheres of the Zagrovyl factory. Frank rolled down his window, spat into the road and continued his journey, turning right into the narrow back lane that plunged into a fertile valley.

Wynyard Hall sat in acres of rolling meadow and woodland. In this secluded haven, Frank could almost forget he was in Teesside.

He parked outside the Palladian mansion which rose above a lake. This was the sort of property Frank imagined owning. Had he chosen to be a property developer instead of an industrial executive, he would have done so by now. His first house, in London, had risen in value tenfold since he bought it. He often checked house prices in the area, a painful exercise since the house was stolen from him in his first divorce settlement. He'd made a healthy profit selling his second property, a Sussex farmhouse, when he moved up north. He'd have done better to hang onto it and not work at all. The increase in value of Home Counties property in the last few years was substantially more than he had earned in all that time. He'd only rented since, waiting for an opportunity as the Northern property market remained stagnant and uninteresting. Investing some of the equity in a yacht had not been, in retrospect, the wisest move. He'd been badly advised. And now he found himself stranded without a property to return to in the south, without assets and, unless he was careful, without a job.

Plan A had always been to stick it out with Zagrovyl. After all, they'd made him move to this godforsaken hole; they owed him at least as much money as he'd lost by relocating. And given what he'd done for them, and what he knew about them, a great deal more. With Graham Dekkers' help that strand of the plan was already nailed.

Plan B was his investment portfolio. Frank had several venture capital investments, including a direct stake in Krixo, the Chinese company set up by Charles Clark. Which aligned well with Plan C – an advantageous marriage, a neat shortcut to get him back on the property ladder without any risk.

He'd been leaving the gym when Sophie called. He ducked back into the lobby, out of the wind and rain, and called her back.

'Can we meet?'

Plan C was looking good. 'Just tell me where and when.'

'Now,' she said. 'Wynyard Hall.'

Frank arrived at the hotel before her. He found a seat by a tall window and opened the paper.

CHINESE GANGS TERRORISE ENGLAND

Is there a link between the murder of a London auctioneer and that of a university professor?

New evidence has emerged that Professor John Tench – emeritus professor at Teesside University, who died in hospital from injuries sustained in a savage attack in his home – attended the controversial auction of ancient Chinese artefacts presided over in London by auctioneer Bernard Ashley-Cooper, who was brutally murdered at his £5 million mansion in Chelsea earlier this week.

Both men sustained multiple knife wounds and, in both cases, a domestic pet belonging to the victims was cruelly dismembered.

Dr David Woolly, a social anthropologist at the University of Salford, and expert in Triad gang activity, speculated that the manner of both attacks is the hallmark of a Chinese gang known as Lingchi. He added that the jade lovers' cup, sold by Ashley-Cooper for £10 million, was once owned by Qianlong, the Qing dynasty emperor notorious for executing his enemies by slow slicing: death by one thousand cuts.

A neighbour, who refused to be named, reported seeing Ashley-Cooper invite a person of Asian origin into his home, shortly after 8 p.m. on the night of his murder. Police declined to comment on the witness statement but confirmed that there was no sign of forced entry.

The attack on the retired university professor, in his £250,000 home in North Yorkshire, had many similar features, including the lack of forced entry and the sadistic nature of the attack, but there were no witnesses.

The value of the auctioneer's London property kept rising. House prices – that was the difference between the South and the North.

Frank put the paper down to see Sophie emerging from a taxi. Did she even have a car? She waved at him through the window. He stood to greet her, waiting while she detoured through the powder room.

'I'm starving,' she announced when she finally emerged.

He patted his gym-toned stomach. 'I'm fine.'

Sophie waved at the waitress. 'Afternoon tea.'

'For two?'

'Just tea for me,' said Frank. 'Decaffeinated.'

'Prosecco for me,' Sophie said. 'Unless you have some of that English champagne?'

'Only French champagne, madam.'

'Prosecco, then.'

'Tough day?' Frank tried, not entirely successfully, to keep the sneer from his voice.

'The Chinese factory has vanished.'

'Vanished?' He reared back. 'What do you mean?' Where did this leave Plan B, his investment in Krixo?

'Pouf!' She snapped her fingers. 'Gone. Operational Monday and razed to the ground by Friday.'

Their drinks arrived. Sophie emptied her glass in one gulp

and signalled for the bottle. Frank poured his tea and wished for something stronger. Bloody doctors.

'Someone's pulling the wool over your lovely eyes,' he said.

'I don't think so.' Sophie handed him the CCS report. 'It was your expert who confirmed it.'

Jaqueline Silver. The interfering engineer. Perhaps it had been a mistake to recommend her to Sophie. He leafed through the report and his jaw dropped. Impossible. Unbelievable. What part had she played in this? She'd already sunk his yacht. Could Silver have spirited a factory away as well, to spite him? She was smart; he wouldn't put anything past her. And fast.

A silver stand arrived, three tiers with sandwiches, scones and tiny cakes.

'I don't understand. Your investment...' And Frank's investment. 'How could this have happened?'

'Oh, don't worry about that.' Sophie spoke with her mouth full. Her table manners left much to be desired. 'Krixo is fully insured.'

Did such insurance exist? In his experience insurers made you pay in good times and ran away in bad. There was always a clause here, a subclause there, hidden deep in the contract. He should know: he was an expert at laying those little traps himself.

'Have you informed the insurers?'

'It's not so much insurance as collateral.'

'What sort of collateral?'

Sophie smiled and tapped her nose. There were many good things about the company of attractive women, but talking business with them was not one.

Frank tried again. 'Have you informed the investors?'

'Why do you think I called you?'

His heart dipped. Was that how she saw him? Just a minor investor in the business? Someone she could use to communicate with the others? Then she smiled, and he remembered that he was special. Of course he would help her. Plan C.

'I'll happily inform the other investors,' he said. 'But first, I think

I need to understand the fundamentals of this business. Can I meet the UK team?'

'I'll set it up for you. When are you free?'

'For you, Sophie' – he tried to look sincere – 'any time.'

'Thank you, Frank.' Sophie leaned forward and laid a small hand on his. A surprisingly cold hand. 'It helps a great deal to be able to rely on someone so much more experienced.' Her amethyst eyes flashed with gratitude.

Good to be appreciated for a change. If Graham Dekkers and Zagrovyl didn't get their act together soon, they might just discover that Frank Good had accepted a better offer.

Durham, England

The Durham University Oriental Museum huddled beside the river, shrouded in mist. Ernest walked briskly from the train station, nodding briefly at the road repair crew manoeuvring their white van into position. With his trainers, jeans and college scarf, he could easily be taken for a student. A memorably beautiful student – medium height with long red hair, freckled skin and startling hazel eyes – precisely why he tied his hair back and hid his slim, muscular body under a shapeless anorak. He pulled up the hood to complete his disguise.

A pair of rowing skiffs raced up the river, the female crews exchanging good-humoured jibes as they jockeyed for pole position. A group of young men followed their progress along the river footpath, striped scarves flying as they ran.

He waited until the students were out of earshot before checking the equipment. The Knightsgate footbridge, a concrete monstrosity, provided the perfect pivot. High above the gorge of the river Wear, it linked the castle and cathedral hill to the eastern town. Last night he'd closed it for maintenance and gone over the side.

The same workmen who'd assisted him then opened the van and began to unload the equipment. In tan riggers' boots, black donkey jackets with orange fluorescent strips and yellow hard hats, they almost looked the part. Although anyone observing closely would have noticed their furtive glances across the river as they set out the cones and barricaded off the work area with incongruous delicacy.

Ernest ignored them, turning his back to focus on his pre-performance stretches. Only when he heard a jackhammer pounding to mask the screaming of the core drill did he begin to run.

The street lamps flickered into life as he crossed the Elvet Bridge and sprinted up the footpath, ears pricked for any shouts of warning or hint of alarm. It took him ten seconds to check the work, in which time he had stripped to his skintight, flesh-coloured leotard. He threw the workmen his clothes and gave a blue, latex-glove-covered thumbs up. The workmen were already speeding away in their van as he made his dive.

The hole in the museum wall was exactly one metre off the ground at its lowest point and roughly fifty centimetres in diameter. A thick wall, so he took a run at it, using his forward momentum to propel himself head first into the exhibition area without touching the sides. Once inside, he moved fast. His hands touched the floor fifty centimetres beyond the hole, and his feet carried over, flipping him into a crab, springing up on his toes and then cartwheeling into a handstand. Upside down, he surveyed the room.

The order was very specific: two jade statues. Each statue was about twenty centimetres high: a man, flanked by a boy and a deer, held a persimmon; a woman in flowing white robes strummed a horizontal harp.

His gymnastic routine had been perfected in an empty basement, with steel wires taking the place of the invisible laser beams inside the museum. The night-time security was simple: a broken beam triggered an external alarm causing steel bars to descend, with less than three minutes before the police arrived. This was to be avoided for as long as possible. The internal alarms were different, impossible to avoid, but the delay before an internal alarm escalated to an external one – an algorithm added after the police became tired of responding every time a cleaner dusted a case, or a member of the public leaned too heavily against the glass – gave him more than enough time.

He stood on tiptoes in front of the case of interest and removed the jemmy from his belt. Deep breaths. This was the moment. Now or never. One, two. He levered the glass case from its base and grabbed the statues as the alarm began to trill. He wrapped each figurine in expanding fibres and slid each one up a sleeve. Left, right. The internal alarm bells were ringing like the clappers. Not long before the external alarm would kick in.

He made his escape, one backflip, one cartwheel, three forward flips, more difficult now with the precious objects rubbing against his forearms, and went backwards through the hole, his arms crossed over his body, protecting the haul above all else.

A second set of clothes – chinos, tailored wool coat, leather gloves and beanie – lay exactly where he had left them, in a bag high up on the west bank, right beside the improvised swing. He dressed quickly, grabbed the swing bar and launched himself across the river, landing on the opposite bank before the external alarm pierced the night.

The swing was easily disassembled. He flipped the catch and pulled the fine steel wire, swing bar first, back through the eyelet he had drilled under the footbridge. The wire spooled onto the bank and he kicked it into the river Wear.

Ernest sauntered back up New Elvet, observing the police cars screaming out of Durham police station towards the museum, and headed back to the train station.

Mission accomplished.

Wilton Centre, Teesside
The Wilton Centre put Frank in mind of a poem from school.

Look on my Works, ye Mighty, and despair!

Replace Ozymandias with ICI and you had a fair picture of the hubris that drove the architects to design such an ambitious fortress, interlocking buildings of tiered red brick arranged around an artificial lake in manicured gardens beside an industrial complex. Now the dregs of the Teesside chemical industry wheezed and gasped with dying, foetid breath.

Nothing beside remains. Round the decay
Of that colossal Wreck, boundless and bare

Frank parked as close to the administration building as he could get, leaving plenty of other disabled parking spaces free. He held his breath as he hurried up the steps. Once the home of cutting-edge research, the Wilton Centre was now almost abandoned, just a few labs and offices for deluded tech start-ups. The dilapidated, half-empty sprawl presented a painful reminder of how the government had wasted his hard-earned taxes, haemor-rhaging money in a futile attempt to cradle invention, to nurture innovation, to create jobs in an industry that was terminally ill, if not already dead.

Since Krixo had moved operations to China, the UK research centre was no more than a toilet-sized lab with a broom cupboard for an office. A handful of employees remained on the books, presumably a condition of the grants, and one of them came to meet Frank. A man in a white coat who introduced himself as Dr Nadim, chief chemist, and led Frank to a Wilton International meeting room.

'So.' White Coat spread his hands. 'Sophie told me you are looking for information on rare earths. Before I start, what do you already know?'

Frank yawned. 'I know they are rare.'

'Wrong.' The geek beamed with triumph. 'They are, in fact, abundant.' He clicked a remote control and the projection of his computer screen lit up one wall. A table with letters and numbers, a few of the squares towards the bottom highlighted in bright colours. 'The rare earths are a series of seventeen metal elements with very special properties, relatively abundant in the earth's crust, but only ever found in very low concentrations in rocks. That makes them difficult and expensive to recover.'

Frank's ears pricked up. Expensive: that was a word he understood. Difficult was just whining, engineer excuses, meaning they hadn't tried hard enough. But expensive meant valuable.

'How expensive?'

Nadim tapped on his computer and a graph appeared on the screen, an x–y plot with a vertiginous slope.

'That's the price of dysprosium. In 2003 it cost less than thirty dollars for one kilogram of metal. This year it reached three thousand dollars.'

Impressive. Frank had pushed through many steep price rises in his time, made the tough choices and hard decisions that his colleagues were too cowardly to contemplate. To achieve such increases for a product that you just dug out of the ground, someone obviously knew their stuff.

'Who controls the price?'

'China.'

Of course. Clever bastards.

'Are there alternatives?'

'People have trialled samarium – cobalt. And—'

'Do they work?'

'Yes and no.'

'Which is it?' Frank snarled.

'Different performance at high temperature. More expensive.'

Frank pointed to the price graph. 'Why has it stopped rising?' Had the peak passed, were prices falling or was it just a false summit?

'There are rumours of a huge new deposit of xenotime on the China–India border. With much higher levels of dysprosium. Our intelligence suggests that the Chinese are deliberately keeping it secret. Allowing the West to spend billions of dollars of research money trying to find alternatives, other combinations. When the time comes, they will flood the market with cheap magnets and cripple their competitors.'

Impressive business acumen. He had to hand it to them.

'Xenotime?'

'A source of yttrium and the heavy lanthanide metals: dysprosium, ytterbium, erbium and gadolinium. Can be radioactive . . .'

Frank shivered.

'Due to uranium and thorium impurities. Chemically it is yttrium orthophosphate, with traces of arsenic, silicon and calcium, but some of the yttrium is displaced by dysprosium and—'

'And all this is important for,' he couldn't keep the scorn out of his voice, 'green energy?'

'Lanthanum and cerium are important for rechargeable batteries, dysprosium and neodymium for wind turbines, and for solar panels you need . . .'

Frank stared out of the window at the grey sky. A light rain was falling. Straight down. Not a breath of wind. He looked up at the spotlights in the ceiling, listened to the whir of the projector fan.

'If the future depends on green energy,' he said, 'then we'd better get used to darkness.'

Christmas, Gothenburg, Sweden

The sanatorium lay hidden in the forest, hunkered down between slabs of granite, the sloping roof slanting towards the beach, wooden slats protecting the windows from the west wind gusting across the North Sea from Scotland. Water that looked deceptively inviting, grey-green and clear, sparkling in the frosty winter light.

A sliding door swooshed open as Jaq approached, closing behind her as she entered a square wood-clad vestibule. A video camera blinked at her from a corner.

'Jaq Silver for Camilla Hatton,' she said.

She'd opted to deliver some of her Christmas gifts in person. Chinese silk pyjamas for Cecile and Lily, handed over before Gregor and his other ex-wife arrived in Paris to 'help' with their grandchild. She took the grizzling baby for a long walk while Cecile caught up on some sleep, earning a grateful hug from her tearful stepdaughter. Lily was out of danger now, but still failing to thrive.

On Christmas Eve, she took the train from Paris to Aalborg on the northern tip of Denmark, and a quiet hotel she'd booked, for two nights' reading and sleeping before taking the Boxing Day ferry to Gothenburg.

It wasn't as if Christmas meant anything to her.

The first Christmas she remembered, really remembered, was in Angola. Her father was away, her mother present in body, absent in mind, leaving Jaq and her brother, Sam, free to roam: the year of the crocodile.

She'd never forget that first encounter: the smell of oleander as she toddled down the bank to investigate the strange reptile with the mesmerising eye, the violent jackknife reaction of the predator as her brother pelted it with sticks and stones, the pain of Sam's fingers on her upper arm, squeezing the soft flesh, dragging her away from the opening jaws, lifting her up and running, saving her life, the roar of his anger afterwards.

Until then, Sam had always been so quiet, so gentle, she took his kindness for granted. Almost four years older, he was the closest thing she had to a parent most of the time – what with her father away with the troops and her mother away with the fairies. Which was why his yelling scared her so. He'd often chided, inveigled, implored, but never screamed like that, never turned on her in such fury. She nursed her bruised arm and cried, not because of the near-death experience, but because he called her a silly little girl.

It was the last time anyone called her a silly little girl.

Later, when the nightmares started, it was Sam who knew what to do.

Where did Sam get the green marble? So unlike the other glass spheres, the ones that came from Europe in an orange string bag: plain, clear glass with little swirls of colour, full of tiny bubbles and other imperfections. This marble was larger, a perfect, smooth sphere, an oval black slit surrounded by a starburst of light in dark green glass.

Exactly like the eye of a crocodile.

He must have traded with the local boys. She never found out what he gave in exchange, but it must have been something precious. On Christmas Eve, when she woke screaming and couldn't get back to sleep, he put it on her bedside table, under the night light. The crocodile was very sorry for frightening her, he said. It had left a Christmas present to make amends, a magic gift that would keep her safe, but only if she kept away from all the other crocodiles, and hippos and snakes, otherwise one of them might try to snatch the magic back. He kissed her, wished her a Merry Christmas and called her his brave little sister.

The nightmares stopped.

He never realised what she was really afraid of. Not the crocodile. Her biggest fear was that her brother had stopped loving her. She was afraid of losing Sam.

And ever since he'd gone, Christmas was not the same.

In the sanatorium near Gothenburg, the flashing red dot on the camera turned green as a wooden wall slid to one side.

Jaq passed through the opening and found herself in a large airy room, a pine-clad trapezium facing away from the sea. Not a soul in sight, only moss-green cushions on rustic wooden furniture. Slanting light came through a smoked-glass ceiling, which flared up and out towards high windows, the clear glass opening into a grove of trees, making it hard to see where the building ended and the forest began.

The vertical lines of pine panelling narrowed as a side door opened. The scent of rose water reached her before the greeting.

'Jaq.' The deep voice carried across the room, full of warmth. 'So good of you to come.'

Camilla emerged from a side door. She moved confidently across the room. Her thick white hair had been cut short again, expertly styled. The prison pallor had vanished, the sharp edges of forced confinement replaced with the softer curves of freedom. The additional weight suited her.

They embraced.

'How are you?' Jaq asked.

Camilla had been working undercover, tracking the movement of illegal chemical weapons, before The Spider caught her. She spent many months imprisoned in the basement of his Crimean villa before Jaq found and rescued her.

'Better, much better.'

Camilla indicated a circle of mushroom-shaped seats, and they sat facing each other across a table cut from a tree trunk.

'I brought you something.' Jaq reached into her bag and pulled out a decorated tin of biscuits from a shop in Yarm.

'Forgive me, I'm such a poor host.' Camilla took the tin and inspected the brightly coloured enamel, embossed with idealised pictures of squirrels and hazelnuts. 'Would you care for some tea to go with these?'

'I'm fine—' Jaq began.

'So polite. You've been in England too long.' Camilla smiled. 'It's no trouble.' She pushed herself from the chair and walked over to a rustic sideboard, opening a wooden door to reveal a kettle and ceramic mugs. She filled the kettle and set it to boil.

Jaq looked around. 'Where are the staff?'

'They come only when needed – isolation is part of the cure.' Camilla held up a tray of coloured paper packets and plastic sachets. 'Darjeeling, Earl Grey, green tea, oolong, camomile, peppermint, liquorice, ginger . . .?'

'Any coffee?'

'Only instant.'

Jaq joined her by the sideboard and inspected the tray. Decaffeinated. Worse than useless, but she shook two sachets of excuse-for-coffee into a mug while Camilla tore open a turquoise packet of camomile tea.

'Allow me.'

Jaq poured the boiling water onto Camilla's teabag, watching the straw-yellow colour deepen as the apigenin, dimethulene and bisabolol were released. She filled her own mug, watching the brown granules dissolve. Chemical Engineering 101 right here on the bench, unit operations in action, extraction, diffusion, filtration, solution, agitation.

They took their drinks back to the tree trunk table.

Camilla spoke first. 'Physically, I'm fully recovered. I can leave here whenever I want.' She paused. 'But I'm not quite ready.'

'Do you want to . . .' Jaq searched for elegant, elliptical words, and found none, 'to talk about it?'

'No.' Camilla grimaced and shook her head. 'Not yet.'

They sat in silence for a while, each lost in their own thoughts, just the sigh of trees in the sea breeze. The sounds of the outside world were relayed into the room through some clever acoustic conduction; the noises matched the movement of the canopy, yet the room was too warm, the air too still for the room to be open to the outside. It felt like floating through the forest in a bubble, full immersion yet completely safe.

'I hear you had some trouble getting back.'

'Shipwrecked,' Jaq said. 'For all the *Good Ship Frankium* looked impressive on the outside, it was rotten underneath.'

Camilla grimaced. 'Just like its owner.'

'Exactly.' Should she tell Camilla that Frank Good was demanding payment for the yacht? Ask for her help? Jaq glanced at the older woman, the slight tremor at the corner of one eye belying the pool of stillness and calm.

No; Camilla had enough to deal with right now. What mattered was her health, her mental health.

They sat in companionable silence until it got dark.

Jaq said her goodbyes and left.

Teesside, England

Despite the cold Tuesday night, Yarm High Street was heaving with scantily dressed revellers. The polyphony bounced between the high Georgian buildings: the syncopated clatter of high heels on cobbles, discordant chatter, a twittering descant, the bellowing of young bulls in search of mates.

Frank entered the restaurant with Sophie draped on one arm. She'd certainly made an effort: dressed to kill.

'Good evening.'

'Table for two.'

'What name is the booking, sir?'

'No booking.'

'We're very busy . . .'

Frank looked around and sneered. 'You don't look full to me.'

'We have several parties arriving soon.'

'Then fit us in in the meantime.' Frank barged past him and pointed at a table set for four in the window. 'This table will do fine.'

'I'm sorry, sir, that table is booked from 8 p.m.'

'Plenty of time.' He strode over to the table and pulled out a seat for Sophie, careful to position her in full view of the window. He took his own seat opposite the mirror with a great view of the glances from the street as passers-by admired his companion. Leave them to their 'grab a granny' night – Frank had a trophy date. Their jealousy and his own reflection made the perfect setting.

The maître d' approached.

'Good evening, Mr Good. I'm afraid—'

'Tonic water.' Frank looked over at Sophie. 'And you?'

'Glass of Prosecco,' she said. 'A big one.'

The maître d' spread his hands, palms upwards. 'I'm afraid there has been a misunderstanding, sir. This table is already booked. We'd be happy to accommodate you for a drink at the bar.'

'No, this is fine.' Frank turned to the menu.

'I'm sorry, sir. The guests who booked this table are due to arrive in half an hour.'

Frank turned his cold blue eyes on the man. 'Then you'd better find them another table, hadn't you?'

'We're fully booked, sir. Maybe if you come back after nine . . .'

'I'm hungry,' Sophie said, batting her false eyelashes.

Frank looked around the room. He pointed to a family group, a couple with two children. 'Isn't it past their bedtime?'

'Mr Good, please—'

'I hope you're not going to give us food poisoning again.'

'Food poisoning? Here?' Sophie pushed away her menu and frowned.

Maybe not here, exactly. Here, there, anywhere. Kitchen restaurants were all the same. He raised his voice. 'Did I tell you about the time my guts turned to water . . .?'

People were turning and staring.

'Sir, please keep your voice down. We don't want any trouble.'

'Then bring us our drinks,' Frank said.

Sophie winked at Frank as the maître d' retreated.

'You look lovely tonight, Sophie.'

'I haven't felt much like going out,' she said. 'Since the funeral.'

What would Nicola the HR dragon say in these circumstances?

'It's important to keep going,' he tried.

When the drinks arrived, Frank ordered a thrice-baked soufflé and a pasta dish. Sophie ordered a salad and rare steak.

'How is probate coming along?' Follow the money.

Sophie shook her head, fair curls bouncing against apple cheeks. 'It's all so complicated.' She sighed.

'Can I help?' Speed this along.

'You've already helped me so much, Frank.' She put her hand over his: false nails, blood-red talons. As she talked, he imagined her nails raking his back. The thought was strangely disturbing. What was wrong with him? Here was a beautiful woman, upset and grateful, and yet he felt no desire. He hadn't been himself for a while.

An altercation at the bar distracted him, broke his train of thought. A party of four had arrived to find there was no table. Frank turned his attention back to the matter in hand: his money.

'The Chinese joint venture partners were trying to cheat my father.'

'Just as well he took action to protect his interests.'

A pretty airhead with a clever father. A father who was no longer around to object to the company Sophie was keeping.

A familiar figure crossed the high street behind him, striding across his field of vision in the mirror, halting suddenly as she spotted Sophie in the window. Her eyes darted sideways to meet his in the polished glass.

Frank leaned across and took Sophie's small face in both hands, pressing his lips against hers in a long, slow kiss.

When he looked back up at the mirror, Jaqueline Silver was gone.

Stockholm, Sweden

The scent of sweet gale, *Myrica*, put Holger in mind of happier times: endless summers spent on the family island, a rocky comma with barely enough room for their summer house. More of a shack than a house, it stood in the middle of the island, between the home-made sauna at one end and the wood store at the other, beside a sheltered deepwater mooring for their little boat.

It was here he learned to swim. As he gained confidence in the water, he swam from island to island, increasing the distance to outswim his elder brothers, uncle and father. Extending the season, swimming in all weathers. The sea temperature didn't bother him; so long as the water remained liquid, he would swim. After Mälaren, swimming pools never felt quite right; he detested the heat, the chlorine and the confinement, although it had won him medals and allowed him to make a living for a time.

The sunlight bounced off a thin crust of ice at the edge of the lake, but the water flowed freely towards Stockholm and the Baltic Sea. Light was both good and bad. It made it easier to see what he was doing, avoiding flashlights which might be investigated by curious soldiers. But it also made him more visible.

Standing six foot eight, with size forty-eight feet and great paddles for hands, he was more comfortable in the water. He hid his pale body and shock of pure white hair under a hooded wetsuit.

The Swedish military provided security for the Royal Family at their permanent private residence and he didn't want to draw their attention.

The Chinese Pavilion, deep in the grounds of Drottningholm Palace, was only a few kilometres from his flat in Stockholm. He hadn't swum all the way; that would be stupid. He had to preserve his energy for the mission.

Entering the water at the Högholmen end of Kärsön, dry bags attached to a floating buoy which trailed behind him just below the surface, he swam round Hundholmen and reached Lovön island at the southern end of the royal estate.

Way ahead of schedule and in no hurry, he sprinted to the rendezvous point just to warm up. From the broad branches of the fir tree he could see the pavilion. Faux Chinese, it made a colourful birthday present for an eighteenth-century queen, with russet panels, yellow architraves and green-hued copper roof. But he also understood the objections. How would his compatriots feel if China had taken Sweden's most precious works of art – raped the Vasa for bronze cannon, or taken the Ramsund Sigurd stone to Beijing? He wasn't stealing. This was an act of restorative justice. And a lucrative one at that.

The next phase was critical, no room for mistakes. Wait until the decoy gang were in place. Then five minutes – six, maximum – to get in and out and back in the water.

He had memorised the order; images were his forte. That and long-distance, cold-water swimming.

Of all the objects listed, the dragon was his favourite, spinach green and sinuous, spiky too, with its sharp teeth and ridged spine, scales and talons. The folded wings looked as if they were about to unfurl and carry it away. The rest of the order was less to his taste: elaborately carved pebbles with 3D relief, bowls and cups and plates and jugs. He could appreciate the skill, but it was the dragon that really spoke to him.

The *puhV-RooPuhHoo* of a two-stroke engine coming over Drottningholmsbron, the route any normal person would take from Kärson, prompted him to check his waterproof watch. Bang on time. And still no soldiers in sight.

Then the *swishslapslap* outboard motor of a speedboat, racing west from Skärholmen. Two minutes later, and the engine went silent. The call. The response. Holger sprang into action.

He wasn't a fast runner, but his height and weight and the fact that he knew exactly where to impact the glass window at the weakest point, carried him through. Now to get the stuff and get out.

He wielded the jeweller's hammer like a twenty-first-century Thor. With the shrieking of the alarm, there was no need to keep quiet. It felt good to bellow as he smashed and grabbed, bellowed and smashed and grabbed. He knew exactly where to go, which cases to target, the mental map secure in his mind, the objects ticked off as he opened each bag and tossed them in to activate the chemical foam that formed around them. Keep going, keep moving. The three-minute alarm sounded on his watch. Time to go. One last bellow and smash and grab, and then reverse direction. Noise receding. Good to be out in the open.

Holger pulled off his gloves, threw the hammer into the bushes and ran for the shore, the dry bags full of protective foam billowing out behind him like balloons.

He heard the decoy moped start up. *Vrooom* and away. He hit the water awkwardly, breaking the ice and swimming strongly for a few minutes. He stopped to check that his haul was intact and then dived towards the deep channel. He didn't make it first time; he couldn't hold his breath long enough to find the submerged mooring. He surfaced and trod water, keeping his movements minimal to avoid attention from the shore. And realised that he was a hundred metres or so off course. He swam breaststroke, just under the surface until the GPS on his watch told him he was on target. The second dive was easy. He secured the bags on the mooring, surfaced with a sense of elation and swam into the darkness.

Mission accomplished.

Teesside, England

A silver cat lay sunning itself on top of the low brick wall outside Eaglescliffe station. He greeted Jaq with enthusiasm, rubbing against her leg before rolling over and purring, offering up his pure white tummy. Jaq bent down and stroked the soft fur. He meowed in protest as she said goodbye and crossed the footbridge in time for the train that would take her on the first leg of her journey to Shetland.

At Darlington she transferred to the Aberdeen train and a window seat. Staring out at the countryside rolling by – so very slow after China – she ruminated on last night's disturbing discovery.

So, Frank and Sophie were lovers. Had Frank played a part in Jaq's selection for a trip to China? What had Vikram said – the job could have been tailor-made for her. All that guff about needing someone with a range of skills, when what they wanted was a patsy, a witness to a vanishing factory. Could Frank be behind its disappearance? Unlikely. He wasn't that smart. Or efficient. No Western company, even directed by someone as ruthless and irresponsible as Frank, with his naked contempt for engineers, could demolish a factory that fast. If anyone could do it – and she still would not have believed it if she hadn't witnessed it with her own eyes – it would be Chinese engineers.

And what of Sophie? What was she doing dating a slimeball like Frank? Sophie was not as dumb as she made out. Her brand was pretty and ditzy; she used her little-girl-lost act to charm and wrong-foot her admirers. A loathsome trope. Not only did it give their gender a bad name – the helpless kitten woman, the ball of fluff that needed supporting and protecting – it was fundamentally

222

dishonest. Sophie was a rich and successful businesswoman, even if she owed some of her good luck to her father. What was she doing with a despicable monster like Frank? And what was Frank Good's connection to Krixo and the vanishing factory?

As the train thundered over the river Tweed and entered Scotland, Jaq made a decision. Time to move on, put the vanishing factory behind her. The Krixo job was done, finished, over with. She'd never know what happened to the factory in China or why it disappeared, but the fact that Frank was involved with its owner was a compelling reason to steer clear. An unresolved mystery, but she could control her curiosity for once. Curiosity had led to trouble in the past. What she needed now were some straight-forward engineering challenges to throw her energy into. Shetland beckoned. Work to do, money to earn, bills to pay.

She admired the bridges as the train crossed the Firth of Forth and then the river Tay. As the train hugged the coast at Montrose, her phone buzzed. Jaq answered without checking the number.

'Dr Silver?' A foreign accent.

'Yes, who is this?'

'Mr Gao Ding, from SEITA in Shanghai.'

For a company that was so inefficient at providing interpreters, they were irritatingly persistent when it came to collecting debts they were not owed.

'I'm trying to clear up a misunderstanding. When you cancelled—'

'I didn't cancel. *You* cancelled!'

'That is the misunderstanding. We received a call just before your interpreter was due to leave the office, cancelling the contract.'

'Who called?'

'You did, Dr Silver.'

'I most certainly did not!' Wait. 'Someone called from this number?'

'No, a local number. I have it here.' He rattled off a number.

Jaq opened her silver card holder to check. *Merda*. Of course.

The unusual interest in Krixo. The cancellation of her independent translator designed to ensure that Jaq had to call for help.

Lulu.

Who the hell was she?

'I see.' Jaq paused. 'There has indeed been a misunderstanding.'

'There is a cancellation charge.' He named a sum that made Jaq wince. Perhaps it was time to renegotiate her own daily rate.

'I'll make sure it is settled.' Would Vikram agree to pay? He hadn't even got around to paying her yet, and there was no dispute.

'Oh, and Dr Silver, one more question. Do you happen to know anyone by the name of Oddo Harkins?'

How very strange. The second time she had heard those names together. The last time was among Dan's ramblings.

Oddo and Harkins: Italian chemist Giuseppe Oddo and American William Draper Harkins, father of the cyclotron, nuclear chemists who never met but whose names were linked by a theory on the abundance of elements. The even-numbered elements being roughly twice as common as the odd-numbered ones. More carbon than boron. Could there be a connection to Dan?

'Oddo Harkins. Yes. Why do you ask?'

'We received a message for him. But we have no client by that name.'

'Is the message in English?'

'It's just a string of numbers.'

A string of numbers. Like the ones Dan was writing in his flat. On the pad that Lulu took away from him.

'I'd be happy to pass the message on,' Jaq said.

'Perhaps you'd like to settle your bill first?'

Jaq sighed. She couldn't afford it, and she might never recover the cost of a cancelled translation service from Vikram. Especially as, through Dan, she was the one who had involved Lulu in the first place.

'Credit card?'

'That will be fine.'

She moved into the corridor to read out the long number, the expiry date and three-digit security. Was Vikram going to pay her soon? The SEITA bill would eat into the credit limit on her last card, and she had no more money coming in until the end of her first month in Shetland.

'That's gone through.' The voice sounded more cheerful.

'And the message?'

'Do you have a pen?'

After the call had finished, Jaq stared out of the window. Raindrops fanned out across the windowpanes, the wind blowing them in all directions. The sky outside was pewter-coloured. Not pollution. The nearest coal-burning power station had converted to biofuels, and most of Scotland's electricity came from hydroelectric or nuclear power. If anyone lit a fire, they used smokeless coal these days. Not many cars, and all of those were fitted with catalytic converters, that tiny bit of precious metal: platinum, palladium, rhodium enough to turn polluting hydrocarbons into carbon dioxide and water. There wasn't enough manufacturing left in Britain to cause the kinds of smog now common in China.

Jaq thought back to the meetings with Dan. His mumblings about leaving Shanghai because of the pollution. Disulphur oxide. What had he been trying to say? S_2O?

She slapped her forehead. *Estupida.*

SOS.

The international distress call. A cry for help.

What else had he said?

71-71.

Porra! Dan wasn't having a breakdown; he was a prisoner.

She opened her laptop to find a periodic table. As it came up on the screen, she marvelled at its elegant simplicity.

Hydrogen, the key to everything, the first element made up of one proton and one electron: atomic number 1, the building block of all other elements. Hydrogen fuses together in the heat of a dying star to form helium, with two protons and two electrons. Atomic number 2. And so on through lithium 3, and beryllium 4, and boron 5, and carbon 6 – six protons, six electrons and six neutrons. The table of elements goes up in whole numbers right up to 118, oganesson, the heaviest element discovered so far. Such a beautiful symmetry in nature. And, with the exception of hydrogen, the elements with an even number of protons are almost twice as abundant as those with a single one: the Oddo–Harkins rule. The elegance of chemistry, the alphabet of life.

And a secret code.

Lutetium, one of the rare earths, had the symbol Lu and atomic number 71.

71-71.

Lulu.

Jaq stared at the numbers she had written down:

71-71
53-61-76-52-75
20-7-73-44-16-90-68
7-8-15-8-3-58
9-53-60-74-47-7
59-8-52-43-54-3-7

And all became clear.

Museu de Arte Antiga, Lisbon, Portugal

It wasn't just the colour of his skin that made Eusébio stand out, but his size. Six foot six with broad shoulders and the muscle tone of a serious athlete, he found it difficult to blend into the background.

Not that he made much effort to hide. With multicoloured dreadlocks and multiple piercings, billowing African robes over tight white jeans and pointed snakeskin shoes, he turned heads wherever he went.

As a professional footballer, he'd once embraced the nightlife of Lisbon. Dinner in the Bairro Alto where the best *bacalhau* – dried salt cod – could be found, then down to the river and one bar after another, winding up at Frágil or Alcântara-Mar, bypassing the long queues, waved inside without charge. When the lights went down, and the volume of the music ratcheted up, Eusébio was the first on the dance floor. He left the club with a different girl every night.

Plenty of people recognised him from his days playing for Benfica, a brief and unhappy promotion after a stellar season with the juniors. A knee injury sent him to the bench before he'd scored a single goal, and then a complication with a botched ACL reconstruction ended his professional football career before he was twenty.

He tried to give something back by coaching kids in the *barracas*, but his heart wasn't in football any more. All that naivety, single-minded ambition, the selfish longing for glory. It was too painful to see his teenage mistakes perpetuated by others.

Even when he'd earned stupid money he'd always felt like a slum kid, a good-for-nothing thief born and raised on the wrong side of the tracks, in the shanty town beside the airport motorway, a kid who'd never amount to much.

A brief flirtation with his mother's evangelical church led him into the arms of Ana dos Anjos and a new start. Manual work by day and back to school at night. He tried to make up for all the lost years of football and sex. The training to become a physiotherapist was tougher and more expensive than he'd budgeted for, and he was glad when the other jobs came along.

The first was dancing in clubs. Initially it involved clothes, but he enjoyed the reaction when it got so hot he was forced to remove his shirt. He'd never seen a strip show, and worried that he might need lessons, but at the audition they said he was a natural.

The second was linked to Ana's job.

The Museu de Arte Antiga, where Ana had a cleaning job, overlooked the busy Alcântara dock. From the elegant garden you could look out over the river Tagus, the beaches of Caparica just visible beyond the grain silos of Porto Brandão and Trafaria. Inside, the museum was deserted most days. A few tourists came to see the fifteenth-century triptych by Hieronymus Bosch, or the Japanese screens, but few spent time in the Chinese collection.

Security was sleepy. Poorly paid, lifelong state employees had little incentive to tackle a determined thief. Even so, Eusébio was not prepared to risk anything during the day.

Ana swung him a job with the gardening contractor. If he was lousy at pruning and weeding, they forgave him for his strength and willingness to do the worst jobs, repointing the stone steps, hauling soil and bags of manure. He flirted with Ana dos Anjos and gained unfettered access out of hours to both the museum and her voluptuous body. A vigorous act of worship among the virgins and icons.

The order was clear, the shopping list specific. Three animal statues, a jug and a set of cups. All carved from jade. The dark green water buffalo looked soft and curvy, but he knew it would be cool and hard to the touch. The little elephant was highly stylised, covered in secondary carvings. The white horse was more realistic, caught in motion, frozen in time. Even he could see they were fine objects, magnificent but also fragile. The trick would be not only to remove them from their glass cases, but to do so without damaging them. And without getting caught.

The replicas were Ana's idea. They'd been fucking in the seventeenth-century portrait room, the leather benches just the right height for more adventurous positioning, and few things are more stimulating than getting butt naked under the gaze of Puritans in dark robes and white ruffs. It was a say-you're-sorry shag. Ana had accused him of using her. The funny thing was, she was much happier after he really had used her, though he supposed she'd used him too. As they lay entwined on the padded bench, she mentioned the warehouse in Odivelas, a place they stored the extra stuff, the objects that there was no space to show. It didn't get cleaned as often, but she'd been asked to go for two days next week.

They went together to find stuff that looked similar. Some of it was so good, he was almost tempted to pinch it instead, but the word on the street was that the buyer wouldn't pay unless he got exactly what was ordered. Ana's plan was much better than a smash and grab. The alarm system was old and prone to false alerts whenever it rained. It might take days, weeks, months or even years before anyone noticed the discrepancies. The seventeenth-century Qing dynasty jade horse in the museum was to be replaced by an eighteenth-century Tang donkey from the warehouse, which had in turn been replaced by an ornament sourced in Ikea. Similar substitutions were chosen for the elephant and water buffalo, jug and cups.

On the night of the job, Ana kicked a pail of water over the main junction box. As the alarms shrieked in every gallery, Eusébio lifted the heavy glass case. In less than three minutes he had removed the objects of interest, replaced them with the alternatives, repositioned the glass and escaped into the garden. He hid the precious things in a wheelbarrow, under a layer of hay and mulch, and locked himself in the garden tool shed while Ana rushed to meet the private security and Lisbon's finest policemen, apologising profusely as she showed them the cause of the false alarm. The security guards made a cursory inspection of the grounds and museum, but as none of them was an expert in Qing dynasty jade, they left quite unaware of the theft.

Eusébio waited until after midnight to retrieve his haul before catching the night train from Alcântara-Mar to Cascais.

One night with Ana, then off on tour to China.

Darlington, England

The golf course, on the north bank of the river Tees just south of Darlington, could only be accessed through the five-star hotel where the president of Zagrovyl global operations had taken a suite.

Frank and Graham shook hands in reception. Gone were the dark suits: both wore the businessman's weekend uniform of light-coloured slacks and polo shirts. Graham's V-necked jumper with its multicoloured diamond pattern was significantly louder than Frank's muted monochrome, but both sported the same logo of finest Scottish cashmere.

A caddy was assigned to Graham, but Frank chose to carry his own clubs as they strolled out into the winter sunshine towards the first tee.

'Heads or tails?' Graham produced a gold Krugerrand and waited for Frank to call.

'Tails,' he said.

The coin spun in the air, catching the sunlight, and landed heads up on the back of Graham's broad, freckled hand.

'My lucky day!' He smiled and pocketed the coin in his pale yellow trousers.

Graham selected a blunt-nosed driver from the cylindrical bag and made a few practice sweeps. *Swish. Swish.* The scent of torn grass filled the air, hints of camomile and mint. He grunted and stepped forward to the tee. A tall man, his Dutch heritage showing in his fair hair and pale skin, he had a smooth, elegant swing.

Thwack.

Frank put a hand to his forehead, shielding his eyes from the sun, following the dimpled white sphere as it flew into the sky, described a graceful arc, cleared the fairway and plopped onto the edge of the distant green.

'Well played, sir.' The caddy got his congratulations in first.

'Nice shot,' Frank added.

Graham smiled. 'Come on then, let's see what you're made of.'

Frank selected a snub-nosed driver. As he prepared to take the shot, a helicopter banked overhead, blades whirring as it prepared to land on the hotel roof. The scar on Frank's left leg began to throb and a tremor ran up through his body and down his arms. The shaft slipped through shaking hands and he let the club fall, wiping clammy palms on his beige trousers.

Buying time, Frank swapped the wooden-headed driver for a hybrid club. Graham was watching him closely now, not yet impatient, but curious, assessing his reaction to the helicopter, his decision to change woods.

Frank fluffed the strike and the ball skittered sideways into the rough.

'Bad luck.' Graham set off after his own ball, the caddy trotting behind.

Nothing to do with luck. Frank had no memory of the helicopter crash – there was a black hole where his memory should be – but he did remember what led up to it. A crippling, paralysing fear overcame him whenever he thought about his narrow escape. He could never speak about it. No one else knew his part in the events leading up to it. No one except Jaqueline Silver.

It took Frank a chip and two more drives to reach the green where an imbalanced putter caused him to overshoot the target on an easy putt.

'Not your day today, Frank?'

Forcing a smile, suppressing his rising irritation at Graham's concern, he finally dropped the ball into the first hole. Seventeen more to go, and his future was still on the line.

The caddy maintained a respectful distance behind them as they strolled round the lake.

The second and third holes were a mess, but by the fourth he had recovered his equilibrium and on the fifth he managed par while Graham had to start again when his ball missed the island green and plopped into the lake.

Frank put a spin on the ball at the sixth hole. He watched with satisfaction as it curved round the dog leg, avoiding the bunkers, and dropped neatly onto the green. An easy putt and two under par.

Graham sank his shot. 'Looks as if you were just out of practice, Frank.'

'A little rusty, yes.'

'Back on form now, though.'

Frank basked in the warmth of approbation.

'Good, I like competition.'

The real conversation started at the ninth hole.

'So, Frank, which part of the Zagrovyl business interests you most?'

'The Green Energy Division.'

Graham lowered his club without taking the shot. 'You surprise me.' He cast Frank a sideways look. 'It's the smallest and worst-performing division in the company.'

'I like a challenge.' Basic chemicals, the core of Zagrovyl operations, might be essential to modern life, but it was a low-margin cyclical business. Not the sort that excited investors. The share price had risen since Graham became president of Zagrovyl global operations and started making radical changes. Frank had done his homework. He took his shot. 'Zagrovyl's future is green.' And that was where the ball landed. Perfect.

'A nice slogan, but what does it mean in practice?'

Careful. The slogan was Graham's. Best not to offend with what he really thought. Frank waited as Graham played. The ball landed close to his.

'What does it mean to you, Graham?'

Graham led on up the fairway.

'Our world is at crisis point,' he said. 'We can't go on living the way we live, doing the things we do. Unless we reduce our reliance on fossil fuels, limit the amount of carbon dioxide we produce, there will be a catastrophe.' They reached the green and he waited as Frank sank his shot. 'Temperatures are hotting up and the deserts are expanding. Glaciers are melting and sea levels are rising. Weather patterns are changing. Our cities will soon be inundated, and we'll be forced to move inland.' Graham selected a putter. Plunk. The ball missed the hole, sat on the lip. 'We'll run out of arable land to grow food. The Gulf Stream will change course and Europe will enter a new ice age. We need a gestalt shift, a mindset change, a leap of faith.' Graham sank his ball with a tap. 'You trained as an economist, right?'

Frank had wanted to study music, but his father had insisted he do hard science or something more likely to provide him with gainful employment. Economics was a miserable compromise. 'Yes.' He collected Graham's ball from the hole and handed it to him.

'People act selfishly, they consume unnecessarily, growth comes at the expense of sustainability. How do we change that?'

'Rare earth metals can change that.'

Graham started walking. Frank hefted his clubs and hurried after him.

At the next hole, Graham made a powerful swing, sending the ball into the bunker just short of the green. 'Damn!'

'Bad luck.' *Thump!* Frank's shot soared over both bunker and green, landing on the rough just beyond. Not as good as a hole in one, but nicely placed for another shot on par.

He followed Graham to the bunker and drew perpendicular lines in the sand. 'Time.' He pointed to the horizontal axis. 'And money.' The vertical axis. 'Here's the price of rare earths from China.' He drew a line that sloped steeply upwards from left to right. 'Prices have risen a hundredfold in the last twelve months, and the rate of rise shows no sign of slowing down.' Not quite true; he was gambling on the peak having already passed. 'The

Green Energy Division relies on stuff that comes from China. Neodymium, dysprosium, praseodymium, cerium and europium prices have increased to stupid levels.' He paused to let Graham chip his ball onto the green. 'We can't be held to ransom, slaves to a monopoly. Someone needs to sort out the supply chain.'

Graham stopped to look at him, then walked on.

With a birdie at the eighteenth, Frank edged ahead. A twist of irritation played across Graham's mouth. A misjudgement? Should he have fluffed the shot and let his boss win?

They turned to face one another.

'Well played, sir.' Graham extended a hand. 'So, you think you can fix this rare earth supply mess?'

'I'm confident of it.'

'Hmmm. There's one condition.'

'Name it.'

'Do you have children, Frank?'

'Yes.' Not that he ever saw them.

'I became a grandfather last year. That beautiful child has changed my life. Thinking about what sort of world she will grow up in. How the decisions we make today will affect her tomorrow. What sort of men she will meet as she grows up.'

Frank's heart missed a beat.

'Harassment claims are nasty things. One person's word against another. Whatever the true facts of the case, it never ends well.' Graham handed his putter to the caddy and waved him away. 'Society has changed, Frank, and you need to change with it. You're a red-blooded male, but you are not an animal. Women at work expect and deserve to be treated with respect. You don't need to like it, you just need to act like you believe it.'

Frank clamped his teeth together to stop the riposte bubbling up from inside.

'The easiest thing is to offer a whacking great financial settlement to make this mess of yours go away. But, against my better judgement, I'm willing to fight it, to restore your reputation.'

Frank bowed his head to hide the anger flashing from his eyes. Between gritted teeth he managed a soft reply. 'Thank you, Graham.'

'I need a man in China. A lateral thinker, someone who can operate outside normal boundaries. Someone who knows when the ends justify the means. I think you might be that man. Are you with me, Frank?'

'I'm with you, Graham.'

'I'll give you a year to sort out the rare earth supply chain.'

If anyone could do it, Frank Good could.

'If you succeed, you'll replace the VP of the Green Energy Division.'

Vice president. Frank felt his chest swell.

'I'm putting my own reputation on the line here, Frank. Don't let me down.'

'You can rely on me, Graham.'

'You have a month to put your affairs in order before you relocate to Shanghai.'

Escape from moribund Teesside to new Eastern promise.

'Now, what do you say to a G&T at the nineteenth to seal the deal?'

PART VII
JANUARY

Brae, Shetland, Scotland

The wind howled across Yell Sound and into Sullom Voe. The small plane from Aberdeen, buffeted by the gale, made two attempts to land at Scatsta airport before being diverted to Sumburgh, fifty miles to the south.

Jaq made it as far as her lodgings in Brae before taking the decision.

Dan's phone was dead, his LinkedIn profile deleted. It was as if he'd never existed.

Except for the coded message.

She'd sat with her student in his Shanghai apartment as he begged her for help, and she'd misunderstood and ignored him. She'd seen only what she wanted to see, abandoned him in his moment of need.

She'd taken the easy decision, just like before.

You've done what you can, others will care for him now.

They lied. But this time, she had a chance to put it right.

The call to Norse Energy didn't go well. She had to leave but couldn't tell them why or for how long. She certainly couldn't tell anyone where she was going, which made the call from Vikram even worse – bridges well and truly burnt. And then she was trapped. The flights leaving the island were booked up for days, so Jaq took a bus to Lerwick and caught the overnight ferry to Aberdeen. From there she took a train to London and booked the earliest available flight to Shanghai.

The only seat left on the plane was near the back. As she turned right instead of left, she glanced longingly at the front of the cabin.

How smug she'd been last time she flew to China, sitting up there in business class, sipping champagne. Spoilt for life.

There was no overhead locker room left and she was forced to put her case under the seat in front. In the middle of a group of five seats, to her left were an American couple, large in girth, height and voice. In the throes of a major dispute, their raised voices attracted attention from all sides. To her right a pair of Chinese businessmen were vying for supremacy in a throat-clearing competition. The one closest to her appeared to be winning. The endless supply of phlegm didn't bode well for the flight.

Immediately after take-off, the man in front reclined his seat as far as it would go, strands of long greasy hair spilling over the top onto Jaq's in-flight entertainment screen. Not that it made much difference to her viewing; the system wasn't working in her section of the plane, which caused the American couple to redirect their wrath at the flight attendant, and a grumpy child behind her to alternate between kicking her seat and screaming in her ear.

Far too cramped to get her laptop out, she settled for a notebook and pencil, going over the numbers she'd written down.

71-71.

Atomic number 71. Lutetium. One of the rare earths, a silvery-white metal. Not so rare – more abundant than silver – but sparsely distributed throughout rocks also containing yttrium. Used as a catalyst in the petrochemical industry, cracking crude oil to make useful products. Lutetium-176, one of the isotopes, has a half-life of 38 billion years, useful in cancer therapy and in dating asteroids. Symbol: Lu.

Lulu.

53-61-76-52-75.

Atomic number 53. Iodine, a superb disinfectant. Symbol: I.

61. Promethium, another rare earth, highly radioactive. Symbol: Pm.

76. Osmium, the densest element found in nature, a hard, brittle, blue-black metal. Symbol: Os.

52. Tellurium, a metal easily absorbed by the human body, causing garlic breath. Symbol: Te.

75. Rhenium, one of the rarest elements in the earth's crust. Symbol: Re.

I Pm Os Te Re.

Ipmostere.

Imposter.

Lulu is an imposter. *Sim, senhor.* That much she'd already worked out for herself. Slowly, far too slowly. When the first story, that Lulu was Dan's sister, began to unravel, Jaq had been too quick to jump to the conclusion that they were lovers. She'd been suspicious from the start, when Lulu came to meet her instead of Dan. She'd let her guard down, her normal common sense distorted by the story of his disappearance.

20-7-73-44-16-90-68.

Atomic number 20, calcium, a soft grey metal, the fifth most abundant element in the earth's crust. Symbol: Ca.

7, nitrogen, a gas that makes up 80% of the air we breathe, symbol: N.

73, tantalum, a rare, hard, blue-grey, lustrous metal used in mobile phones, DVD players, video game systems and computers. Symbol: Ta.

44, ruthenium, a silvery-white metal found with platinum. Symbol: Ru.

16, sulphur, brimstone, the foul-smelling 'burning stone'. Symbol: S.

90, thorium, a radioactive metal, more abundant than uranium, co-fuel for future nuclear reactors in China. Symbol: Th.

68, erbium, a rare earth metal used in lasers. Symbol: Er.

20 Ca, 7 N, 73 Ta, 44 Ru, 16 S, 90 Th, 68 Er.

Ca N Ta Ru S Th Er.

Can't trust her.

Couldn't get clearer than that. Lulu was one person Jaq would not be contacting when she arrived back in Shanghai. Once bitten, twice shy.

7-8-15-8-3-58.

    7, nitrogen, N.

    8, oxygen, O.

    15, phosphorus, P.

    8, oxygen, O.

    3, lithium, Li.

    58, cerium, Ce.

    N O P O Li Ce.

No police.

Yes, that also figured. Jaq's only contact with the authorities had been the tall policeman with perfect English who ran her out of town. Yan Bing, the recently appointed head of the Art Police, his photo was everywhere, posing with Ming vases and silk paintings, the treasures of China recovered for the nation. So, what had he been doing in Shingbo? And why had he interfered with her Krixo investigation?

9-53-60-74-47-7.

9	*fluorine*	F
53	*iodine*	I
60	*neodymium*	Nd
74	*tungsten*	W
47	*silver*	Ag
7	*nitrogen*	N

F I Nd W Ag N.

    Find Wang.

Wang, as in the Chinese boss of Krixo?

59-8-52-43-54-3-7.

59	praseodymium	Pr
8	oxygen	O
52	tellurium	Te
43	technetium	Tc
54	xenon	Xe
3	lithium	Li
7	nitrogen	N

Pr O Te Tc Xe Li N.
Protetc XeLiN.
Protect Xe Lin.

Something about the name Xe Lin had rung a bell. On the train from Aberdeen, she typed it into a search engine. Two thousand hits. She tried Xe Lin and Ning Dan. Still hundreds of hits. What about Xe Lin and Krixo?

Claro. There it was.

Dr Xe Lin, PhD in chemistry from Teesside University, supervisor Charles Clark, now research director at Krixo. What was her connection with Dan? Judging by the dates, they were contemporaries at Teesside University. Had their paths crossed? When Jaq asked about Krixo, had Dan realised he knew their research director? Had he decided to go and see Xe Lin in person?

Or had he met a monk on a train and gone to an island monastery?

As she couldn't reach him by phone or email, there was only one way to find out.

Shanghai, China

The immigration official put up a hand to stop the next passenger from advancing. She switched her booth light to red, picked up the phone and dialled.

'*Ni hao.*'

'Yes? What is it?' The deep male voice was brusque.

'You asked to be informed of certain arrivals.'

'Who?' The head of the Art Police sounded bored, impatient.

'Number forty-seven. Arrived a few minutes ago.'

'Any problems?' A spark of interest.

'No problems.'

'Good.' Yan Bing's voice softened for a moment. 'Well done. Border control keeps China safe.' The line went dead.

After a moment of pleasant reflection, the official switched her booth light to green and waved the next passenger forward.

In the arrivals hall, Bluetooth earpieces were winking.

The square-faced driver scanned the emerging passengers. It wasn't an easy job – Westerners all looked the same – but he spotted No. 47 without too much difficulty.

He touched his earpiece twice for the others to stand down and followed at a safe distance.

Shanghai, China

The balcony of the old Spanish signal tower overlooked the busy Huangpu river. A flat barge, piled high with sand, chugged round the bend, trailing a cloud of red-gold glitter. Faster barges gave it a wide berth, hurrying to supply the massive cranes of Pudong with cement and gravel, wood and steel, copper and glass, all racing to add another skyscraper to the Shanghai skyline. The perfect view for an engineer trying to stay awake.

Unable to sleep on the overnight flight, crammed in between noisy travellers in cramped and uncomfortable seats, Jaq felt wretched. Immigration had taken forever; she was among the last to disembark and the queue moved at a snail's pace. Avoiding the expensive Maglev, she took a bus from the airport to a mid-price hotel in the suburbs. A far cry from the luxury that Sophie Clark had enabled. After a shower, it took all her willpower not to lie down on the bed, not to slip between smooth sheets, not to close her eyes. Her body was in turmoil, biological alarms screaming for sleep. Her period had started, and her lower back ached. Everything ached. What harm could there be in a short nap? So tempting. And the worst way to prolong the discombobulation. Sleep now would come too late and too briefly to do anything except befuddle. Best to keep going, hit the wall of weariness and punch through, go with the light and reset the body clock by delaying sleep until it was night again, China time.

She dressed in clean clothes and walked to the metro, changing twice to get to a more familiar part of town. Her body needed to move and stretch after being confined for so long, but her brain had been replaced with cotton wool somewhere over Mongolia. Every step was a mental as well as physical effort.

She walked as far as Huangpu Park at the end of the Bund, where she was confronted by an abstract concrete monument: three giant rifle barrels, with their tips meeting high above her. Dizzy from looking up, she sat on a step to study the bas-relief at the bottom. A monument to the people's heroes, the plaque told her, to those who died in wars and the victims of natural disasters. It didn't mention the man-made disasters.

Heavy traffic rumbled on Zhongshan Road behind her. Fog limited the view beyond the river. She could just make out the skyscrapers of Pudong disappearing into a grey sky. Her eyelids began to droop. Get up. Keep moving. Every movement was in slow motion, the air a soup of cold treacle.

The smell of roasting coffee drew her to the old Spanish signal tower – a small oval building made of alternating red and white stone. The slim tower, topped by a crow's nest and mast, had been converted into a café and bar.

She took a seat with a view of the river and ordered a double espresso. A poster caught her eye: a louche-looking group of Western men dressed in dinner jackets with dress shirts open and bow ties suggestively untied. She stood up and inspected the poster for the launch of Hop!, a new brand of light beer for women. She recognised the fake priest from her previous flight, Timur, one of five strippers. The Masters of Disguise were going on a pan-China tour. So, he'd got the job after all.

The purple-bordered card was still in her silver case. In different circumstances she might have called him. But right now, she had more pressing matters to attend to.

She called SEITA.

Gateshead, England

A black limousine cruised over the Tyne Bridge and pulled up outside the glittering snail shell of Sage Gateshead, its tinted glass lit up from within. The chauffeur sprang out, opening the door for his female passenger – pink stiletto heels followed by long bare legs, a short cream dress and white fur stole – and then for her more soberly dressed companion.

'Have a great evening,' PK said, touching his cap. 'I'll be waiting out here from nine.'

Frank ignored him. Although he always asked for PK by name when he booked with Chariot Cars, it didn't mean he was obliged to make conversation with his regular driver. PK was a reliable man of few words and boundless discretion.

Frank took Sophie's arm and led the way towards the auditorium.

'Are you sure I'll like it?' Sophie hesitated outside the revolving door. 'I've never been to a classical music concert before.'

Frank pushed ahead. 'What harm does it do to try?'

In the mood to celebrate, he checked his pockets for the ring. Plan C. Sophie would come to Shanghai with him. As his wife. His rich and beautiful wife. Not exactly cultured, but he could change that.

He'd selected the easiest programme he could find, the musical equivalent of baby milk with soft white bread, no crusts and a little crash-bang-wallop tomfoolery to help the paps down. God give him strength: *Classical Music's Greatest Hits* was not the programme he would have chosen, given a free hand.

One drink at the bar – a double Bloody Mary for Frank and a large Chardonnay for Sophie, the same on order for the interval – and he began to feel a little more optimistic as they took their seats in the familiar wood-clad auditorium.

'How will I know when to clap?' Sophie asked.

Frank shuddered. 'Just don't, OK?' Nothing worse than an audience who couldn't count and applauded between movements, breaking the spell, ruining the magic. 'Follow my lead.'

At the interval, Sophie went to the bathroom while Frank collected the drinks from the bar and took them to a shelf overlooking the river.

The melee at the bar was reflected in the glass. Depressing to see how popular this concert was proving. Compared to the superb Baroque season he'd attended last year, the audience was both larger and younger. And clearly stupider.

Frank looked out at the dark river and illuminated bridge, now a shade of magenta, and his own reflection in the curved glass. A striking Chinese woman met his eyes and kept her gaze fixed on him as she approached from behind, swaying on killer heels, her blue sheath dress with thigh-high split tight on her body as she moved. She came so close to him that he could feel the heat from her body, smell her perfume with hints of lavender. He didn't move away. *Take your time, Sophie.*

'Your friend,' she said. 'Tell her to be more careful.'

Frank turned and appraised the stranger. Even more desirable in the flesh than her reflection. Pulsating with repressed desire. Or anger. Hello, what was all this about? Some sort of catfight in the toilets? Had Sophie trodden on someone's lipstick, spilled their face powder, nudged an arm while they were applying mascara?

'Pardon?'

'Is this hers?' The Chinese woman extended a small hand towards the large glass of white wine, the short fingernails painted a shade of blue that complemented her satin dress.

Without waiting for a reply, she curled her slim fingers around the stem, raised it to her crimson lips and slowly, deliberately, her eyes never leaving his, took a long sip.

Frank was lost for words.

'It's not nice to take other people's things, is it?' She placed the glass back on the shelf, a smudge of lipstick on the rim, before opening a black sequined purse and removing a coin. 'You have to pay for the things you steal.' She dropped the coin into the wine. A little crown of golden liquid formed and then plopped back. 'Or better still, give them back.' She spat into the wine, a stream of saliva coalescing into a fat globule that bobbed to the surface.

The interval bell rang, and she was gone.

Frank remained at the window, gripping the rail. Where the hell was Sophie? What sort of trouble was she mixed up in? This was not going to plan, not at all. If she was as rich as he suspected, he was willing to overlook the mysterious case of a vanishing factory. But what else was she keeping secret? He moved away from the sullied wine glass and downed his vodka.

The second bell rang.

If Sophie didn't come back in the next five minutes, he was tempted to return to his seat without her. It was perfectly obvious she had a tin ear, although she seemed pleased when she recognised a tune. '*Platoon!*' she whispered excitedly after Samuel Barber's interminable adagio for strings. '*Elvira Madigan!*' Truth be told, he could happily give the second half a miss; there was something profoundly depressing about a meal that consisted of nothing but puddings, only so many times the bloody lark could ascend. But he wasn't here to enjoy himself, he was here to tighten his hold on an heiress.

He strode to the entrance of the women's toilets and accosted a middle-aged woman as she left. 'My companion,' he said and pointed inside. 'Can you check if she's OK?'

'No one there,' she said. 'I'm the last out.'

The third bell rang.

'Oops, better hurry.' She bustled past him.

Frank found a steward and explained his plight. She entered the toilet. He heard her knocking on the door of a cubicle.

And then she screamed.

Mount Putuo, China

The giant statue of Guanyin towered above a sea the colour of mud. The gender-bending deity gleamed after an ill-judged regilding, the bright acid gold clashing with the subdued greens of the tropical vegetation and turbid sea below. Bodhisattva Avalokiteshvara shone with a harsh quality of mercy.

Jaq's head ached, and her eyes burned. She'd returned to her hotel too tired to seek dinner and fallen asleep. With the result that she woke at midnight, tossing and turning, hunger pains gnawing at her stomach, drifting off just as an alarm pierced her muddled dreams with a shrill peal.

The journey to the island had been easier than Jaq had expected, a bus most of the way and then a short ferry ride, a trip she could easily have managed herself. But now she was saddled with Chang En, English name Brad. If he was named after the actor Brad Pitt, it had been an ironic appellation. She quickly developed an antipathy towards her SEITA interpreter, and as far as she could tell, the feeling was wholly mutual. One of the first truly overweight Chinese men she had ever met, there was something floppy about him that went beyond his paunch. Everything she said made him screw his face up with puzzlement or cause him to break into peals of high-pitched laughter. When he spoke, it was to trot out stock phrases, whether appropriate or not. He put her in mind of a weak-minded sloth. And moved at the same speed.

Brad the Sloth slept through the bus journey and waited until they were on a crowded ferry before explaining to her that most of Shanghai and Ningbo would be converging on the island tonight for a grand karaoke party on one-thousand-step beach. This crowd were going to make the full-moon parties of Ko Pha-Ngan in Thailand look exclusive and refined.

She had imagined Dan in a tranquil place, empty except for a few monks, silent apart from the tinkling of temple bells, remote from the city with only the scent of wood fires and incense. Had she known it was a crowded tourist trap, she would have reconsidered.

The Sloth ushered Jaq onto a tour group that involved traipsing from one monument to another. He translated the local guide's animated descriptions into a monotone, a litany of dates and periods: 'Built in Ming Dynasty, 1368–1574. Renovated in Qing Dynasty, 1904.' Everywhere they went, hundreds of people went with them. The temples had been refurbished in faux ancient style.

Jaq refused to join the cable car ride. The peak was less than three hundred metres high; she could have bounded to the top of the island in less than the time it would take to buy a ticket. If there weren't so many people on every step, every path, she would have done just that. The Sloth cleared his throat and spat into the undergrowth.

'Very beautiful view.'

'I don't want to be with a tourist group. I want to talk to the people who live here.'

The Sloth scowled. 'If a stranger approach to you and starts up a small talk with you, then be vigilant.'

The chances of her striking up a conversation with anyone were vanishingly small. The plan had seemed sensible. Start with the last-known place Dan had been. Said he'd been. He'd sent her a coded message. A cry for help. He was being held prisoner, against his will. She had to find him, find a way to talk to him.

'I want to find an active monastery.'

'Remember, no free lunch.'

The Sloth was more of an impediment than a help.

A monk dawdled outside the Buddhism museum, a swarthy man in a shiny orange robe. Jaq nudged The Sloth in the ribs. 'Let's ask that monk.'

'Often too good to be true.' Chang En giggled. 'Fake monk.'

'So, where are the real monks?'

'Four sacred mountains,' he intoned. 'Mount Putuo the smallest. Maybe real monks at Mount Wutai or Mount Jiuhua or Mount Emei.'

'Let's go back to Shanghai.'

'Later.' The first sign of emotion. 'After the party.'

'We're leaving,' she said. 'Now.'

'Are you sure?'

The only thing that Jaq was sure of was that they were in the wrong place. Dan was not here; she knew it in her bones.

Gateshead, England

'There now, that's the bleeding stopped.' The young first-aider secured the bandage on Sophie's upper arm. 'The ambulance is on its way.'

'No need.' Sophie's voice was a whisper. 'I'm OK.'

'You are most certainly not OK,' Frank snapped. He loathed the sight of blood, and there had been an awful lot of it. Her white dress and her fur stole were covered in the stuff. 'This is a police matter. My companion was attacked!'

'No police.' Sophie put up her good hand. 'It was an accident.'

'An accident?' The first-aider bit his lip. 'Can you tell me what happened?'

'There was a Chinese woman . . .' Frank started.

'Frank, NO!' The power of Sophie's protest took him by surprise. 'No one else was involved. I cut myself. By accident.'

The first-aider opened his eyes wide. 'There's something sharp? In the toilets?'

Sophie's eyes darted around, searching for an excuse. 'My nail scissors . . .' It sounded impossibly lame to Frank, but it seemed to reassure the first-aider, who was presumably most concerned about liability. 'They slipped.'

'You must go to hospital. You may need stitches.'

'I'll go to A&E. We have a car.' She looked at Frank, he nodded and dialled Chariot Cars. 'No need for an ambulance,' she said.

The first-aider frowned and bit his lip. 'Well, if you are sure.'

'I'm sure.'

The limo drew up outside and PK rushed to assist Sophie, exclaiming with horror as he helped her inside. She collapsed onto Frank's lap inside the car.

'Accident and Emergency!' Frank ordered.

'I just want to go home.'

'Be sensible, Sophie. You lost a lot of blood. That wound,' he shuddered, 'needs attention.'

'I can't.' She was sobbing now. 'Frank, I'm scared. She tried to kill me!'

Frank held her close. His favourite dinner jacket would be ruined, but needs must. 'A Chinese woman in blue?'

'You saw her too? Wang must have sent her.'

Wang? The mysterious joint venture partner. The Chinese owner of 51% of Krixo.

'But why?'

Sophie let out a moan. 'Please, Frank, take me home.'

'I'll take you home,' Frank said. 'But only if you agree that we call a doctor when we get to your house, OK?'

'Can we go to yours instead?'

Not the circumstances he'd envisaged, but a bird in the hand . . .

'Of course.' He barked instructions at PK.

'What happened, Sophie?' he asked. 'What's all this about?'

But Sophie was already fast asleep.

Shanghai, China

The Shanghai traffic roared past the hotel, making the thin walls vibrate. In Jaq's hotel room, the only window looked out on to a blank wall and the bedroom grew smaller as the night progressed, as if the walls were creeping inward, squeezing, suffocating.

Unable to sleep, awake at 2 a.m. for the second night running, Jaq got out of bed and dressed. She put on her running shoes and shorts and pulled a sweatshirt over her vest before heading out into the night. The streets were still full of traffic, and the pavement blocks too short to get up to a decent speed. She decided to head back to the river.

The metro was half-empty at this hour of the morning. A bunch of well-dressed twenty-something party animals held a drunken conversation at shouting pitch, ears still deafened from high-decibel music, pupils dilated with narcotics. A few men and women in drab clothing, on their way to work, gazed on impassively.

The river didn't sleep either. Barges shuffled up and down, some with lights, some without. She was drawn to the Bund like a magnet, a place where she could move freely, could think. As she ran past the Spanish tower for the third time, a barge came round the bend in the river and caught her attention.

Initially professional interest. The barge carried the sort of equipment she was familiar with: long silver absorption columns laid on their side, glass-lined reactors – the cobalt blue of the glass just visible against the rust red of the carbon steel – carbon block heat exchangers, cylindrical tanks. Such a smart way to move heavy equipment. Too wide for rail, transporting on land meant damage to roads, but barges just floated along. And could be any size. Why didn't they sink?

Steel is eight times as heavy as water. A tonne of steel, in a solid block, a cube measuring 50 centimetres on each side, will sink like a stone. Flatten it into a sheet, 5 metres long, 5 metres wide and 5 millimetres thick, and it will still tip and plummet to the bottom of the river. But bend the sides of the sheet 2 metres in four directions and close the gaps at the corners, and suddenly it floats. Why?

Enter Archimedes and his bathtub. When the Greek philosopher immersed himself in a bath that was already full of water, he displaced not his weight, but his own volume in water.

The volume of our steel cube is 0.5m x 0.5m x 0.5m = 0.125m³. One tonne of steel displaces 0.125m³ of water, which weighs only 125kg. The steel is denser than water, so it sinks. The volume of the flat sheet is 5m x 5m x 0.005m = 0.125m, exactly the same, so it sinks too. But the volume of the crude boat you make by bending up the sides is 2m x 1m x 1m = 2m³, and that could displace 2 tonnes of water, which is more than it weighs. Hey presto! It floats. In fact, the water will come to halfway up the side, and you can carry up to an extra tonne of cargo before it will sink.

As dawn broke over Shanghai and the barge drew level with the Spanish tower, Jaq saw something that made her gasp. Something in the water. Someone in the water? *Diabos me levem.*

Alarmed, Jaq ran back along the pedestrian walkway, past the Spanish tower until she found the steps, stumbling down the worn stone treads, grasping the iron handrail to right herself. She glanced right and left. The river was busy. The barge was moving slowly towards her.

She was aware of warmth beside her.

'Hello, Jaq Silver.'

Timur, looking even better in a dinner suit than a priest's robe. Now was not the time for distractions.

She acknowledged him with a nod of her head, returning her eyes to the river. 'I thought I saw someone in the river.'

'That would be Holger.'

She saw movement again, a flash of white hair, then a curling arm, elbow high, fingers pointed as they entered the water. She hadn't imagined it. There really was a man swimming front crawl across the Huangpu river. A madman. She stood transfixed, watching the evenly spaced splashes as he advanced towards them, an exceptionally strong swimmer.

'Who the hell is Holger?'

'The Swedish water baby. He always goes for a dip in the morning.'

She thought back to the photo on the poster, the baby-faced giant with white hair. Another one of the Masters of Disguise.

The barge drew level and blocked the swimmer from view. Something about the equipment looked familiar. As Jaq moved to get a better look, a ferry set off from the pier. With the barge in between, it was unlikely the swimmer had seen it.

'Timur, look.'

Holger had passed through the wake of the barge, swimming strongly. On a collision course with the ferry.

'Shit.' Timur had seen the danger, too. He jumped down onto the boardwalk, put two fingers to his lips and whistled.

She covered her eyes as the sharp steel prow approached the path of the unprotected man. When she looked again, Timur, and the man in the water, were gone.

Teesside, England

Frank cradled Sophie's head against his chest in the back of the chauffeur-driven limo as they sped down the A19 from Gateshead to Stockton. Her skin was pale, but her breathing was steady as she slept. He called a consultant he knew from the golf club and persuaded him to make a house call.

PK helped Frank to get Sophie up the stairs and she was awake by the time the doctor arrived. The old sawbones caused no end of trouble, but after cleaning the wound and checking her blood pressure, he eventually accepted her refusal to go to hospital. Sophie slept in Frank's bed upstairs and he took the sofa downstairs. Not so much out of propriety, but because of the noises she made as she slept, low groans of pain and little yelps of terror.

He woke to find her downstairs, barefoot and wearing one of his shirts. She looked younger, smaller, more vulnerable without clothes, heels and make-up, and he felt an unfamiliar surge of affection.

He sat up and ran his fingers through his hair.

'How are you feeling?'

'Better,' she said.

He slid on his dressing gown and pointed to a stool at the breakfast bar as he filled the kettle.

'Coffee? Tea?'

She winced as she pulled herself onto the seat.

'Hot chocolate,' she said.

Frank spooned the powder into a mug, added milk and put it in the microwave before making his own coffee.

'Who was that woman?' he asked. 'The one in the blue dress?'

'I don't know who you are talking about.'

He handed her the steaming mug.

'She accused you of stealing something.'

'A case of mistaken identity,' Sophie said, sipping the hot drink.

'She said you should give it back. What did she mean?'

'I have no idea what she was talking about.'

She met his eyes. Sophie was a remarkably good liar.

'Last night, you said that Wang must have sent her.'

'I was in shock. Confused.'

'If you want my help, you're going to have to level with me. Who is Wang?'

She sipped her drink in obstinate silence.

'Is Wang connected to Krixo? Does this have something to do with the Chinese joint venture?'

Sophie slammed the mug onto the counter.

'Why would your own company send someone to threaten you? What do they want? To scare you? To kill you?'

'Stop!' She slid down from the stool and faced him, angry now.

'What have you stolen, Sophie?'

She turned on her heel, bare feet squealing on the laminate floor. 'I need to wash.'

Frank waited for the click of the bathroom lock and the splash of water before opening his laptop. Whatever mess Sophie had got herself into, chances were it would take more than his power shower to wash it away.

Shanghai, China

Standing at the edge of the Huangpu river, Jaq doubled over and clutched at her stomach. Had she just watched a man drown?

With daylight came noise. The rumble of traffic was now a roar. People moving on the Bund, a group of elderly women doing tai chi. Where was Timur? What had Holger been doing in the water? And what did it have to do with a barge full of factory equipment? She stared at the barge as it receded into the mist. She rubbed her eyes. When she looked again, the barge was gone. Was she so tired, so jet-lagged, she had started to hallucinate? Had she imagined the whole episode? She scanned the water. Full of boats, but no sign of a swimmer. She turned away from the river.

When Timur swam up behind her, she almost lost her balance and joined him in the water.

'Pass me a towel, Jaq Silver.' He pointed to where she had last seen him crouching down. Tucked away under the pier was his dinner jacket and a sports bag.

Too startled to do anything other than obey, she found a towel and handed it down. Timur pivoted himself onto the wooden ledge in a smooth movement. His dress shirt clung to his chest as he held out a hand for Holger.

If Timur was a beautiful man, Holger was extraordinary. The Swedish water baby was a perfectly proportioned giant, tall with broad shoulders, a swimmer's well-developed chest, lean stomach and narrow hips, skin so white it was almost translucent, hair like a sable shaving brush.

'Hello, Jaq Silver,' Holger said. 'I've heard lots about you.' He took the towel from Timur and wrapped it around his hips. 'Thanks for the warning.'

'I thought you'd drowned.'

'I went underwater. Those ferries have a shallow draught.'

'What were you doing in the river?'

He looked down at her and frowned, bushy white eyebrows meeting in the middle.

Timur interrupted. 'Holger likes to swim.'

'That was stupidly dangerous,' she said, unable to contain her anger. 'You both need your stomachs pumped and a tetanus shot.'

'Hot shower, cooked breakfast and warm bed?' Timur suggested.

'Sounds good to me,' said Holger and winked at her.

Timur had replaced his wet shirt with a dry dinner jacket. He climbed up from the pontoon back onto the boardwalk and held out a hand for her. She ignored it. Vaulting easily over the fence herself, she walked away, delayed shock making her suddenly furious.

Timur shouted after her. 'You're welcome to join us, Jaq Silver.'

She didn't deign to reply, striding away and giving him the finger.

Teesside, England

While Sophie showered, Frank made fresh coffee and microwaved a packet of scrambled egg. He laid two places at the kitchen bar and stuck some bread from the deep freeze into the toaster.

Sophie appeared in the doorway. 'I need to go.'

Frank pulled out a stool and pointed at the place setting.

'You need to eat. Restore your strength.'

She dragged her feet, but she followed his direction. He'd found some clothes left behind by a previous overnight guest. Rather more casual than Sophie's usual style, but with her pink stilettos and freshly applied make-up, the mask had returned.

He poured orange juice and coffee for both of them. She shook her head at the scrambled egg and opened a jar of jam, spreading it thickly on her toast. A little colour began to return to her cheeks.

'How can I help you?' Frank asked.

She looked up at him with soft violet eyes. 'You would help?'

'We're in this together now, Sophie.' He laid a hand over hers.

'That means a lot.' She sipped her coffee. 'Tell me again what the woman said to you.'

'That you should be more careful. That it was wrong to steal, and you should pay for it or return what wasn't yours. What was she talking about?'

'I really don't know.' She stood up, but he grasped her shoulders and brought her to face him.

'Sophie, what happened to your father?'

As she glared at him, he recognised something in her eyes, something feral, something furtive, followed by a veiling that was not grief: far more calculating than that.

'Wang poisoned him.'

He released her arms but held her gaze.

'Dad was fine when I left China.' She rubbed her wrists. 'But then things seemed to change. He would call at odd hours. He seemed worried, distracted, unhappy.' She put up a hand to smooth her hair. 'Afraid.' She sighed. 'By the time he flew to England, he was already ill. He went to hospital, but they couldn't find out what was wrong, couldn't help him.' Her voice broke and she covered her eyes. 'He never came out again.'

'I'm sorry.'

Frank handed her a clean handkerchief. The staccato of her sobs put him in mind of a piece of music. He put an arm around Sophie's shaking shoulders, holding her close as she wept, silently replaying The Basle Concerto to distract himself.

By the time he reached the end of Stravinsky's score, she was calm again.

'Sophie, what did you take that wasn't yours?'

'I don't know what you mean.'

'You stole something. What was it?'

'It wasn't me!' She stamped her foot, eyes ablaze. 'It was my father who took the jade lovers' cup.' She collapsed back onto the stool. 'Remember I told you about insurance? The cup was collateral.'

'But you sold it.'

'Dad was dying. It couldn't wait.'

'Ten million pounds.' Frank whistled through his teeth. 'You have the money?'

'Most of it.'

His eyes narrowed.

'Well, some of it . . .' She dropped her gaze. 'I had debts to clear, bills, commitments . . . Oh, God.' She pushed away her plate and dropped her head into her hands. 'What am I going to do?'

'What do they want? Money?'

She shook her head. 'No, they want the lovers' cup.'

'They want you to tell them who bought it?'

'They already know who bought it. But the buyer has vanished.'

'Sophie, you need to go to the police.'

'Never!' She slid down from the breakfast bar, wincing as she approached him. 'If I don't do exactly what they say, they'll kill me, just like they killed my father.'

Shanghai to Shingbo, China

Back at the hotel, Jaq undressed – shivering as if she had been in the filthy, dangerous water herself – washed and got into bed, but sleep eluded her.

Where to go next? What to do?

Coming to China had been unplanned, a knee-jerk reaction, a mistake, but what choice did she have? Dan was in danger. She'd missed his cry for help, ignored it for weeks. Now she understood what he'd tried to tell her, how should she respond? She couldn't go to the police; Dan had made that crystal clear.

She had several options. The first, and her original intention, had been to visit the monasteries of China until she found Dan. He wasn't in Mount Putuo, so next stop Mount Wutai or Mount Jiuhua or Mount Emei? The thought of touring China with The Sloth as translator made her heart sink. It was pointless anyway. Lulu had been lying and Dan dissembling. The whole monastery story had been a ruse to get her to back off and go home.

Dan had asked for her help. But not for himself. He'd asked her to find Xe Lin. The research director at Krixo. And how was she going to do that?

Her second option was to find and confront Lulu. Assuming Lulu still used the same phone number, then she should be easier to find. But what then? Lulu was an imposter. A consummate liar. Why should she help? She'd tricked Jaq before. Why would Jaq believe anything she said now?

The third was the most pointless, and the most dangerous. Go back to Shingbo. Visit the empty factory site. See if she'd missed some clue. Hope to avoid the sinister policeman, Yan Bing, and the fate of the sweet men, Mr Smiles the translator and the sharply dressed driver, who had tried to help her. But how to get there?

Call SEITA again? Spend another day with Brad the Sloth? Or try a private tourist agency? She was almost out of money. How to find someone willing to take her to an industrial estate? The taxis in Shingbo had refused. But perhaps someone from out of town wouldn't have the same problem.

Jaq dressed and returned to the hotel lobby. The receptionist smiled. 'Can I help you?'

Out with it.

'I'm looking for transport, with a driver who speaks English. It's a private day trip.'

'When?'

'Now.' Ridiculous.

'Who?'

'Just me.'

'My cousin has a motorbike.'

'He speaks English?'

'Better than me.'

'And he's available?'

'Wait.' She dialled a number and spoke rapidly, before covering the mouthpiece and looking up. 'One thousand renminbi.'

A fraction of the price of The Sloth.

'Fine.'

'Wait.' The receptionist put up a hand and listened. 'And petrol, and any tolls.'

'Sure. When can he get here?'

'You pay me.'

'Put it on the bill?'

'You pay me.'

'Card?'

'Cash.'

Jaq opened her bag and extracted her purse. She unrolled

ten 100-renminbi notes. The bundle was a lot thinner when she returned it to her bag.

'His name is Peng Ran. Everyone calls him Speedy. He's outside now.'

Speedy was as good as his name. A young man of few words and twinkling black eyes, he gave her a full-face helmet, listened to her detailed instructions and roared off the moment she hopped on the back.

It was a bright, clear day and he manoeuvred expertly through the traffic, taking back roads and shortcuts, weaving through the bottlenecks. As they accelerated onto the freeway, she leaned forward and held onto his waist. Partly for warmth – it was cold without leathers – mainly for safety. She thought about Petr, the last man she had ridden a motorbike with; he kept his body away from hers when he rode pillion. Petr was dead now. Was she leading Speedy to the same fate?

The site was exactly where she remembered it, close to the Changtai expressway and bordered by the river estuary, with a huge red-and-white-tipped chimney behind. Empty. The Krixo factory had not reappeared as magically as it had vanished.

The whole industrial estate stretched as far as the eye could see, a hive of activity, a constant stream of barges loading and unloading. New buildings had appeared even in the short time since she'd last been here. What was it that allowed China to move so fast? Streamlined regulation? Hard work? Planning? It wasn't as if it was fast and shoddy – the new infrastructure looked as good as anything in Britain. Better, in fact.

Speedy pulled off his helmet. 'This it?'

'Yup.'

'Nice,' he said, and offered her a cigarette. She refused and he lit up.

'There was a factory here once.'

He looked around. 'Not any more.'

'I need to find out what happened to it.' And more importantly, what happened to the people inside it. Dan, Xe Lin.

'What do you want me to do?'

'Can we visit all four sites around this one, ask and see if anyone knows anything?'

'Sure.' He flicked his stub and ground it out with his foot.

Jaq waited by the bike as Speedy tried one gatehouse after another.

'No joy, I'm afraid. They know something, but they are not saying anything.'

'Would money help?' Not that she had much left.

'The other foreigner tried that. It didn't go down well.'

'What other foreigner?'

'Some young guy, speaks fluent Chinese, asking questions. Looking for someone called Wang.'

Someone else was looking for the joint venture partner of Krixo. A little shiver ran down Jaq's spine.

'Did he leave a number?'

Speedy returned to the gatehouse and emerged brandishing a card.

A card with a purple border.

She pulled the silver card holder from her bag and compared cards. Same name, same number.

Timur Zolotoy. A Russian stripper.

What was he really doing in China?

Vladivostok, Russia

The mournful hoot of a ship approaching Golden Horn bay rose up to the palace high above Vladivostok. After losing the Second Opium War with Britain, Qing dynasty China was no longer able to defend itself and ceded Outer Manchuria to Russia in the 1860 Treaty of Beijing. Chinese *Hǎishēnwǎi* – 'sea cucumber cliffs' – became Russian Vladivostok.

The snow was falling again, settling on the window ledges, dusting the branches of the swaying trees of the palace where the old man sat in his rocking chair, his mouth twitching as he dreamed.

She came to him, dressed in her work clothes: high collar, long sleeves, shapeless tunic and trousers, shabby rough cotton that served only to accentuate her grace. It had been so long since he'd seen her, he'd almost forgotten how beautiful she was, still standing where he left her, in their secret place beside the lake, beckoning to him from the other side of the dam, trying to tell him something, something important. How to get to her? He had no boat. He daren't swim; the underwater currents near the hydroelectric plant were too strong. He stood still, unable to decide, unable to move, trapped in a stasis of longing.

And guilt.

'Nina, I'm sorry. I'm so sorry.'

'Good morning, Dmytry.'

He woke to the stink of incense and mealy-mouthed sanctity, a great black vulture waiting to pounce: the priest again.

'I'm not dead yet.'

'Timur asked me to look in on you.'

'Thanks.' Dmytry waved him away. 'You can go now.'

'What's he doing in China, anyway?'

'None of your business.'

'How about a game of chess?'

'Think you can beat a blind man?'

'Scared of losing? I'll let you be white.'

The clatter of resin pieces on a wooden board roused him from his fug. A game he loved and loathed in equal measure. Not a game: a fight, a battle.

Dmytry nodded. 'E4.'

The priest moved the white pawn, and then mirrored it with his black one. 'E5.'

'Nf3.'

'Nf6.'

'Petrov's defence?' Dmytry moved his fingers over the board, tracing remembered patterns. 'Let's spice this up. Nxe5.' He closed his fist around the black pawn.

'Hmm.' The priest sucked air in through his teeth. 'Have you told Timur yet?'

'If you lecture me about Timur again, I'll stop playing. Come on, it's your move.'

'Nxe4. You were speaking Chinese again, old friend.'

'When?'

'While you were sleeping.'

'Mind your own business.'

'Is there something you need to get off your chest?'

'Confess before I die? You old soul sucker. I'm not going yet.'

'Tell me, what weighs on your conscience? I can provide absolution.'

'You think you can forgive my sins? You think that if there is a God, he is so benevolent that, whatever I have done, I can just confess at the last moment and go straight to heaven?'

'The Almighty has infinite compassion, infinite wisdom.'

'And you talk an infinite amount of crap,' Dmytry said. 'Qe2.'

'Nf6.' The priest clucked his tongue. 'When were you in China? The Great Leap Forward?'

Dmytry snorted. 'Giant Slide Backward, more like.'

'Is that where you met her?'

'Met who?'

'Nina.'

Dmytry fell silent and closed his eyes and there she was in front of him, as if it was the first time.

The light was fading, just a band of pink on the horizon as the sun sank level with the fields, the mocking shadows of the stalks lengthening the stunted plants, creating the illusion of a healthy crop. The peasants were out banging pots together, scaring the birds, keeping them away from the fields, leaving the other pests to eat their fill. His throat went dry as he removed his cap with trembling fingers and knocked at the door.

Nina answered, opening the door with a frown that turned into a broad smile when she saw the basket of food he had brought. It had been a hard year, and the poor harvest was going to make things worse.

A young man, a long way from home . . . if the locals acknowledged him at all, it was with suspicion and distrust. But Nina and her father were different. Educated. Cultured. Open. Wang Jun spoke some Russian and played a Chinese variant of chess called Xiangqi which he had promised to teach Dmytry.

She led him to the hearth, where Wang Jun was already setting out the chess pieces. Her scent lingered as she disappeared behind a curtain to make tea.

To cover his beating heart and blushing neck, he inspected and admired the pieces.

'Are these jade?'

'No.' Wang Jun shook his head. 'Are you interested in jade?'

Something about the boyish enthusiasm from the older man snagged his interest.

'Yes.'

'I'm the temporary curator of a very fine collection. Ask Nina to show you sometime.'

His heart skipped a beat at her shy smile.
And that's how it all began.

Dmytry coughed, gesturing for water to ease his dry throat. He gulped it down and leaned back. 'I played chess with Nina's father – he was twice the player you are.'

'How did you like China?'

Dmytry blew through his lips. 'It's a hard life, you know, living off the land.'

People romanticise farming. They imagine lowing cattle in grass meadows, rolling fields of grain, orchards laden with fruit, forests full of game, rivers stocked with fish. Not in China. It took back-breaking labour to eke out a precarious subsistence from depleted soil and capricious rivers.

'Some people are born to it.' The priest rubbed a hand over his skull, smoothing what was left of his hair.

'What sentimental bullshit! The best you can wish for is to survive it. Natural selection. Survival of the fittest. You are born weak, you die. You become weak, you die. You need extra food to survive the spring, you die. You are reckless and break a leg, you die. You need warmth over winter, you die. It's not that you are born to be a peasant, it is just that your forefathers, hundreds of generations of peasants – small, stocky, cautious and wiry – survived. Nc6.'

'Damn!' The priest realised his mistake.

'It was hardest on the intellectuals.' People like Nina and her father turfed out of the city to toil on the land. The work was hard enough, but the insanity of the central plan made it intolerable. The peasants understood the land; the intellectuals understood the science. Everyone understood that the new policies were suicide. Everyone except those who enforced them. Or perhaps they knew and didn't care.

'Weren't the Russians there to help the Chinese modernise?'

Dmytry sighed. 'That was the worst of it. Some of us had

been through it all ourselves. We knew the dangers.' People's communes, the party exhorting the natural world to bend to the will of communist science. Had nothing been learned from the Ukrainian famine decades ago? Did anyone still take Lysenko and his pseudoscientific claptrap seriously? Discredited in Russia, and yet China rushed down the same disastrous path.

'Out-of-date Russian policies, recycled in China?'

'And some uniquely Chinese ones. Do you know how to make steel?'

'No.'

Dmytry gave a snort of bitter laughter.

'Nor did the peasants.'

Shanghai, China

Outside, the sky was dark, but the Bund was a magnificent light show. Shifting artworks displayed on the giant canvas of one skyscraper after another, each with their own rhythm, all bursting with stroboscopic pride. Jaq caught her breath. Pointlessly beautiful, like the fireworks that suddenly crackled and popped over the river, great chrysanthemums of golden sparks.

Timur had responded to her call with enthusiasm.

'Jaq Silver! I was wondering when you'd be back in touch. You want a ticket to the show?'

'Not really, I was wondering if we could meet.'

'A private dance? Fine by me.'

'Stop it.' It came out fiercer than she intended. 'I want to talk to you.'

'Sorry.' She could hear the contrition in his voice. All that crude flirting was just a cover; a more complex man was hiding under that bravado, she was sure of it. But what that complexity meant, she wasn't sure. Bad or good? Was she predisposed to like him, just because he was gorgeous? She'd made that mistake before. This time she would be more careful.

'We're rehearsing till six. Then I have a couple of hours before the show.'

He was waiting for her outside the Spanish signal tower on the Bund.

'Hungry?'

She had barely noticed until now, but she hadn't eaten all day. 'Starving.'

They crossed a busy intersection and he led the way up a flight of narrow stairs into a dimly lit room full of Chinese groups. A queue of people waited to be seated, but he went straight to the waiter, who waved them to a small table beside the window.

'Anything you don't eat, Jaq Silver?'

'I avoid endangered species, genitals and foetuses,' she said.

Timur ordered, exchanging incomprehensible pleasantries in Shanghainese with the man who poured tea into porcelain bowls.

The food came, a fiery Sichuan stew with floating chilli peppers, and Timur spooned it into their bowls.

Jaq took a mouthful. Delicious. She let the heat wash over her, the capsaicinoids in the chilli triggering the pain receptors in her mouth, quickly balanced by a flood of endorphins, nature's painkillers, with a chemical surge of happiness and well-being. She finished her bowl, helping herself to more. Clicking her chopsticks, she extracted a small bone. 'Chicken?'

'Frog.'

'To help you launch Hop!' She laughed. 'How's it going?'

He told her about the show, made it sound less sleazy than she had imagined, the pride of a performer shining through.

'Enough about me.' He flashed white teeth at her. 'Where have you been, Jaq Silver?'

'Work, you know.'

'All work and no play?'

'I did manage a day trip to Mount Putuo.' She described her visit with The Sloth in graphic detail.

Timur laughed, then put his chin in his hands and gazed at her. 'I like you,' he said. 'You're different.' He smiled. A good smile. The sort of smile that was part bashful question, part mysterious promise. Hinting at things to come. Good things. The gentle, wavering smile amplified by the desire that shone from his green eyes. Not some unspecific craving – the desire of an athlete for physical release after a race, or a near miss with a river barge. Not just the glow that follows a good meal, the warmth of a full belly lulling inhibition, hushing whispered warnings. Not just the recovery from the spicy assault of Sichuan pepper, the senses reeling from the heat, suddenly alert to new possibilities. His eyes, his lips, his body all spoke of yearning, a powerful need completely focused on her.

Careful.

She allowed his desire to wash over her like warm silk. It had been a long time since a man had looked at her like that. Too long. She gazed deep into his green eyes, jade flecked with amber, interrogated his confidence, his constancy, his integrity, waiting for him to look away first.

Crash!

Jaq jumped as a clatter of clean cutlery was thrown onto their table. '*Nǐmen xiànzài zǒule!*' A small man blocked Timur from view as he leaned over to wipe the surface. '*Ren zai deng chifan.*'

'They're busy,' Timur said, and threw down some notes. He checked his watch. 'I have to get ready for the show.'

They strolled into the velvet night, crossing over Zhongshan Road to a pedestrian walkway that ran along the Puxi side of the river, side by side, not touching, but close enough to sense the heat of the other. Jaq caught her breath at the light show, skyscrapers blazing into the night sky.

Barely aware of the promenaders who crowded the Bund, families from the country who stopped and gawped, children who skipped and sang, Shanghai sophisticates who glided past on roller-skates, the man beside her filled her thoughts.

'If you don't want to come to the show, will you meet me afterwards?'

There was a moment, a fork in the road, when she could have made a different choice, listened to the alarm bells ringing in her brain. She could have waited for him, gone for a drink in a cool Shanghai bar, told him the truth and openly enlisted his help. Perhaps then things would have turned out differently.

She put her hands to his face, feeling the light stubble, drew him towards her and kissed him. Gently at first, tentative, exploratory.

His scent was new, spearmint mixed with spice, but the rush of desire was disturbingly familiar. Everything peripheral disappeared as she moved closer, pressing her breasts against his overdeveloped pectorals, running her hands lightly over the athletic body under his coat, closing the contact, chasing the electric tingle, melting inside.

She pulled away suddenly.

'I have to go.'

'Jaq, wait . . .'

'Good luck!' she called over her shoulder, turning to hide his mobile phone as she slipped it into her bag.

Shanghai, China

The square-faced driver raised his phone and took a burst of pictures. The quality was poor, the bright lights of Pudong throwing Puxi into relative darkness, but he'd captured enough to remove any doubt.

So, suspects 47 and 69 were in cahoots. No doubt about it. He thought his boss was paranoid, that they just happened to travel on the same flight, but perhaps that's why Yan Bing was the boss and he was just a hired hand.

And what would his favourite fighter, Mico, make of all this? She had a soft spot for the 'Masters of Disguise'. She'd hired them for the Hop! tour and was attending every date throughout China. She had her favourite, that much was clear. Would she tolerate a rival?

Mico might just pay him for the information. And pay even more to make the problem go away. Nothing better than having two sources of income for the same task.

Maybe Yan Bing wasn't the only smart one.

Shanghai, China

Back in her tiny hotel room, Jaq set Timur's phone to silent – it had been ringing almost continuously since she'd got off the metro – and set about unlocking it. A six-number PIN with ten options for each number – zero to nine – meant a million possible combinations. If she entered one every six seconds, it would take her sixty-nine days to crack the code. And if the security setting was on, the phone would lock down after a handful of failed attempts. Fortunately, she'd watched him unlock it over dinner. Middle right, bottom right, repeated three times.

Her own phone rang. She ignored it. Timur had probably figured out who'd liberated the phone from his inside coat pocket. But he had a show to do, and she had a couple of hours' grace before he came after her. An engineer knows how to plan.

She connected the two phones with a short cable and started to copy his data. Flicking through the different apps, she saw that it was light on email traffic but chock-full of photos, which is where she started.

The first picture to capture her attention was a factory entrance, a large sign with three green recycling arrows inside a triangular flask: the Krixo logo. There was no doubt that Timur had been to Shingbo, and no doubt that there had been a working factory there at the time. The photos were grouped in files; the Master of Disguise was clearly a well-organised chap.

In a folder marked 'Shopping List' were high-quality pictures of museum exhibits, ancient Chinese jade: a horse, a water buffalo, a dragon, an elephant, jugs and cups, plates and bowls, carved figures. Lists of sizes and weights. Then the names and addresses of museums in Europe: Durham, Stockholm, Lisbon. Floor plans, wiring diagrams, alarm specifications.

In another folder, a set of newspaper articles.

She stared at the headline from the *Northern Echo*. The theft from Durham University Oriental Museum happened on the day she went to tell Vikram and Sophie that the Krixo factory had vanished. She remembered seeing it on the news that same evening. And suddenly a piece of the jigsaw snapped into place. Of course! The young man at Durham train station, the one she'd assumed was a student – she'd seen him again, more recently.

She clicked on the 'Swim Team' folder and flicked through the pictures. What a very beautiful group of athletes they were. A tragedy that they were reduced to stripping for money. She stopped and stared at the red-headed Adonis. No doubt about it – that was the man she'd seen on the day of the robbery.

She scratched her head. So, the Masters of Disguise were art thieves as well. Masquerading as strippers. Sounded improbable, and yet . . .

She flicked forward to 'Active'. A folder with the floor plan of the Hénán Bówùyuàn Museum in Zhengzhou. Wiring diagrams with Chinese annotations. Were the swim team also stealing to order in China, using the Hop! tour as a cover?

Or was it worse than that? The older newspaper articles were far more sinister.

CHINESE GANGS TERRORISE ENGLAND

Is there a link between the murder of a London auctioneer and that of a university professor?

New evidence has emerged that Professor John Tench – emeritus professor at Teesside University, who died in hospital from injuries sustained in a savage attack in his home – attended the controversial auction of ancient Chinese artefacts presided over in London by

auctioneer Bernard Ashley-Cooper, who was brutally murdered at his
£5 million mansion in Chelsea earlier this week.

Both men sustained multiple knife wounds and, in both cases, a
domestic pet belonging to the victim was cruelly dismembered.

Dr David Woolly, a social anthropologist at the University of
Salford, and expert in Triad gang activity, speculated that the
manner of both attacks is the hallmark of a Chinese gang known as
Lingchi. He added that the jade lovers' cup, sold by Ashley-Cooper
for £10 million, was once owned by Qianlong, the Qing dynasty
emperor notorious for executing his enemies by slow slicing: death by
one thousand cuts.

A WeChat notification flashed across the screen of the pilfered
phone.

She clicked on the app. Her heart raced at the sender's icon –
green recycling arrows inside a triangular flask – the Krixo logo.
She couldn't read the Chinese characters that made up most of
the brief message, but the arabic numerals gave a date and a time.
A meeting? Where? And why was someone from the elusive Krixo
arranging to meet with Timur? She took a picture of the message
with her phone.

Who was Timur? An athlete? A stripper? A thief? Part of a gang
of sadistic murderers? And what was his connection with Krixo?

Vladivostok, Russia

An eagle rose from the sea, wings spreading to the full two-and-a-half-metre span, dark brown feathers flanking snow-white shoulders, a silver fish writhing in its yellow talons. It soared up the hill above Vladivostok and passed over the hospice, the Palace of Death, where the old man lay on his narrow bed. As he slept the dream came again.

Nina, by the lake. Sitting this time. Something in her arms wrapped in muslin. The lovers' cup! She has the lovers' cup, and it is perfect, exactly as it was when they first met. She reaches in, detaches the first lid, the circle of flowers. She pins it to her tunic. She reaches back in, removes the second lid, the circle of fire, and holds it out to him. He is running, running, but not moving . . .

He woke with tears streaming down his cheeks and memories shredding his soul.

They met after work one day, walking by the side of the Ru river, near the power station. Beyond the transformers was a set of outbuildings, which were always locked. Nina led Dmytry to the furthest one, deep in the forest, an old switch room no longer in use.

The room was bare, empty apart from an old electrical panel. Nina slipped behind it, propped a bamboo ladder up against the back of the old panel and climbed up, sliding a concealed trapdoor aside and climbing into the roof space. Dmytry followed and she pulled the ladder up and closed the hatch behind them.

'Wait here,' she said.

Dmytry crouched in the darkness and tried to regulate his breathing. His heart was beating so loudly, the blood coursing through his veins faster than the mighty river outside. Could she hear it?

The loft space smelt of sun-dried straw and pine needles. A match flared and fizzed, the burst of bright light softening into the warm glow of an oil lamp.

It took a few minutes for his eyes to adjust. The loft was bigger than he would have guessed. There was room for a small trestle table and chair, and a series of wooden crates.

'Come,' she said, indicating the chair for him to sit.

She unpacked the first box, wiping away the straw dust with a soft white cloth. The little statue stood six inches high, pale celadon, a man and a boy and a deer. She placed it on the table in front of him.

'May I touch?'

Did she blush, or was it just a trick of the light?

'Yes,' she whispered.

He inspected the carving, holding it to the light, turning it slowly.

He felt Nina's breath on his neck, smelt her honeyed fragrance, and his own fire burned brightly.

'So beautiful.' He stared into her dark eyes as he held it out to her.

'Shhh.' She put a finger to her lips and snuffed the lamp. In the darkness, he heard it too. Thwack, thwack. *The sound of an axe chopping through a fallen branch. Voices. Men gathering firewood for the furnaces.*

When he first saw the backyard furnace arrive in the village, he couldn't believe his eyes. Even as a civil engineer, he knew enough about steelmaking to realise that something so primitive wouldn't produce anything useful.

But no one at the commune would listen to him. People turned white, began to shake, whispered stories about what happened to those who tried to reason with the authorities. And what happened to their families.

At night the town glowed orange, red sparks and flames lit up the sky. By day they cut down more trees to keep it stoked up like an enormous, insatiably hungry baby. And all the baby produced was excrement – nu shi ge la.

The pig iron they produced was brittle, useless. But the party officials were only interested in the weight of production, not the quality. They had targets, meaningless numbers, quotas that had to be met.

When the villagers ran out of scrap iron, they started to bring their *cooking pots and hoes, their hammers and plough blades, nails and animal halters, water pipes and wheels, bicycles and bed springs. The things they needed to live, to farm, to cook, to repair their houses and keep their carts on the road.*

And still they were out there, stripping the lovely mountain forest bare. The Chinese had been expert steelmakers since 500 BC. How could they forget so fast?

He let out a sigh as the footsteps receded. They waited in silence until the only sound was the water lapping against the shore, the wind in the trees and their own hearts beating in unison.

'Look at this,' she said, lighting the lamp again.

The green jade shimmered as if it had a life of its own, a fire inside. The serpentine body, layered with scales, rose from muscular legs, the broad feet ending in curved talons. The wings were partly folded against its back, and the long neck and head were ridged with triangular thorns, the mouth slightly open to reveal sharp teeth. Almost alive in his hands, the artist had captured the sinuous movement, a moment of action frozen in time, solidified into one of the most beautiful objects Dmytry had ever seen. So intricate, so delicate, there were patterns within the patterns.

The dragon was exquisite, but Nina took his breath away. He closed his eyes and breathed in her fragrance.

A rustling sound told him that Nina was packing the dragon back in its bed of straw. 'We should go,' she said.

His heart sank in disappointment. 'We can come again?'

'There's more to see,' she said. 'And touch.'

His heart skipped a beat. He blinked hard as the harsh light of the switch room invaded the darkness. Nina held the trapdoor open for him.

'Be careful,' she said.

If only he had heeded her advice.

They met as often as they could, in the loft of the old switch room beside the power station, away from the prying eyes of the villagers, away from her father's trusting smile. The forest had gone, the trees chopped down to fuel the backyard furnaces that turned useful metal objects into brittle pig iron, of no use to anyone except the party statisticians.

They would arrive separately. Dmytry first, careful that no one saw him, carrying a concealed picnic inside some rolled-up drawings or a tripod case. Nina would watch and wait. If it wasn't safe, she would go home, and he would loiter in the emptiness where the old electrical panel used to be before it was taken apart and fed to the furnace.

But usually, he didn't have long to wait.

They would eat first. The visiting Russians were well supplied, but he could see that the villagers were desperately short of food. Dmytry loved the moment when Nina chose an object. This was their pretence for coming here. Chinese lessons, through the stories of priceless objects. The unspoken rule was that he could hold her while she talked. Sometimes he pressed his chest to her back, his chin resting on her shoulder, his lips nuzzling her neck, his hands around her waist. Sometimes she would sit beside him on the chair, a warm thigh pressed against his; if he was lucky, she would sit in his lap. When she finished the story and he'd answered her questions correctly, she allowed him one long kiss before pulling away to leave first.

He fell in love, head over heels.

Zhengzhou, China

The town of Zhengzhou was gridlocked. Car horns beeped, windows were lowered and heads leaned out, shouting, coughing and retreating.

Jaq emerged from Zhengzhou train station into a diffuse yellow light and stood blinking in surprise. The capital of Henan Province – the most populous region in China – boasted a spacious, modern town centre with a tall central tower and several buildings that resembled giant alien eggs scattered around a lake. A city of ten million people, and yet she had never heard of it until yesterday.

The receptionist at the Shanghai hotel had translated the WeChat message on Timur's phone. He was meeting Wang from Krixo in the forest of pagodas at the Shaolin Temple complex, Dengfeng. And Jaq planned to be there.

Before leaving Shanghai, Jaq had employed Speedy and his motorbike to return the phone to Timur. With strict instructions to wait until the next call, answer it and say he'd found it on the Bund before arranging its return. On no account should he mention her involvement. Once she'd got that job done and paid for, she'd texted Natalie for advice, checked out of the Shanghai hotel and taken an overnight train west.

'*Gōngjiāo zhàn?* She knew the Mandarin word for bus station, but her enquiries were met with blank stares. A few fellow passengers replied to her question with questions of their own, and then she was completely lost.

'*Dengfeng?* Her destination. The officials seemed disinclined to help, even though their main occupation appeared to be staring into space. One after another they waved her back towards the train station with a frown. Language was her superpower, but China was her kryptonite. Jaq had never felt so helpless, so alien in another country.

'Can I help?' A Chinese man walked towards her, moving upstream against the crowd, dressed in a sharp business suit.

'I'm heading to Dengfeng.'

'To the Shaolin Temple?'

Timur was meeting Wang at the Shaolin Temple. But how did this stranger know where she was going?

She narrowed her eyes. 'What makes you think that?'

He laughed. 'You want to go to Dengfeng. No one goes to Dengfeng unless they're going to the temple. It's famous.' His accent was American. Probably he learned his English from the TV.

'So how do I get there?'

'Best pick up an organised tour from your hotel.'

Jaq shook her head. 'I haven't got much cash.'

'You need a cashpoint?' He pointed to the hole in the wall.

She shook her head. Vikram still hadn't paid her and she'd reached the limit on all her cards.

He frowned. A foreigner in China without money must be a novelty.

'Just point me in the right direction for the bus.'

He waved a slender hand back the way she'd come. 'The bus station is inside the train station.'

Of course, how stupid. China was brand new; all this infrastructure had been built in the last decade. If you could start from scratch, on a blank canvas, why not integrate everything? Connecting the airport, high-speed train, bus and bicycles for hire at every intersection.

The businessman consulted his phone. 'The fast buses leave every half hour. Get off at the last stop, the old bus station in Dengfeng, and then pick up a number eight to Shaolin.' He opened a notebook and scribbled something down in Chinese characters. 'Here.' He tore the page from the notebook. 'Show this to the driver.'

'Thanks,' Jaq said, taking the paper. 'You speak good English.'

'I should hope so.' He smiled. 'I'm an American citizen.' And he was gone.

Bolas. What an ass. Don't judge by appearances alone. Jaq hid her embarrassment in brisk steps in the direction the businessman had indicated. The bus to Dengfeng pulled in a few minutes early. Jaq joined what looked like a queue, standing behind a young woman with a crying baby. The gap between Jaq and the young mother was clearly misjudged, based on an English sense of personal space, and within minutes half a dozen people had forced their way in front of her. A crowd of people pushed and jostled forward as the bus doors hissed open. Jaq stood back and let them go, waiting until the end. The only seat remaining was right at the front, next to the mother who was now discreetly nursing her baby.

As Jaq sat down, she accidentally caught the shawl draped over baby and mother, exposing a white breast. The bus driver turned and began to remonstrate with the woman.

'*Duìbùqǐ, hěn bàoqiàn,*' the woman said. Her drooping shoulders and anxious expression spoke of embarrassment.

Why should she be sorry? A baby at the breast, the most natural thing in the world. Jaq smiled reassuringly and helped the woman to reposition the shawl.

The man behind them pitched in, striking the young woman on the shoulder, making her wince. The baby pulled away and began to howl.

'It's OK.' Jaq turned and made the universal sign, first finger and thumb forming a circle, other fingers elevated. But the passengers on the bus were not remotely interested in her opinion on the matter. A raucous discussion erupted in the bus. The woman ignored them, and the baby resumed feeding.

The bus joined a motorway. Visibility was poor, a light brown miasma hanging over the flat plain of the Yellow river. The valley of coal-fired industry.

Coal, the most natural of products, is a concentrated form of solar energy. Millions of years ago, in tropical wetlands, plants used energy from the sun to trap carbon and oxygen from the air in the process we know as photosynthesis. Dying plants fell to the bottom of the swamp, new ones took their place faster than the old ones could decompose, layer upon layer pressing down and compacting into peat. Over time, bacterial action, high pressure and temperature squeezed out the water and concentrated the vegetable matter into coal.

You burn coal to heat water, the water boils to becomes steam and the steam turns the turbine, magnets rotating inside stationary copper coils to generate electricity. If coal was just carbon, hydrogen and oxygen, then it would be bad enough. Hydrogen plus oxygen to water, no problem. But carbon plus oxygen equals carbon dioxide, and poisonous carbon monoxide if you don't get the ratio right: greenhouse gases.

And coal is not just carbon, hydrogen and oxygen. It is a natural material made of fossilised plant matter. And living plants once contained sulphur, as did the bacteria that fed on them as they decayed. Burning sulphur gives SOx, oxides of sulphur, leading to acid rain.

Coal contains more than sulphur, it has traces of other elements. Nitrogen. Selenium, in tiny quantities, essential for plant and animal growth. The dose makes the poison. Released into the air in large quantities, it's toxic, just like mercury and arsenic. That's the trouble with nature; it's messy.

Much of China was still burning lignite, brown coal. The haze was composed of microparticles – unburnt fuel, soot, liquid droplets – emitted from a coal-fired power station. Particles so tiny that they could penetrate the lung's natural defences.

The great smog of London, in 1956, caused countless deaths and led to the Clean Air Act in England. The new constraints were midwife to the birth of new technologies and the golden age of chemical engineering: clean coal combustion in a fluidised bed with slaked lime, natural gas from the North Sea desulphurised with precious metal catalysts, expansion of the chemical industry to meet the new demands of the Anthropocene – the age of humans and their insatiable demand for nutritious food and clean water and safe medicines. Regulations tightened, forcing polluting industries to close. And who meets the demand today? China.

Now China was coming to terms with the price of progress and moving fast to halt pollution. But was it fast enough?

Jaq was the last off the bus, the only way she could be sure it was the right stop. She shivered in the wintry smog, flapping her arms around to her back to keep warm while she waited for the number eight bus. Several taxis drew to a halt, beckoning, offering to take her to the temple. She ignored them. The little cash she had left needed to last.

Her teeth were chattering by the time the bus arrived, packed with monks. They wore dark red robes and sneakers and sat in silence. When they got off, she followed them. Not that she could have missed the entrance to the temple. A statue of a monk towered over the road, imposing black metal atop a stone plinth, palms touching and raised in greeting or prayer. The noise of people rose to a hubbub as she approached. A mass of Chinese tourists swarmed in a vast, paved square bordered with souvenir shops and noodle bars, sealed at one end by ticket booths and turnstiles. Her heart sank. What had she expected? An isolated monastery in the hills? Just the river and the trees and some fighting monks? She hung back. Even after the disastrous visit to Putuo island, she was still surprised by the scale of domestic tourism in China.

A signpost displayed the distance to the major cities: 960km from Shanghai, and thousands of miles from home. Wherever that was. She shivered. *Move, keep moving.*

More tour buses arrived and disgorged their shrieking, throat-clearing and spitting passengers. *Chato*, it was only going to get busier. Jaq bought a ticket with the last of her folding money, throat-tighteningly expensive at 100 yuan, and pressed through the turnstile and under the huge grey archway with elaborately carved roof. She ignored the electric shuttle bus and followed the able-bodied hordes down a paved, tree-lined path beside the dry riverbed.

To the right was the first of the martial arts – wushu – schools. A group of children in red sweatshirts and black tracksuit bottoms ran in wide circles, windmilling their arms.

The temple was big business. On a huge parade ground four groups, separately identifiable by their coloured costumes, were already hard at work. A group of teenagers in yellow were exercising, working on flexibility and strength. Star jumps, sit-ups and press-ups, handstands and backflips, aerial kicks and somer-saults – tong zi gong. The group in white were halfway through a recognisable version of the tai chi long form, just moving from diagonal flying to wing-spreading. The grey group, who looked to be the oldest, were working in pairs, on elaborately stylised hand-to-hand combat, each wielding a short stick as they twirled and attacked. The *clack, clack* of weapon on weapon, with the occasional cry where a blow landed undefended, rang out across the huge open square. The last group, all in red with shaved heads, looked to be the Shaolin kung fu specialists. This group was mixed, male and female, young and old, Chinese and foreign. And yet the most advanced. Diversity in action.

She bypassed the Martial Arts Gym. Her ticket entitled her to a thirty-minute display which she had zero interest in attending. Passing a ginkgo tree with indented bark, she climbed the stone steps leading up to a deep-red building with tiled roof and mouse hole entrance, guarded on either side by statues of fierce warriors.

Monks in grey and orange robes bustled this way and that, the scent of incense mingled with the susurration of chanting.

Timur was meeting Wang here. Thanks to Natalie's kung fu connections, a cut-price temple hostel with a bed and hot meal were waiting for Jaq. Once she'd located the meeting point in the forest of pagodas, she could afford to wait.

The attack came from her blind side, the low mustard-coloured sun making an inconvenient appearance, burning through the smog before sinking below the horizon, making it hard to estimate the speed or direction of the dark shapes that flitted across the diffuse light.

The smell of male sweat – testosterone and its derivative, androstenone, on heavy cotton, river-washed and not completely dried – reached her before the noise of soft shoes on gravel.

Deus me leve.

Some sixth sense, intuitive self-preservation, made her stop in her tracks, ducking just in time to avoid the first blow. Her swift evading action took the first attacker by surprise. His motion propelled him across her path, giving her just enough time to swing her bag and whack him hard across the side of his head. He tumbled to the ground and remained there.

She took a step back and stared at him. Han Chinese with a round face, razor-cut black hair, dressed in a loose tunic and trousers which failed to hide the overdeveloped muscles. More gym beefcake than a real kung fu acolyte. And not some lone maniac, either; there were others in the trees. Regrouping. Waiting for her next move.

Jaq shielded her eyes and debated her options.

The path had cleared of tourists as she had wandered further into the forest of pagodas, a cemetery for monks, the tall stupas built to venerate the dead. No help was coming from that quarter.

The living emerged from the trees, four of them, dressed identically to the man on the ground. One stepped onto the path ahead of her, the leader judging by his nods and gestures to the others. Hard to judge his age, but his hair was badly dyed and a slight paunch hung over his cloth belt. Another stepped onto the path behind her, blocking any possibility of retreat. Taller than either the first attacker or the boss, and smarter, judging by the way he moved smoothly into a defensive crouch. The youngest members of the gang formed the wings of the ambush, twigs snapping and leaves rustling as they emerged from the trees on either side of the path. The two older men showed no interest in their fallen companion, who lay motionless on the path, but the eyes of the younger ones strayed there repeatedly.

Delaying tactics. Jaq knelt to the ground and felt the man's pulse. She shook her head.

'He needs a doctor,' she said. What was the Chinese for doctor? '*Yīshēng*,' she tried, '*kuài*.' Quickly.

At a nod from Paunch Man, the wingmen approached. Jaq stepped back from their fallen companion, but they adjusted direction. No compassion in their advance, they weren't coming for their comrade, they were coming for her. The one to her right raised his hands, crossing them in front of his face.

There are three things that matter in a fight. Size, speed and technique. Apart from numbers, size is weight and height. Simple physics. The energy delivered in a blow is force times distance. Force is mass times acceleration. Jaq was outnumbered, but the young man approaching from her left was shorter than her, and slighter. She faced the one on her right, listening out for the other. At the first jab, she feinted, swivelled and high-kicked. Her steel-capped boot caught the smaller man under the jaw before he could strike. He went down without a sound, just the *whoomph* of his slight body hitting the leaf mulch, the smell of forest damp intensifying. A knockout blow. The chin is the furthest point from the base of the skull, causing the maximum rotation of the head and subdural haematoma in the brain. Nasty.

Two down, three to go. The young man on her right attacked again, but he was slow, landing only a glancing blow to her left arm as she parried, not enough to stop her striking back.

She needed to take this one down, move his centre of mass away from his feet. He might be stronger, but she was faster. She danced from foot to foot, keeping her muscles loose. High-energy strikes, localised tissue damage, make him angry, before tightening her muscles to become a single solid object, concentrating all her mass behind a single punch to the gut. He staggered on impact but didn't fall, turning and snarling, his face flushed red, his breath coming in short, sharp jabs.

Good. The angrier he got the easier it became. Angry men are irrational. Their brain floods with catecholamines, their muscles tense, heart rate accelerates, blood pressure rises, rate of breathing increases, attention narrows. She waited for his counter-attack. He roared as he rushed her, and she used his momentum to throw him over her shoulder. The fall wouldn't stop him, so she kicked him in the groin before he could get up.

The first man was back on his feet, and now the other two were closing in. Three big, angry men. She thought of Natalie, hairdresser and kung fu instructor, and wished she'd attended more classes. A different technique was called for.

Jaq ran.

She dashed into the forest, tearing down the wooded bank, weaving through the trees, away from the thugs. At the bottom of the valley an irrigation channel provided a smooth concrete track. She splashed through the cold water, running with the flow, moving downhill, towards the sounds of temple bells and the chatter of people.

She almost made it.

Teesside, England

The plane was airborne now, and Frank opened his laptop to review the documents he'd collected, tapping his fingers, first in impatience and then in alarm.

The £10 million sterling sale at auction of an eighteenth-century Chinese lovers' cup was fifth-page news. Until the murder of the auctioneer, and that of a retired university lecturer known to have attended the auction, brought it to the front page. How could he have known there was any connection with Sophie and Charles Clark and his own investment in Krixo?

There were other articles on Chinese jade: a spate of thefts from European museums, objects thought to be stolen to order. Was there a link to the Krixo lovers' cup? Or had the record sale value simply sparked a new understanding of the value of ancient Chinese artefacts, and made them more attractive to criminals?

He pressed the buzzer above his head and ordered a fresh drink.

His concerns were threefold.

First, his own investment looked to be in jeopardy. It wasn't a vast amount, but it was a lot more than he could afford to lose. He scratched his balls. Given the progress he had been making with Sophie, it was not completely irrecoverable. Unless Wang had her murdered before Frank could get control of her money.

Secondly, the investors were going to be furious when they found out that not only had their factory vanished, but the collateral had been pissed away by the new owner. How on earth had Sophie managed to make a dent in ten million pounds? He needed access to her bank accounts, and fast. But however angry the other investors proved to be, they were unlikely to resort to murder.

The third concern was the most alarming. Someone had murdered the auctioneer and one of the auction attendees. Why? Revenge? A warning to others not to mess with China's ancient heritage? Then why was Sophie – the person who put it up for sale – still alive? The incident at the Sage had been a warning, not a hit. What did it mean for him? If he remained close to Sophie, was he putting himself in danger?

Sophie was trouble. Time to put some distance between them.

Slow slicing – death by a thousand cuts – was not on his agenda.

Frank had decided to escape from England and its knife-wielding assassins. He was about to revive his career with Zagrovyl, and he was going alone.

In eleven hours, he would be in Shanghai.

A new beginning.

Zhengzhou, China

The founder of the Shaolin Temple, Dharma, brought Buddhism from India to China 1,500 years ago and developed kung fu to improve both the monks' health and security. The temple was now big business, but away from the crush of tourists, there were many hidden corners.

A group of men dragged their captive to one of these quiet places, to what looked like a gymnasium, a flat-roofed concrete box with a sprung floor and wooden climbing bars covering one wall. They tied her wrists and ankles to the bars with cable ties.

Jaq struggled in vain. After they left, it took a few minutes for her breathing to return to normal, but as it did, she began to shiver. There was no heating in the gym, and the temperature was close to zero. Her clothes were soaked from running down the river channel and her teeth were chattering of their own accord. She looked left and right, craning her neck to try and see out of the high windows. The light was fading. Soon it would be dark. Did they plan to leave her here overnight? Would she survive?

'Help!'

When the men in black robes arrived, she felt a moment of relief. At least they weren't going to freeze her to death. Then she saw them line up, seven of them, and raise their sticks.

'Guys, you are making a mistake. Let me go.'

One of their number stepped forward and drew out a short-bladed knife. She shrank back against the bars and closed her eyes, but he simply cut through the cable ties, first the ankles, then the wrists, and stepped back before she could punch him.

She rubbed the welts on her wrists, the pain more intense now the broken skin was exposed to the chill air, and looked around for a way of escape. The windows were high, two metres off the ground, and the only door was behind the line of seven men.

She walked towards them, hands in the air palms outward, to show that she meant them no harm, heading for the exit. When she was almost level, the first one gave a cry and they surrounded her.

The beating was vicious. She put her hands up to protect herself, but the blows rained down. They made no attempt to question her, so she knew to expect the worst. They were going to beat her to death. A painful and humiliating way to go. She sank to her knees and curled up into a ball, hands over her head, knees up to her chest, and prayed for a miracle.

She didn't see the women at first, but she heard them. Light footsteps, thin rubber soles slapping the wood, followed by blood-curdling cries in a higher register.

The men ignored them, continuing to hit her in a perfect chore-ography, taking turns to raise their sticks and thwack them down on her broken body. The first man went down, his legs scissored from under him by a ball of yellow energy. She saw a flash of dark pigtails as the ball uncurled into a young woman, no more than four foot high. The second man staggered back as a short-haired woman jumped on him from behind. She climbed onto his shoulders and grabbed his raised stick, pulling it across his neck and garrotting him. The circle was broken, and the remaining men paused for a moment, long enough for the other women to surge forward and stand between the men and their victim.

For a while her rescuers seemed to be gaining ground. The women were lithe and well trained; their opponents undisciplined thugs. But the men fought dirty, and the women were tiring.

A vicious blow caught her on the temple. Jaq began to float in and out of consciousness, unsure if she was dreaming this whole improbable fight. How could these slight women possibly overpower the fully grown, brutal men?

Until the white angel joined them, a vision in flowing white silk, her silver sword cutting and slashing. The assassins fled from the whirling dervish.

Jaq tried to reach out to her, but the pain came in a wave and everything went black.

Shanghai, China

'Welcome to China, Frank!'

A small, rotund Chinese man bustled through the airport crowds, beaming through thick-rimmed spectacles.

'My name is Joe, and I'm in HR.'

Frank took the proffered hand and gave the plump white flesh a firm squeeze, letting go only after some discomfort passed across Joe's smooth features. He hated the word Human Resources, and its abbreviation, HR, almost as much as he loathed the people drawn to it.

'My name is Mr Good.'

'I'll be happy to show you around Shanghai.' Joe gave a nervous giggle. 'Mr Good.'

Frank yawned. 'Take me to my apartment.'

The uniformed man holding the Zagrovyl sign tucked it under his arm and seized the luggage.

'This is Tsin Ding.' Joe introduced Frank to his official driver. 'We'll go to Jade Villas. It takes about an hour, OK? Very nice. Very top-class. Very convenient.'

The apartment was part of a gated community in the south-east of the city. The car stopped at a security checkpoint to be searched before being allowed to meander slowly through cast-iron gates, past tennis courts and an outdoor swimming pool to a clutch of apartments and villas in shady gardens.

Joe waited by the lift while Frank checked his new accommodation.

'Everything OK?' he called through the door.

Everything very much OK. Much more spacious than expected, given the price of Shanghai real estate. The apartment was on the top floor, with a large living room and terrace looking out over

Century Park to the west and Pudong golf course to the east. It had a well-equipped kitchen, the fridge already stocked with eggs and bacon and milk and a range of ready meals, separate dining room, a master bedroom with en suite bathroom, two further bedrooms, a family bathroom and a study. Graham had done him proud.

'It'll do, I suppose.'

'And now? You rest? Meet later?'

Frank refused Joe's offer to take him to dinner. He wasn't going to celebrate his first night in Shanghai with a minder from Zagrovyl. He had other plans.

'Tell the driver what you want. He'll take you where you want to go.' Joe handed Frank a new phone, already programmed with the driver's number.

'Hamburger, hotpot, massage . . .'

HR obviously meant something different here.

'Anything you want, just say the word.'

After a shower and a nap, Frank did exactly that.

'*Xīnǚ.*'

The card came from a man at the golf club who was often in Shanghai on business, a discreet and exclusive nightclub. And the best knocking shop in town.

Zhengzhou, China

The bare room contained a narrow metal bed with a thin mattress, a washstand with a basin and jug. Watery winter light filtered through the bars of a small, high window. Hospital or prison? A cast-iron radiator clunked and clanged as hot water mixed with steam, but Jaq was glad of the noise. The room was so cold, she could see her breath as well as hear it. Small puffs of steam after each ragged gasp. It hurt to breathe, it hurt to move, it hurt even to remain still. She tried to move her limbs only to find that her wrists and ankles were tied to the bed. She called out, begging for some relief from the awful pain.

The woman who tended her, a nun with shaved head, dark red robe and brown woolly cardigan, was as unsmiling as she was efficient. She put warm poultices on the bruises and gave Jaq a potion to drink, some ancient Chinese herbal medicine, perhaps – it certainly tasted godawful. What Jaq needed right now was codeine, ibuprofen, paracetamol, aspirin. But the nun spoke no English and Jaq was trapped in this spartan cell until she could move again. She gave in to sleep.

By the time Jaq knew which day it was, she had missed the meeting. The event that had brought her to the Shaolin Temple, a meeting between Timur and Wang, had taken place without her. She had come all this way only to get the stuffing knocked out of her. Someone had beaten her up to keep her away.

From Krixo?

Or from Timur?

The nun showed her the photo that the men had left beside her beaten body. Despite the poor quality, it was easy to identify both

Jaq and Timur as they kissed. Was that why she'd been beaten up? A jealous lover? A nervous tour promoter who didn't want anyone spoiling the illusion that the Masters of Disguise were only here to please Chinese women? To sell them beer?

The next time she woke, a woman was sitting on her bed. She wore a loose white tunic and matching trousers. Her long black hair was tied back in a ponytail.

'How are you feeling?'

Jaq tried to sit up; pain flooded her body and she sank back down, defeated. 'Wretched.'

The woman patted the bed. 'I'm Mico, by the way.'

'Jaq.'

'I know. You're the one who was kissing my employee.'

Jaq's eyes flew open. Was this the jealous lover, come to finish the job? Play for time.

'Your employee?'

'I hired the Masters of Disguise for the Hop! tour.'

So, this was the deluded Svengali who imagined that naked Western men could entice Chinese women into drinking beer.

'And their contract forbids them from fraternising while on tour.'

'It's not what you think.'

'You have no idea what I think,' Mico said. 'Or what I do.' She turned sideways so that Jaq could see the scabbard slung across her back.

Was this the murderer? The woman who had travelled to England to torture and kill?

'Are you a thief, too?' If Jaq was about to die, she might as well understand why.

'My, someone is well informed.' Mico frowned. 'I think of it less as theft and more as repatriation on behalf of the Chinese people.'

'You employed the Masters of Disguise to "repatriate" ancient Chinese treasures?'

'Very good.'

'But what is your connection with Krixo?' Why had Timur arranged to meet the boss of Krixo here at the Shaolin Temple? What was the link between the jade treasures and a vanishing factory?

'Wang has the missing piece of the collection. We're negotiating its return.'

Negotiating. It sounded so reasonable coming from this softly-spoken woman with her perfect English. Was it negotiation when she sliced the young auctioneer to death? Or cut the retired metal-lurgist to pieces? And what about their innocent pets? Jaq felt sick at the thought. Was Wang in danger from this fanatic? Is that why the factory disappeared overnight?

'How can a few bits of ancient rock justify so much harm?'

'Sometimes the end justifies the means.'

'And do the proceeds of their sale get "repatriated" to your pocket?'

Mico chuckled. 'It's so much more fun than that. Not only did my trusty band of light-fingered athletes have to break into Western museums to acquire the treasures, they are going to break into a Chinese museum to return them. Nothing if not brilliantly symmetrical.'

'That's absurd.'

'You think? Perhaps because you have no idea of how China works. To return the treasures through formal channels risks their disappearance. No: this is the only way. Imagine the surprise after a burglary to find that nothing has been taken. On the contrary, you open your museum one morning to find that the Qianlong jade collection has been returned, intact, to its former home in Henan. Once social media get wind of that story it'll be harder to disappear those objects into the coffers of corrupt government officials.'

The penny dropped. 'People like Yan Bing?'

Mico narrowed her eyes. 'Perhaps you know too much, Jaq.' She raised her hand to her left shoulder and pulled out a sword, the blade glinting in a shaft of sunlight that slid between the bars of the window. 'More than is safe.'

'Are you going to kill me?'

Mico threw back her head and broke into peals of laughter.

'Oh, but you are precious! If I wasn't already spoken for, I might just fall for you. Don't you remember? I'm the one who saved you.'

The white angel, the sword-wielding dancer, this was the woman who had intervened to stop the death-beating.

'Lucky for you my stunt team were filming here. Lucky for me that Yan Bing's idiot henchman tried to make some extra money by showing me the photo of you and Timur.'

Ah, the photo again. Perhaps she wasn't safe yet. Had she been saved only to be tortured afresh?

'The kiss,' Jaq said. 'It meant nothing.'

'Poor boy,' Mico said. 'He obviously thought differently. In fact, he's on his way to rescue you right now.'

Mico raised the sword.

'Alas, I can't wait for him.'

Jaq closed her eyes.

Shanghai, China

Frank gave Tsin Ding the card for the club and relaxed into the leather seat to watch the city unfold. The driver kept up a running commentary as they approached the river, pointing out the sights of Shanghai.

A giant pagoda sparkled with golden light. Jin Mao Tower, the Golden Prosperity Building, 420 metres high with its spiky tiered roofs and needle spire, looked like a huge prickly cactus.

The iconic Pearl Tower glowed pink. Tonfon Mintsyta, a mad confection of eleven spheres linked by slender columns. Little lights sparkled, moving upwards from Space City, through the twenty-bed Space Hotel, up to the revolving restaurant and then the Space Module, rising up the slender antenna to a height of 468 metres. Up went the lights and then down again. Pink and cream pearls rising and falling, the lights reflected in the smooth jade plate of the Huangpu river.

Nicknamed the Bottle Opener, the only building in the world with a trapezoidal aperture near the top, the Shanghai World Financial Centre had been transformed into a 500-metre canvas of shimmering lights.

The Twisty Turny Tower, tallest of them all, was lit up by ascending red bars which drew the eye to the Chinese characters circulating like a crown at the top, a giant stairway to heaven.

And still under construction, the Shanghai Tower seemed almost organic in form, the circular glass sheath twisting through 120 degrees as it soared 632 metres above the river.

His heart beat a little faster as the car pulled over and his driver pointed to the sign. Frank descended the steps to the basement club, his finger trembling as he pressed the intercom. A shutter opened and closed, and the steel door slid open.

It took time for his eyes to adjust to the low lighting inside. On a central stage three pole dancers, in high heels and stockings, gyrated to the music. Above them a series of cages held other girls in various stages of undress.

A man in a waistcoat bowed and directed Frank to a booth. He demonstrated the function of the console in the middle of the red velvet horseshoe, flicking through pictures of drinks, food and other delights.

Frank used the screen to order a beer and a light meal, ignoring the languid performers on stage. So far, so dull.

He checked his watch. Not long to go until the auction.

At midnight, the volume and tempo of the music increased and new girls, fresher ones, joined the pole dancers. They wore costumes that were crying out to be removed. A dominatrix led the way, a tall black woman in a black leather catsuit with zips in interesting places, cracking a bullwhip. Chinese twins in pyjamas, conjoined at the hip, clung to one another and the soft toys they carried. Frank followed the progress of a buxom girl in a blonde wig and shepherdess costume, leading other girls dressed as sheep, wriggling their bare arses as they crawled behind her on all fours, naked except for fluffy white hoods. Each of the girls had a number sewn to their costume and their details flashed up on the screen in front of him. One by one they paraded past the booths, the occupants hidden from one another, but the raucous shouts and lustful bellows perfectly audible.

Two girls slid into the booth, one either side of Frank. Both impossibly young and slender, with spaced-out dark eyes and vacant expressions. They wore striped corsets and tight red shorts, Tweedledum and Tweedledee. The one on his left whispered something, but the music was too loud. Frank turned to the other girl, on the side of his good ear.

'Which one do you like?' Tweedledee brushed her pouting lips over his.

Tweedledum laid a small hand on his knee and began to stroke his thigh.

'Or you prefer à la carte? Something not on the menu?' Tweedledee nibbled his earlobe, her breath hot and heavy. 'Or something right here?'

Perish the thought. Skeletal children with a drug problem was not Frank's idea of a good time, however adroit the technique.

His eyes were drawn to the shepherdess, admiring the milk-white thighs spilling over the tops of her pink stockings and vanishing enticingly into frilly panties. A very short skirt led to a tight, low-cut bodice. This one had more curves than all the other girls put together.

'That one?' whispered Tweedledum, following his eyes and finding details of the pert little newcomer on the screen.

'First fuck is on the house!' Tweedledee said, and touched the big green tick on the console. A light went on above the booth, a number flashing.

The parade finished and the shepherdess approached. With her blonde wig and pert body, she reminded him of Sophie. The wave of sadness that washed over him was as unexpected as it was disturbing. Frank waved her away and got up to leave.

Too late. The woman who pushed him back into his seat was not dressed for a nightclub. Surprisingly strong for her size, she wore a simple black trouser suit with a high-collared turquoise blouse. It wasn't until she spoke that he realised who she was. Those sharp little features, the short bob of glossy black hair, the broken English. The maniac who'd attacked Sophie and threatened him was back.

'Where is your friend?'

'I don't know who—'

'Sophie Clark will come to Shanghai. She will bring what she stole.'

'We're not seeing each other any more. We broke up.'

'Then make it up. A man like you will find a way to persuade her, I'm sure.'

'This has nothing to do with me.'

'Oh, but it does.' She laughed. 'If you want to live.'

'I can't . . .'

She laid an ice-blue velvet tube on the table, unrolling it to reveal a set of knives of increasing blade length.

'Unless she comes before the Spring Festival starts, I will find you.

'I will torture you.

'And I will kill you.'

Zhengzhou, China

Jaq kept her eyes closed until she was sure that Mico was gone. She moved her limbs carefully, to find that the restraints had been severed. Bloody overdramatic way to release her. Mico had a lot to answer for.

Timur arrived a few hours later.

'Good Lord, Jaq Silver.' He opened his eyes wide. A shade of green that reminded her of a storm at sea. 'You certainly take your martial arts training seriously. You look terrible.'

'You should see what I did to the other guys.'

The nun said something in a low voice.

Timur looked around. 'Mico was here?'

'Your boss?' Jaq shivered. 'I thought she was going to kill me.'

'Mico?' Timur laughed. 'She wouldn't hurt a fly. Lots of bluster and make-believe, but underneath it all she's OK.'

'She used her sword to trim my bandages.' Jaq held up her hands to show the neat cuts. 'I think it was a warning.'

He approached the bed and knelt beside her, his face suddenly serious.

'They tell me a bunch of thugs nearly killed you.' He ran a hand through his short dark hair. 'Shall we get you out of here?'

Was it wise to go with him? The nuns had been kind to her, in their own way. Why not stay until she'd recovered, involve the British Embassy, ask to be repatriated? Because she still hadn't found Dan. And because Timur was in contact with Wang, the Chinese boss of the vanishing factory. And Wang was the key to Dan and Xe Lin. Timur knew more about Krixo than he was letting on.

'Where to?' she said.

'Our show is in Zhengzhou this week. We have a place near here, up in the mountains, where the air is cleaner. Just the Masters of Disguise and a driver.'

The driver appeared in the doorway. Jaq recognised him immediately – the motorbike man from Shanghai. 'Speedy?' The words were out of her mouth before she could stop herself.

He shook his head, a warning.

Too late.

'You two know each other?' Timur frowned.

'We met in Shanghai,' Jaq said. 'Speedy gave me a lift on his motorbike.'

'I have a car now,' Speedy said. 'Official driver for the Masters of Disguise.'

Timur glared at Jaq. 'My phone.' He slapped his forehead with the palm of his hand. 'So it *was* you who took it? And you gave it to Speedy to return? We liked him so much we gave him a job.' He fixed her with a cool gaze. 'I think you have some explaining to do, Jaq Silver.'

'As do you, Timur Zolotoy.'

She bit her lip to stop herself crying with pain when they carried her to the car. Lying on the back seat, she slept as Speedy drove them into the mountains, waking when they stopped outside a stone-clad guest house. The view over the valley was obscured by thick mustard-coloured smog. Four men came out to greet them. She recognised Holger, the giant water baby, and Ernest, the redhead from Durham, but the other two, one dark-skinned, one Chinese, were just a blur of beauty. Timur introduced her to Eusébio and Ting Bo. Alone in a house in the mountains with five beautiful men, and she couldn't even breathe properly. What a bloody waste.

A burst of warmth enveloped her as Timur opened the door to a ground-floor bedroom. He pulled back clean sheets and deposited her on a soft bed.

Eusébio, a former footballer and physio in training, asked her permission before undressing her, unwrapping the bandages and gently probing each bruise with detached professionalism, before applying ice packs on the worst of the swelling.

'Nothing broken,' he announced. 'But you haven't half taken a beating. That must hurt like hell.' He turned to Timur, who was hovering anxiously. 'The things we do for love.' He opened a medical box and fished out some painkillers. 'You taking anything already?'

'Some disgusting herbs.'

He laughed. 'Allergic to anything?'

She shook her head and then wished she hadn't. Something had worked loose inside her skull and continued banging against her temples even after she stopped moving. Flashing lights and blinding pain made her cry out.

'Let's try some conventional medicine.'

She swallowed the tablets he gave her, let him re-bandage her wrists and hands and then sank back into crisp cotton sheets, asleep again before she could even thank him.

She woke to a breakfast tray and Timur sitting by the window. Sunlight streamed through a chink in the curtains, illuminating his sharp cheekbones. She tried to sit up and groaned out loud.

'Morning, Jaq Silver.'

'Morning, Timur.'

She managed to eat the porridge he gave her, balancing the bowl between bandaged hands and slurping it from the rim. Timur wiped her face with a damp cloth.

His gentleness touched her. Had she misjudged him?

'Why were you meeting Wang from Krixo?' she asked.

He reeled back. 'So that's why you are here.' He crossed his arms. 'Why should I tell you anything? All you have done so far is trick me.'

'I didn't know if I could trust you.' And yet she did.

'Well, I am absolutely sure that I can't trust you.'

Time to come clean. 'I'm looking for a student of mine, Ning Dan. I taught him in Teesside before he returned to China. I was hired by the English owner of a joint venture company called Krixo and I asked Dan what he knew about the Chinese operation. Next thing I know he's vanished, just like the factory in Shingbo. I got a message from him, in code, asking me for help, imploring me to find someone called Xe Lin. As far as I can tell she was a former classmate of his working for Krixo, and he was worried about her. Is she OK?'

Timur shook his head. 'I don't know. I didn't meet anyone called Xe Lin.'

'But you met Wang from Krixo?'

'Yes.'

'Why?'

Timur stood and walked to the window. 'Do you know your parents, Jaq Silver?'

'Know them? Well, yes, of course . . .'

'I don't know mine,' Timur said. 'My grandfather told me they were killed in a car crash, but the woman who raised me, and taught me to speak Mandarin, says that my mother abandoned me after my father abandoned her.'

It explained something about him at least, this striking, sensitive man with his almost childish desire to please, to impress, to be desired, be loved. 'Perhaps your parents had valid reasons . . .'

'Exactly. And that is what I'm here to find out.'

'I don't understand.'

He turned to face her.

'There's a link between my father and the Qianlong lovers' cup.'

'What sort of link?'

'That's what I'm trying to discover. I came to China to find the buyer. Sun Chang, Mico's father, was one of the last two bidders.'

'The successful one?'

'No.' His mouth twisted into a rueful smile. 'But I met Mico at her father's office and she offered to help me.'

'In exchange for . . .'

'In exchange for the Hop! tour.'

'But you and your friends don't just strip for her. What about the thefts?'

'You're a nosy parker, Jaq Silver.' His shoulders dropped, as if the air had gone out of him. 'Mico made a deal with Wang. The lovers' cup in exchange for the rest of the collection.'

'You stole to order? The Qianlong jade from foreign museums?'

He sighed. 'Yes.'

'And now you have the lovers' cup?'

'I'm not finished yet.'

He stood beside the bed, leaned down and took her face in his hands.

'Did the kiss mean anything?'

'Absolutely nothing,' she lied.

He released her and left the room.

Holger brought lunch, a clear broth in a sippy cup that she managed to hold between her wrists. Perhaps the giant water baby would be more forthcoming. *Be direct.*

'The day we met,' she said, 'what were you doing in the river?'

'Bargespotting.' Holger had a voice so deep it was part rumble. 'A bit like trainspotting, but more exciting.'

'But why were you in the water?'

'Attaching a tracker,' he said. He flipped open his mobile phone. 'That barge is now a long way upstream.'

He showed her a map with the flashing dot indicating the barge. It had moved from Shanghai to Wuhan.

'That was an incredibly dangerous thing to do.' She was unable to keep the admiration out of her voice.

'I get paid for it. There's not much call for synchronised swimming champions, especially male ones, so I tend to get odd jobs.'

Odd as in peculiar. Odd as in dangerous. 'Are you really a synchronised swimming champion?' she asked.

He nodded.

'Why that barge?'

'It belonged to a company called Krixo.'

Her pulse quickened. 'The equipment from the Shingbo factory?'

'I have no idea. I just track what I'm told to.'

'By who?'

'Insurance companies, generally. It is amazing how often a vessel magically reappears after being reported as sunk.'

If only Holger could magically restore the *Frankium*. 'Where do you think the barge is going?'

'We'll know when it gets there.'

Vladivostok, Russia

The wind was howling outside the palace high above Vladivostok. The Siberian High met cyclones from the Pacific, west and east clashing with raucous commotion. The old man lay on his narrow bed and slipped in and out of consciousness.

'Good morning, Dmytry. How are we today?'

The patient muttered something, and the doctor bent her ear towards him as she checked the dressing on his chest.

'They are falling from the skies,' Dmytry whispered.

'Are they indeed?' She straightened up. 'Well, you're safe here. Nothing to worry about.'

'I can't stand the noise,' he said.

The doctor took a step back. 'What noise?'

'The shouting.' His voice was clearer now. 'The clapping.'

Nurse and doctor exchanged a silent glance.

'Stop banging!' Dmytry raised his voice. 'STOP CLATTERING!'

'You must rest,' the doctor urged, taking his wrist and checking the pulse.

Dmytry screwed his face up. 'Such sweet little birds, all plump and honey-coloured, short tails, strong beaks.'

'Ah, you're a birdwatcher, are you?' the doctor said. 'Why don't you tell us more after you've had a good sleep.'

'*Passeridae, Passer montanus, shù má-què.* Why sparrows?'

Dmytry's eyes opened and shone with a wild light. The doctor moved her hand across his field of vision, but his pupils remained unfocused.

'Can you see me, Dmytry?'

'Sparrows have an extra bone in the tongue, you know.' He

sounded almost lucid now. 'The preglossale to hold the seeds. They eat grain, it's true, but they eat pests too.'

'Can you hear me, Dmytry?'

'STOP BANGING! STOP CLATTERING!'

The doctor nodded to the nurse.

'If you kill the sparrows, the pests will flourish,' Dmytry said.

'Will they now?'

The nurse plunged the needle of a syringe through the rubber membrane of a glass ampoule.

'What about the locusts?' Dmytry asked.

'What indeed.'

The nurse retracted the plastic plunger, filling the syringe.

'What about the bed bugs?'

'No bed bugs here.'

The nurse held the needle upright and tapped the syringe.

'Why would you kill the sparrows? Why?' He banged his head against the pillow, up and down, left and right. 'STOP THE NOISE! STOP BANGING POTS! STOP SHOUTING! STOP CLAPPING! STOP!'

The nurse administered the injection and Dmytry fell back onto the pillows.

'They are falling from the skies!' the old man muttered. 'She will starve.'

The doctor shook her head.

'Nina, Nina!' he shouted. 'I'm sorry! So sorry.'

The nurse put her hand on his brow. 'Shall I call his family?'

'I think it's time.'

Zhengzhou, China

A crescent of moon cast a silvery glow onto the garden. Jaq lay on the bed, in darkness.

She had barely moved since they'd brought her here. It all hurt too much: the cuts to her hands, the bruises on her skin, the welts round her wrists and ankles, the ache in her bones. But worst of all was the knowledge that she had failed, that she hadn't been enough. Once again, she'd tried to go it alone and, once again, she had done too little, too late. A washed-up, broken, penniless engineer, who couldn't even support her own mother.

Jaq heard the Masters of Disguise returning from their show. She called out as they entered the house. Timur appeared at the doorway.

'How did it go?'

'Police closed it down again. Offences against public decency.'

What to say? She wasn't entirely unsympathetic. The libertarian in her believed that consenting adults should be allowed to do whatever they liked in private, or in a private club for that matter, and yet her moral compass was disorientated by the idea of paid strippers, male or female.

'They seemed to like us, though. The Hop! publicity team say news of the ban sent the campaign viral. Makes the offering a bit edgy. Good for selling beer, apparently.' He took a step into the room. 'I'm glad you are awake. I wanted to say goodbye.'

'You're leaving? Did you get what you came for?'

He shook his head. 'Not yet.'

'You're giving up?'

'I have to go back to Vladivostok. My grandfather has taken a turn for the worse. The boys are going back to Shanghai for a few days, but Speedy will stay with you until you are well enough to go home.'

The slow wave of sadness took her by surprise. 'Timur, I'm sorry.'

'Sorry for what, Jaq Silver?'

'For everything. For not trusting you. For tricking you. For stealing from you.'

'Jaq Silver, steady on.' He came into the room. 'This is not like you. Are you OK?'

He sat on the bed and she caught a whiff of his scent. Mint and clove with hints of musk. Despite herself, she leaned into him and allowed his arms to envelop her. She pressed against the human warmth and let her head drop against his shoulder.

'Have you been able to wash?'

He must be able to smell her.

'No.' She sighed. 'Not since I got here.'

'Do you want to?'

'Yes, but . . .' She held up her bandaged hands to demonstrate her inability to perform the simplest of tasks.

'I can help.' He paused. 'If you'll let me.'

He waited for her assent and she nodded.

'Here's what we are going to do,' he said. 'I'm going to bag up your bandages to keep them dry. Then we're going to get in the shower together and I'm going to wash you. OK?'

Forget embarrassment. So badly did she need to get clean, she was beyond caring how it happened.

'OK.'

He undressed her carefully, draping a quilt over her shoulders to keep her warm, and taped plastic bags over her bandaged hands. But when she tried to stand, her legs gave way and she would have fallen if he hadn't been there to catch her.

'Wait.' He helped her back onto the bed and fetched a plastic chair which he placed in the shower. He opened the taps, tested the water and then came back for her.

She looked away as he took off his shirt and trousers. When he picked her up, his bare skin was warm against hers as he carried her to the shower.

'Temperature OK?' he asked.

She tested the water with an outstretched foot.

'Could be hotter,' she said.

He sat her in the chair and adjusted the taps until the steam rose and the shivering stopped.

'Hair first?' he asked.

He stood behind her to shampoo her hair, massaging her scalp with deft fingers. He rinsed it before combing conditioner through it.

'Leave that on for a few minutes, OK?' he said.

'OK.'

He cleaned her face with a flannel and then patted it dry with a hand towel. Careful to avoid getting water on her hands, he washed her arms, her armpits, her neck and her shoulders and then rinsed off the conditioner.

'Lean forward.'

She obliged, and he rubbed her back, using long firm strokes with the heels of his hands.

'Now the rest, OK?'

Taking the soap, he knelt in front of her and washed her feet, careful to go in between the toes, gentle with the welts on her ankles, then her calves and thighs.

He smiled up at her.

'Do you trust me, Jaq Silver?'

'I trust you, Timur Zolotoy.'

He was quick and firm, washing her torso, her breasts. Lifting her to wash between her thighs. The sensations from his hands, fleeting, impersonal, efficient, made her both grateful and sad. The shower water bounced off her body, splashing him.

He left her seated in the shower while he brought towels.

'Ready?'

'Just a moment longer.'

She threw back her head and let the hot water cascade over her face and body. How had it come to this? How had she become so helpless that she was dependent on the kindness of a virtual stranger? Why did she never learn? Wasn't it time she faced up to the fact that she wasn't cut out for this sort of thing? She should have remained in Europe. Forget contracting – she should have found a steady job in Teesside. And if there were no jobs in manufacturing any more, then something else. Something low-risk. Something she could learn to do well. In an engineering drawing office, perhaps? When this was over, she would remake her life. Start from scratch.

'I'm ready now.'

He turned off the water, draped a large bath sheet over her shoulders and twisted her hair into a smaller towel.

'Let's get you dry, OK?'

'OK.'

He wrapped the towel around her and knelt to pick her up.

'Are you and Mico lovers?' she asked.

Timur laughed. 'If there's one thing erotic dancing has taught me, it's how to recognise which team people bat for. Mico has no interest in men.'

Oh, why was she so bad at this? What had Mico said to her? *If I wasn't already spoken for, I might just fall for you.*

'You, on the other hand, can barely keep your eyes off the Masters of Disguise.'

'Stop it.'

'Were you jealous?' he teased.

'Don't flatter yourself.' It came out sharper than intended. 'I don't want you to get hurt, that's all. Mico might be a murderer.'

Timur shook his head. 'You misjudge her. She's a stuntwoman. And a consummate actor.'

He deposited her on a stool in front of the dressing table. She watched him in the mirror as he combed her hair.

'What about those men in England, murdered by a thousand cuts? Bernard Ashley-Cooper, Professor John Tench?'

'The auctioneer and the metallurgist?' He tested the warm air from the hairdryer. 'I wondered about them, too. But Mico was in the US in October. Some Hollywood film awards. She was in all the papers.'

Whoever had killed those men, it wasn't Mico.

Her scalp tingled as he began to dry her hair. 'Thank you, Timur.'

He grinned. 'I'm only just getting started.'

She felt a little stirring. Bad idea, neither the time nor the place.

He brushed her hair until it was dry, then removed the plastic bags from her bandaged hands, unwrapped the towel and carried her, naked, back to the bed.

'I'm sorry I stole your phone.' She swallowed. 'The kiss did mean something.'

'I know.' He smiled. 'Think you can sleep now?'

Truth was, although she felt better, sleep was still far away.

'I can try.'

'You want me to stay for a bit?'

What was the point of dissembling? She didn't want to be alone right now. 'Please,' she said, and tears came again.

'It's OK, Jaq Silver,' he said, wiping them away.

'It's not OK,' she said.

'But this is OK?' he asked, stroking her hair.

She sighed.

'Do you trust me, Jaq Silver?'

'I trust you, Timur.'

'Those hands of yours are no use right now. Let me help you to relax so you can sleep.' He tightened the towel around his hips. 'This isn't for me, OK? It's a private dance, just for you.'

It had been so long. Why resist?

And yet resistance was inevitable. He slipped into the bed beside her, kissing her neck, her breasts. This was a bad idea. What had she been she thinking of to permit it? However experienced, however technically gifted he was, this was just a transaction. Whether or not money changed hands, there was an unbridgeable gulf between intimate pleasure mutually exchanged in love and sexual gratification given for any other reason. And what was driving him? Pity? Friendship? Or did he just want to prove a point?

She trusted him; he was hers to command. This was a strange new experience. Did she like it? Not really. The imbalance of power was a turn-off. All she had to do was tell him to stop. And she would. In a minute. Once she had thought this thing through.

He slid under the sheet, licking her belly button, and she felt herself yielding as he moved down. She had to admit it felt good. Oh, so good. The ache easing, the stinging soothed, the discomfort forgotten. It was getting harder to remember why this had to stop.

Phenylalanine, the essential α-amino acid $C_9H_{11}NO_2$ Jaq had ingested with her dinner of egg noodles, was undergoing rapid oxidation to $C_9H_{11}NO_3$. Tyrosine, one of the twenty standard amino acids used by cells to synthesise proteins, was in turn oxidising to $C_9H_{11}NO_4$. Levodopa, a short-lived intermediary, expelled a molecule of CO_2 to make $C_8H_{11}NO_2$. Dopamine brings a rush of pleasure as the reward pathways in the brain go into overdrive before oxidising again to form $C_8H_{11}NO_3$. Norepinephrine is sometimes called the fight or flight hormone, but Jaq wasn't leaving, and she certainly wasn't fighting. There's another response they don't mention in the textbooks: sexual arousal.

A moan escaped her lips. *Treacherous body.* Yielding to the pressure of his fingers gently parting her legs, keeping his hips away from her as the stubble of his cheek grazed her inner thigh. A runaway chemical reaction had taken hold of her body.

Another α-amino acid from her food, tryptophan, $C_{11}H_{12}N_2O_2$, was undergoing hydroxylation to form the intermediate 5-hydrox-ytryptophan $C_{11}H_{12}N_2O_3$, followed by decarboxylation to produce

$C_{10}H_{12}N_2O$. Serotonin – one of lovemaking's most important chemicals, chasing away our wits, making us temporarily insane.

And now resistance was futile, response was instinctive, primeval. Unable to help herself, she lifted her hips towards his tongue, flitting from one frisson of pleasure to the next. The warmth rose up, spreading to her core, rolling in ripples across her body.

Transported to a beach, warm sand between her toes, hot sun on her naked body, whole again, she surrendered to the swell of the ocean. At first the little waves nibbled at her ankles, then they lapped around her knees, the waves increasing in power until her feet were sucked from under her and she was floating.

Carried out to sea, the waves were bigger now, the warm water caressing her breasts, surging between her thighs.

Just when she thought the pleasure was over, a new swell rose, the summit just over the horizon. And then the aching and yearning started all over again and she was diving back into the water, swimming out through the surf to find where the clear green water crested, twisting to attain new heights as wave after wave of pure delight crashed over her.

Her pituitary was in overdrive, flooding her brain with giant molecules of $C_{43}H_{66}N_{12}O_{12}S_2$ – a peptide of nine amino acids in the sequence cysteine-tyrosine-isoleucine-glutamine-asparagine-cysteine-proline-leucine-glycine-amide. Oxytocin for orgasm.

And bonding.

She had no idea how long it was before she washed back onto the beach, exhausted, utterly spent.

'Sweet dreams, Jaq Silver.'

She could taste herself on his lips as he kissed her goodnight.

'Goodnight, Timur,' she whispered, drifting into sleep in his arms.

When she woke, he was gone.

PART VIII
FEBRUARY

Vladivostok, Russia

A bitter wind blew in from Siberia, bringing daggers of ice. The snow was falling faster now, dusting the branches of the swaying trees, settling on the window ledges of the palace where the old man lay dying.

He kept his eyes closed – what use were blind eyes? – as he took stock of his surroundings: a different room, the echoes suggesting somewhere smaller. A machine wheezed and beeped. The medical wing? A light breeze cooled his lips and something pressed against his face, as if his glasses had slipped, tightening across the bridge of his nose and wrapping themselves under his chin.

Whatever they had done, the pain had gone and his mind was clear again.

Only the guilt was left.

Guilt, Dmytry reflected, comes in many forms: guilt for things you did, guilt for things you failed to do, and survivor guilt.

He felt no guilt for the things he had done in his life, the decisions he made. Nothing is without risk; everything comes at a cost. Take the fortune he'd made. If he had continued as a civil engineer when he returned from China, he would have remained in the one-room flat above an Irkutsk power station until he was carried away by ambulance to exhale his dying breaths on a trolley in the corridors of the state hospital.

It was his willingness to take risks, risks far beyond those allowable in his original profession, that had enabled him to accumulate so much wealth. More money than one man could ever need had passed through his fingers.

In the chaos after the Iron Curtain came down there were easy pickings, rich pickings. All you needed were connections.

He bought a grand house, a big car, rented an office in a good part of town, hired young escorts to accompany him to functions – appearances were everything, and an older man with a young woman on his arm was the perfect demonstration of power.

That's how he met Svetlana. He thought her different from the others, until she got pregnant with his child. After Timur was born, he gave her money to go away. He found a nurse, a gentle woman who reminded him of Nina, and let Timur call him grand-father. It was so much easier than trying to explain. He raised the boy by himself.

Would he tell the boy the truth? Why? What was there to be gained?

He felt no guilt for the things he had chosen to do. But guilt for the things he had failed to do, now there was a thing to haunt a man. He'd allowed structures to be built too fast, turned a blind eye to the shoddy materials used, left poor workmanship unchal-lenged. If the design was right, those things could be remedied. When the cracks appeared, they could be plugged by the right mix of mortar, the right depth of injection, the right supervision of the repairs.

If the design was right.

Could he have challenged the design of the dam? Supported his Chinese colleague, who, Cassandra-like, warned of the danger and was sidelined for his pains? Refused, point-blank, to strengthen the lethal structure? It wasn't as if he hadn't been warned.

It was Nina's father who cautioned him.

Dmytry toppled his king as he admitted defeat, cursing the distracting effect of his opponent's daughter.

Dmytry and Wang Jun played chess every week. In exchange for teaching Dmytry the Chinese game of Xiangqi, Nina's father insisted on learning federation chess. He had a fine, strategic mind and the two were closely matched, although Nina's presence caused Dmytry confusion and defeat on more than one occasion.

'*This chess set, it's not part of the collection?*'

Wang Jun shook his head. 'A good fake, but a fake nonetheless. So, Nina showed you?'

Oh, yes. Nina had shown him. He had to fight not to blush. Nina was slowly introducing him to the jade collection. And to so much more. His lips still tingled from her butterfly kisses.

'*The little water buffalo. That's one of my favourites. Deceptively simple. Takes real skill to carve such flowing lines from such hard stone.*'

'*Your collection is exquisite.*'

'*It's not mine. I'm keeping it safe until the museum is rebuilt and I can return everything. I rescued it from the flood.*'

A biblical reference? 'The flood?'

'*At the start of the war. You were too young to fight?*'

'*I lived through the hardship.*'

His mouth tightened. 'What do you know of China's war?'

'*I know that millions died fighting the Japanese.*'

Wang Jun snorted. 'It wasn't only the Japanese. Our own armies contributed with their scorched earth policies. Or flooded earth, in this case.'

'*Tell me about the flood.*'

'*The nationalist army decided to use water as a weapon. They breached the dam on the Yellow river near Zhengzhou and let the water pour out to halt the advancing Japanese.*'

'*Ingenious.*'

'*Disastrous. The peasants received no warning. Hundreds of thousands drowned. Millions were made destitute. Our own people.*'

Such numbers were unbelievable. How could water, the stuff of life, cause such a disaster? 'It's hard to credit . . .'

'*Twenty years ago, and already no one remembers. And here you are, you Russian engineers, helping us to build new dams, bigger ones.*'

'*Stronger ones!' Dmytry reassured him.*

'*And what happens if the waters breach them?*'

What indeed. His skin prickled. 'Did it halt the invasion?'

Wang Jun shook his head. 'The Japanese army changed direction and attacked Wuhan instead.'

Survivor guilt. That was the worst. He had survived where others had died. His inaction had killed them. So many of them. His bony fingers closed around the pyramid of white jade carved into a circle of dragon fire. He brought it to his upper lip, rubbing it across the skin where a moustache bristled, losing himself in the familiar texture of memory until the tears came freely.

When he told her he had to leave, Nina said nothing. Instead she unpacked the lovers' cup. That day she told him the story of everlasting passion, transcending time and distance, overcoming geography and politics. She filled each cup with rice wine, and they drank together and made their vows.

The first time they made love it was slow and soft and oh, so sweet. She smelt of jasmine, tasted of honey. Her dark eyes were fathomless, filled with curiosity and devotion. 'Be careful,' she whispered, and he pulled away just in time.

Afterwards, he detached the two lids, small discs of white jade, threading a strand of fine straw through each eyelet. He fastened the circle of flowers round her long slim neck as she wept, and allowed her to hang the pyramid of dragon fire around his own.

'One day,' he said, lifting the cup, 'I will make this whole again.'

They made love again, a sort of desperation overtaking them, losing themselves in one another's bodies, forgetting everything in order to remember.

He never saw her again.

Except in his dreams.

Nina is hovering above the lake, folds of green silk billowing around her, her long black hair streaming up and out like a fan. He stretches out his arms. Every fibre in his body aches to hold her again. It has been so long. He is trapped, unable to move, but it is all right, she is coming to him, flying to him. He tries to take her in his arms, but something comes between them. He can feel it pressing against his chest as she moves closer. The lovers' cup! She pulls away, leaving him the muslin-wrapped bundle. He is surprised at the weight, the warmth. What is this? He opens his mouth to ask her, but she is fading, wasting away before his eyes, thinner and thinner, her brown eyes huge, her cheeks sunken. The silk blows tight against her and he gasps in horror to see her ribs forming a cave of bones over a concave belly, her arms and legs stick-thin, her hip bones protruding. And all the while, the bundle in his arms is growing heavier and heavier. And starting to move. With trepidation, he peels the muslin aside. A pair of bright green eyes stares back at him.

A little mouth opens and starts to howl.

Dmytry woke to the murmur of conversation.

'Mr Zolotoy had a very bad night, I'm afraid. He's taken a turn for the worse.'

A muffled voice. 'Can I sit with him?'

Was it the damn priest again? Offering false promises?

'He needs to rest.'

'There is something he asked me to do. Something that was very important to him. He'll want to know right away.'

Dmytry's eyes flew open. 'TIMUR!' The cry was lost in a pyramid of plastic, the breathing mask tight around his mouth and nose.

He struggled to free his arms, the sheets pulled so tight they imprisoned him, cursing at his own weakness, gasping for breath. Sparrow wings inside his ribcage beat a new rhythm. He fumbled under the bedclothes for the alarm. His fingers closed around the jade pendant. He pushed it aside, found the plastic button and pressed.

Footsteps approached.

'There, there, Mr Zolotoy. Calm yourself.'

Dmytry swore into the mask. '*Otvali!*'

A warm hand squeezed his shoulder. '*Dedushka*, it's me.' Sensing his struggle, Timur loosened the sheet, allowing his hands to break free.

Dmytry pulled the mask from his mouth. 'You found it?'

'I found it.'

Eagle wings entered his chest, beating hard and fast, preparing for flight.

'You have it?' Dmytry held out his hand. 'Here?'

'Not here.'

'I don't have much time left.'

Timur squeezed his hand.

'Before I can bring it to you, there's something I need to ask.'

'Ask me anything.'

'You're my father, aren't you?'

Dmytry couldn't deny it, so he said nothing.

'And my mother?'

What point was there in keeping secrets now? 'A girl who comforted me for a time.'

'Is she really dead?'

Dmytry sighed. 'The priest will find her, if you must know.'

'Why did she . . . leave me?'

'I made her go.' Perhaps the truth would help them both. 'I gave her money to leave you with me. I'm sorry.' For the first time he meant it. 'I couldn't love another woman after Nina.'

He blinked repeatedly, his eyes smarting.

'Nina gave me this' – he held up the circle of dragon fire – 'and took the circle of flowers. We promised to reunite them with the cup.' *And with one another.* He scrunched up his eyes to stop the tears.

'What happened to Nina?'

'She died. Along with our daughter.'

Timur took his hand.

'Ru?'

Ru. The river. Their river. 'How could you know her name?'

'I met a woman with bright green eyes, just like yours. She has the circle of flowers. Her name is Ru.'

His heart was leaving his body, taking off like a rocket. It wasn't possible. Not after all this time. His voice broke as it rose in pitch. 'Where is she now?'

'A place no one has ever heard of, in the middle of Henan Province.'

'Where!'

'Banqiao.'

There was no escape after all.

Ice in his veins, frozen arrowheads speeding towards his heart. Powerless to stop his legs twitching, his arms flailing, the pressure on his chest like a truck slamming into him, squeezing him against a wall, the convulsions taking control of his body.

Suiping, Henan Province, China

The moon rose behind the mountain casting a pale shadow over the valley. A huge fair man with a shock of platinum hair sat at a table beside an open window, staring at a map on a computer screen. A woman came up behind him, moving slowly as if each step caused her pain.

'You're all leaving?' she asked.

'Timur gets back tonight. Time to move on.'

'Can I come with you?'

Holger shook his head. 'Jaq, you're not well enough to fly. Stay here and recover. Speedy will stay with you. We'll be back in a few days.'

She pointed at the screen. 'How's the tracking?'

'The factory is still moving.' Holger pointed at three blinking dots on the screen. 'The green one, that's the limpet tracker. I stuck it on the side of the barge you saw in Shanghai.'

'And now it's going backwards?'

'Offloaded at Wuhan, going back to Shanghai with a different cargo.'

'And the red one?'

He checked the legend. 'A least five signals in that one dot. I hid a bunch of them inside the equipment.'

'You got onto the barge?'

'I threw them in.' He demonstrated, raising an immensely long arm, swinging it back and flinging it forwards. 'I got one inside the big metal tube' – the extraction column – 'and maybe two into the big red pots with blue edging' – the glass-lined reactors – 'and the big black cubes' – graphite heat exchangers. 'The rest probably bounced back into the river.'

'Is the equipment still travelling by water?'

He zoomed in and checked the speed. 'Yes, they must have offloaded onto another boat. The red signals separated at Jiujiang, were static for a while and now they are moving slowly again. Down the Poyang lake.'

'And the turquoise one?' The smallest dot was moving north.

He checked the legend. 'The big wooden crate. Something fragile and precious inside, it was boxed up pretty good.' He mimed throwing a dart. 'I got it with an arrow-tip tracker.'

'Speed?'

'Faster than the other two. Probably on a truck.'

'Show me the map again.'

Holger enlarged the map on the screen. To the south, Jiangxi Province was dotted with names she didn't recognise: Fujuo, Longyan, Ganzhou. Then he moved the cursor to the north, back into Henan.

When she saw the names of the towns – Suiping, Zhumadian – she suppressed a cry.

Nineteen seventy-five. The Banqiao Dam disaster.

Now she knew where the precious crate from the barge was going.

But she had no idea why.

Jaq said nothing to Holger. She waited until the Masters of Disguise had left for the airport before going outside to find Speedy. He was smoking a cigarette in the moonlight.

'How far is Banqiao from here?' she asked.

'Never heard of it.'

'It can't be far away. It's in Henan Province.' She racked her brains. 'Near Suiping.'

'South of here, a six-hour drive.'

So easy to forget how vast China was.

'We need to go.'

'Are you fit to travel?'

She'd been inactive for long enough. A new energy was flooding into her veins, wiping out the lassitude of pain. 'I can manage.'

They set off early the next day, before it was light. Once they left the highway, the road deteriorated. Winding through fields of corn, the rutted, potholed roads made the last few kilometres a teeth-chattering, bone-shaking, muscle-aching endurance test.

Given the enormous size of the structure, she expected to see it from a distance, but they arrived in the small town of Banqiao without spotting the dam.

'There's some sort of memorial here.'

Speedy pointed to a sign and turned sharp left. The noise and juddering stopped as the car rolled onto smooth tarmac, passing through an avenue of trees, a well-maintained lawn on either side.

At the end of a long, straight road, a grass-covered barrier stretched as far as the eye could see. Below it stood a granite block, engraved with a message, the characters picked out in gold. They got out of the car and stretched their legs with relief.

'What does it say?'

'Banqiao Reservoir Dam. Reconstruction Memorial.'

Beside the memorial stood a taller structure, blocks of pale limestone, one straight edge, the other curved into a wave.

Jaq walked round to the other side. 'Come here, there's more.'

Speedy translated.

'The Banqiao Reservoir Dam, originally built in 1952, was one of the earliest large-scale reservoirs built after the establishment of the People's Republic of China. It was extended, constructed and consolidated in 1956 and was destroyed by a disastrous flood on August 8, 1975.'

Nineteen seventy-five. That was why she was here. Dan's clue. But this was no natural disaster; it was a man-made tragedy. The iron dam. The worst confluence of Sino-Soviet engineering. Chinese tofu construction concealed by Russian concrete.

Too fast, too shoddy, a triumph of political optimism over the harsh reality of hydrogeology. The disaster was wholly predictable.

The Chinese expert on the project, Chen Xing, mandated twelve sluice gates. He was sacked and only five were built. As the first cracks appeared, he was reinstated and repeated his warnings. Sacked again, and a primitive design was shored up with advanced Russian technology, concrete pumped in to strengthen a structure that was fundamentally inadequate.

Speedy continued. *'August 8, 1975, during a period called "ten years of turmoil" when ineffective rescue was provided, so the lives and properties of tens of thousands of people were taken away . . .'*

Tens of thousands? Or hundreds of thousands? Or closer to a million people? Do you only count those swept away as the Ru river burst its banks, or do you include those who drowned as sixty-two dams collapsed downriver? What of those who died of famine and disease in the days that followed? And the eleven million who lost their homes and livelihoods, scattering, never to return?

'It was rebuilt in January 1987 . . .'

To a new design, with the correct number of sluice gates to release water before the pressure could build up to danger level.

'The note is here to help us remember this lesson for life.'

Yes? So why place the note on the back of the monument? So the official cars driving up this elegant road to the offices of the water board could only see the celebration of construction? How many got out of their cars to read the *lesson for life*?

Speedy shuffled his feet. 'What are we looking for, exactly?'

Dan – what were you trying to tell me? Why did you bring me here? Where are you?

'I don't know.'

Speedy stretched. 'I'm hungry. Let's find somewhere to eat.'

The town of Banqiao was little more than a village. A strip of shops along a badly maintained road with some houses and blocks of flats clustered behind. Nothing but garages and electrical workshops, an oil press and a haberdashery. All closed, and not a soul in sight. Speedy parked in front of the only business with any sign of life. An Arabic quotation from the Qur'an announced it as a Muslim restaurant.

'Is this OK?' Speedy looked doubtful.

Jaq peered through a window blurred with steam. 'I just want a bowl of soup.' She pushed at the door. The clack of chopsticks stopped as everyone in the room looked up and stared, a hundred eyes fixed on the foreigner, fifty shades of brown plus a flash of green as an old woman turned away.

A rotund man with a bristly moustache came forward, shooing a white kitten away. After a rapid-fire *rat-a-tat-tat* exchange with Speedy, he showed them to a table, whisking away a soiled paper tablecloth and replacing it with a clean one.

It might not be fine dining, but something smelt terribly good. The dishes arrived one by one. First a plate of spiced aubergines in a rich tomato sauce, followed by a carpaccio of beef on a green salad. And finally, the soup, a great cauldron of lamb broth with giant flat home-made noodles.

Speedy devoured everything with gusto. Jaq took her time, gazing around the room. Everyone had returned to their food, a hubbub of conversation, only the occasional glance to check on the peculiar visitor.

Nineteen seventy-five, less than forty years ago.

The waiter came to clear away her plate. He must be in his fifties or sixties. Perhaps he remembered the disaster. Jaq nudged Speedy. 'Ask him if he remembers the 1975 flood.'

Speedy barked at him, aggressive, staccato.

The waiter shook his head and pointed to someone else, an old woman hunched over a mound of noodles.

Speedy translated. 'This guy moved here from the mountains, in the eighties when they were rebuilding the dam. But he says that the lady over there' – a pair of narrow green eyes flashed up at them – 'Madam Ru, she witnessed everything.'

Suiping, Henan Province, China, 8 August 1975, 2 a.m.

The growl of the river dragon woke the green-eyed girl. She sat up straight and listened.

The pigs were awake, splashing through puddles in the byre below, snuffling and grunting. Thunder rumbled in the distance, on and on. Or was it thunder?

In her dream, the dragon had landed on the opposite bank, where the river used to flow. She had hurried towards him, a fellow monster, fascinated by the flaming pearl under his chin. Strong legs propelled her across the dry riverbed, her feet suddenly sure and nimble on the uneven stones. But as she got close enough to make out the emerald scales on his sinuous body, he arched his back and unfurled his wings. He flapped them once and the sky collapsed, smothering her. He flapped his wings again and the earth cracked open under her feet and she was falling, falling.

Wide awake now, breathing hard and slick with sweat, she pulled the hay from her hair and rolled over, opening a shutter to escape the smell. After days of torrential rain, a few stars had braved the night sky, winking at the receding storm clouds. A light breeze brought warm, moist air that caressed her skin. She stretched her bare arms through the open window and slipped out onto the roof.

The villagers mocked her strong arms. Gorilla Girl, they called her, but her legs didn't work properly so other limbs had to compensate. She pulled herself upwards, scraping the bare skin of a polio-withered leg against the crude thatch of the barn. She stopped on the ridge to catch her breath, inhaling the warm scent of an osmanthus tree that trailed yellow flowers smelling of apricots and honey.

Not thunder. The growl had grown to a roar, and now the earth was vibrating, too. The stones were singing, singing for her. It was a long time since anyone had sung to her. Alone in the darkness, she peered into the night, down towards the village, up towards the mountains – and that's when she saw it.

When the water came, she was ready. She threw up her arms, welcoming the spray that cooled her burning skin. The great wave crested, the water lifted her up and carried her away.

She didn't have to walk any more; she was flying.

'Chu Jiaozi!' *The river dragon has come!*

Suiping, Henan Province, China

A tall bird lurked in the shallows, perfectly still, waiting for the silver ripple of a fish. As the thrum of an outboard motor intensified, the bird turned its head this way and that, forming a question mark with its long neck. The approaching boat ploughed a deep furrow through the water, cascading waves spreading out behind. A dog barked. The bird raised a razor-sharp beak in protest, bending its long legs and springing into the sky, huge wings unfurling – cream feathers fringed with charcoal – trailing its long legs like streamers over the vast reservoir, flapping south towards the forested slopes to find a fishing spot in quiet streams that tumbled from cone-shaped hills.

Madam Ru had not been disposed to talk to them. She berated the waiter, a torrent of abuse streaming forth, before she threw some coins onto the table. As she stood up, her chair clattered to the floor and she banged the door as she stormed out.

The waiter had apologised to his guests. A young man picked up the fallen chair and spoke softly to Speedy.

'I guess it is still too painful for some. But this guy,' he nodded at the beaming man, 'he's offered to take us out in his fishing boat. To look at the dam from the reservoir side. What do you think?'

They'd come all this way, and Jaq had no idea why. She wasn't leaving yet.

Sitting in the front of the fishing boat, a fibreglass dinghy with an outboard motor, Jaq shaded her eyes against the sun and followed the heron's flight, marvelling at the power that had allowed it to rise from the water. Power. A curious concept: rate of work, energy

341

divided by time, joules per second. She turned back to the dam. It stretched east and west, a vast concrete wall that held back 178 billion gallons of water. Water that appeared so benign, the smooth glittering surface broken only by the ripples from the boat.

The reservoir was not just storing water, it was storing energy. A giant battery composed of only the purest, cleanest material.

The pagoda-style roof of the power station came into view as the boat swept round the island. Under the wooden shingles and curling eaves, spinning turbines were converting the energy of flowing water into electricity. Hydroelectric power, cleanest of all forms of energy generation – no greenhouse gas emissions, no waste – and the most versatile: easy to vary the production rate to match the peaks and troughs of demand. Excess energy from other sources can be stored by pumping the water back up to the reservoir. The power output is entirely proportional to the flow of water through the turbines, giant spinning water wheels which turn magnets to produce an electrical current in stationary coils of wire. Power equals flowrate times height of fall times density of water times acceleration due to gravity. Everything is fixed except flowrate, which can be varied by opening and closing the water gates. In a perfect system, with no energy losses due to noise or heat from friction, one cubic metre per second of water with a density of one tonne per metre cubed falling ten metres from reservoir to riverbed gives 98 kW of power. Enough to run fifty electric fires, 500 fridges, 20,000 charging mobile phones. That's 130 horsepower – the work rate of 130 farm horses – all that just from a one-metre cube of water, weighing a tonne, falling from a four-storey building every second. When you think about it like that, it is easy to see just how dangerous hydroelectric power is. In fact, more people have been killed, per kilowatt hour generated, as a direct result of failures of hydroelectric dams than by any other form of energy generation. Water is essential to life, and deadly to it. A few litres are enough to kill you. Every year 350,000 people die from drowning – that's forty people per hour, many of them children.

The fisherman pointed at the power station and shouted, '*Wǒ bùnéng zài kàojìnle.*'

'What is he saying?'

'He can't go any closer,' Speedy said.

'It's OK,' Jaq said. Under the deceptively still water, powerful currents were racing towards the turbines. Best to keep well clear.

'Have you seen enough?'

A good question. Why was she even here? A hint, a hunch. She thought that Dan had directed her to this place, but why? There was nothing to see but water. Had she misunderstood his coded message? Read too much into it because of her fascination with man-made disasters? She gazed across the reservoir, up to the distant hills and then back to the impassive dam.

Something caught her eye. A flash of turquoise. Curiously familiar.

She pointed. 'Can we go over there?'

The fishing boat wheeled round in the direction she indicated, a great arc of spray catching the sunlight. Through shimmering drops of gold, Jaq glimpsed another boat emerging from behind the island. A faster, sleeker craft, jet black and low in the water, silent and powerful, heading straight towards them.

And, standing at the prow, a man with a gun.

Suiping, Henan Province, China, 8 August 1975

The green-eyed girl rode the river dragon. Water everywhere, smashing and swirling, powerful currents sucking her under and spitting her out. Danger all around. A tree, torn up by its roots, snagged her trailing shirt in its branches, rolling her under. She tore herself free, her clothes ripped to shreds, and grabbed hold of a bamboo fence that slithered past. She could hear other people, sobbing and screaming, crying out to one another.

'Oh, my baby! Help me find my poor baby!' A wailing woman swept past clinging onto a wooden door, an ill-designed raft that flipped over as the water surged around some obstacle. When it bobbed back up the woman had gone. Reunited with her baby.

Something blunt and heavy crashed into Ru and the water closed around her. She lashed out, searching for a handhold. Which way was up? The top of her head bumped against a large, soft surface, her hands finding the hide of an animal, a cow or an ox. Everywhere she swam there were more of them, lifeless corpses, moving with the water, trapping her under.

Lungs bursting, aching for breath – she'd never been under the water this long – desperation gave her new strength. She kicked against the animal carcasses, but it was no use. She rolled with them, moving herself sideways until she found a gap.

She surfaced, gasping. The new moon was a sliver of light, but the stars were bright in a clear, mocking sky. I've sent you all my water; it's your problem now.

Around her, others tried and failed to stay afloat. She kept her distance. There was no love lost between Ru and the villagers, but she had to look away, avert her eyes from faces that she knew: the boy who threw stones at her and called her a freak, the girl who brought the swill she was meant to share with the pigs. The lucky ones must have been asleep when the tidal wave hit them; they would never wake up. The less fortunate struggled on through the nightmare, but all were doomed.

Ru had one advantage. She'd learned to swim long ago, when she lived with her grandfather beside the reservoir, in the same water that was now tearing up roads and carrying away whole villages and their farms. Perhaps the water remembered her because, bit by bit, it allowed her to move to the fringes, away from the arrowhead with its waterborne shrapnel and missiles.

But she was tiring. Each time something crashed into her, it took her a little longer to recover, increasingly difficult to time her breathing to miss the standing waves, going under more often, taking longer to surface. Coughing out water only to take it into her lungs again. Her arms ached, their movements weakening.

When she smashed into a tree, her instinct was to push herself away. But she no longer had the strength, so she wrapped her arms around the trunk instead. The water pummelled her, pressing her chest against the smooth bark, while debris slammed into her back, knocking the breath out of her.

The world began to spin. Was this any worse than drowning, finding refuge above water and yet being unable to breathe? If she let the water take her, the end would be quick. She slackened her hold and the current spun her round the trunk. The pressure eased on her chest and she was able to take in great sobbing lungfuls of air. She hung onto the trunk, not giving up, not ready to stop fighting yet. Her arms ached; the effort of pulling against the current was too much. Only two ways out. Down or up. A low branch touched her face and she reached up to grab it, praying it would hold as she heaved herself upwards.

'Go away.'

A moon face appeared in the darkness. A boy, younger than her, kicked at her with a dangling leg.

'This is my tree,' he said. 'I was here first. It's not strong enough for two.'

He was probably right; the slender trunk was bending in the current now that her full weight was suspended from it. But what choice did she have? There were no other trees near, and she didn't have the strength to continue.

'Please,' she begged. 'Just let me rest a while.'

'Get lost.'

As kicks and blows rained down on her, she grabbed a thin ankle to make it stop. He screamed as he lost his balance and fell into the torrent.

It took forever to haul herself up to the spot he had occupied, a saddle between higher branches. Using her arms to swing a leg either side for balance, she jammed her back against the larger branch while holding onto a smaller one. It was a young tree, the type that shoots up tall before filling out. Other structures had attempted to resist the onslaught and snapped, but this tree had bent under the initial wave – she could see debris among the topmost leaves – and sprung back as the torrent abated. Slender and flexible, rather than thick and sturdy, it might survive. As might she. For the first time that night, she began to believe it. Her breathing slowed. She closed her eyes.

When she woke, she saw that a pale band of light had appeared at the eastern horizon. She looked back towards the mountains. The river dragon was sleeping. The water that should have been confined in a reservoir now lay spread across the fields. There was little sign of the towns and villages that had once dotted this land, no landmarks to tell her how far she'd travelled. The first wave had torn into the sleeping settlements with brutal force. Anything anchored to the ground was flattened; everything else was swept away.

As the sun rose, she took stock. Her village was gone. She wouldn't miss most of the people, but she was sad for the animals. The pigs had been her friends, especially the new litter of piglets. Since her grandfather had died, the pig barn was the only home she knew.

Ru stayed in the tree all day and a second night. It rained a little and she opened her mouth to catch the water, then licked it from the leaves, but she was still so terribly thirsty. She knew better than to drink the flood water. The swollen things bobbing around below her were beginning to smell and she tried not to look too closely at their faces. Insects crawled in her hair and buzzed around her eyes and nose. She tried to eat them, but her mouth was too dry to swallow the disgusting dry morsels.

By the third night she knew she would have to move in the morning. The waters must be receding; perhaps she could swim to safety.

Suiping, Henan Province, China

The black speedboat approached the fishing boat, and the fisherman shrank into his seat, head bowed, shoulders hunched, suddenly diminished. His hand trembled on the tiller.

The man standing on the prow of the speedboat lowered the gun and lifted a loudhailer to his mouth. The message was both distorted and clear. The boatman reached behind him and cut the engine.

'What's going on?' Speedy turned to Jaq. 'Who is that? How does he know your name?'

With a sinking heart, Jaq recognised the man standing on deck. Polished shoes, neatly pressed uniform, black gloves, police cap. Yan Bing, the policeman who had run her out of Shingbo. What was he doing here?

The speedboat came alongside, and another uniform grabbed the rail of the fishing craft and secured it with a rope.

Yan Bing spoke to the boatman. Clipped, precise words. The fisherman recoiled, each staccato burst from the thin lips of the policeman the lash of a whip.

Yan Bing turned to Jaq.

'Dr Silver,' he said. 'What an unpleasant surprise.'

'The dismay is mutual,' she said.

'Please, step across into my boat.'

'And if I don't?'

'Then I will arrest you all.'

'On what grounds?'

'This man here,' Yan Bing waggled a dismissive foot at the boatman, 'is profiteering. He has no licence to take tourists onto the reservoir. In fact, foreign tourists are banned from this area, so he is also breaching national security laws.'

Yan Bing nodded his head at Speedy. 'And your translator, Peng Ran, is from Shanghai?' Speedy nodded his head. 'Therefore, not licensed to work in Zhumadian. Aiding and abetting a spy.'

'A spy?'

'Yes, Dr Silver. I have reason to believe that you are engaged in industrial espionage.'

'That is ridiculous.'

'I'm willing to hear your side of the story, but only if you come with me.' He raised his voice. 'Step across, right now.'

'Jaq,' Speedy whispered. 'There's something not right here.'

'Silence!' The click of a safety catch as Yan Bing raised his gun. He pointed it at the boatman. 'Either you come with me, or your fisherman friend will suffer a most unfortunate boating accident.'

Jaq stepped sideways, directly into the line of fire. 'Hardly an accident if you shoot us at point-blank range.'

'By the time you've gone through the turbines, the bullet will be lost in the human mince, and no one will be any the wiser.'

Jaq shuddered. What sort of a mad bastard was this man? 'You leave me little choice.'

Speedy grabbed her hand. 'I'm coming with you.'

Jaq jumped across onto the black speedboat. Speedy followed.

'This way.' Yan Bing opened a door.

Jaq stepped inside, turning back at the cry, followed by a splash. 'Speedy!'

Yan Bing stood in the doorway, blocking out the light.

'Your translator fancied a dip in the water.'

'You bastard.'

'This reservoir has taken so many lives over the years.' He shook his head. 'Tragic, really.'

Jaq faltered as he raised his gun and pointed it at her.

'Some people need to be protected from their own stupidity,' he said. 'Those who have no idea just how dangerous water can be.' He stepped back from the door frame, into the light.

Jaq rushed towards him; the door slammed in her face.

She tried the handle. The door was locked. She put her ear to the keyhole, but all she could hear was the distant barking of a dog.

Suiping, Henan Province, China, 10 August 1975

Ru was woken by the sound of a dog barking.

'Yinling!' The call came across the water. A man was rowing a boat towards her, the sun behind him. All she could make out was the silhouette of arms even stronger than her own, his muscles bulging as he pulled the oars through the water. 'Yinling, is that you?'

Her throat was so dry, she could only croak, but the boat came faster now until it was under the tree. She looked down to see a sturdy man, his square chin covered in dark stubble, a golden-haired dog barking wildly.

'Oh.'

As their eyes met, a sob escaped him, then a long sigh as he caught sight of her withered leg. Double disappointment. Not only was she not his Yinling, but she was a cripple. He began to row away.

Ru dropped into the water and swam after him, grabbing the stern of the boat.

'Help me,' she begged.

He shook his head, rowing harder. 'I need to find my wife.'

She gestured at the vast expanse of water, nothing above the horizon except for a few slender trees, the water heaving with bodies and flies.

'The river dragon spared me for a reason,' she said. 'I can help you.'

He paused at this, then relented, holding out a hand to help her into the boat, balancing it as she struggled over the side. The dog licked her face as she flopped, like a huge fish, into the bottom.

'Water,' she begged. He handed her a stone bottle and she drank deeply. 'Enough!' he shouted and pulled it away from her, his eyes narrowing. 'I'll take you to land. Then you're on your own.'

He wore a thick gold band on one finger. She eyed the contents of the boat. Fishing lines and nets. Clay pots which might hold food.

'Where are you from?' he asked.

She named the village, and then, in response to his blank expression, added the nearest town. 'Near Suiping. And you?'

'Banqiao,' he said. 'Upstream of the flood.'

'But your wife, Yinling?'

'She went to check on her mother last week. Near Zhumadian.' He shook his head. 'I told her not to go. The weather was too bad, flooding everywhere. I need to find her.' He began to row again, calling out his wife's name. 'Yinling!'

She took advantage of his distraction to open the seal on one of the clay pots. Dried fish sprinkled onto a cold maize porridge. She kept her back to him and scooped handfuls into her mouth. The dog watched her, quietly complicit, so she allowed him to lick the pot before stowing it back with the others. Now she was thirsty again. But when she asked for water the man shouted at her instead. She lay down. The dog stretched out beside her and licked her face, as if to apologise for its master. She closed her eyes.

She woke to the rumble of the boat sliding onto gravel.

'This is where you get off,' he said.

She sat up and looked around. A slight rise in the middle of the water. An artificial island miles from anywhere. No village, no people, no fresh water, no food. Nothing to see in any direction except bobbing black pillows, where flies feasted on putrid corpses.

'You can't leave me here.'

'The water's going down. You'll be able to walk to safety.' He picked her up and heaved her over the side. The dog whined.

'Wait!' she screamed. 'I can't walk.'

He ignored her and pushed the boat back into the water, rowing like a demon while the dog whimpered.

Anger gave her strength. She hauled herself back into the water, slowly at first as she pulled herself over gravel and then sludge. But once the water was deep enough, she swam fast, long, clean strokes underwater, trying to avoid the buzzing carcasses each time she came up for breath.

If he'd seen her coming, he could easily have escaped, but after ten minutes' hard rowing, he'd stopped to eat out of sight of the rise. On discovering a bowl of food licked clean by a canine tongue, he started beating the dog, first with his fists and then with an oar.

His brutality gave her strength. She caught the oar as he swung it sideways, pulling him off his feet. He hit the side of his head on the transom and shouted out in anger and pain. Pulling the side of the boat towards her, she rolled him overboard. He made a grab for her, but she dived under and pulled herself in on the other side. Desperation made her fast and strong. She hefted the other oar and lashed out at him as he tried to climb back in, smashing the hands that grasped at the boat's ribs until he let go. She propelled the boat away with the single oar.

'Wait,' he cried. 'I can't swim.'

She held onto the dog as they listened to him drown, then she took a long draught of water and went back for the other oar.

And his gold ring.

The fever started that night. However careful she'd been, she'd ingested several gulps of contaminated water. Every part of her body ached, and her skin burned with fire. The dog sat beside her, licking the sweat from her brow as the boat meandered wherever the weak currents took it.

The river dragon returned. She begged it to take her, let her fly away on its scaly back. But Moon-faced Boy appeared and whispered to the dragon, telling tales and lies, so it flew away. As it crossed the waxing sliver of moon, she saw that Stubble Man was on its back, brandishing an oar, towing a woman on a wooden door like a magic sleigh. The woman was holding a newborn baby, cradling it, singing to it, loving it. She dreamed of a place where her parents loved her. Surely she must have had parents once. Was she abandoned as a baby because she was a girl, or later because of the sickness that had wasted her leg? Tears streamed down her cheeks.

On the fifth night, the fever broke. The dog whimpered until she fed it, and then she ate a little herself. She nestled into his warm fur and then the shivering started.

They didn't stop at the first village – she could see they were as wretched as she was – or the second. She waited until the food and water were finished and the putrid lake resembled a river again. Before they reached the next village, she found branches strong enough to act as crutches. She lashed the boat to a post and, with the dog by her side, limped her way into the village.

The ring was almost worthless. Law of supply and demand meant that plenty of destitute people were selling jewellery, and all anyone wanted was food.

So, she sold the dog instead.

Suiping, Henan Province, China

Jaq rattled the shackles that imprisoned her in the cabin of the police boat, her hands and feet cuffed to a sturdy metal post. It had taken three of them to restrain her, but now Yan Bing sent the other two away.

Breathe. Through the soles of your feet. Stay calm. Feet apart, chest forward, chin up. Drop your brain into your stomach. Quench the anger. Slow down. Now is not the time to lose your head.

'What do you want?' Jaq's voice was low and calm.

'Information,' Yan Bing said. 'Why are you here?'

Why dissemble? 'I'm looking for the factory that vanished.' *And for my student who vanished with it.*

'You think I am stupid? You think I don't know who you are working for? You and that disgusting bunch of perverts who take their clothes off for money.' He spat on the ground. 'You were with them in Durham on the day of the theft from the Oriental Museum. You were in Lisbon for the switch at the Museu de Arte Antiga, and in Sweden to collect the Drottningholm Palace haul. So where's the stuff you stole?'

'I have absolutely no idea what you are talking about.' *Oh, Timur, what have you done?*

'I already know who ordered the theft.'

'What theft?'

'There's no point in protecting Wang.'

Wang? The Chinese owner of Krixo, the shady joint venture partner who remained hidden?

'I'm not protecting anyone.'

'Where is Wang?'

'I have no idea.'

354

'Why are you here then?' Yan Bing sneered. 'What is your real interest in Krixo?'

So, she was close.

'What I'm really interested in is rare earth metal recycling.' Not a word of a lie. If only it wasn't for this damn mystery, she could be spending a lot more time on the things she cared about, like how to bring safe, clean energy to the world without destroying the planet. 'I'm a chemical engineer.'

Baotou, Inner Mongolia, China, 1985

The wind cut like a razor, chilled and sharpened by its journey across Siberia. It howled across the dark lake, whipping up clouds of black dust at the shore. Through the grey smog wafting over from the distant factories, a long line of workers snaked up from the pits, each one carrying a hessian sack. Men, women and children queued outside the shack, bent double from the back-breaking labour, the exposed skin of their faces livid and scarred from the acid fumes, their ragged clothes filthy from scavenging the tailing ponds of an opencast mine.

Inside the shack, an abacus clattered, black beads sliding smoothly over wooden shafts. Ru pulled the cloth cap down over her ears and blew on her hands. The heat from the furnaces didn't reach the intake bay.

Baotou, this godforsaken mining town in Inner Mongolia, was her reward for surviving the flood. In the end, it wasn't the dam bursting that caused most of the deaths. Many more perished in the aftermath. Slowly. Painfully. Hopelessly. With no fresh water, scant food and medicine, disease spread quickly. Messages were sent out, but any help that came was too little and too late. The victims of the flood had been forsaken, left to die. For Ru, it was not the first time she had been abandoned, not the first time those with a responsibility to care for her had walked away. She was better prepared than most.

Leaving Suiping for the mines was her idea. Before the flood, a few men from her village had returned rich after only a few years away. A few boys, those who had lost everything, with no ties left, showed interest, but muttered among themselves that a cripple girl would be a liability. Ru showed them the ring, and persuaded them she had more treasure, enough to pay for the first mining concession, her only condition that they took her with them, convincing them that the river dragon was on her side.

And it was true: she had brought them luck.

Every few years they moved on, a cohesive group bound by the trauma of the flood. The band of peasants-turned-miners were used to hard work. Lean and wiry, they could survive on long hours and little food. She lost a few to sickness, injury or love, the latter being just another form of injurious sickness, replacing them with new recruits as news of success reached their poverty-stricken villages.

Ru learned to make herself invaluable. She couldn't cook and didn't fuck, but she made sure they were well supplied on both counts. She traded with villages far enough away not to be corrupted by the mining economy. She distilled crude spirit, keeping a small ration of the purest liquor for her men, selling the rough stuff to their rivals. She knew which palms to grease and which to avoid. She found ears receptive to vicious rumour, destroying the careers of government officials who could not be bought. She acted as banker, guarding her men's earnings, controlling their expenditure, exchanging tokens for silver and gold and investing it.

Her new weighing scales consisted of two brass pans suspended by ropes from either end of a wooden beam, pivoted on an iron stand. The balancing weights were blocks of metal, each one stamped with a number. She had several sets of weights, one for the government inspectors, one for the suppliers, and now, one set for herself.

She'd learned early on that the mines were poorly run, all brawn and no brain. They relied on an inexhaustible supply of labourers: men and women who started with little choice, and as the mining and extraction activities destroyed their fishing lakes, hunting grounds and farmland, ended up with no choice at all. The methods used to extract the metal from the rock were dirty and inefficient, leaving much of the value behind. She knew there was money in muck.

Now it was her turn to prosper.

As each scavenger poured the detritus from the burlap sack into one brass pan, they watched as she adjusted the weights on the other. Once satisfied with the quality, she noted the quantity in a ledger, clicked the abacus and paid in tokens. Tokens could be exchanged for food and other benefits at a rate that she controlled.

The air in the shack was thick with dust. It would be cleaner to weigh the rocks inside the sacks, but the lazy workers often cheated, filling sacks with bricks and any old rubbish. Ru had learned how to distinguish one grey-brown particle from another, to recognise quality.

And value.

She knew the names of her products now: kàng, yǐ, lán, shì, pǔ, nǚ, pǒ, shān, yǒu, gá, tè, dī, huǒ, ěr, diū, yì, lǔ. *Better than a Tang dynasty poem, those trim little syllables tinkled with the sweet sound of money. She followed the prices of each metal. Hoarded a little as prices fell, sold when they peaked. Her luck changed when demand rose for* nǚ — *neodymium. That's when she realised that the money was not in the hard, dirty work of mining. Viewed from Shanghai, she was just another filthy labourer in that long, grubby food chain. The people who became rich were not the miners, but the traders, those who speculated on the Shanghai metal exchange.*

She didn't tell her partners, the men who had come with her from Suiping, that she was selling up. They'd long outlived their usefulness, broken by a quarter of a century of hard labour, as crippled now as she was then. Thanks to a leg brace and many hours of physiotherapy, she had learned to walk. She didn't need them any more.

Time for a change.

Suiping, Henan Province, China

The grinder whirred and sparks flew, illuminating the cabin as the policeman sharpened his long knives.

'Interesting, isn't it,' Yan Bing said. 'I studied art history at Durham University, you know. My final year dissertation was on the history of China as misrepresented by the West: fascinating stories of cruel and unusual punishments.' He placed a book on the table, open to reveal an eighteenth-century woodcut. 'Have a look at this. *Lingchi*. Slow slicing. Death by a thousand cuts.'

The picture showed a naked man tied to a tree. On the ground were his clothes, a priest's collar and crucifix. The drawing was crude but explicit. It showed a Chinese swordsman, dressed as a soldier, removing slices from his victim. Blood poured from shoulder and thigh, and the man's mouth was open, a black hole where his tongue should have been, in a silent scream. Jaq swallowed hard.

'Barbaric.'

'Was this really any worse than some of the things practised in your country? Hanging, drawing and quartering?'

He ran a finger along the text beside the picture.

'Your missionaries were terrible journalists. They had a vested interest in making us seem like savages.' His eyes narrowed. 'But I'm happy to fill the stereotype. If we go for *lingchi* as reported by Friar Martin, then we should start with the eyes, prise out those lovely round eyeballs of yours.'

'Spherical,' she said. Even native English speakers confused two- and three-dimensional words. Round instead of spherical, spiral instead of helical, square instead of cuboid.

'Pardon?'

Perhaps now was not the time to correct him. 'Nothing,' she muttered.

Yan Bing stared at her with such loathing, it was almost solid in the air between them.

Play for time. 'Please continue. All this history is very absorbing.'

He was back in the flow again. Perhaps he had excelled at amateur dramatics at Durham. He was certainly full of himself. Wordy thugs were the worst. It was one thing to have grown up hopeless, helpless, fighting for survival, but anyone who had benefited from further education should know better.

'I imagine the enucleation will hurt, though not enough to kill you, unless the knife slips, of course. You must stay still and listen – the noises will be so entertaining.'

He inserted a finger into his mouth and made a slurping, popping sound.

'As will the fact that you can't see what's coming next. Which should add to the entertainment.'

'I never took you for a coward,' Jaq remarked. 'Only a craven weakling would think it necessary to blind their enemy.'

'Oh, you're not my enemy, Jaq. You are my friend. You're going to tell me everything. Tell me where Wang is.'

'I don't know where Wang is, and I don't care.' If she never heard the name Wang again, it would be too soon. All she wanted was to find Dan, safe and sound.

'Why is it that I don't believe you?'

He steepled his hands. 'You are clever, I'll give you that. And calm. Perhaps because you don't believe that I will do what I say.'

'Let me out of here.'

'And you are quite right. I don't practise *lingchi* myself.'

Jaq narrowed her eyes.

'I have an assistant who is much more experienced than I am. It takes a special sort of skill to maximise the pain while delaying death.'

She looked around for a way to escape. Keep him talking.

'How did your assistant learn this skill?'

'It's an interesting story.' He beamed. 'Her mother owned a butcher's shop in Yulin, her father ran a restaurant. She worked in both, gained early experience. Her family were brutally slaughtered during a Lychee Festival riot – their daughter was the only survivor.'

He stopped and stared at her, judging her reaction.

'How terrible, but—'

'After she decapitated the daughter of her foster-family, the police reopened their investigation into the festival murders.'

Yan Bing let out a long, low cackle.

'Too young to be tried as an adult, she was sent to a special school. Where I sought her out. I take a keen interest in admissions to juvenile detention. You never know where you will find your next protégée.'

'She follows your orders?'

'Indeed. We usually start with some little cuts, places with the highest concentration of nerves. A slice from the pad of the finger, the ball of the foot, maybe a few fingers and toes,' Yan Bing laughed and broke into song, affecting a childish falsetto, 'and eyes and ears and chin and mouth and nose.' He cackled. 'They taught us that in language school, y'know.'

'What else did they teach you, Yan Bing? That it's wrong to hurt people?'

He came closer, little flecks of spittle from his mouth dampening her cheek. 'After the little slivers, she'll take some chunks of flesh, go deeper with the slices. But don't worry, she won't let you bleed too much, not at first. We have until the Spring Festival, all the time in the world. You don't have to worry about dying any time soon. Although you will die eventually. Only a thousand cuts to go.'

'You don't want to do this.'

'In a way, you are right. My ancestors didn't do it. It was all a foul rumour. Yes, people were executed. In my country as well as yours. A stab to the heart. The thousand-cut mutilation came post-mortem. But your sort always told lies, terrible lies. They were the real barbarians.'

'I agree,' Jaq said.

He reeled back in exaggerated surprise. 'You agree?'

'Yes.' Jaq sighed. 'The British introduced opium to China. A deliberate enslavement. We couldn't live without your tea, your silk, so we made addicts of you.'

Yan Bing nodded. 'You were too weak to fight, you had little else of value, so you chose the drug trade, the lowest, most underhand form of commerce. And then you stole the tea plants and the silkworms and introduced them to India.'

'Stealing technology. Something you Chinese have excelled at ever since. Learning from the masters.'

Yan Bing studied the picture. 'Maybe she'll start with the tongue. So we can work in silence.'

'Then how will I tell you what you want to know, Yan Bing?'

'I thought you said you didn't know anything.'

'We could help one another.'

'So, you *are* looking for Wang.'

'I don't care about the vanishing factory or its mysterious boss.'

'Then what are you doing here? In Banqiao?'

'Looking for my student, Ning Dan.'

'And what makes you think he is here?'

'Something he said.' True strength – yielding, not breaking. The danger of letting the pressure build up. 'The year 1975.'

'What happened in 1975?'

How was it possible that he didn't know? 'Haven't you seen the memorial to the disaster?'

'What disaster?'

'The great flood of 1975, when the Banqiao Dam burst.'

Yan Bing shook his head. 'I've never heard of such a thing.'

Exactly why Dan had got away with the coded exchange.

'Go now. Go and see it. The block of granite below the dam. Walk round to the back. Read what it says.' *A life lesson.*

'You're lying.'

'I'm offering you a fair exchange. You help me find Dan, I'll find Wang for you and leave China.' *And never come back.*

'Why do you care so much about a student? A student is nothing.'

'Why do you care so much about Wang?'

'Wang is everything.' The policeman advanced. 'Wang has the wedding cup.'

'How do you know?'

'Mr Bernard Ashley-Cooper. He told us who bought the wedding cup at auction.' He laughed sourly. 'Just before he died.'

'Then why did you kill Professor Tench?'

He didn't deny it.

'To err is human, to forgive, divine.' He shrugged. 'We went after the seller, the last one to leave the auction.' He laughed. 'Turns out the old man was not the last. Someone else remained behind.'

'Ever thought your interrogation methods might be part of the problem?'

'Where is Wang?'

She locked her gaze with his, so tightly that a knock at the door made them both jump. A shouted exchange through the door made Yan Bing put the sharpened knife down.

'Are you a dog or a cat person, Dr Silver?'

'Why do you ask?'

'Preparation. My assistant finds it helpful to warm up, to provide a little demonstration. We find it concentrates the mind.'

Bernard Ashley-Cooper's cat, Professor Tench's dog. Jaq swallowed hard.

'You see, I supervised my assistant's education, gave her all the anatomy books she wanted, the dogs and cats she needed for practice. Of course, she came to me with extraordinary natural talent, but I like to think I played some part in shaping the woman she is today.'

'I don't approve of cruelty to animals.'

'Oh, nor do I. You are forcing my hand. Think about what I said. If you tell me what I need to know, we might be merciful.'

He moved towards the stairs.

'We might kill you faster.'

Shanghai, China, 2000

Before the flood, Wang Ru had several friends. The fisherman's boy who sometimes lent them a boat. The teacher at her school who had once been a doctor. And her grandfather who, although wrinkly and stern, was the only family she'd ever known. Sometimes, when they were fishing by the reservoir, he would talk wistfully about her mother, Nina, although it made him cry to talk about the old days. After recoiling from a blast of anger, she learned not to mention her father, the man who had tricked and abandoned them all. Others in the village taunted her about her green eyes, told her they were a curse bestowed on her by a bad man from far, far away.

But the flood changed everything.

After the flood, Ru found a new friend. What had started out as a necessity grew to an interest, matured into a passion and flipped over into obsession.

At first it was the coin that provided food to eat, firewood to keep warm, bribes for the gangmaster in return for work for the crew. Coins trickled through calloused hands back into a clay pot for safekeeping. After the stabbing, when Ru took over the management of the night girls, the notes came, too, soft and torn, crumpled and sticky from all the hands that had fondled and groped and held on tight until the transaction was completed. The filthy notes were invested, multiplied and came back crisp and glossy. No longer just security against cold and hunger, but a source of power, buying protection against rivals and thieves who might steal the hard-earned wealth.

Then it was numbers glowing on a computer screen. Share prices, bonds, equities, gilts, spreadsheets, double entry. Counting the money every night before sleep was as close as Ru ever got to lovemaking. Less messy. As a lover, money was often fickle – a tumble in the stock market, a project that was stillborn, a business venture that had to be terminated like a baby girl.

Ru was tenacious, making money by working at it. Day and night. Night and day. Nothing else mattered. And careful with it, mean even, never spending it unless forced to. Accepting risk, taking bold decisions, picking investments shunned by others with better education and deeper prejudice, spotting an opportunity and moving swiftly. Competition was there to be eliminated, and all was fair in love and war. Ru became ruthless.

Ru was fundamentally honest. If a street thug was paid to deter a competitor, then the outcome hinged on how much money changed hands. The sum would determine whether he received a fright, a beating or a fast track to the afterlife. It was an honest transaction when the compact was clear, and no one pretended otherwise.

Ru was fundamentally corrupt. If you pay low wages to public officials in positions of power, then they will supplement their wages. It may start out with favours, small gifts. The Jianli *on the construction site will find a pot of rice wine in his dormitory after he approves the concrete mix. He will find a bed full of dead rats on the occasion he stops the substitution of structural steel with stolen railway track. He learns quickly. If he uses his authority just enough, he will be able to eat and send money home to his family in inland China. If he fails to accommodate the needs of the contractor, his wife and son will receive news of a tragic accident.*

The officials who signed the permits – land, utilities, design, construction, fire protection, export – they became experts in balancing the huge potential for wealth against the risk of one day being made an example of. The wise avoided flashy cars, large apartments, but few could resist private schooling for their sons.

Ru understood the business environment, how to get what was needed without giving away too much.

Until the day she met Xe Lin.

Suiping, Henan Province, China

A patrol boat bobbed on the grey, silk-smooth waters of the Banqiao reservoir, tied to a jetty with long orange ropes. Two uniformed policemen stood guard. Both men wore dark glasses, blue shirts, black belts and holsters with sidearm, grey trousers over black boots. One leaned against a post on the wooden pier and smoked a cigarette. The other sat on the foredeck and gazed out over the tranquil water, whistling a tuneless dirge. The patrol boat, around forty feet long, fast and powerful, was equipped with a main cabin, small galley and makeshift torture cell with adjoining heads, a small bathroom which was securely locked from the inside.

Jaq had no idea how much time she had before Yan Bing returned. And whether his fantasy of slow slicing was about to become a reality. Neither of the two options he had presented – tortured to death or murdered quickly – were exactly appealing. And the second option wasn't even open to her, given that she had no information to trade. No clue where the mysterious Wang might be.

It hadn't taken her long to get out of the handcuffs – what else are earrings for? The first ratchet mechanism was tricky to hook, but as soon as one hand was free, the others were easy. Thank heavens for good-quality jewellery.

Barricading herself in the bathroom was a futile gesture, the lock mechanism so flimsy it would not withstand any determined assault. But it gave her the illusion of separation, a haven to facilitate a few moments of thinking time.

Yan Bing claimed responsibility for the torture of the auctioneer and metallurgist, murdered along with their pets. Was that just to frighten her? Would he really use those knives? Who was the assistant that he had gone to collect? Best not hang around to find out.

Jaq sat on the edge of the bathtub. She could hear the banter of men outside, incomprehensible words. At least two guards. Possibly more. Even if she got through the cabin door, she wouldn't get any further without overpowering them.

So how to escape?

The heads contained a marine toilet, sink and a three-quarters bathtub. There was little in the way of fixtures: a mirror above the sink, a twelve-volt light fitting above the mirror, a rubber-headed plunger and a gas-fired water heater fixed to the wall. She traced the flexible supply line from the heater as it coiled and disappeared through the wall. There must be a gas bottle in a locker somewhere beyond. Propane. Assume a nine-kilogram propane cylinder. And there were probably two cylinders piped in parallel. No one wanted to run out of hot water mid-shower. More than enough.

It looked as if another New Year's resolution was about to be broken.

Once she'd formulated the plan, Jaq didn't hesitate. She pulled off the rubber dome from the plunger and fashioned a crude plug before turning on the cold tap. As the small bath filled with water, she carefully dismantled the light fitting, stripping back the positive and negative wires to bare metal. She tied the positive wire to the wooden shaft of the denuded plunger, so that the bare metal protruded from the end like a snake's forked tongue. She looped the negative end round the sink tap so that it dangled just below the bath. She adjusted the position until it was within easy reach of the bath. When one wire touched the other, it made a satisfying spark.

Jaq took a deep breath before disconnecting the gas supply from the heater. It had to be detached upstream of the safety shut-off, the valve that stopped the flow of gas if the pilot light went out. This was no CORGI installation; the gas hose screwed into the water heater with a simple brass olive, quickly loosened. Thank heavens for shoddy plumbing. The escaping gas hissed as she dropped the open end of the hose to the floor.

One and two and . . .

Holding the makeshift igniter, Jaq slid into the bath, careful not to let any water slop over the sides, and counted.

Ten and eleven and ...

Propane, C_3H_8, forms an explosive mixture in air at concentrations between 2.4% and 9.5%. The bathroom was no more than two metres wide by two metres high and one metre deep. Four cubic metres. If the propane behaved as a perfect gas, 44 grams would occupy 22.4 litres and 9 kilograms would more than fill the room, displacing the air Jaq needed to breathe. Too rich a mixture, no ignition and she would suffocate. Too lean a mixture, no ignition and Yan Bing would kill her. Just the right amount, a successful ignition and the explosion might still prove fatal. But it was her best chance. Assuming a pressure in the cylinder of 40 bars with a standard regulator, it wasn't hard to estimate the flow. Timing was everything. *One hundred seconds.*

Fifty and fifty-one and ...

The chances of the explosion killing her were pretty good.

The primary shock wave might perforate her eardrums, collapse her lungs, lacerate her intestines and cause her brain to haemorrhage.

Sixty and sixty-one and ...

Then there were injuries from flying fragments, missiles shaken free and launched at speed, penetrating her skin and entering the soft tissue, shattering bones.

Seventy and seventy-one and ...

Or she might be lifted by the blast and slammed into a wall, impaled on protruding objects like taps, the door handle or coat peg.

Eighty and eighty-one and ...

And finally, there were the flash burns and smoke inhalation, not to mention being crushed as the structure collapsed around and on top of her.

Ninety-eight and ninety-nine and ...

And every possibility of drowning if the boat sank while she was trapped.

It still sounded preferable to death by a thousand cuts.

Jaq took a deep breath and slipped underwater. She brought the pole down against the metal sink and waited.

Nothing.

She resurfaced. The smell of gas was strong, choking. She looked for the wire – it had moved round the tap. She would have to bring the pole lower. One last chance.

She slipped under the water and tried again.

Silence.

Merda. Why hadn't she made a snorkel? She could have wrenched one of the water hoses free, threaded it into the bathroom vent and breathed through the other end. Too late now.

One last desperate effort.

BOOM!

Jaq sprang from the tub and walked through the jagged hole where the door had been, crossed the office into the main saloon and stepped up into the helm station. Looking aft, she could see the shock wave had thrown one of the police guards into the water, and the other was attempting to rescue him, throwing a floating ring on a rope from the pier.

The key was in the ignition. She turned it and the engine spluttered into life.

'*Tíngzhǐ!* A gunshot cracked and a bullet whistled overhead.

Jaq pushed the throttle forward and the boat took off. A moment of resistance as the boat reached the end of its tether and was held by the dock, but the flimsy structure and rotten supports were no match for the powerful engine. The boat broke free, bounding across the water with three metres of the severed wooden jetty trailing behind.

The two policemen were hanging on. One was in the water trailing behind the severed boardwalk, clutching a red and white ring on a rope. The other was still dry, both arms wrapped around a wooden post that flipped and bucked and leapt in the water as the motorboat gathered speed.

Jaq set the course and flicked on the auto-helm. Clipped to the bulkhead beside the wheel was a fire axe. She walked calmly to the back of the boat and raised the axe.

Could they swim?

The policemen shouted in protest.

They were close to the dam now, near the point where those men had thrown Speedy into the water. Their chances were the same as his, no better and no worse. If they couldn't swim, they would be dead in a few minutes. If they could swim, they would still be conscious when the powerful current sucked them under and carried them into the giant turbine to be minced by the rotating blades.

The closest guard, still bouncing around on his slatted wooden monoski, pulled a gun from his holster and pointed it at her.

'Me or you,' Jaq muttered, and brought the axe down with all her might. 'This one's for you, Lai Lang.' Mr Smiles. A bullet whistled past her ear. 'And this one's for you, Pang Mo.' The Shingbo driver. It took three blows to sever the rope. 'This one's for you, Peng Ran.' Mr Speedy. The split rope flew into the air. Jaq turned her back and returned to the helm, swinging the boat round towards the power station.

Ignoring the screams from the water, Jaq Silver entered a narrow creek and approached the bungalow with a turquoise fountain that had vanished from Shingbo and rematerialised a thousand miles away on the shores of the Banqiao Dam.

Shanghai, China, 2005

Ru first saw Xe Lin in Shanghai. They didn't meet, both preferring to keep a low profile.

On the day of the presentation, the hotel ballroom was buzzing with people anxious to attract attention. Suited lackeys from the management consultancy and investment banks, young men, green about the gills, meeting and greeting the great and the good and pinning name badges on them. Young women in high heels who could barely walk, breasts thrust forward, mincing along with exaggerated hip movements.

Ru, in her loose trouser suit and cloth slippers, watched them with dismay. Why did women do this to themselves? Why would anyone voluntarily squeeze their feet into such instruments of torture? As bad as foot-binding. Long outlawed in China, there were still a few old women with lotus feet, three inches long, their feet repeatedly broken and bound as children to prevent normal growth. A barbaric practice prohibited by the communist party. And yet, high heels achieved the same effect, stopping women from moving freely, reducing them to erotic objects.

Ru slipped into the audience unseen and found a place in the shadows. Despite the number of chandeliers, there were plenty of shadows.

The event opened with an effusive introduction from the Inward Investment Directorate, followed by a series of dull official speeches. Finally, they invited Charles Clark, founder of Krixo, and his translator, Xe Lin.

Charles Clark himself did not impress: an ugly old man, tall and bony with childish round eyes. Another naive Western businessman who claimed to be looking for a Chinese partner. He clearly had no idea what that entailed. For all the potential Chinese investors in the room, the proposition was purely defensive. Krixo was making headlines with a prototype technology for recycling neodymium and dysprosium. If it worked, it would have a disastrous effect on metal prices. That is, unless it was carefully manipulated by someone who understood the market. It was clear from the start that Clark was an idealist, besotted with the science, cavalier about the commercial implications to the point of imbecility. How can smart people be so stupid?

Xe Lin, on the other hand, was fascinating. Not just a translator, it turned out, but also a research chemist with a doctorate in the chemistry of interest. Small and slender, dark hair cut short, modestly dressed in flat shoes, she surprised Ru when she spoke with complete authority: she had a voice that could command armies. Ru leaned forward, entranced. Xe Lin was quick and graceful, but also smart and savvy, the ideal person to do business with. Long before the presentation was over, Ru had decided.

Of course, the deal didn't run smoothly. What deal ever does, when investment banks, management consultants, tax accountants, lawyers and politicians are involved? It dragged on and on, with 175-page contracts full of gibberish, decorated with meaningless official stamps, and all the while Ru sat back and waited until the leeches and the parasites had sucked their fill.

When the one-page summary of practical arrangements was presented, the Englishman nearly walked away, complaining that if he was never to meet his joint venture partner in person, then the deal was off.

Bluster. Charles Clark was not a complete fool. The deal was not off. The art of negotiation is . . .

Timing.

Charles had many strange ways. He appeared oblivious to the fact that, as boss of the organisation, his job was to know what to do, and then shout at the workers until they did it. Xe Lin quickly became the de facto boss. And she was brilliant. Endowed with an extraordinary insight into what made others tick, she had the gift of making other people want to do what needed to be done. Most of the time. And when things didn't go to plan, she could be swift and ruthless. A steel fist in a velvet glove.

Did she guess? She said not, but it was hard to believe, given what followed. Was she especially empathetic? Or simply part of a new generation who had never been exposed to a relentless diet of brutality from an early age? Perhaps the first generation in China's violent history who had been raised with unconditional love. A single child, a girl at that, she had been allowed to live. Someone must have loved her to take that risk.

And she gave that love back. Even to Ru, the crippled old woman who cleaned the lab.

One night, Xe Lin was working late. She'd been running an experiment, and something had gone right. Such was her excitement that she'd danced around the room, grabbing Ru and whirling her around, whooping with excitement. And then pausing, apologising, before explaining. Explaining her joy to Ru as if Ru mattered. Treating her as an equal, a fellow human being. Not a cripple. Not a useless old woman. Xe Lin wanted nothing from Ru. And Ru was content to ask for nothing in return.

Her love was as pure as spring blossom. She loved, protected and cherished Xe Lin as if she were her own daughter.

And even if Ru had loved her in another way, Xe Lin only had eyes for Charles. What she saw in him, no one could understand, but they were good together.

For Ru, Charles was convenient. A simple, academic man. A trusting scientist. No business sense or understanding of the real world. No feel for how China worked. The perfect joint venture partner. He didn't even notice that Ru was building a second factory, mirroring everything that went on at Shingbo. Well, not everything. Charles insisted on Western-style waste; what Ru built in Gangzou was simpler, more efficient.

When Charles Clark died, Xe Lin was inconsolable. She wanted to go to England, to be at the funeral. That's when Ru stepped in. To protect her.

The poison that killed Charles Clark was meant for Xe Lin.

Ru brought her back home.

Suiping, Henan Province, China

The house was perfectly camouflaged. Not only did the bulk of the hydroelectric power station mask it from the north and east, but the folding geology of a narrow creek also hid it from the south and west.

The fountain had moved to a location completely unlike that of the Shingbo industrial park, where Krixo had once announced its presence with pride and giant lettering. Was this where Wang planned to rebuild the factory? The site had the two things it needed most – electrical power and water. But would a factory be allowed here?

In the rush to industrialise China, the obvious place to site power- and water-hungry factories was beside hydroelectric power plants and their watercourses. But the danger of flooding exacerbates the risk of chemical release. This looked less like a factory site and more like someone's private estate.

Was Dan here? Only one way to find out.

Jaq cut the engine, tethered the boat against a wooden pole and jumped ashore. A modern bungalow, roofed in traditional style with ridged tiles and flying eaves, was set back from the lake, guarded by a fence and gatehouse. A security guard emerged.

'*Ni hao!* Jaq held up her arms to show she meant no harm.

The security guard walked towards her, surprise turning to bemusement as she rattled the fence.

'May I come in?'

He retreated into his office to make a call, casting glances at her as he spoke into a telephone. Eventually he opened the gate and pointed to the main building, accompanying her through an arch across a courtyard and into a room as wide as the house, with a polished floor, exposed beams and a full-height picture window.

The room was simply furnished: a wooden table and chairs; hanging scrolls on the walls with *guóhuà* paintings, black ink on cream silk, depicting dramatic landscapes; a group of two padded chairs and a sofa set round an Aubusson rug in front of the window, its grand view of the reservoir diffracted through vertical blinds of pale green silk.

Another security man entered.

'Yes?' he barked.

'I'm here to see Ning Dan.'

'Why?'

Why? Why was she here, beside the Banqiao hydroelectric power station, when she should be building wind turbines in Shetland? Jobless in the centre of Henan Province when she should be earning money to meet her obligations in the far north of Scotland. Why? Why had she thrown caution to the wind to return to China? Penniless? Clueless?

Because of Sam.

Because she'd failed her brother when he needed her most. Because she'd made the wrong decision when he'd been too ill to make his own.

She'd put her trust in others, those who were meant to be in charge, those whose job it was to protect the weak and vulnerable: Sam and Jaq, two lost children trying to find their parents in the middle of a civil war.

She'd taken Sam to safety, to a refugee camp on the border.

'You've done what you can,' they told her. 'We'll care for him now.'

'Go, Jaq,' he said. 'Stay safe.'

He'd put his trust in her and she'd let him down.

The camp was crowded, filthy, violent, full of desperate people fighting to survive. The hospital was overrun. Sam's bullet wounds became infected.

There was something about Dan that reminded her of Sam. The way he trusted her. A level of trust that was unearned, undeserved, unjustified.

And in Sam's case, fatal.

How could she live with herself if she did nothing?

'I'm here to find Ning Dan.'

The man shook his head. 'Not possible.'

Jaq stood her ground. 'Then I want to see the boss.'

A cleaner entered the room with a mop and bucket. Jaq moved out of her way as she limped past, dragging a withered leg. *Santos*, they worked till they dropped in this country. Then again, it was difficult to estimate a person's age in China. Anyone over forty had seen harder times than it was possible for her to imagine.

He shook his head. 'No appointment.'

'Tell Mr Wang either we speak now, or I go to the police.' *Yeah, like Yan Bing is going to be any help here.*

'Why?'

'I don't care why the factory was moved. I don't care about the stolen jade. I only care about Ning Dan.' Jaq took a deep breath. 'He was my student. He trusted me. I need to see him, to hear from his own mouth that he is OK. That he's here voluntarily, not under duress. I just want to know that he is safe.'

'You are his teacher?'

Too complicated to explain. Once a teacher, always a teacher. 'Yes. And I care about my students.' She'd been lazy and careless, accidentally sending him on a fool's errand, straight into danger. 'I have to be sure he is OK.'

The swishing of the mop stopped.

Something tugged at Jaq's memory. The irritating cleaner in the Shingbo meeting. The customer who'd stormed out of the restaurant in Banqiao. She turned to look at the old woman. And saw her for the first time. *Porra*, how could she, of all people, have been so blind? Every bit as prejudiced as the worst of them.

The hunched old woman with the withered leg straightened up. A pair of clear green eyes met Jaq's.

'I am Wang Ru.'

The boss.

Suiping, Henan Province, China

A shout rang through the air.

Wang Ru, the Chinese boss of Krixo, limped to the window and pulled back the blinds. Below the window, the reservoir stretched as far as the eye could see, a smooth sheet of silver disturbed by an interwoven pattern of ripples. A boat? Too small. A bird? Too large. It took Jaq a moment to realise what it was, who it was, coming towards them across the water.

'Wait!' Jaq was out of the house, sprinting towards the security guard.

'Bùyào kāi qiāng!'

A woman was already at the water's edge, shouting orders at the guard that made him run to the boathouse. Jaq recognised the woman from her LinkedIn profile. Charles Clark's PhD student. Research Director for Krixo. She was even more beautiful in real life, and her advanced pregnancy suited her.

'Dr Xe Lin.' Jaq held out a hand. 'At last.'

'Dr Silver, I presume.' Xe Lin frowned. 'Are those friends of yours?' A tiny dog ran around her in excited circles, barking and leaping as the swimmers approached.

Jaq suppressed an exasperated smile. There was no mistaking the smooth, synchronised strokes of Timur and Holger. A madly dangerous swim, even though they had taken the long way round, keeping clear of the dam and the power plant intake. And nowhere near as dangerous as dodging the barges and ferries of Shanghai's Huangpu river one thousand miles downstream.

The two men emerged from the water in their wetsuits, and the security guard handed them towels. Timur strode over to Jaq and gave her a damp hug. 'Jaq Silver. What's a nice girl like you doing in a place like this?'

'I don't need your help, Timur.'

His dark brows met. 'I'm not here for you.'

He turned to Xe Lin.

'I bring a gift for Ru, from her father.'

Jaq jumped at the sudden burst of gunfire, automatic and from the direction of the mountains.

'Quick,' Xe Lin shouted. 'Inside.'

She picked up the little dog and ran, Jaq, Timur and Holger following.

The first security guard fell as they entered the courtyard, crimson petals exploding from his chest. The second guard cowered inside the gatehouse, the glass panes smashing around him.

Xe Lin locked the door as they entered the house, but the bolts and chains were useless against the bullets which shredded the wood. They joined Ru at the far end of the room, watching in horror as the inner door flew open and uniformed police strode into the room.

Yan Bing carried a gun, a large semi-automatic already drawn and pointing. His assistant had something worse in her hands: an ice-blue velvet knife roll.

Of course. The perfect undercover agent. Highly intelligent. Deeply disturbed. A chameleon in appearance and character. One minute an innocent student, the next a femme fatale. Highly efficient, utterly ruthless. Completely deranged.

She had been working for Yan Bing all this time; Lulu was his murdering assistant.

'Well, well, well,' Yan Bing said. 'What do we have here? A bunch of perverts, thieves and liars.'

'Get out of my house.' Ru advanced, fearless.

'Give me the Qianlong wedding cup, and I'll go.'

'I don't have it.'

'You're lying.'

Yan Bing pointed his weapon at Xe Lin.

'On the floor.'

'I can't . . .' Xe Lin protested.

'Now!'

Jaq helped the pregnant woman to the floor. Xe Lin lay on her side, cradling her belly with her hands. Jaq took up position in front of her, shielding the unborn child. The little dog broke free.

Lulu cooed at the pug, who trotted towards her.

Yan Bing muttered an instruction; she laughed and bent down to pick up the dog.

'Where is the wedding cup?' Yan Bing repeated.

'I don't have it.'

Lulu put the dog under one arm and began to unroll her knives.

'No!' Xe Lin watched, appalled.

'Where is it?'

Lulu pulled on a pair of latex gloves before selecting a small filleting knife.

Sensing that something was wrong, the little dog struggled to escape. Lulu tightened her hold. It yelped and started to whimper.

'One last chance.' She brought the knife close to the struggling dog and it shrank away.

'Stop!' Xe Lin was struggling to sit up.

'Stay down,' Jaq hissed.

'I know where it is!' Xe Lin got to her feet.

Lulu released the dog. It whimpered and ran under the table.

'Don't do this!' Ru begged.

'It's not worth a life.' Xe Lin walked to the table. 'There has been too much death already.' She seized the TV remote, and at the touch of a button a silk wall hanging rolled slowly upwards, revealing a safe.

Yan Bing leapt onto a chair and inspected the keypad.

'Combination?'

Xe Lin threw him a glance of contempt and unlocked the safe using the remote. The door swung open.

Yan Bing reached in and recovered a small wooden box, reinforced with strips of iron. He set it on the table and opened the shutter door. Straw spilled out as he extracted the contents, sunlight catching the carved feathers of a wide-winged bird, the scales of a snaking dragon, the soft curves of flowers and pearls. He set the wedding cup down on the table and turned to Ru.

'Give me the lid of flowers.'

She clutched at her brooch. 'It's all I have left.'

Lulu pointed her knife at Xe Lin's swollen belly.

Timur and Holger began to move, but Yan Bing raked the beams above their heads with bullets, the huge window shattering, showering them with glass as they dropped back to the floor.

Ru detached the circle of flowers and handed it to Yan Bing.

'Now you.' Yan Bing pointed to Timur.

Timur sprang to his feet. Ignoring Yan Bing, he advanced towards Ru, unzipping the front of his wetsuit to reveal a jade disc, a circle of dragon fire, on a slender gold chain.

He pulled the chain over his dark hair and handed it to her.

'Your father, Dmytry Zolotoy, sent me. He wanted you to have this. To prove he loved your mother, Nina, as he would have loved you if he had only known you. Banished from China before you were born, he believed that you died with your mother. He has never stopped trying to keep the promise he made to her, to reunite the three parts of the lovers' cup.'

'The dragon fire.' Ru took it from Timur. 'Who are you?'

'Timur Zolotoy, your brother.'

'How sweet.' Yan Bing swung the butt of his weapon towards Timur, who ducked just in time.

Lulu advanced with a knife. 'Get back.'

Yan Bing grabbed the jade from Ru.

'Pack it away,' Yan Bing ordered. Xe Lin began to wrap the jade in straw, starting with the lids.

The little dog continued running around in circles, yapping excitedly. Yan Bing kicked out at it and it sank its teeth into his ankle. With a cry of pain, he picked it up and grabbed a knife from the table.

The shimmering steel, hurtling through the air, took everyone by surprise. Yan Bing's gun clattered to the floor as the sword passed through his throat, pinning him to the wall.

A woman in flowing white robes did a backflip and kicked the knife from Lulu's hand, a second kick to the jaw sending her sprawling. 'Sadistic psychopath.'

'Mico!' Jaq sprang to her feet. 'Am I glad to see you!'

Mico extracted her weapon from Yan Bing's throat and his lifeless body slumped to the floor, his mouth fixed in an O of surprise.

Ashen-faced, Mico turned to the wall and retched. The little dog skittered away to escape the spreading pool of blood and bile, jumping onto the table.

The wedding cup began to topple.

Timur made a desperate lunge towards it, but his movement only hastened the fall.

The Qianlong wedding cup fell to the floor and shattered into thousands of pieces.

In the confusion, no one noticed Lulu until an outboard motor roared into life. The police boat was moving away, back down the creek, towards the reservoir, Lulu at the helm.

Jaq stood at the broken window and watched a new drama unfold.

The damage to the boat had not been repaired. The trip across the reservoir had been fast, well ventilated enough to prevent further build-up of combustibles.

Lulu was not so lucky. The boat had been sitting at the pier, the propane still leaking into the heads, torn fuel lines after the explosion adding to the incendiary mix. An accident waiting to happen. The fire started in the engine but spread quickly.

As the boat emerged from the creek into the reservoir, the flames took hold. The blazing boat began to drift towards the dam.

Lulu screamed as she launched herself into the water.

Had she seen Timur and Holger swimming? Did she think she could do the same? Did she not realise that the men were professionals? Or was she unable to bear the pain any longer: the heat on her face, the smoke in her nostrils, her clothes on fire, the polyester police uniform melting onto her skin?

Holger was the first to move. He made to go after her, but Jaq grabbed him by the arm.

'It's too late.'

The current took Lulu, pulling her in the direction of the dam, sucking her towards the intake of the hydroelectric power plant, the long tunnel leading to whirling turbine blades.

They saw her go under. She surfaced once, and then she was gone.

Death by a thousand cuts.

Ganzhou, Jiangxi Province, China

Jaq and Xe Lin travelled together in the Krixo private plane, a light aircraft with amphibious landing gear, leaving Timur and Ru behind. By the look of it, they had a lot to say to one another. The two women sat at the back, a new security guard in front with the pilot.

The factory was hard to miss. In a wasteland of scarred earth, the shining towers stood out like a spaceship on Mars.

As they circled overhead, Xe Lin pointed out the tanks of solvents and acids used to dissolve salts from the rock, huge silver towers filled with special resin beads to extract and capture the metals from the liquid, mountains of slaked lime, calcium hydroxide, to neutralise the steaming black liquor, banks of filters to remove the waste solid, a side factory to turn it into inert building material and circular ponds to clean and purify the waste liquids for recycling back into the process.

They landed in a quarry, a runway cut deep into the earth where a car was waiting to take them up to the factory.

There was movement everywhere: diggers and bulldozers with wheels the height of a man, an army of trucks to transport the feed to the main factory, and smaller-scale, mobile units that followed behind, cleaning as they went: vacuum cleaners that sucked and slurried and extracted and polished and discharged.

Those who came before didn't care about the land, neglected to fill the holes they dug, failed to replace the earth they removed or treat the water or clean up the air: strip, lay bare and plunder, exploitation as old as time.

Cheaper to haul stuff out of the ground and move on. Even if there were some who tried to do the right thing – pay a fair wage, extract with care, landscape the land, leave the earth as they found it – someone else, somewhere else, would do it cheaper and drive them out of business.

But one man's waste is another man's treasure. The early mining was crude. Gallons of acid were pumped into the hillside; streams of black sludge were channelled into steaming, leaky ponds. The extraction process was inefficient. Mountains of waste remained, containing valuable metals in concentrations that were viable for recovery, given the right technology.

And that was the brilliance of Wang Ru. The Krixo technology had been designed to recycle metals from obsolete electronic devices: batteries, phones, tablets, laptops, games consoles, TV screens. But collecting them was difficult, and separating them from other materials proved expensive.

Wang Ru had seen the opportunity to use the technology for something else, something dull and unsexy, something completely essential: land remediation.

Jaq stared down at the valley. In one direction, a blasted heath. But in the other, where the mining waste had already been removed, green shoots had started to appear. People would follow, farming would return. Wang was bringing this land back to life.

The most sophisticated technology to undo the crudest harm.

There was dysprosium and neodymium in that waste; europium and cerium. Wang Ru was making a fortune.

She was no eco-hero, no saint; she was a businesswoman with a keen eye for an opportunity. But was she something worse? Was she a killer, too?

Dan came to meet them as the jeep entered the factory gates. He held himself with new confidence. Gone were the hollow cheeks and grey skin of the pale wraith she had seen in Shanghai; he was back to the sparkling bundle of intensity she remembered from his student days in Teesside.

His face lit up at the sight of Xe Lin, his expression turning to surprise as Jaq emerged from the jeep behind her.

'Dr Silver!' They embraced, but as he pulled away, his brow furrowed. 'What are you doing here?'

'Can we talk privately?'

Dan spoke to Xe Lin and then opened the door. 'Come with me.'

Jaq followed him up some stairs to a conference room with a bird's-eye view of the factory.

'You got my message?' Dan asked.

'*Lulu is an imposter. No police. Find Wang. Protect Xe Lin?*'

His face paled. 'That was months ago. While I was in police custody.' He ran a hand through his short black hair. 'I sent you a message after that. To tell you I was OK.'

'I didn't believe it.'

He bowed his head. 'I am horrified to have caused you more trouble. Please . . .' He gestured to a table with two chairs, pulling one out for Jaq and taking the other.

'What happened, Dan?'

'From the beginning?'

'Yes, from the beginning.'

A young man filled teacups with hot water, placing two on the table before bowing and withdrawing.

'After you contacted me, I did some research. Discovered that an old friend worked at Krixo as research director.'

Xe Lin.

'We knew each other in England. I had tried to contact her a few times back in China.' Dan blushed and cleared his throat. 'But she never replied.'

Xe Lin had been in Teesside at the same time as Dan. He was sweet on her, but she ignored him. She did her PhD with Charles Clark and then worked for him at Krixo. That at least explained why Dan had made the trip to Shingbo in person.

'I turned up at the factory. Said I had been sent by my teacher from England, asked to speak to Xe Lin. They asked a lot of questions about you, then told me Xe Lin had moved on. I remembered that she was from Banqiao, so I asked if she might have gone back home. That's when things started getting strange.'

'Strange, how?'

'As I left the factory, I was arrested and held in prison. The interrogation was weird – it was led by the head of the Art Police in person.'

Yan Bing.

'I had no idea what he was talking about. He had a scary woman working for him, knife-obsessed, unhinged.'

Lulu.

'She tried to get me to trap you. They seemed to think we were working together, trafficking ancient jade.'

The art squad hunting down the Qianlong collection.

'They released me from prison and held me under house arrest. I was watched all the time. But the knife woman left things lying around – a card from the translation agency SEITA. I guessed it was your interpretation service. I managed to write a message in code and seal it in an envelope with SEITA's address. If the police found it, it wouldn't make any sense. I dropped it out of the window. And prayed that someone would pick it up and post it.'

'You sent that message before I came to your flat?'

'Yes. Your visit surprised them. They made me dress up in a curtain and say I'd been at a monastery. Told me if I said anything more, they would kill you. I tried to give you a message in code.'

SOS. 1975.

'When you left China, they let me out. Just like that.' He clicked his fingers. 'I wasn't giving up on Xe Lin. I tracked her down, here at the other Krixo factory.'

'There were always two factories?' Identical twins. One known to the joint venture, and the other a secret.

'It's more common than you think, Jaq.' Dan at least had the grace to look embarrassed. 'Western companies manage things differently because they are used to labour that is slow and expensive.'

Expensive? Or paid its worth? And slow? Is it slow to plan, to design on paper before launching into construction with concrete and steel? Is it slow to do things right first time? China was the hare to the West's tortoise.

Except that China was winning the race.

'Here in China we have many willing, deft hands.'

Wang Ru built a shadow factory, a place where the Chinese team could run things the way they wanted, without interference from the joint venture partner. Jaq shook her head. Would she ever understand this bizarre country?

'And, before you judge too harshly, have a look at what the English joint venture partners were up to.'

'What do you mean?'

'The English investors didn't like the way things were going in Shingbo. No progress had been made recycling consumer goods. It cost too much to collect and sort them. They were worried they would lose their investment. The Clarks stole something that belonged to the boss. As collateral.'

The Qianlong lovers' cup. The object that Timur and Mico and Yan Bing had all been searching for. The Clarks had stolen it from Ru Wang.

'There's more to this than you are telling me, Dan. Why did you warn me off?'

'I sent the letter telling you I was returning to the monastery to make sure you didn't come back and lead them to Xe Lin.'

She bit her lip. Dan was right. By rushing to Banqiao, she had put Xe Lin, put everyone in danger. Yan Bing had followed her, bringing psychotic Lulu. Without Mico they might all be dead. Jaq shivered.

'Xe Lin is safe.' It was all over now. 'Yan Bing and Lulu are dead.'

Dan shook his head. 'That's not who she is afraid of.'

Dan left the room and returned with Xe Lin.

'Who is it you are afraid of, Xe Lin?' Jaq asked.

Xe Lin shrugged. 'I don't know what you mean.'

Dan took her hand. 'Tell her.'

Xe Lin whispered something in Chinese.

'Is it true that you are working for the English investors in Krixo?' Dan asked.

'Not any more,' Jaq said.

'She's afraid that whoever killed Charles Clark—'

Jaq opened her eyes wide. 'Charles Clark was murdered?'

'Stop!' Xe Lin cried.

'Yes, and whoever did it wants to kill Xe Lin too,' Dan said.

Jaq scratched her head. 'But Charles died in England.'

Xe Lin bowed her head. 'He was given poison in Shingbo.' Her voice was barely a whisper.

'By whom?'

'I can't be sure.'

'Your boss, Wang Ru?'

'Never. They were friends.'

'Even though he stole the lovers' cup from her?'

'Charles Clark didn't steal the lovers' cup.' Xe Lin spoke more confidently now. 'Ru gave it to him, in exchange for his share of the joint venture. SAFE foreign exchange rules make it easy for foreigners to bring money in, but much harder to get it out. The only condition Ru made was that he had to sell it to a museum. They trusted one another.'

'But he betrayed her. He put it up for public auction.'

Xe Lin shook her head. 'Charles would never have done that. He was very ill at the end. It must have been done without his knowledge.'

Jaq admired her faith in the man. In her experience, people followed their own self-interest. Or that of their family. Promises are easy to make, even easier to forget.

'So, if it wasn't Wang, then who killed him?' Jaq asked. 'Yan Bing?'

Xe Lin laughed. 'The police are too crude and stupid to hide something like that. Look how they operate. Their wake is littered with butchered bodies.'

Mr Smiles and his driver, Speedy, the boatman, an auctioneer, a metallurgist, the hapless security guards. Who else?

'Mico?' The sword-wielding stuntwoman who had employed the Masters of Disguise to repatriate the jade? She was more than capable of operating outside the law. And she'd killed Yan Bing in front of Jaq's own eyes.

'Possible. Capable. But why? Charles was poisoned before he took the lovers' cup out of China. What motive would she have had before that?' And poison, in the hands of the best stunt fighter in China? Not her style.

She couldn't leave them out. 'Timur? The Masters of Disguise?'

Xe Lin laughed. 'Fine athletes, gifted thieves, but not killers.' Indeed, their mission had been to repair, not to destroy.

'So, who killed him?'

'Charles was murdered by the person who still has the real lovers' cup.'

'The real lovers' cup?' So, they hadn't *all* been fooled. Jaq smiled. 'Not the glass replica that smashed in Banqiao.'

'You knew it was a fake?'

'Only when it broke,' Jaq said. 'Nephrite doesn't shatter like that.' A hard mineral, a silicate of calcium and magnesium: $Ca_2(Mg,Fe)_5Si_8O_{22}(OH)_2$. Cool to the touch. Tough as nails. 'Did Wang Ru buy the fake at auction?'

'No, the auctioneers certified it as genuine. Experts can tell the difference between jade and glass. The weight, the thermal conductivity, tiny bubbles and other imperfections. The switch must have been made after the auction, but before delivery.'

'Then who has the real lovers' cup?'

'The same person who commissioned the fake and sent it to Wang Ru. The same person who brought me a box of sweets, laced with thallium.' Xe Lin's voice broke.

Thallium. A tiny dose of poison administered in China, effective weeks later in England, with the doctors still scratching their heads. Unless you know what you are looking for, hard to diagnose. It brings an excruciatingly slow and painful death.

'Charles was not the target,' Xe Lin said. 'I was.' She crossed her arms across her swollen belly. 'Because I'm carrying his child.'

This had nothing to do with rare earth prices or stolen jade.

Someone else had wanted Xe Lin dead.

What had Martin at Selkie let slip? That the new English owner of Krixo, Sophie Clark, had come to supervise a difficult job. What job? Spare parts for mechanical seals? That didn't sound like Sophie. Something else. Selkie had sophisticated tomography and 3D printers; they could scan and copy anything.

Even a Qianlong lovers' cup.

And suddenly it all became clear.

Motive – the fear of losing an inheritance.

Means – a chemistry lab.

FINALE

66
Dy
Dysprosium
162.50

Kowloon, Hong Kong

The club took up most of the top floor. Glass walls afforded spectacular views over Victoria Harbour. The stage, a raised circular dais with four catwalks, extended out into the room like the spokes of a wheel or the rays of the sun. Four bar stools had been placed around the circumference, along with a man-sized Perspex cylinder and other props. A curtained crown concealed the gangways, lighting rigs and hoists suspended from the ceiling. Around the stage, smaller-diameter tables nestled between larger ones, tessellated to leave a corridor for the waitresses to serve drinks, and later, for the performers to interact with the audience.

Crystal glasses clinked. The air was heavy, the aroma of ginger and star anise lingering as the banquet was cleared away, along with the fragrance from the elaborate flower displays on each table, but most of all with the scent of the audience: so many individual perfumes, so much anticipation.

The music changed in tempo, from the tinkling of a *yangqin* to the thump of a disco bass. As it rose in volume, the lights dimmed and the compère ran onto the stage, illuminated by a single spotlight.

'Good evening!'

Dressed in a tuxedo, dark trousers, white shirt, waistcoat and bow tie, he greeted and bowed to each section of the audience in turn: north, south, east and west – the four winds. A slight man, Han Chinese, his deep voice carried over the chatter.

'Welcome, ladies!'

From a lighting box, on a platform high above the stage, Jaq scanned the room. The audience really was all female. Some of the women had dressed to kill: strapless, backless, glittering dresses, high-heeled shoes, false nails and eyelashes. Those who had come straight from work or after-work studies wore smart suits and carried briefcases. The noise rose and fell – there was no shortage of testosterone in the room.

Curious, how many times in her professional life had Jaq found herself the only woman in an all-male gathering. More times than she cared to remember. Was this the first time the situation had been reversed? Almost certainly. Women clustered in small groups, but they didn't often flock en masse like this.

Jaq moved aside to let the female technician work the spotlight. No sign of the star guests, not yet. Just two empty seats either side of Mico. The film stuntwoman who rescued Jaq from the attack at the Shaolin Temple, and again at the Banqiao Dam was in her element here. An elegant woman with a cerise handbag leaned across the table, relaying something to Mico which caused both women to throw back their heads in laughter.

'And now, to business!'

The compère held up four golden tickets; he had the undivided attention of the audience now. Nothing much to look at, yet he was skilled at this sort of foreplay. The auction for the prime seats was hotly contested, and by the time the lights went down, the whole place was pulsating.

'Wish me luck!' Ernest emerged from the access galley and climbed onto his swing.

'Break a leg!' Jaq whispered.

One technician worked the spotlight as another lowered him from the ceiling to rapturous applause. Dressed in a shimmering leotard, he used the bar of the swing to perform a series of spectacular acrobatics mid-air, swinging over the audience in all directions, to gasps and cheers. Once his gymnastic routine was over, he jumped onto the stage to take a bow, releasing his long red curls from the band that held them back. Ernest was the smallest of the Masters of Disguise, but he stood a good head taller than the compère. Followed by the spotlight, Ernest ran onto each of the catwalks in turn, progressing with backflips and aerial somersaults right to the end of each one, finally landing in the lap of the woman who had won the first golden ticket. To squeals of excitement, he led her to a chrome stool on stage and danced just for her.

Jaq pressed the first detonator and a firework show exploded on the stage.

Holger joined Ernest on stage in a fake fireman's uniform, descending from the rig by shimmying down a red hose. A platinum-haired giant of a man, he had the audience relaxing into chuckles as he chased the compère around the stage. When he turned the hose on the audience, mirth turned to alarm. The front rows shrieked and ducked under tables as he sprayed them with what looked like water but turned out to be fluidised glitter. After kneeling in front of her, asking and receiving permission, he slung the second winner over his shoulder and brought her onto the stage. He ended his routine by climbing into a Perspex cylinder and inviting her to drench him in real water as he danced. The seams of his uniform jacket dissolved and fell away, the shirt sticking to his impressive chest, swimming muscles rippling for the entertainment of the crowd. His trousers turned out to be painted on, washing away to reveal the briefest of crotch-hugging swimming trunks.

Lost in the show, Jaq missed the arrival of the special guests. She'd never doubted that Frank would accept the invitation; the one thing Frank always protected was his own self-interest. She'd been less sure that Sophie would take the bait. Frank must have made her an offer she couldn't refuse. The empty chairs at Mico's table were now occupied. Sophie wore a tight black cocktail dress and a pink satin jacket, her fair curls piled on top of her head under a fascinator that matched her glossy lipstick and pink stiletto shoes. Frank looked uncomfortable in a short-sleeved white shirt and tan chinos. It was interesting to follow his dawning reactions. The smile of the cat with the cream on surveying the table to find several beautiful women staring at him, the mounting confusion as he noticed that all the other tables in the room were occupied by women only, the disquiet as he understood the nature of the floor show and the horror when he realised that he was the only man in the room with clothes on.

Jaq pressed the second detonator, and a river of silver sparks cascaded down the Perspex tube, a pyrotechnic waterfall. The light and noise concealed what was going on inside Frank's chair, the liquid $C_5H_5NO_2$ seeping out through the seat, the arms and the legs of the chair. The hidden camera pointed at Sophie began to whir and click. Mico bent over and whispered something. Sophie looked around, furtive, anxious, but all eyes were on the stage. Sophie couldn't see Jaq watching her from the gods.

People stood up to clap when Timur appeared in karate robes, performing a scintillating display of strength as he set up and then smashed through boards with the sides of his hands, kicked down walls with leaping feet. He collected the winner of golden ticket number three, carrying her on his shoulders to the seat on the stage. The audience clapped to the music as he began his whirling dervish routine, his karate tunic flying off with the centrifugal motion, leaving him bare-chested. The boy could dance, she had to give him that.

Jaq looked back at Sophie. With the audience distracted, Mico retrieved the package from under her chair. It was wrapped in coloured paper and decorated with ribbons, just as it had been when Sophie presented her father's girlfriend with the gift: a box of marzipan fruits laced with thallium. Xe Lin had been too nauseous with early pregnancy to eat any, but Charles had eaten three or four, enough to kill him. Slowly. Painfully. The rest were still in the box.

The chance to recover the incriminating evidence had persuaded Sophie to come to Hong Kong. That, and a generous offer for the real Qianlong lovers' cup. Sophie nodded at Frank, and he slid a wooden box over the table. Mico passed it on to the elegant woman sitting opposite her, to check the contents. At a nod of confirmation, Mico handed a red envelope to Sophie. She opened it, checked the figure on the bank draft and smiled. The exchange was swift, all over before Timur had finished his dance.

Frank whispered something to Sophie. It was only when he tried to stand up to leave that he realised he was glued to his seat. Methyl cyanoacrylate, $C_5H_5NO_2$, more commonly known as superglue, is useful stuff. Frank wasn't going anywhere unless he left his trousers and shirt behind.

Sophie jumped to her feet, ready to abandon him, but Ting Bo ran towards her in police uniform waving a truncheon and blowing a whistle. Mico feigned alarm – the consummate actor – and Sophie slumped back down, her pretty face distorted in terror. For a moment, the rest of the audience also fell silent, wondering if this was a genuine police raid. As Ting Bo passed each table, the laughter of relief was almost hysterical. The police uniform was perfect apart from the bare bottom he wiggled as he ran. He stopped at Sophie's chair and whipped out a pair of manacles. Kneeling at her side, he swiftly attached her slim left ankle to the table leg. The audience roared with approval as he placed the key in his crotch. He ran onto the stage and then disappeared.

Jaq smiled. Ting Bo had played his part to perfection, the women screaming for him to return and take off the rest of his clothes. Sophie sat frozen, staring around wildly, a rabbit in headlights. Mico smiled and patted her hand, pouring her a drink and encouraging her to relax.

Finally, it was Eusébio's turn, stripping off his faux African robes and performing astonishing feats of weightlifting, culminating in connecting the four hot seats by a crossbar and lifting them, and their squealing occupants, into the air and twirling them round.

Mico vacated her seat and Jaq took her place. Sophie's expression of confusion turned to one of complete horror, Frank's to one of anger.

Jaq handed them the legal documents that she had had Emma

prepare. Sophie's confession set out in detail the bungled attempt to murder Xe Lin which had led to her father's death.

Frank's document was simpler: it released Jaq from any responsibility for the loss of the yacht, the *Good Ship Frankium*.

Intent on savouring Frank's fury, Jaq missed Sophie's final, desperate act. Before anyone could stop her, Sophie had opened the box of sweets and stuffed half a dozen of them into her mouth. Preferring to poison herself rather than go to jail? Perhaps she hadn't observed her father's last days closely enough; perhaps she had forgotten how bad thallium poisoning could be – the slow advance of fever, excruciating pain in the palms of the hands and soles of the feet, like tiny creatures with burning-hot needles raking the skin from the inside; a racing heart, ulceration of the lips and tongue, constant stomach pains, diarrhoea and vomiting, confusion, loss of balance, loss of memory, and then the awful side effects of a slow shutdown of the organs, one by one.

Sophie started to sweat, her lipstick smearing as she gulped more champagne to wash down the sweets, the tears running down her face smudging her mascara, forming rivulets in her thick foundation. Jaq felt not a single gram of pity. The sweets she was eating were perfectly normal; the thallium-contaminated ones had been sent to a forensics lab in England. Sophie would be serving her time back home. But let her suffer for a while.

The final number before the interval was an intricate dance that used the whole room, the men moving in perfect synchronicity on stage before leaping into the audience to work the floor. And work it they did. Jaq suppressed a grin as she watched how they teased, focusing on one woman at a time, flirting as if she were the most irresistible object of desire, changing the tempo if the group began to thump the table or bray in savage arousal, controlling the temperature with artistry and charm. Steady work, getting the crowd on their side, the climax was still to come.

The number finished with a synchronised stage strip. Each

performer left the stage still wearing a thong. Saving the best to last.

Except who really wants to see a penis in public? When all is said and done, is it really an object of beauty? The Greeks rendered it inoffensive; in sculptures copied by the Romans and perfected by Michelangelo and Rodin, the male member nestles in a forest of curling hair. An anatomical fact, but not the main attraction. So why is the promise of full-frontal male nudity in a strip show such a big deal? Curiosity? Every man is different. Taboo? Not normally sanctioned, the very scarcity making it appealing. Or power? Paying another human to do something that most would find excruciatingly humiliating? Pushing the boundaries of natural reticence, privacy and modesty, giving in to the worst kind of bullying mob power?

After rapturous applause, prolonged by feet drumming the floor and appreciative whistles, the audience fell to laughing and chatting as the house lights went up and the waitresses moved around the tables serving drinks.

It was time. Jaq gave the signal to the lighting box to activate the third detonator and clouds of gold exploded above the tables, showering the audience in glittering confetti. The envelope with the bank draft began to sizzle before bursting into flames.

The beauty of the alkali metals is their high reactivity. The first chemical warfare Jaq ever waged, substituting potassium for sodium in the chemistry lab, got her chemistry teacher fired.

Jaq doused the fire with a glass of champagne and left the table.

Timur and Ru were waiting in a private room. Timur in a silk robe and Ru in her usual simple tunic and loose trousers.

Ru opened the wooden box to reveal the real Qianlong lovers' cup. She handled it with reverence. This tiny Chinese woman with a polio-withered leg was a survivor. She had outlasted the banishment of her father, the death of her mother, recovered from the effects of polio, endured starvation and been swept away on a tidal wave from the worst man-made disaster in the world. This was a woman who had worked the mines of Baotou, speculated on the stock exchange, made and lost many fortunes and allowed wicked things to happen in order to survive. A woman who had found the strength to change and embrace all that was new and good about China.

She opened her silk purse and removed the pendant that Timur had brought from Russia.

'Tell me again who sent this?' she whispered.

'Dmytry Zolotoy. Your father,' he said.

They embraced.

For the first time, Jaq could see the family resemblance between them. Those green eyes.

'You brought me something far more precious than a piece of jade,' Ru said. 'Proof that my father loved me. Something I never knew.' She wiped a tear from her eye. 'My father didn't abandon my mother. He loved her to the end. My mother didn't abandon me – she sacrificed herself so I would live. And now I have a brother.'

There was silence in the room as Ru replaced the lids on the lovers' cup: a circle of fire and a circle of flowers, the perfect fit.

More beautiful than in any picture, lifelike and intricate, unlike the fake, the true wedding cup sat on a base of honey-coloured crystal. Carved from a single piece of milk-white nephrite, a rare jade with just a tinge of sea green, two slender cups were joined by phoenix wings. The male cup encircled by a dragon, its jagged spine coiling around the cylinder in a graceful helix, head raised, mouth open, breathing out a lid of fire. The female cup laced with strings of carved pearls, a trellis of flowers curling round to a lid of petals. The Qianlong wedding cup was finally complete.

Ru held it up.

'The age of greed is over. No more rapacious development without thought for the land, the water, the air, the people. The dynasty of money is ending as the dynasty of love and generosity, truth and beauty finally dawns.

'I promised my grandfather that I would take care of this. The Qianlong cup belongs with the rest of the collection, along with the story of how it was lost and found. This is the story of a new China.'

The cup was going back to the place it had come from, to a public museum where it could be admired by everyone, not just the beer and metal barons, but the ordinary people of the most populous province in China.

'Brother, I need your help to smuggle this into the new Henan museum.' Ru looked him up and down. 'But first, I am curious to see the rest of your show.'

Jaq remained seated, allowing herself a momentary flush of triumph.

Mystery solved.

Factory located.

Dan safe.

Yan Bing and Lulu dead.

Sophie about to be convicted for murder.

Timur and Ru, half-brother and half-sister, united in the knowledge that they were always loved, never abandoned.

There were still many loose ends to tie up. Vikram had finally paid Jaq for her first trip to China, enough money to cover Angie's care for the next few months. Frank had released her from the punitive contract. Time enough to figure out how to discharge her ongoing financial responsibilities once she left China. For tonight at least, she was going to celebrate the things that had gone right.

A roar erupted from the crowd, followed by rapturous applause, signalled the end of the show. Jaq waited for Timur outside his dressing room.

'Put some clothes on,' she said. 'And then let's go and celebrate.'

Ten minutes later, Jaq opened the door into the vibrant Hong Kong night and led the way.

Zhengzhou, China

There was a moment of silence after Mimi raised her bow from the strings. The final chord of Ligeti's Cello Concerto reverberated around the atrium of the Zhengzhou museum before the audience burst into rapturous applause.

In the balcony Yun reached across to take Mico's hand.

'Thank you,' she whispered.

Mico smiled. 'Don't mention it.'

Yun stood to applaud her daughter, the rest of the audience rising to their feet with a whoomph.

The gifted young cellist, recently accepted at the Beijing conservatoire, stood to take a bow. Behind her, the Qianlong jade collection, each piece newly cleaned, gleamed inside individual glass cases. The prize exhibit, the wedding cup, had pride of place in the centre. The two lids – a spiral of dragon fire and a coil of flowers and pearls – had been connected to the cups with tiny gold hinges. The damage to the base, where some vandal had hacked off a chip of xenotime, had been buffed and polished away.

Yun straightened her new police uniform. After the Spring Festival, the Women's Federation would have to look elsewhere for a Sunny Women Program Director.

Shanghai, China

Frank took the rock and held it up to the light. There they were, dotted throughout the grey lump: honey-coloured crystals that glowed, as if lit from the inside. None as large as the xenotime crystal that formed the base of the lovers' cup, but even to his inexpert eyes, clearly the same family. The source.

'Careful. It contains thorium. Some uranium, too.'

A white-coated technician passed a portable instrument over the ore.

Click . . . click . . . CLICK CLICK CLICK

The rattle of a Geiger counter triggered a memory he would rather forget. The old fear grabbed him by the throat, a dry pressure that could not be swallowed away. Beads of sweat blossomed on his brow and began to trickle down his temples. Before the trembling in his limbs took control, he let the lump of ore fall to the bench and looked around for a seat.

CLICK CLICK CLICK . . . click . . . click

'Turn that thing off!'

Using the laboratory benches for support, hand over hand, Frank manoeuvred himself towards the desk where he sank into a chair in front of the computer. He took six tablets and his breathing gradually returned to normal.

The Chinese Zagrovyl technician brought the screen to life.

'Radioactive decay. That's how we found where your crystal sample came from.' He pointed to the fragment Frank had brought to the lab. The piece Frank had hacked off from the base of Sophie's jade cup before returning it. 'The isotopes all have different rates of decay. The ratio gives us the age of the rock.'

'And?'

'Your sample is about sixty million years old. Formed in pegmatite, slow-cooling igneous rocks. And with a unique signature. See here.'

He pointed to a table with the results of the analysis, a list of elements and their percentages.

'The highest levels of dysprosium and holmium I have ever seen. Incredibly pure. Just as you thought. A real game changer.'

'How big is the deposit?'

'Huge. These rocks have been shredded by glaciers. Now the ice is melting, the rivers have washed and sorted the heavy minerals. The sands rich in rare earths stretch right across the border.'

Say goodbye to your monopoly, my friends. Rare earth prices are about to take a dive.

Say hello to the new vice president of Zagrovyl Green Energy.

Once again in control.

Once again unstoppable.

Vladivostok, Russia

The old man lay back on his pillow.

He stroked his neck where the jade pendant once lay. Giving it away had lifted a burden from his soul. Acknowledging Timur as his son had brought him Nina's child, Ru, the daughter he thought was dead.

All this time amassing stuff. For what? You can't take it with you. Why had the realisation come to him so late?

He'd done what he had to do. Now he could let go.

His life had been far from perfect; he'd been part of things he wished he could undo. But time moves forward, not back.

No one knows what is going to happen next.

He took his last breath and prepared to find out.

Author's Note

As a professional engineer, I have been involved with projects in China for over thirty years. The speed of change has been extraordinary; I might not have believed it possible had I not witnessed it with my own eyes. This is a story; I made thing up. But sometimes truth is stranger than fiction.

Art thefts

The Qianlong emperor ruled China for sixty years from 1736 to 1795, at a time when China was the wealthiest and most populous nation in the world. He studied Chinese painting, was an expert calligrapher, a passionate poet and essayist and an astute collector of art, as well as one of China's most successful rulers, the fourth and longest-living emperor of the Qing dynasty (1644–1911).

After the Opium Wars, and the 1860 Treaty of Peking (which ceded Outer Manchuria including modern-day Vladivostok to Russia), French soldiers sacked the Summer Palace in Peking, stealing the Qianlong art collection housed there, some of which found its way into European museums.

A spate of thefts from European museums starting in 2010 exhibited a pattern suggesting that specific ancient Chinese objects were being repatriated to order. Thieves first smashed their way into the Chinese Pavilion in the grounds of Drottningholm Palace, Stockholm, Sweden. They fled by moped to a nearby lake, ditched their bikes into the water and escaped by speedboat. The heist took less than six minutes, and the thieves were never caught.

A month later, in Bergen, Norway, intruders descended from a glass ceiling and plucked objects from the Chinese Collection at the KODE Museum. In England, the Oriental Museum at Durham University and the Fitzwilliam Museum at Cambridge University were targeted before a hit on the Château de Fontainebleau, just outside Paris in France.

Floods

The rivers of China bring both life and peril to the agricultural communities they sustain. Floods in 1837 and 1931 killed millions. But not all the river disasters in China were natural.

In 1938, a terrible act of 'sacrifice' was inflicted on Chinese civilians by the retreating National Revolutionary Army led by Chiang Kai-shek. In a futile attempt to halt the Japanese invasion, a dam was breached at Zhengzhou. The surge of water flooded the plain, drowning all in its path, and shifted the mouth of the Yellow river hundreds of kilometres to the south. Official government estimates put the death toll at 800,000 Chinese civilians, with a further 10 million displaced. The invading army simply took another route.

In 1975 the 'iron dam' at Banqiao failed. Freak weather conditions caused unusually high rainfall, which exceeded the design capacity of the dam. Blame the weather? Or blame the design? A huge programme of dam-building began in the early 1950s with the help of Russian specialists. But there was insufficient surveying or planning, and the advice of the expert Chinese hydrogeologist, Chen Xing, was ignored. His repeated warnings proved tragically prophetic. In the disaster of 1975 at least 26,000 people drowned (other estimates put the number at 230,000), and perhaps as many as one million people died from the subsequent famine and disease, with 11 million people becoming refugees in their own land.

Strippers

It was common practice in rural China to hire female strippers for large events, even for funerals. A public decency campaign led to a ban on nude women appearing in corporate advertising, but no similar restriction was applied to naked men. Western male models

FIONA ERSKINE

were hired to add sex appeal: Budweiser launched a new beer with a male strip show as part of a pan-China tour and a publicity stunt by Sweetie Salad featured food delivery by Spartan warriors, bare-chested western men in cloaks, tabards and sandals parading through the streets of Beijing bearing lunch for office workers. The police intervened, wrestling the scantily dressed Russian models to the ground before arresting them, adding to the press attention.

Lingchi
Lingchi – death by a thousand cuts (also known as slow slicing or lingering death) – was an ancient form of torture and execution officially outlawed in China in 1905.

Female murderers
Sasebo, a small city in the Nagasaki Prefecture of Japan, was the location of two murders of female children by their classmates, a decade apart. In 2004 an eleven-year-old girl murdered a twelve-year-old in an empty school classroom during the lunch break, slitting the victim's arms and throat with a knife, before returning to afternoon classes covered in blood. In 2014, a fifteen-year-old schoolgirl invited a classmate to her apartment, where she beat and strangled her, before decapitating and partially dismembering the body. She had bought the tools herself with the intention of committing murder, after studying medical textbooks and killing and dissecting a cat as practice. The age of criminal responsibility in China is fourteen.

Lychee Festival
The Lychee and Dog Meat Festival is celebrated annually in Yulin, Guangxi, China, during the summer solstice in June. During the ten days of festivities, dogs are paraded in wooden crates and metal cages and are taken to be skinned and cooked for consumption by festival visitors and local residents. Opposition from inside and outside China has led to violent incidents.

Sinking yachts

In May 2014, the sailing yacht *Cheeky Rafiki* capsized in the middle of the Atlantic Ocean with the loss of four experienced English sailors. Investigation showed that the keel had parted from the hull. The connection between hull, matrix and keel had been repaired several times after repeated prior groundings.

Rare earth metals

Most of the seventeen rare earth metals (fifteen lanthanides (atomic numbers 57–71) plus yttrium (39) and scandium (21)) are not actually rare at all, but as they exist in low concentrations in minerals in rock, they are extremely difficult to extract.

Neodymium (60) and dysprosium (66) are essential components for wind turbines, hybrid and electric car batteries, computer hard disks and mobile phones. All of the world's heavy rare earths (such as dysprosium) come from China.

In 2010 the Chinese authorities imposed strict quotas on the export of rare earth metals in order to conserve scarce resources, increase prices to cover the environmental costs of production and encourage the growth of domestic high-tech industries.

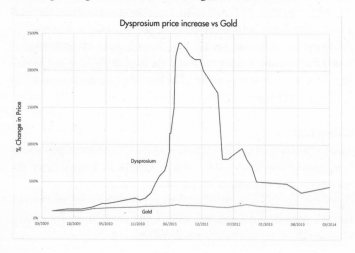

Prices rocketed. The price of dysprosium rose over 2000% in six months.

In 2015 Chinese export restrictions were lifted after a ruling from the World Trade Organization (WTO) and prices stabilised.

Oddo–Harkins rule

Named after two scientists who never met, the rule states that elements with an even atomic number[1] are roughly twice as abundant as adjacent[2] elements with an odd number. The exception to the rule is hydrogen (1) which is the most abundant element in the universe. For all other elements, proton pairing enhances stability.

Shetland wind farm

I had the great good fortune to work on Shetland, and I can confirm that it is both breathtakingly beautiful *and* breathtakingly windy. Located just a few miles outside of Lerwick, the first three wind turbines – Mina, Betsy and Brenda (660kW turbines with 47-metre rotors) – were commissioned in 2000 and soon achieved a world record of 57.9% availability (or load factor = the actual output of a turbine divided by its theoretical maximum output in a year); the UK onshore average is less than half of that. The 2005 plan to build further large-scale wind farms on Shetland (150 turbines, 600MW of power) has been challenged, delayed and reduced in scope, but ultimately sanctioned. Construction work is about to start at the time of writing.

Green energy

The Anthropocene, the age of human control of our environment, has brought light and power and warmth and connectivity to

---

1 The atomic number is the number of protons in the nucleus. The periodic table is a map of all 118 elements organised in rows by increasing atomic number and in columns by common properties.

2 Adjacent here means side by side in the periodic table.

billions of people. But no technology is without risk. Stored energy of any sort – in oil, gas, coal, uranium, wind, sun or water – must be carefully controlled. Based on deaths per kilowatt hour generated, hydroelectric power remains the most dangerous form of energy, and based on the number of deaths by drowning every year, water continues to be the most dangerous substance on earth.

As Ella Fitzgerald sang, 'T'aint What You Do, It's The Way That Cha Do It'.

Teesside energy

A parmo is a Teesside delicacy, served in restaurants, pubs, works canteens and from food vans in and around Stockton and Middlesbrough, England. It consists of a piece of chicken breast deep-fried in breadcrumbs, topped with a white sauce and cheese and served with chips. A typical takeaway dish contains 2,600 calories and 150g of fat. It is delicious.

Bibliography

Mr China by Tim Clissold (London: Constable, 2010, new edn) tells a rip-roaring tale of greed, skulduggery and cultural conflict. A Chinese-speaking Englishman, Tim Clissold, acted as an adviser to foreign investors who flocked to the new Wild West between 1995 and 2005.

River Town by Peter Hessler (London: John Murray, 2002, new edn) shows China through the eyes of an American schoolteacher, who slowly begins to understand just how far the group matters more the individual.

The Elements of Power: Gadgets, Guns, and the Struggle for a Sustainable Future in the Rare Metal Age by David S. Abraham (London: Yale University Press, 2017) explores the sourcing of rare metals essential to modern technology and delves into the political, economic and environmental implications of their scarcity.

Wild Swans by Jung Chang (London: William Collins, 2012, new edn) is still banned in China. A deeply moving personal history, it also covers key historical events in detail: the overthrow of the Qing dynasty in 1911, the rise of Communism, the Japanese invasion starting in Manchuria in 1931 and the Second World War, which continued into a civil war ending only after 1949 when Mao Zedong founded the People's Republic of China.

In the 1950s the USSR sought to strengthen ties with its neighbour and sent Soviet engineers and scientists to assist in modernising newly communist China.

Mao Zedong's 'Great Leap Forward' (1958–1962) was an attempt to industrialise China. Instant results were required – 'Survey, Design and Execute Simultaneously'. The Great Sparrow Campaign (part of the Four Pests Campaign) resulted in ecological imbalance. The 'backyard furnaces' turned useful agricultural implements into useless pig iron. The collectivisation of agriculture, along with communist pseudoscience, led to a catastrophic drop in crop yields and the famine of 1959–1961.

The Russian experts were recalled in 1960 after Mao and Khrushchev fell out.

The Three-Body Problem by Cixin Liu (London: Head of Zeus, 2018) brilliantly translated by Ken Liu is a Chinese science fiction novel. It opens during the Cultural Revolution (1969–1976) and charts the attack on science by extraterrestrials ahead of an invasion. Using the freedom of science fiction and a mind-bendingly surrealist plot, the story charts the rise of opposing extremist factions in response to the perceived threat, revealing a great deal about China yesterday, today and tomorrow.

From the Chinese invention of gunpowder in 220 BC to the development of plastic explosives after the Second World War, *The Chemistry of Explosives* by Jacqueline Akhavan (Royal Society of Chemistry, 2011, 3rd edn) is my go-to reference book for things that go bang.

Acknowledgements

Thanks:

To Sensei Matt Zahand, former US Navy sailor and karate instructor moonlighting as a stripper, who took his clothes off beside a pool in Los Angeles and shared his life story.

To all my wonderful Chinese colleagues, especially to those who indulged my peculiar wish to visit the Banqiao Dam in Henan Province, China, and made it such a memorable day.

To my Beta Readers: Dr Lorraine Wilson, who stopped me burning an early draft; John Schofield (www.saltyjohn.com) who turned my flimsy dingy into a powerful yacht and then helped me blast it to smithereens (his blog and free book, *Sailing Snippets*, is heartily recommended for sailors and landlubbers alike and can be found at www.saltyjohntheblog.com); Joanne Morgan for luxury yacht tips and the tragic story of *Cheeky Rafiki*; Ian and Claire Barnard, who make me laugh while pointing out my errors and are actively making the world a cleaner place, reusing valuable resources rather than throwing them away (Right to Repair manchesterdeclaration.org and www.facebook.com/creditonrepaircafe); Barry Hatton for advice on all things Portuguese; Helen Greenough, for being young and whip-smart and multilingual – the most insightful millennial reader you could wish for; Ivan Vince, for being wise and patient enough to check some of my calculations; Mark Dufty for crucial advice on geology and mining; my favourite uncle, Laurie Fairman, for last minute metallurgy and ornithology; Marjory Flynn, my best friend, for reading despite eye surgery and always telling it like it is; one day I'll listen.

All mistakes are my own.

To Viv Groskop for her inspiring book on public speaking, *How to Own the Room*, and William Gibson for his unrivalled description of jet lag in the brilliant *Pattern Recognition*.

To KLM and Grand Central for keeping the outside world connected to Teesside. To the Raby Hunt Restaurant for its second Michelin star, and The Waiting Room, Café Lilli, Muse, The Devonport and many others for culinary inspiration.

To the crime writing and reading and blogging community: what an extraordinarily friendly and supportive bunch of people you are. To all the brilliant bookshops including Drake in Stockton, The Golden Hare in Edinburgh, Far from the Madding Crowd in Linlithgow, Forum in Corbridge and the knowledgeable and helpful staff in Waterstones everywhere. To all the friendly book groups, especially the Belmont Babes and the Stockton Specials.

To the team at Oneworld – Jenny Parrott, my fabulous editor, Harriet Wade, her insightful assistant, Jenny Page, my copy editor, Molly Scull, Thanhmai Bui-Van, Anna Murphy, Margot Weale, Paul Nash, Ben Summers and too many others to mention.

I owe a special debt of gratitude to my agent, Juliet Mushens. Her perceptive comments galvanised me at a key stage of the project.

And finally, to my family: Spike the magic cat and feline muse, my beautiful sons, Andrew and Joseph, who tolerate endless embarrassment from their mother with perfect equanimity, and to my husband, Jonathan, the love of my life.

Fiona Erskine is a professional engineer based in Teesside, although she travels frequently to Brazil, Russia, India and China. As a female engineer, she is often the lone representative of her gender in board meetings, cargo ships, night-time factories and offshore oil rigs, and her fiction offers a fascinating insight into this traditionally male world. She is the author of *The Chemical Detective*.